AMBASSADOR 11: THE FORGOTTEN WAR

PATTY JANSEN

GET FREE EBOOKS

DID YOU KNOW?

Ambassador 11: The Forgotten War is also available in audio.
Click the image or visit https://pattyjansen.com to find out more.

CHAPTER ONE

THERE WAS a headless dinosaur in the courtyard underneath my balcony.

A giant chicken with a red rubbery comb that bobbed with the chicken suit occupant's movements was doing up the straps over the dinosaur's shoulders while the dinosaur's head lay on a chair that stood outside the entrance to the storage container that —evidently—held all the performers' props. A monocycle leaned against the wall which separated the hotel's courtyard from the courtyard of the next hotel.

Instead of working on my urgent and very boring messages, I was looking down in fascination, wondering how someone wearing a dinosaur suit with a giant head and awkward tail was going to ride a monocycle.

Welcome to the New World entertainment precinct, and welcome to Los Angeles.

Strains of cheery music drifted between the buildings, where, if yesterday was anything to go by, a show was taking place in the square outside our hotel.

The dinosaur head went on, the tiny Tyrannosaurus paws adjusted the visor, the chicken grabbed the monocycle, jumped on, and then the dinosaur ran after it through the alley along the side of the hotel with a speed that would make me freak out.

A cheer went up when they arrived, a few seconds later, in the square at the front of the building and I could no longer see them.

Sigh.

Back to my messages and attempting to be polite to a man who, frankly, had not deserved my politeness.

Although I had no illusion that if I let it fly and wrote *Why the fuck won't you respond to my correspondence?* it would have any more effect than my previous messages to Nations of Earth president Simon Dekker had. All nine of them, since we'd prepared for this trip.

I'd started off asking for a meeting, when we were still in Barresh, saying that we were coming through the Exchange, and I could drop into Rotterdam for an informal chat, to tell him that there were a few things I'd like to touch base on, just like I'd do with his predecessor.

And he had continued to ignore me. And now we were out of range in the northwestern corner of Mexico to honour my promise to a Coldi family—it was a long story. We were also about to go even further out of range, if I was successful at procuring a trip further inland, which might or might not breach a raft of international laws. I didn't want Dekker to find out I was here, and that we were doing this, but I did want to talk to him once we came back to Rotterdam, but either way, he continued to ignore my messages.

The performers of the previous act now filed into the area around the storage container, cordoned off from people on the ground by screens, but visible for me, three floors up. They peeled off colourful jackets and tossed hats aside. Someone passed around a tray with cups of water.

A mother and a small child had come to the pool on the other side of the barrier. It was early March, and I didn't think it was that warm, but I guess they thought differently. The mother spread out a towel on one of the deck chairs that stood on the fake grass.

Damn, I was really not getting any work done.

I picked up my reader and went inside.

As Earthly as the courtyard outside of my balcony had been, the inside was all off-worldly. Thayu and Sheydu had moved the table in front of the window, and they had set up as much security equipment as they could fit on it. Sheydu was on her knees under the table, trying to connect leads to a power box that led from a very old-fashioned power point. I hadn't seen any of those in many years.

After arriving yesterday, she had complained bitterly that the level of power was not up to what she needed to operate her scanners, chargers and transmitters, and she had borrowed or purchased or otherwise acquisitioned a box to make this happen.

"Is it working now?" I asked Deyu, who stood watching the goings-on.

She shrugged. "This is only the first step. Connectivity is poor and there is next to no Exchange coverage."

Yes. I knew that and we'd known that, coming into this area. Somehow, I'd not expected that to be such a major issue, because I'd expected to have made arrangements with Dekker by now.

"People are watching us," Thayu said.

"Yes. People are always watching us, aren't they?"

"It would be nice to know who they are."

"I can make some guesses," I said.

Asto military, people sent by the Exchange out of pure curiosity about what we were doing in this unusual part of the world, people sent by local authorities to follow out of curiosity about what we were doing here. Those were just the ones I could think about off the top of my head.

"Those are only guesses," she said.

"We're on a fun trip. Just do the best you can," I said.

"There are people on the register," Sheydu said from under the table, apparently her preferred option.

The register of Coldi people on Earth that assist in case of an emergency. But there was no emergency, and I preferred solving this via Earth channels, even if only not to put any pressure on any Coldi who lived in this very strange city in a very strange place where people wore chicken suits and performed for the rich, while many others lived in the endless dusty slums we had passed on the roadsides while coming into this place.

"The guide said she'd be here soon," I said, as a warning to my team to make sure that their most obvious off-worldly items were packed away. Like readers, like spy equipment.

In the room behind the table, a full scale security meeting was still underway.

Isharu and her team had put their readers on the bed, with the screen up, and they had somehow rigged them up so they joined and formed one projection in the air. Anyu was there, trusted Anyu with her extensive knowledge about communication. Zyana was there, because as ex-guard of the Athyl Third Circle, he had some sort of loyalty towards one of our young charges. I hadn't asked about it, and my team had found it unnecessary to bother me with the details, but he was very handy with equipment and because he was an ex-guard, he made for a formidable presence.

Most of the rest of Sheydu's association had remained in Athens, including Leisha, our pilot.

Reida was in the room, and Veyada.

I couldn't see what was being projected, but again it would be about security and people following us or listening in to us.

Isharu nodded to me that she acknowledged my words and continued the briefing.

I went into the small hallway to the apartment.

In the adjacent room, Nicha and Mereeni were preparing for

today's trip, a preparation that involved electronic trackers and spare clothes, nappies and tubs of safe food.

Jaki stuck his head into the room.

"How long before the guide is here?" he asked. His tail waved at waist height, showing that something bothered him.

"She said she'd entered the precinct and would be here soon," I said. The guide had only communicated with me. I hoped she understood what the makeup of my team was and that it included some unearthly visitors.

Then Jaki asked, "Have any of you seen the kids?"

Oh.

To be honest, I had not. And we had too many kids on this trip to keep an eye on all of them.

Nicha said, "I gave them a card, because Larrana wanted to get some trinket from the shop downstairs."

"Did they all go out?" Jaki asked. His tail hit the door frame when he turned around.

It was his task to look after the younger kids, but Ileyu and my daughter Emi were still too small to take part in any of the older kids' mischief.

We shared joined responsibility over Ayshada, Larrana Azimi, who we'd agreed to take, and Thayu's son Nalya. Those two were a few years older than Ayshada, and Ayshada had picked up a lot of their naughty habits. And there were also two Pengali youngsters—I wasn't sure if they were Ynggi and Jaki's children or if they knew or cared about their parentage in an utterly Pengali way. Both Pykka and Amay were born in the same cycle and had lived at my house with Ynggi and Jaki for the last few months. They were hard to keep up with, even when they were at my house in Barresh.

And this band of kids had gone down to the hotel foyer to buy some souvenir, because Larrana was obsessed with this strange part of Earth culture that involved plastic figurines, and had not come back.

Right before the guide was supposed to arrive to take us for our long-awaited trip into the park, too.

Typical.

I blew out a breath. "I'll go down to check on them."

Nicha handed me a tracker. "Take this."

I stuck it in my pocket.

"Do you have the gun?" Thayu asked from near the window where she and Sheydu had progressed to connecting the devices on the table to the power box.

I wanted to say, "I'm just going to the foyer," but I knew what she would say, that there was never a "just going" in terms of security, that we should stay vigilant, especially here, and that this was not a friendly place.

Yes, yes. I collected the weapon. I'd probably be carrying the damn thing all day.

I left the unit. One of the hotel staff was cleaning the apartment next to ours. He had wheeled a trolley onto the balustrade that ran outside the front doors of all the units.

The young man gave me a nervous look, one I'd sadly grown used to.

"Do you want me to clean your accommodation, sir?" he asked.

"No, we will be fine."

I had to speak really clearly. They didn't speak Isla here, but an archaic form of English, one of the languages that made up Isla. Other people spoke Spanish, but I wasn't familiar with that either.

"I'm sorry, sir?"

"No cleaning."

He nodded.

"Have you seen a group of children come this way?"

"You should probably get them, sir. People might complain, sir."

"Are they making too much noise?" I asked.

I didn't think the noise had been as bad today as it had yesterday, when the kids had put on very loud music and attempted to sing to it at the tops of their voices and I'd needed to intervene to tell them that people in the building didn't like the noise.

"No sir, it is about the kids outside sir."

He seemed decidedly nervous.

"They went outside?" I thought they'd only gone to the foyer.

I walked down the balustrade, and down two flights of stairs, then through the accommodation's reception area and out the front.

The sunlight hit the square, and it was already hot.

It was busy in the square. I'd known this because of the dinosaur activity going on in the hotel's courtyard. A sizeable group of tourists had gathered around the performance. Music drifted over the square.

It was always busy when those performers were here. I'd seen a schedule of performances displayed, which I meant to obtain, because the children loved it.

As soon as I entered the square, a man in dark clothing came to me.

"Are those your kids?" He spoke Isla.

"My kids? I don't know what you mean. They could be." I was getting an ominous feeling about this.

"Come with me."

He pushed between a couple of tourists, who all turned around with slightly disturbed looks on their faces. There was something uncomfortable about how quickly they moved aside to let through the security guard with me following in his wake.

We came to the middle of the crowd and I saw that what the people were watching was not the regular performance at all.

The chicken and the dinosaur stood to the side. Both had taken off their heads. A woman occupied the chicken suit. Both were speaking into headsets, presumably to security.

In the middle of the square, a bunch of kids on unicycles

raced around in a big circle. Some of them were our kids. Nalya was riding a unicycle, and Larrana's wheelchair was already a tricycle with independently moving wheels. A group of scruffy and skinny little kids had joined them with unkempt hair, many of them brown-skinned with mismatched, patched and too-large clothing.

Ayshada walked around the middle of the circle with a basket full of the type of plastic toys they had gone downstairs to purchase. He was throwing these with deadly precision to the young kids on unicycles, who caught the toys that Ayshada was throwing them. They then juggled all the toys in a great tangle of colourful plastic objects over Ayshada's head. One occasionally hit the ground, but Ayshada would run to pick it up.

They had turned the music up really loud.

The two Pengali kids were both dancing. They swung their hips and tails in time with the beat. Neither of them were wearing anything, which probably caused part of the consternation.

Larrana came into the group and started dancing with them.

Asto wheelchairs were not at all like the earthly ones. They resembled scooters, with the person strapped in and attached to the motor with nerve sensors that controlled the chair in a way that made riding one almost better than walking. It allowed the wearer to jump, to dance and do all kinds of things that people with normal feet and normal legs would have trouble doing, or at least have trouble doing for an extended period.

He was bouncing up and down in his chair, walking on his hands, flipping backwards and forwards, somersaulting.

Heavens. It's even looked like an actual performance. I was unfamiliar with the music they had chosen, but it all looked very real.

The people cheered and clapped.

"Are these your children?" the guard asked.

"Some of them."

"I mean the ones with the bike and with the toys."

"Yes, some of them are with us. I don't know the other children."

"We're familiar with the young rascals and will pursue this with their families." It all sounded very serious.

"They haven't done anything, have they?"

"This space is for authorised performers only. Our performers are professionals who are getting paid for their efforts. You wouldn't want amateur medicine men to attend to you when you go to the hospital."

"Er... I guess not." I was struggling to see the point of his argument. They were only kids, and they were only having fun. "I'm sorry. I didn't know the kids were here." There were no signs that people weren't allowed to hold impromptu performances, especially kids. I didn't think they were breaking any rules.

"Please tell them to go back to their families."

"We're about to go out for the day," I said.

"Good, the performers want to continue with their act."

Those performers were standing at the side of the circle. The dinosaur and the chicken had put their heads back on, but there were a few others in green outfits with bits of fabric dangling off their arms and legs, and they looked bemused more than anything. But they kept glancing at the guard.

There was some strange, uncomfortable dynamic going on. I assumed that the guards meant to keep the square free so that the performers could do their jobs. The performers might even give the guards a percentage of their takings—and a little device stood at each corner where people could give money, even if entrance to the park and accommodation already cost a fortune.

But maybe the guards were here to make sure that nothing inappropriate happened and that the performers didn't go off-script. The thought chilled me.

"I'm sorry. They are just kids having fun," I said.

"You might also tell them not to treat their toys like this. They might get damaged."

I walked into the circle and clapped my hands. "Kids, this man here says you have to stop this."

Nalya turned to me, and as his face took on a disappointed expression, one of the toys thrown by a dark-skinned unicyclist hit him on the side of the head and bounced over the ground. *They might get damaged.* What? Pieces of coloured plastic? Why did he care anyway?

"Can we come back here later?" Nalya asked.

"I don't know." I sighed. "I don't think they like it when you perform their show." And they didn't like the fact that they played music in the wrong way and treated toys in the wrong way.

Or something. I was struggling to comprehend these people.

The young rascals on their unicycles jumped off their bikes.

The legitimate performers rushed into the square. They reset the music, pushed the toys aside and took up their positions to start dancing.

CHAPTER TWO

LARRANA COLLECTED his toys and put them in Ayshada's basket.

Whenever he passed, people retreated as it dawned on their faces that this boy did not ride a tricycle for fun, but that it was part of him.

"You shouldn't encourage those kids," one tourist said to me. He was very tall and broad, but walked with a walking stick. He wore a hat with the New World Entertainment logo.

It was probably stupid, but I couldn't keep my mouth shut. "I don't think they were doing anything wrong."

He snorted. "It looks like fun to be a performer, but these people get paid next to nothing and treated like dirt." He nodded at the square where the chicken-and-dinosaur routine had made way for a song performed by young women in butterfly suits.

"Oh, do be quiet, Hank," a woman said next to the tourist, presumably his wife. "They have paying work. They will be grateful for that."

The man eyed me. "You're not from here, mister. I can hear that by the way you speak."

"Just visiting. Have a nice day."

I was going to leave it at that. Besides the fact that Ayshada and Larrana had collected all the toys, and we needed to get going, I didn't think there was anything to be gained by holding this conversation.

It could go in any of three or four directions, and neither the *Tell me all about it*, the *How long are you there for?* or *I'm glad that those aliens don't live here* lines of discussion were particularly appealing to me.

I gathered the children, who were now watching the officially approved show where the performers danced in approved ways to approved music and juggled approved items.

So they got paid a pittance?

Typical. Everywhere we'd been so far, we'd met people who worked in expensive accommodation and still *begged* for money.

It annoyed me. I also felt sorry for them. Not sorry enough to succumb to this system.

"Let's go. Our guide may already be at the apartment."

"Why can't we play?" Nalya asked.

He had very large dark eyes, and when he looked up at me like this, I could see so much of Thayu in him.

"I'm very sorry. This is not our world, and they don't like it if we use their songs and their images for things they are not intended for."

"But it's just for fun," Ayshada said.

But the Coldi word for fun also meant frivolous, and these people here did not think fun was frivolous. Fun was serious, fun was prescribed, fun was smiling even if there was nothing to smile about.

Fun was *Have a nice day*, the ultimate fob-off that killed any opportunity for a serious conversation.

Like all those little scrawny kids with their unicycles would have a nice day, or would even be employed, or their parents would be paid fairly.

Where had they come from?

They all stood in a group, some of them with their unicycles folded. One or two had already run. A young boy was standing out the front, his eyes wide. He was staring at a man on the other side of the square who wore the same uniform as the fellow who had attached himself to me and was still watching us.

Some of his colleagues moved through the gathered onlookers. Most people ignored them, or nodded polite greetings. Others slunk into the crowd and disappeared. Undesirable elements?

All this was happening while cheerful music blared over the square and the female dancers with butterfly wings were singing about flowers and sunshine.

It felt decidedly weird.

I met the eyes of the urchin at the front of the group. He was about the same age as our eldest youngsters, eleven or twelve, had dark skin and arms as thin as sticks.

"I hope we didn't cause too much trouble," I said.

He looked so terrified, and I had no idea where all these kids had come from. They couldn't be employees of the resort, because they would never have been allowed into the precinct dressed as they were.

The kid just looked at me. I don't think he understood me at all.

He eyed the uniformed man who stood behind me. Did he want anything?

When the uniformed man took a step forward, he tucked his unicycle under his arm, and the entire group ran out of the square.

"They won't bother you anymore," the uniformed man said.

Telling him that the kids weren't bothering me would be a waste of breath, so I didn't.

I led our group back to the hotel.

Our kids followed me, except the Pengali, who ran ahead, evoking squeals from tourists, and enjoying every bit of it. They'd be climbing over the balcony railings, raising alarm from fellow guests. I was tired of trying to stop them after two days of this. You couldn't. They were Pengali.

"What were we doing wrong?" Nalya asked, walking next to me.

His voice was soft.

He was the oldest of all the kids, but you would never tell from his behaviour.

He watched, listened, barely said anything and rarely questioned anything.

His family was extremely strict, and he was used to getting lectured when he had done something wrong. It showed. I'd been apprehensive about having him along—being from a rival family and all that—but the only thing I'd had to worry about was that he was too quiet.

"I think only approved people can do performances out here."

To be honest, I suspected what was at the heart of this slap-down. It was about licensing and intellectual property. The park owned everything: the characters, the music, the dance moves, the costumes and didn't allow anyone—not even a bunch of kids —to use it in an unauthorised fashion.

This was such an alien place.

Now that the staff had cleared the disturbance, the square returned to normal. Sweetly, sickly normal. With people in their costumes smiling with not a speck on their shirts or hair out of place, with not a wrong word or heaven forbid a wrong image, with spectators in the audience where they belonged.

I felt alien. We might as well have landed on another planet.

"I'm not sure I like this place," Nalya said. "Everyone is supposed to be happy, but a lot of the people here are not happy. They just pretend to be happy."

In Earth years, he would be about twelve or thirteen, and him spending time with us was part of his mentoring agreed to by his family.

It amazed me that a young boy from another world could see those things. Many of the holidaymakers appeared to be oblivious to the fact. Or maybe they liked pretending to be happy.

They were families on trips of nostalgia. Many were rich people, because it wasn't cheap to stay here.

I promised the kids a snack, and we went back into the apartment.

"How did you meet those other kids?" I asked when we were walking across the hotel foyer.

"They work here," Nalya said.

I was pretty sure that was impossible. The rules for children working were very strict, even here.

"Where?"

"At the back of our accommodation."

"What were they doing?"

"Riding and playing."

But I gathered he didn't know where the kids had come from and what they were doing here any more than I did.

I surmised that when Larrana, Nalya and Ayshada had gone to the foyer to look at the souvenir shop, the kids with their unicycles had been there. Kids being kids, they were attracted to each other, even if they didn't speak each other's language or, for that matter, they came from the same world.

Back in our apartment, Ynggi was happy to see everyone returned in one piece. He doled out my promised snack in the kitchenette—bananas. The kids *loved* bananas, and they all collected as many as they could and proceeded to peel them—reminded by Jaki to please put the skins in the bin. Not that Pengali were familiar with the concept of rubbish bins.

Calm returned while the kids ate, and it lasted a blissful few minutes until an argument broke out between Ynggi and the Pengali kids about wearing clothes. I made my exit to the hall.

My security team had packed up all the equipment and were getting ready for the day. We would spend it in the park, having fun with the kids. The long-promised trip was part of my attempt to placate the Azimi family, Ayshada's clan, and that of his demanding, unreasonable mother, who was also Larrana's aunt.

Larrana had already forgotten the incident and his disappointment, because I had promised him that there would be a lot more of his favourite cartoons and he would be able to purchase a lot more figurines for his collection.

He had transferred a whole damn catalogue of the things onto his reader and had shown me which ones he still lacked. The prices for the things were ridiculous.

So he was soon again bouncing off the walls practicing dance moves, Nalya and Ayshada were egging him on, Ileyu was squealing at the top of her voice, and Emi, being Emi, sat in the middle of it, legs spread, on the floor taking it all in.

The security staff had gathered in the hall. They were ready.

I didn't miss the concerned look on Sheydu's face.

"No luck restoring connectivity?" I asked her.

"Their systems are rubbish," she said. "I'm sure someone is following us. Someone is blocking our equipment and blocking our communication. I don't understand. If your president had any sense, he would be glad to talk to you. He wouldn't ignore you, only because of what you are."

But of course what I was might be part of the problem. Dekker and Nations of Earth would not acknowledge that I had become a major representative, and that I worked closely with Ezhya. Dekker and his people distrusted Asto and anything to do with *gamra*. His predecessor had presided over Earth's decision to join *gamra*, in a different time that seemed years ago. And all the time that he had been in power, Dekker had done nothing about furthering the cooperation. He had put the joining process on the slowest burner possible.

He now refused to speak with me. I didn't think that his lack of communication had anything to do with the equipment. Although I granted that there were probably issues with the equipment as well. If the antiquated power point on the wall was anything to go by, the level of communication in this place was probably just as bad as Sheydu said.

"Any other news?" I asked.

"Nothing shocking. We crosschecked a few of the references we found yesterday."

We had visited a location we had *really* come here to visit, a building and warehouse in San Diego. According to my research, the location used to be an office of the Southern California Aerospace Corps, but the building itself had changed hands a few times since their alleged ownership and no one knew anything about the Corps or why there was a half-buried space ship of theirs in the rainforest in Barresh.

The current owner had allowed us to look around. My team had pulled up some old electronics, and the owner had let us photograph old items that had been inside the office when he moved into the warehouse, and my team had pulled some pieces of equipment apart and had sent snatches of code to the Exchange for analysis. Those results had now come in.

"Anything useful?" I asked.

"Nothing beyond what we already knew. They owned the building for a few years and manufactured small electronic parts."

"Not any that happened to contain Coldi routines?"

She flicked her eyebrows up. I wasn't supposed to know this, officially. "You have a very high opinion of Asto's omnipotence."

"I would be right for most of this world."

"Most of this world. Not this part."

Well, that was disappointing. Was she insinuating that this group, this semi-private militia about whom we knew little, had been smart enough to realise the spying potential of imported electronics? Or that this was just a sign of their general paranoia?

We needed to put all the information we had found on the table about how these people had ended up in Barresh, why no one had noticed except a remote Pengali tribe, and what had happened to this space force or private militia, or whatever they were.

"Anything else?"

"We've had a short message from Amarru that came to us not via the regular channels."

"Does that mean anything?"

"She just said she'd be in contact. I'm not sure if that meant anything."

"No, I meant the fact that the message didn't reach you through regular channels."

"It means that communication here is rubbish. Normally we can use the local network, even if they don't want us to, but that doesn't even seem to be a functional local network."

Yes, yes, I had heard it all before. This was not a particularly modern part of the world, and we had several pressing problems bearing down on us, and it would be helpful if Dekker pulled his head out of his arse and started talking to us, so we could, for example, discuss our joint responses to the unidentified space vehicle that was approaching Earth from the outer solar system, that we knew nothing about, and that both Nations of Earth and *gamra* played tag with.

"Have you heard anything about our other activities?" Being deliberately vague here.

"Nothing." She sounded disappointed. "The people we tried to contact just vanished."

When I was in Barresh, a few people from this area had been willing to talk to me, but with the prospect of a visit from us, most of them had stopped responding. I'd even found some of their contact addresses disabled.

Since I'd started investigating the Southern California Aerospace Corps, I had found that, despite the name, the organisation had never spent a long time in southern California. Their main locality was in a small inland town across the border in America Free State. I wanted to visit it.

I didn't know if many people from the organisation were still here, but at the very least, I hoped to speak with local historians about why and how a ship of theirs had crashed in the rainforest near Barresh about fifty years ago.

But America Free State was one of the hardest countries in the world to get a permit to enter.

We weren't getting anywhere with our usual contacts.

I knew Sheydu wanted to be out of here. She didn't like this place any more than I did, but we promised, and we were here for the kids, so we packed up all our things and got ready for a day of being tourists.

Tourists with listening equipment. Tourists wearing armour under their regular clothes. Tourists with hidden guns and explosives.

Someone knocked on the door. Reida went to open it, and came back a moment later, announcing that our guide had arrived. When we booked the accommodation, I'd been informed that groups over a certain size qualified for a guide courtesy of the hotel, and I'd accepted their offer.

The woman was in her thirties.

She had olive skin and a mass of black curly hair. Her eyes were black and clear and reminded me of Thayu's eyes. She had broad hips underneath the regular service uniform, blue trousers and a black-and-white striped shirt, which all people working in the precinct wore. I had noticed that they used different coloured lapels on the shirts and presumed the different colours denoted difference in position.

She smiled at me. Her smile was genuine.

"Are you Mr Wilson?"

"Yes, I am."

Although I rarely used the name any more. I'd changed all my official documentation except my Earth ID to Aveya Domiri.

"I am Mariola, your guide for today." She spoke decent Isla. That was a relief because I wasn't looking forward to attempting conversation with someone in the archaic forms of the local English dialect.

"These are all the kids? The message I received said there were seven, so I took seven satchels of gifts for them."

"There are seven."

I hadn't spotted the Pengali kids since the banana-eating extravaganza, but as I said that, the door opened to Ynggi and Jaki's room and two very grumpy youngsters came out, both dressed in identical bright purple jumpsuits, their tails dragging over the carpet.

I had to make an effort not to laugh.

I'd chosen the colour so that we could easily spot them when they escaped our attention, but they looked rather comical in those suits.

And they'd be grumpy because they didn't like wearing clothes.

Visiting a theme park was not high on the Pengali list of priorities either.

To her credit, Mariola did not freak out at the sight of them.

She introduced herself to the kids, who gave her a bewildered look. I had to translate for her.

I could see Nalya think about whether she was seriously friendly, or only pretending to be friendly. Now I wished I hadn't acknowledged that to him. He was a deep thinker and he would think about this and talk about this and bring it up at inopportune moments, for the next few days, and possibly the entire trip.

Mariola handed out her gift satchels, which were received with wide eyes by the older kids and suspicion by the Pengali kids.

Larrana opened the zip and took out a headband with two

black ears and pencil set with a colouring book. His mouth formed the letter O and his eyes were wide. He carefully folded the ears back up and put the treasure in the satchel he wore around his waist.

"The book is a puzzle," Mariola explained, and I had to translate. Coldi understood puzzles. "And if you hand in the colouring page, you can win prizes."

I translated that, too, but I wasn't sure that the meaning landed.

Never mind.

Ayshada was fascinated with the ears, and Mariola adjusted the headband so it fitted him. He ran to the bathroom to climb onto the cabinet so he could look in the mirror and then chased after Larrana while jumping and singing out of tune, very much like Larrana had done during most of the trip.

The Pengali youngsters had also opened the satchel and discovered a piece of plastic like a spoon with a hole, one in each satchel. One was bright green, the other bright pink.

Mariola showed them that the handle opened and contained similar "spoons" with multiple holes and also a fold-up plastic satchel of see-through material with a spout at the top to attach a tube.

Pykka had already figured out how to put the thing together using the schematic instructions on the back of the satchel, but neither could work out what the contraption was for.

Mariola said, "It's for the bubble machine."

I had no idea what that was either, so I couldn't translate for them.

Emi did the only thing she knew what to do with unfamiliar things: she put the corner of the satchel in her mouth, but pulled a face at the hard feel of the zip on her tongue.

I introduced Mariola to Thayu and to Nicha, Veyada and Mereeni, and she seemed to understand that the rest of the team were security and therefore faceless people. Even though I had instructed them that they were not to wear black, but had to wear holiday clothes. This was rather amusing because I had never seen Sheydu or any of her team in anything other than security uniforms. Their choices of outfits were interesting, to say the least. Sheydu wore a pair of purple trousers. Anyu had chosen a dress of fabric too thin to hide the fact that she wore her black outfit underneath. Reida and Deyu wore matching outfits that would look better on a pair of toddler twins, and Zyana looked only marginally less threatening than usual in khaki.

All the monitoring equipment in the living room was shut down, the door of the apartment locked and double locked, and I was sure that people had various other devices that would warn them if someone was trying to get into the apartment, but all that security business was now finished and we were going to have a day of fun.

CHAPTER THREE

IT TOOK us quite some time to make our way out of the accommodation. The lift was too small to fit everyone.

There was a stairwell, but using it apparently set off an alarm in the office that the staff needed to reset and investigate. It was "For Emergencies Only". It even said so on the door.

So we took the lift down in three batches, because the lift advertised it held eight people at a time, but the weight of Coldi people, like Deyu and most in Sheydu's team, reduced that to seven.

When we finally made it into the foyer, it turned out that our guide had procured an electric trolley that was waiting under the awning outside the entrance.

I protested that we could walk.

"I know you can, but, take it from me, the children will get tired," Mariola said. "And you'll have a place to put your things, like your extra clothes when it gets warm. Many people use these trolleys."

Two similar vehicles waited under the awning, one of them being boarded by a group with an elderly man and a woman who walked with a stick.

Well, yes, it was understandable for them. Many of the tourists I'd spotted in the hotel were not in good health or elderly, and clearly Mariola hadn't experienced the boundless energy of the Pengali kids.

Having sensed that the vehicle was intended for us, Ayshada had already climbed on the outward-facing seats and he patted the seat next to him for Nalya and Larrana to join him. The two Pengali youngsters sat perched in the middle where the backrests touched each other. Their tails waved excitedly in the air. They had dropped their satchels on the seat, but still carried the spoon-like contraptions. At some point, we would find out what they were for.

I guessed we were stuck with yet another item on the ever-increasing space our party took up.

Ileyu also climbed on the seats. Emi was too small to climb the first step into the vehicle, so she held her arms up and yelled.

Thayu lifted her up. She sat primly like a princess, wearing her headband with the black ears, her dark eyes taking in everything around her.

Larrana wanted to sit next to Nalya, but the step was too tall for his wheels to negotiate.

"There is a ramp that slides out from the back." Mariola rushed to show it, but Larrana snorted. Nalya and Ayshada hoisted him onto the seat, with Nalya pulling him up by his shoulders and Ayshada pushing him from behind.

They were partners in mischief, those three.

The vehicle came with a driver, a young man in the same service black-and-white striped uniform that Mariola wore. She said he went by the name Chickadee, but I suspected it was a nickname.

"It's a kind of bird, isn't it?" I asked him.

"That's it. That's my name."

Like many of the service staff, he was dark-skinned, had glossy black hair and spoke with a curious accent.

While I'd been talking and watching the kids, Deyu had run into the hotel and now returned—panting—with the bulky backpack that contained the field transmitter hub. She'd done that very quickly. I suspected the hotel reception would have a thing or two to say to me about not using the stairs—again.

She shoved the pack in between the seats, with the bags of spare clothing, extra food in case we couldn't find any that was certified not to contain artificial sugar, because it did unpleasant things to the digestive tract of Coldi kids.

Deyu glanced at me, giving a small nod.

Yes, that was good thinking on her part. We could now have a fully operational local hub. We hadn't planned on taking the equipment, because it was heavy and would cause raised eyebrows.

And we were on a holiday, right?

But this vehicle was too good an opportunity not to take it.

Then, finally, with squeals from the kids, we were off.

The trolley had broad wheels and travelled at walking speed.

It went first. We followed behind, walking along the lush green street with tall trees and tropical flowers. Drops of water glittered on the bushes. I'd heard the sprinklers come on in the morning, a cacophony of hissing reflected by the canopy that enclosed the street like a glasshouse.

The air was pleasantly cool, a difference from the fierce dry heat on the balcony of our accommodation.

From what I'd seen coming into the precinct, most of the streets which housed accommodation or attractions were at least partially covered. Mariola explained that during the fierce heat of summer, the roof of the canopy could be changed so that it didn't let through as much sunlight. We also passed a giant cooler on a street corner, blowing cool air into the intersection where people and electric trolleys were all going in the same direction, like a trail of ants to their nest.

A garishly colourful statue of a yellow dinosaur stood outside the park entrance. It carried a bunch of flowers and a chicken sat on its head. That explained this morning's performance outside our hotel.

Larrana wanted off the trolley, and zoomed around on his wheels, recording the thing from all angles. Nalya had to take a picture of him standing next to it, and wanted to send pictures to his friends on Asto.

"Come on, we haven't even gotten in yet," Mariola said.

A decent line of people was waiting to get into the park.

Larrana joined us, bouncing on his wheels.

"That really is an amazing wheelchair," Mariola said, looking at me. "I mean—it is a wheelchair, right?"

"Yes, he had an accident when he was little."

Coldi didn't always treat people with disabilities very well. Most of these kids were ignored and forced to do dumb jobs, unless they were from a rich family. Larrana *was* from a rich family. I still didn't think they treated him as fully equal.

We waited in the line.

I told Mariola about Larrana's collection of figurines. She seemed surprised.

"You mean, he collects these things all the way on Asto?"

"Yes, it's big over there. Coldi like displaying items in their hallway that reflect the mood of the house's occupant to visitors. Often these items arouse curiosity and are a starting point for discussions. I think this is how those collections started. There are extensive catalogues of collectible items and some are worth a lot of money, especially the original figurines from the twentieth century."

"That's amazing! I didn't know that."

"Most of the collectors are older, but Larrana is not your normal kid."

"I can see that."

"He's also from an influential family. This trip is part of my promise to that family in return for things they have done for us."

Not quite, but there was no point in spending more time explaining it.

Mariola wanted to know more about where we came from, and what those "little monkeys" were. I warned her to never assume that Pengali were animals, although she'd probably have learned that by the end of the day. I would have added that I disliked it when people called them monkeys, but I was the only one who cared about that.

"And you, what are you, really. Your name is very... normal, but you look like..." She shrugged.

Questions like these irritated me, but to be frank, we *were* in a very backward place and her interest probably came from genuine curiosity. Did they ever see *gamra* people here?

So while we waited, I told her of my varied and tangled work history and allegiances in a nutshell.

Her eyes were wide. "Wow. I've never left this area. We don't have the money to travel, and I can't take that much time off, anyway."

She told me that her family lived in the streets around the precinct. Her mother had come from Mexico City in search of better opportunities. Her father had been a refugee from America Free State who proudly identified as a native American. He managed to get out of the country as a young man. He'd met her mother while working as domestic staff for the park's managers. He used to look after their dogs, but he'd retired a few years ago. Now, he made little souvenir trinkets to sell in the shops on the kitchen table of their home.

"Did there used to be much traffic across the border in those days when your father came?" I asked.

"There are still people who go across. The people in America Free State need to buy stuff from us. They say it's not always easy, and sometimes they need to give the border guards money, if they strike a bad one. I don't know, you come from a rich place and probably think our lives are crap. That's nothing compared to their lives. If you try to cross and get the wrong guards on the other side of the border, they will ask for money, because they have none and it's worth a lot to them. It means they can buy stuff we sell to them, like medicines."

"Do you still have relatives there?" I asked.

"Some."

"Do you get to see them?"

She glanced aside. I swore she was looking to see if the people behind us were listening.

I didn't think they were. They were a group of elderly women, all of them wearing bright pink hats, and all of them giggling like they'd had too much to drink already.

"Sometimes," Mariola said, in a low voice.

"Can they come here?"

Again she looked around.

"No. We go there. We bring them canned food and stuff like that. We're not supposed to, because there is a boycott. But every time someone visits, we take stuff. You just have to hide it well."

"Is it possible to visit? I thought you couldn't cross the border, not even to see family." The stories of the separated families were one of the few things I'd learned about this region at school. It had shocked me as a young kid growing up in New Zealand, that people could do things like that to each other.

My teachers held it up as an example of how people were mistreated, but I didn't think it was that simplistic.

Mariola said, "You can't visit without an acceptable reason. My cousin operates a business. He can travel. America Free State likes the money he brings in."

"What sort of business?"

"He takes rich people out for scenic flights."

"You mean to see the Grand Canyon?"

"Anywhere they want."

"Anywhere? I've been trying to find a way across the border, but all the tour drivers said they couldn't do it."

"No, you can't hire a driver. There is a very strict no passenger rule and none want to lose their licence. We still supply America Free State with fresh food, so they need the trucks to come in, but they'll shoot any stray passengers on the spot."

"But passengers in a plane are fine?"

"These are rich people, understand. It's kept quiet. All my cousin does is take them to these spots. Most of them are remote and have been deserted since the start of the war. My cousin owns a plane and some gyrocopters. He owns places where people can stay and hunt."

"Hunt?"

This reminded me horribly of Minke Kluysters and his vast property in South Africa where rich people came to hunt.

"Anything they can shoot. Dogs, in that area, mostly. Not much else left. And the dogs are pests. They come into town and raid people's houses."

I nodded and understanding passed between us. If it was hot and dry in this dust bowl, it was nothing compared to the situation further inland.

But my mind was whirling. We'd been looking for a way to cross the border. This might be a better option than all the other avenues we were trying.

I guess we qualified as "rich people" in Mariola's eyes.

The line shuffled forward, and we followed the trolley. The driver stared into the distance, doing his best to ignore our conversation. He worked for Mariola, I guessed.

"The Chickadee is a bird, right?" I asked her.

She nodded.

"Now extinct?"

She nodded again.

"And Mariola is also a bird?"

"It's a plant. They're a bit tougher than birds. Still hanging on."

We arrived at the front of the line and had to stop talking. But this talk was proving to be more interesting than I'd expected.

Mariola had contacts, she was a local but not someone from the Coldi register. She and her co-worker were named after a plant and an extinct bird. That had to mean something, right?

I wasn't terribly rich and maybe the places we wanted to go were truly off-limits, but the seeds of a plan grew.

Better still, she was spending the entire day with us and I could ask her more questions without arousing suspicion.

CHAPTER FOUR

WHEN WE GOT CLOSER to the end of the line, Mariola went to speak to the entrance guards and arranged for us to bypass the ticket and bag checks. She told me she had a special relationship with the park employees because she brought in so many tourists.

The guards asked other visitors in the queue to unpack bags, hand in bottles of fluid—because apparently it could contain dangerous poison instead of water—and explain their need for items that could be used as weapons. At least I guessed the latter, because I had no idea why else anyone would have a loud argument in Spanish about a bright blue umbrella.

I remembered these types of bag checks at Nations of Earth when I was little, but these days, most building entrances had sophisticated scanning and detection equipment that analysed people while they walked past.

At *gamra*, this even included a person's ID.

I also wondered, as we were ushered past the checkpoint and guards opened a gate for the trolley to get through, why Mariola had said nothing about Deyu's backpack because surely she would have seen that Deyu had added the bag, and that it looked black, heavy and menacing.

I was confident that it would pass security, because on the flight here, Nations of Earth guards had checked and unpacked the transmitter several times. They'd asked questions and made Deyu walk through special scanners with it and had allowed it through. But wouldn't these guards want to know what it was?

Or was Mariola one of the people keeping an eye on us? Because there *were* those people, Thayu had said, and she had let it shine through that my team were uncertain about their identity.

And while people *always* spied on us, and most of the time, we didn't know who they were, or ever came into contact with them or their bosses, it was of greater concern to me here, in this place, where we were out of our comfort zone. Moreover, if we needed to do something about those people who followed us, it would raise a forest of eyebrows within Nations of Earth—which I could explain if only they agreed to talk to me.

Suspecting Mariola to be part of a spying ring was not helpful because most likely, one, she wasn't, and two, I'd contacted the park and asked for a guide, they had provided one and hadn't swapped her on me, or had displayed any of the runaround trickery that would normally go with inserting a spy in a group.

Anyway, I appreciated that we didn't have to wait, because Larrana had spied some images of his favourite characters and had gotten the other kids excited, and as soon as we were inside, they raced off looking at this thing or that thing.

We were in a quaint, old-fashioned street with shops along the sides that sold sweets and souvenir items like shirts and posters and mugs. So many mugs.

We adults had a heck of a job keeping everyone together.

Larrana showed every poor kid he met in the shops pictures of his collection. He cared little about his victim's reaction because he couldn't understand anything they said. They couldn't understand him either, which was probably just as well, because he commented if the kid had bought cheap replica souvenirs that were displayed in overflowing bins at the shop entrances, and not the real deal, displayed in glass-fronted cabinets at the back.

His family had supplied him, through Amarru, with a more than decent amount of credit to buy stuff. We traipsed in and out of shops and the pile under the seats in the trolley grew.

He ticked off items in his catalogue to make sure that he didn't buy anything he already owned.

He knew all the names of the characters, the different movies they were in and what they represented. This part of Earth's culture was utterly alien to me. It disturbed me that someone from off-world knew so much more about it than I did.

Meanwhile, an old-fashioned tram had stopped in the street, and people dressed up as dogs had come out of the carriage to perform a show.

Several of us placed ourselves strategically in the crowd to watch, not in the least because the Pengali kids had discovered a tree and had climbed onto the branches. Both were dancing to the music, waving their tails. Fortunately, they hadn't yet found it necessary to remove their jumpsuits.

The gathered audience alternated between watching them and watching the show.

Two uniformed women walked past, giving them, and Ynggi at the bottom of the tree, the stink-eye.

We finally dragged Larrana out of the shops with the promise of going on the rides.

Mariola told us about the history of the park while we walked from one to the other.

I was sure it was a rehearsed and approved speech, but I found it quite interesting, because I'd never been here or had anything to do with this industry.

She said that in the twentieth and twenty-first century, people from all over the world used to come here, and that these parks were considered entertainment for the masses. The era of the great amusement parks had ended in the mid-twenty-first century, after a series of cataclysmic events had stopped mass tourism. Of course I knew about those events. Armed conflicts, great trade wars, massive displacement of people because of hunger and war. Border closures relating to conflict and boycotts and the protracted wars in Western Asia and Northern Africa made air travel risky, because people never knew whether flights would leave or they'd end up stranded in foreign countries.

The—far too tardy—move away from fossil fuels had caused a crater in the airline industry because air travel remained dependent on fossil fuels, but mining those fuels became uneconomic, causing a sudden collapse of companies that sold them. Biofuels were big until worldwide droughts forced people to use the land for producing food.

When the second American civil war broke out, Mexico was quick to scoop up this part of the country that used to be known as the United States of America. Because of Mexico's annexation, this region surrounding Los Angeles escaped the worst of the violence, but that didn't mean it didn't suffer. When the tourists stopped coming, a lot of the parks fell into disrepair. The companies that owned them went bankrupt or were absorbed into larger companies and vanished quietly. New World Entertainment had bought up a lot of the parks and brought together the most endearing features of all into this precinct.

The park and surrounding area was home to thirty thousand people, most of whom were employed or otherwise supported by the park.

They had to be, because the world outside was a dusty, desolate desert that, frankly, resembled something out of a dystopian show.

In the Bay of Islands, where my father lived, a warming climate had caused more rain and had brought colourful fish and corals into the shallow waters.

It was good to be reminded that for much of the world, the changing climate had meant desertification, hunger and misery.

Once the Earth had supported seven billion people. It was now struggling to support half the number.

While I listened to Mariola, members of my team were doing other things. Ynggi and Jaki kept their kids out of the garden beds. Pykka and Amay then discovered a poor park-employed woman who was entertaining young kids with a bubble machine. After being told that jumping on the barrel of the machine to pop the bubbles was not acceptable—and not pleasant either when rubbing their eyes with their soap-covered hands—they resolved to figure out how the machine worked. Mariola showed them how to use the spoon-shaped contraptions in their satchels, and how to fill the reservoir bag with soapy fluid and blow through the holes in the "spoons". The one with the little holes would make a lot of small bubbles, and the single hole would make a very large bubble.

The soap solution was not regular dishwashing soap—which my mother used to give me to blow bubbles, but a solution that dried quickly and produced a coating around the bubbles, making them less likely to pop.

The two Pengali youngsters really got into bubble blowing, and we had to beat our way through the park surrounded by a cloud of bubbles, even to the point where it was hard to see.

Deyu's transmitter went through phases of having weak Exchange coverage. Each time this happened, there would be a flurry of activity around the trolley, with Sheydu and Isharu listening in on some conversation and replying in serious tones, or Reida studying maps or scans. Once, Zyana sped ahead of our group, presumably to clear the way of spies or watchers.

I also hoped there would finally be news from any of the people we hoped to hear from.

Thayu and Nicha and Reida entertained the kids by going on rides with them. Thayu's eyes shone, her cheeks were rosy.

Ayshada had the uncanny ability to charm the socks off guards, and Zyana was no exception. When a ride scared him, Ayshada made Zyana go with him, even if Zyana was always watching every corner and every roof.

Who knew that serious security people could be so enamoured with roller coasters that they went in them not once or twice but three times, and that they enjoyed being pretend-dropped from a tall tower in a wire cage, or trying to find their way out of a virtual reality maze?

And it was entertaining, even if only for Emi's squeals. Our life must be terribly boring for these poor kids.

Even the Pengali got into it, although the rollercoaster's attendants didn't appreciate the youngsters getting out of the restraints and dangling on the backs of the seats. Nor did they appreciate the enormous cloud of bubbles that Pykka produced by taking the blower on the ride and using a sheet of paper to funnel air through the spoon-like contraption while racing around on a rollercoaster. The effect was spectacular, to say the least. The staff had to shut down the ride while waiting for the bubbles to dissipate.

I hadn't looked forward to this part of the trip, but it was strangely relaxing.

When we got tired, we attended a live show with singing and dancing, even if few of us recognised or understood the words in archaic English.

The costumes were dazzling and the musical performances very good. It was amazing how these people could sing in tune while dangling from a rope off the ceiling. The kids thoroughly enjoyed it.

Gradually, during the day, it had become busier with more and more families coming out.

Most of them had hired trolleys and a driver. The vehicles came in different sizes.

Larrana was also interested to see how many people used

wheelchairs. He asked me why there were so many. I couldn't answer that question and felt ashamed admitting that.

When I translated the question for Mariola, she said that many people suffered debilitating diseases. Some were brought on by deficiencies in diet. Older disabled people had likely been injured in the civil war. She also said that if you were on a special pension, you got discounts for coming to attractions like this. She said that many people from across the border had come for that reason alone, because they claimed dual citizenship.

"Mexico was handing out dual citizenships?" I asked.

"Yes. Our government sees it as our duty to help people who escape across the border. Because despite all the stuff that's gone on, our countries are very closely related."

"Are there's still battles going on? I thought the creation of the four countries was the end of the civil war." It was what I had learned at school.

She snorted. "That's what they say. It made everyone feel good about having stopped the fighting. But it went on in other places. Trade wars, boycotts, attempts trying to steal resources and influential people."

I had to admit to not fully comprehending why the civil war had started, despite reading up on it. I thought *gamra* and Nations of Earth were steeped in ideology, but the clashes over the role of religion in government and discrimination against certain groups of people were a level of parochialism I never hoped to attain.

I knew that *gamra* had little interest in this part of Earth and were not keen for the four nations to join Nations of Earth either, fearful that religious ideology—which was alien to *gamra*, but always under the surface at Nations of Earth—would dominate the discussion.

"So how would you describe the current relationship between the four countries if you don't think they're at peace?" I asked Mariola, aware that it was a question she might not want to answer.

She shrugged. "We're in Mexico. Mexico is a fine place."

And Mexico, of course, was a powerhouse member of Nations of Earth, the home of the man who occupied its first presidency, Pedro Gonzales. Mexico had been instrumental in establishing Nations of Earth out of the ashes of the United Nations, to guard against the conflict spilling out across their northern borders.

"But you just said you have relatives across the border. Don't you feel worried about them?"

"My younger cousins will find a way across. There is a large expat community here."

"Is everyone trying to leave?"

"Everyone under the age of forty I know. You may not understand, but America Free State is a very poor country. The government—if you can call it that—only serves those people who can pay."

"Governor Patterson, right?"

She nodded, glancing aside. This was clearly an uneasy subject for her.

"I don't like to talk about politics. It can be dangerous."

"I'm trying to understand the situation."

She nodded.

I continued, "So we have Governor Patterson of America Free State, Governor Schuster of the Dixie Republic, Governor Sukar of Prairie and Celia Braddock of Atlantia. Out of these, Prairie and the Dixie Republic feed the other two countries, Atlantia is the de facto liaison with Nations of Earth and America Free State is... simply trying to survive while also being a chunk of inhospitable desert and mountainous terrain largely unsuitable for farming."

"If you know so much, why do you ask?" Mariola said. "So that you can laugh at us? You know that we got the worst end of the deal from the hallowed Nations of Earth. They kept us stupid by denying us collaboration in science and education. They told us lies that we didn't have the knowledge and courage to debunk. They walked away when things went wrong, when the land burned, and other countries stopped buying oil, and the water dried up. But you know what? You can blame us or call us stupid, but we're still a proud people. We don't need any other countries to help. Because they all betrayed us."

By *us*, she very obviously meant America Free State.

"I don't call you stupid at all. In fact, we would like to visit there," I said.

She gave me a suspicious look.

I continued, "You told me that you have a cousin who does scenic flights. I'd like to know about booking such a flight. This is a once in a lifetime trip mostly for the young boy. If you think the scenery is worth it."

The excuse about Larrana and his once in a lifetime trip was a very handy one.

"There are several scenic flights you can do," she said, suddenly all business-like. "There are a few areas that are open to visitors. They're like small islands where tourists can still come. They're crazy across the border, but not that crazy. They still like making money from people who want to see the countryside. You will see genuine beauty and real wilderness. "This—" She waved her hand at the park attractions. "Is all fake. That, across the border, is real country."

"Do contact your cousin and let us know what he says, preferably tonight. You know where we're staying."

"Sure. I have to warn you it's probably not going to be cheap, but if you're okay with that, I can make some inquiries."

"Yes, sure. Do that."

Of course. Money was always the first consideration. No matter where you were in the galaxy, you could buy everything for money.

The kids had fun.

We prevented some disasters, such as when the Pengali kids discovered a poor squirrel in a tree and chased the poor thing into a shop.

Or when Ayshada became hyperactive and ran around yelling and almost upset a family's lunch.

It was amazing how much energy the kids had when they were enjoying themselves, but after many hours of rides and shows and many unhealthy snacks that Deyu needed to test for anything Coldi children could not eat, even the older ones grew tired and allowed themselves to be driven on the trolley.

Emi and Ileyu had crashed a long time ago and lay on the seats of the very handy trolley fast asleep.

It was going dark, and I was keen to get back to the accommodation so that I could check if any messages had come in.

Mariola sent Chickadee home and drove the trolley herself. It seemed like an innocent enough action, but all members in my team were suddenly alert. She had intended to get us by ourselves in a place where no one else could overhear what she told us.

"My cousin has agreed to meet you," she said. "I'll take you to the hotel and you can decide who will come to talk to him. It's a rough place."

"I thought you lived in the area that serviced the park?"

"We do, but that is the real world out here. There is no cover, no cooling, and no pretty plants."

"I'm game."

CHAPTER FIVE

MARIOLA TOOK us back to the accommodation, where we dropped all the debris we had collected during the day and delivered the tired children to the room. Ynggi and Jaki would get them fed and bathed, although, with the amount of junk food they'd eaten, I doubted they would be hungry.

I was a bit jealous of Emi, who collapsed in her cot and looked unlikely to wake until morning. I wanted to go to sleep, too, but we had this meeting still to attend. I'd have to be alert to make sure we didn't walk into a trap. But I would much rather go to bed.

Out the window, sparkling fireworks rose over the roof of the accommodation block to the left. We decided earlier that we were too tired to stay to watch them.

In the hallway of our apartment, we held a brief meeting, deciding who would come and how much we'd reveal about our plans. The locations we wanted to visit were very specific, deep into restricted territory, and might pose a risk to any genuine tourist operators.

"They're not simple tour guides," Evi said. "None of them are."

He and Telaris had spent much of the day monitoring the newsfeeds that Deyu's receiver had picked up. They'd picked up how Mariola had contacted her cousin and had discussed arrangements for a trip for us.

Was it normal that families of park guides hawked their business?

Apparently. Like the dancers and singers, they didn't get paid a lot, and made extra money off supplementary business.

Anyu handed out listening bugs for each of us to carry under our clothes. Mine came with a sticky pad that I attached to my chest. Thank the heavens for the lack of chest hair that had resulted from my genetic treatment. I'd not been able to find the time to go back for the laser treatment.

We decided that myself, Sheydu, Evi, Deyu and Nicha were going to come. I was keen to have Nicha, although I hated to take him away from his son, who had woken up again and complained that he wanted his father. I told Ayshada that Thayu would put him to bed, but that only resulted in Ayshada becoming more awake and stubborn.

Nicha told him to play with his cousin Larrana, to which Ayshada replied that Larrana was only interested in his collection, and Ayshada was getting bored with plastic figurines.

I gave Thayu a satisfied look. Earlier today, she'd expressed her concern that the kids would forever be interested in this "useless junk", as she called it, but this was evidence that we were not in danger of cultural infiltration.

But just when I feared that a tantrum was imminent, a cloud of bubbles drifted from the bathroom. Amay ran from the room holding her bag with liquid soap attached to a piece of tubing—where the hell had that come from?—blowing air through the solution and spewing vast quantities of bubbles out of the nozzle that was used to fill the bag. She had attached the spoon-like contraption to it.

Holy crap.

Jaki blundered after her into the bedroom, batting away bubbles and trying to keep them out of his eyes. Several got stuck in the short hair on his tail. They also clung to the back of his shirt.

He caught Amay and took the contraption off her with much squealing.

One rarely saw Pengali berating their youngsters, but she copped an earful and then moped off carrying a towel to wipe the soap off the furniture in the room.

Relative peace returned.

While we were putting gear in our pockets, I realised something else: I should take also Ynggi on this night-time excursion.

Mariola had told me about her cultural heritage, which was obviously of importance to her. The park was a bastion of cultural heritage, and the history of her varied family was another. These people might appreciate seeing different cultures represented in our group.

So I fished Ynggi out of the kids' room, where he was playing a game with Nalya and Ileyu was watching them.

The game involved sets of little wooden triangles that you could stack in different ways to produce the tallest structure. It was a Pengali agility game, and I'd seen them play it at home in Barresh, usually when their concoction collapsed on the tiles with a great clatter, and wooden triangles bounced everywhere.

Nope, not much risk of a cultural takeover by plastic figurines happening here.

The kids' faces fell when I asked Ynggi to come. Both he and Jaki were very popular with all the kids. Because of the Pengali system with karrit points that governed an individual's standing in the tribe, they taught the kids, both Pengali and Coldi alike, a lot about responsibility and consequences of their actions. Employing them had been one of the best things I'd done.

Ynggi told them that Jaki would continue to play once he had put the younger kids to bed, and then he came with me into the hall. He asked what I wanted him to do.

"Listen and observe. I want to know if we can trust these people or if they have an ulterior motive."

"I'm not great at those things. Sheydu is much better."

"I don't want you to do the security stuff. Sheydu will do that. I want you to look at the people. How they react to you. How they dress. How they treat each other. How they treat their children or their elders."

Comprehension dawned on his face. Yes, he understood. And no, Sheydu did not do any of those things.

Sheydu handed him the listening bug which he stuck onto the inside of his Pengali belt that sat over the top of his jumpsuit and from which dangled not the traditional glass-stone knife, but a satchel of cloths to wipe spills and sticky fingers, a bundle of spoons and a little holo-sheet that contained key terms to look out for in local eatery menus for things that would cause trouble if the kids were to eat them.

To be sure, his knife had still travelled with us, as had the fishhooks and the lines, but they were in our luggage, packed in a travel case that stood in the hall.

We filed out of the apartment.

It was now dark, and fellow hotel guests we met in the foyer were going out for dinner. They gave our party a wide berth. Dressed in plain dark clothing and with several of our team imposing in stature, no one could pretend we were simple tourists.

Mariola waited outside under the entrance awning with the trolley. She was talking to another woman, leaning against the vehicle.

When we approached, the other woman scurried away, giving Mariola a wave. She wore a uniform that differed from the park standard outfit that Mariola wore.

Mariola said, "Get in everyone and keep your belongings

inside. I'm going to put up the sides of the vehicle. It's going to be a bit hot for you, but this way, there shouldn't be any questions about what you're doing as park visitors in the residential area."

We all climbed into the benches where the children had sat during much of the day, and with a click and a zoom, the sides of the vehicle, the boards that had formed the safety railing unfolded. They formed into a cabin which displayed the New World Entertainment logo on the outside.

They enclosed us in a stuffy bubble of darkness.

The trolley wobbled when Mariola jumped in the driver's seat. We started moving.

I could see a little strip of the street in between the panels of the vehicle. We turned away from the hotel, in the opposite direction from where the park entrance was. We had come in that way yesterday, in a dedicated bus service that ran from the beachside suburbs where we had stayed a few days. On the way, we had traversed some utterly desolate country: dry fields, cracked and abandoned roads, dilapidated housing estates, abandoned business parks with windows smashed in.

Once the greater Los Angeles area had housed over ten million people. Just two million lived there today, and I had my doubts whether this area would even support that many. Athyl was a desert city, but there was evidence of food production in alleys, inside indoor farms, in the aquifers everywhere. There was none of that here. The food, apparently, came from elsewhere.

We had entered the resort through the main road and the main entrance, a large arch to give visitors the illusion that they were entering a fantasy castle.

Mariola took us out via a bumpy back road. She stopped several times when she would speak to someone. Once I could hear a gate opening and closing. We left the zone of covered streets and cooling. It grew hot inside the cabin with all of us in the small space.

The trolley proceeded slowly.

An avalanche of sound washed over us: people talking and yelling, motorbikes and other engines, some of them quite noisy, loud music, people laughing, a noisy party with blaring music, and people talking.

The small strip between the panels allowed me to see coloured lights illuminating houses painted in bright colours. Blue, yellow, pink, green.

We drove for what felt like a couple of blocks before Mariola turned off the road, into a driveway, and stopped.

A man approached the vehicle and spoke to Mariola in a language I didn't understand.

She then let down the sides.

We stood on a paved driveway with different-coloured tiles arranged in patterns. The house was two floors high, painted bright orange with electric blue window sills—seriously—with a porch and two sets of windows on either side on the ground floor. The front yard was small, all-paved, but several large pots stood around the edges, filled with palm trees and flowers.

Another electric trolley stood in the yard, and Mariola's driver Chickadee was washing it with a cloth and a bucket.

He greeted us.

A man came down the steps that led down from the set of double doors that looked too large for a house this size.

He was tall, dark-skinned, wore his curly hair in a ponytail and wore a pink shirt with blue flowers.

"This is my cousin, Swallow," Mariola said.

Totally in keeping with the tradition of using animal and plant names.

The fellow came into the yard.

He stuck out his hand, and I shook it.

He met my eyes. His expression was intelligent, shrewd almost.

A second man watched from inside the open door to the house.

"Good evening. How can I help you?"

His voice was deep.

"I heard that you organise trips across the border," I said.

"We do, yes. We do sightseeing trips of the parks and canyons, the natural wonders of the world. We can do one day and multiple day tours, depending on where you want to go."

"Do we have options?"

"Yes, if you're a serious customer, we can take you pretty much anywhere you want. Different places will have different rates. We can also advise you on the best places to visit."

"I would like to discuss a number of options."

He jerked his head to the door. "Let's go inside."

The second man had already disappeared into the house, and we followed Swallow up the steps into a broad hallway with gleaming tiles and a carpet runner. There were gold rimmed light fittings along the sides of the walls with lights that spread a warm glow through the hallway.

Several doors on the sides were closed, but one door was open and gave a view into a lush dining room, where several young kids sat watching a screen.

"Do you live here as well?" I asked Mariola.

"No, I live around the corner with my family. My husband's father and aunt live with us, and we also live with his sister, and her children."

I wondered how many people lived in this house. It looked much bigger than it had appeared from the outside. I definitely hadn't expected the richly appointed furnishings. I wondered if the other houses in the street—which looked fairly similar—also contained such elaborate interiors. Maybe it was a status symbol associated with the part of the street. Maybe it was because people would spend a lot of time inside during the day when it was hot and there were dust storms.

Swallow opened a door to the side, letting us into a palatial office. White tiles lined the floor, and in the middle sat an enormous desk made of dark wood with ornately carved wooden legs, polished within an inch of its life, and a leather chair.

One wall contained a large screen, and heavy blinds hung over the window. Through a crack between them, I could see the house next door, which was roughly an arm's length away. These people obviously had little use for outdoor space. The weather might be quite pleasant at the moment, but the summers would be ferocious.

Two couches faced each other in one corner of the room. Swallow waved his hand for us to sit down.

As was usual, Evi remained at the door, and Ynggi joined him.

I sat down on one couch, and Swallow sat on the other couch, with a low table between us. Sheydu, Nicha and Deyu remained standing, but Swallow offered them a seat at the table in another corner. A man he didn't introduce also remained at the door. His security guard, I guessed.

A young woman scurried into the room with a tray with glasses and a carafe containing an amber fluid.

"Drink?" she asked.

"Yes, please." Because it was impolite to refuse.

As she poured, the scent of alcohol drifted on the air. I had better be careful and not drink too much of this.

Swallow waited until the young woman was gone. She left the door open.

"Now we can talk about your proposed trip. We have all the facilities to make you comfortable and to provide an exciting trip. If you want to go walking, we can arrange that, we can also arrange boat tours in the canyon, we can arrange horse riding, or camel riding if that is your thing, or we can arrange speedboat racing on the lake."

"Actually, there are a few specific locations that we would like to visit."

I took out my reader and put it on the table, and found the

maps that Deyu and Reida had prepared. Several locations we had already crossed off as being not significant or we had already visited.

I enlarged the area I was interested in across the border.

His eyebrows flicked up.

"Why would you want to go there? There is nothing to see over there."

"It's close enough to the tourist spots, isn't it?"

"I guess, but..."

"You said you could take me anywhere?"

"We can, but I don't understand why..."

"We're not here as tourists. There is a mystery that we would like to solve. There used to be an organisation called the Southern California Aerospace Corps. They were initially based in San Diego, in a location we have already visited. That visit didn't answer our questions about the organisation, so we're now looking at additional locations. They used to operate a factory in this location."

"Huh." He stared at our map.

"Have you heard of them?"

"Heard, yes. Aren't those the group that was going to take us all for trips to the Moon?"

"I'm pretty sure that's the group," I said. "They took over a lot of technology once the space exploration institutes fell victim to the civil war." Mainly from NASA, but there had been other, related, institutes.

Swallow snorted. "You're putting it politely. They stole a lot of the stuff. They squirrelled it across the border. They were going to build space bases and all that. They even got money for it. But nothing ever came of it." He frowned at me. "But why would you worry about that? I mean—you come from..." He spread his hands.

"It's a fairly long story," I said. "In short, we found some stuff that we think may have been theirs and we want to know more."

"You found stuff? You mean, out there?" He glanced at the ceiling.

"Yes. We need to know how seriously to take it."

"Huh. They kind of disappeared."

"Do you know what happened?"

"Ran out of money and out of people who wanted to support their crazy dreams, that's my guess."

"Do you know anyone who used to work for them?"

"Not really."

This had been our reply, everywhere we went. People knew of the organisation. No one knew anyone who had worked for it. The youngest of those employees would now be in their seventies, and average life expectancy was seventy-one, so it was not surprising.

"I want to find some of those people who can tell me more. I want to look at this place that used to be the base where they put space craft together and test the vehicles. Perhaps someone in the town has an old vehicle in a shed at their house. Perhaps we can find someone who used to work at this factory. According to my information, thousands of people used to work here. Does that explain to you why we want to go there?"

"I guess. It's not a pleasant area, though. The townsfolk are fond of roughing up strangers."

"I'm not expecting a welcome committee. I just want to see what we can find out."

"You said you wanted to find people who used to work there and kept stuff in their garage."

"Get us a good local guide. That's all we need."

"Huh."

And then he said nothing for a while.

"So can you do it?"

He shrugged. "This is a long way to travel, and these localities are not easy to get to. They're well off-limits, and not even we have easy access to them. We might need to bribe an administrator or two. You have to understand that this is deep into enemy territory. We'll also have to get local guides and they don't come cheap."

"I also understand that not terribly many people live in these areas."

"With good reason. They're hellish deserts."

"It's not summer."

His mouth twitched. He didn't look entirely convinced and was still stalling. It was time to bring out the heavy-duty tactics.

I asked, "How much?"

"Just you and these people?"

"No. There will be two parts to this trip. We'll start off doing the usual sightseeing. There is a fairly large party in our hotel. Mariola knows them. They will want to come on the sightseeing part. Then I want you to take myself and a smaller group to these sites while the children and the others come back here."

He eyed my map. "You'd need two days for your part."

"That's all right."

"You'd need on-ground vehicles, and guides."

"That's all right."

"It will cost."

"I understand."

"No, I don't think so, Mister. I'm allowed to take people on scenic tours. This here..." He waved at the map. "Is crazy territory. You never know what you might find there. Bands of rogues, coyotes."

"Make it happen. I'll pay you fairly, for your knowledge and your silence."

He eyed the other man who still stood at the door, and then Mariola, also at the door. She gave a tiny snort, as if she wanted to say: "You wanted a job. I give you a job, now take it."

He nodded. "All right. Tomorrow."

CHAPTER SIX

WITH THAT SETTLED, we went into the details of the planned trip, and other people came into the room. It so happened that Swallow had a guide on the books who had grown up in the area where the factory was. There was a lot to organise for so many people to go out tomorrow. Swallow gave orders to his people, all of whom took their tasks without asking questions, except to ask if there was anything that people in my team couldn't eat or didn't like.

Mariola was the central tent pole of the business.

In this house, Swallow was the boss, and the others were his servants. We were keeping alive an entire ecosystem.

He said that he would come to pick us up in the morning and gave us a list of all the things that we should bring.

We already had most items, but it might be a good idea to swing by the shop on the corner and pick up some insect repellant, if we could find any that was safe for everyone to use. It might also be a good idea to stock up on some non-perishable food.

I asked if we would camp overnight and needed to bring sleeping bags, but Swallow said he'd look after it.

Then it was time for us to go back to the accommodation, because we had a lot of packing to do ourselves.

Evi and Ynggi were still in the hallway, but the children who had been watching the screen earlier were now with them, playing another Pengali game. The children were all laughing and running after the bouncy balls he flicked through the hallway with his tail.

They looked disappointed when we entered the corridor.

We made our way back out of the house. A lot of curious people had gathered in the street. They all remained outside the gate and started calling as soon as we came out.

Swallow yelled something at them. They shuffled aside, off the driveway. Some continued calling.

Then the other man, the guard, strode down the steps, across the yard while yelling at them. Some people started leaving before he reached that gate, but others argued back at him, but eventually left, too.

What was all that about? People wanting work?

Chickadee was still cleaning the other vehicle, now vacuuming it out. He gave us a brief nod. Another servant.

Mariola drove us back to the accommodation. She didn't close the sides of the vehicle this time, because she said the curfew had ended.

I asked her what curfew, and she said the park owners didn't want the guests to see anything related to the maintenance and upkeep of the place, so this all happened after a certain time when all the guides had ushered the visitors to their rooms or the approved evening venues.

I had noticed that the restaurants advertised session times, and that they were all the same time slots. So the guests had set times to eat, and the workers would then scurry out of their way when the change-over happened? Just so that the rich visitors wouldn't see anyone sweeping the streets or, heaven forbid, cleaning the toilets? And these people who cleaned the place were faceless grey ghosts, very poorly paid grey ghosts at that? People who, judging by the spectacle outside Swallow's house, were even begging the family to give them jobs?

I felt sick.

Houses like the one we had just visited lined the street. They were all in different bright colours. People sat on the verandas, and music spilled out. Children played in the yards.

These were proud people, business people, who relied on the tourists. They were brown people who didn't speak Isla, or the old English. But they were tough people, with their own language, originated from Spanish.

We got many curious looks as we passed. The houses grew smaller as we came closer to the park entrance where a maintenance crew was at work cleaning the signs and sweeping sand off the road.

I guess we weren't meant to see that, either.

"The dust blows in all the time," Mariola said. "They employ a lot of people to keep it clean."

"You mean, people sweeping up sand by hand? Can't they use machines?"

"They make too much noise. And most machines use water, and we have severe water restrictions."

"But what about the sprinklers that come on in the morning?"

"That's all harvested and recycled here. Wait."

She turned the vehicle onto a side road. After another turn, we came past sets of huge tanks with large pipes leading to them.

"All the water and garbage from the park is taken here and sorted, cleaned, reused and recycled."

Deyu was giving me a blank look. Her translation module didn't cope well with Mariola's accent. Nicha explained it to her.

But to someone from Asto, recycling water was not a new concept. To be honest, even the small coastal community where my father lived in New Zealand did it.

We arrived in the park through a back entrance where

Mariola opened the gate with an access pass. It was amazing how the scenery changed. Cheerful colours, neatly paved streets, green gardens.

It was busy on the main thoroughfare with tourists ambling past the restaurants and shops that stayed open until late. I hadn't noticed this yesterday, but now saw that the tourists were kept in the main street through temporary barriers across the side streets, except where there were entrances to accommodation.

In the square in front of the hotel, scores of service people were sweeping and watering and pruning the plants, cleaning the benches and emptying the rubbish bins into trucks.

There was an entire army of these people, chatting and working hard. A bunch of kids on monocycles were playing with a ball, all of them racing around on their bikes. These were the kids we had seen earlier that day.

Our apartment was also a hive of activity.

We had not planned to stay here another day, regardless of whether we could arrange for the trip, and so we needed to pack everything up. As per our tradition, a pile of bags had appeared in the hall.

I went into Sheydu and Isharu's room, intending to ask her if any messages had come in. I found most of the team in the middle of some sort of security briefing. Thayu, Deyu, Zyana and Reida sat on the bed, while Anyu had projected something on the wall.

"Oh, sorry. I can come back later," I said. "I just wanted to ask if any messages had come in."

Reida said, "No, but we were just discussing some messages we intercepted."

"Anything important?"

"That's what we were discussing."

I went over to the bed and sat next to Thayu.

The projection showed a couple of lines of text in English. The translation function had produced some corresponding

Coldi text, but I ignored it, because the translations from Isla to Coldi were bad enough. I had no faith in the device's capability to translate from English to Coldi. I had to read it a few times before I understood.

Movement across the border has our troops on high alert. Patterson denies any activity. Braddock says military exercise in progress. Sukar confirms.

I checked the Coldi translation, which was garbage.

"Is it something important?" Reida asked.

"I doubt it has anything to do with us," I said. "It seems one country is holding a military exercise and the others want to bicker over it."

I had no idea what this out-of-context snippet meant. Maybe this type of bickering was normal. Who knew?

I explained to the others what I made of it.

"So they're not about to go to war?" Isharu asked.

I checked the translation and noticed it mis-translated military as war. The Coldi word for military could be described as "going to war", and it was a term of potential or threat, while "war" was a definitive term and meant that a war was already happening. Ah, I figured why this alarmed them.

"I don't think there is anything to worry about. We are in a strange place. Our translation parameters will not work like they do at Nations of Earth. This message is talking about military exercises."

"Ah," Sheydu said.

They understood exercises.

The other members of the team came in. The room was not terribly big, and it grew very crowded, especially with Evi and Telaris in there.

I told the team that the trip was on, and we needed to do some planning.

We had to divide the team and decide who would come with me tomorrow afternoon and who would come back to the city with the children. I wanted that party to be the biggest, because we needed a small, powerful and nimble team to travel into the restricted zone.

We settled on Sheydu, Anyu, Veyada, Evi, Reida and Ynggi.

I packed a few things and then discussed the arrangements with Thayu.

To my surprise, she didn't mind not coming with me.

"I don't understand these people. I can hear what they're saying behind our backs, and they don't like us at all."

That was true. We were going to have enough "aliens" problems, because I was definitely going to take Ynggi.

After crashing out earlier in the evening, Emi had woken up again, and I gave her some fruit purée mixed with the supplements she needed, and told her a story.

The pictures I showed fascinated her, very proper pictures from Asto, and once again, she did not embody any of Sheydu's fears that we would corrupt our children with another culture of which she disapproved.

I thought it was important that the children learned about culture. Any culture. Sheydu also had a problem with Pengali culture when we first involved them in our team, but she seemed to have warmed to their presence in my household.

The two Pengali youngsters had also woken up, and came to listen to my story, both of them curled up with tails around them in my lap.

Then Thayu and I retreated to our corner of the room, and I read through my notes on this old factory we intended to visit.

I'd found out about this complex in my tedious and often frustrating research on the Southern California Aerospace Corps.

The international efforts to salvage NASA's work was the side of Earth's space program I knew: the settlements on Mars and the Moon, the long-distance ships to travel to the natural jump point in the outer reaches of the solar system, Midway Space Station, Arkadia and New Taurus.

But apparently some of NASA's technology and hardware had been sold locally, or, if some reports were to be believed, had been stolen.

The Southern California Aerospace Corps had originated out of San Diego. We had already visited the building that used to be their headquarters and had found little of use.

News reports of the time spoke of them as being a group of enthusiasts who, with the help of rich donors, had tried to keep the pride of the original program alive.

There were some problems: after the Second Civil War, California became part of Mexico, and Mexico was keen to add the space program to their industries. But Mexico was a prominent member of Nations of Earth, and a significant number of the organisation's members saw Nations of Earth as their enemy.

What exactly had happened when the first launch of their new space vehicle had gone wrong was unclear. Official reports said that the vehicle had come down on the other side of the border and had crashed, killing all on board.

However, others said that the crew had taken off with their technology and set up a new base in America Free State where they employed thousands and produced space ships. Whether the locality of the ship-building plant and the accident were related was a matter for debate. But the fact that the plant had existed was undisputed. This was where we were going.

The official records maintained that the organisation had never left Earth and had fizzled out after a number of years, having neither the workforce nor the resources required, but yet, there was that spaceship in the forest near Barresh. Also, the aforementioned official records meant Nations of Earth records, and they weren't particularly accurate for North America.

Ezhya had asked me to investigate the origin of the ship because while it wasn't unusual for unknown items of technology to turn up in unusual places, it was unusual for them not to be traceable to a known source.

Historians in Barresh had confirmed my estimate that the ship was about fifty years old. Where had it come from, and what was it doing there? Worse, why had the occupants passed technology to a Pengali tribe that made them think they could take on their rivals?

Ezhya had given me a very poignant explanation why he wanted this investigated:

"If a family lives isolated from other people, they will spend most of their time gathering or growing food. If a group of people live in a small community and have no contact with other people, they will develop small tools for building and harvesting and working the land. There will be no time or resources for detailed teaching or major technology, because if one member of the community is smart and can figure this out, this member will still need to explain the concepts to the community in a way that they're on board with it. Most communities will just tell this member not to be silly. The smaller the community, the less chance that the ideas will take root. A small town may develop crude vehicles for transport. They may have factories to mass-produce things so that their people's time can be freed up from doing menial tasks like harvesting. A city in isolation will have people who specialise in things and become really good at those things. But because there is no market for the specialist stuff, it will be scarce and expensive. Space travel needs a lot of really specialist knowledge, and people who spend their time doing just that, so it needs lots of people who grow the food, harvest the food and prepare the food so that these very specialist people can worry about how to get vehicles into space. It needs a society that understands and agrees about the importance of sending people into space. Space travel needs a *huge* population base. So if we find a vehicle, and we cannot trace it back to known technology, this means that somewhere in the galaxy there is a huge population that we don't know about that can do this kind of stuff."

This was not a fun archaeological trip. It was finding that link, probably tracing it back to the Aghyrian ship, or the Tamer Collective, which was also related to the Aghyrians, just so that we could rule out the existence of some sort of shadow society that we didn't know about.

But for now, it was time to go to bed. We were all tired, and tomorrow would be a very long day.

CHAPTER SEVEN

THE NEXT MORNING we all got up very early, because there was a lot to do that my team hadn't been able to do the previous night.

As well as getting the kids ready with the right outfits, because Swallow had warned us it might be cold, we had to get ready for our investigating trip.

Sheydu and her people had already collected a bunch of gear in the hall, hidden in innocent-looking bags that looked like simple travel luggage.

That illusion only held until you tried to pick one of the bags up. This gear was all extremely heavy.

Outfits included having to wear armour and wearing clothes over the top that accommodated for it.

Most of the clothes I had bought to look like a local were too tight, so I had to resort to wearing a grey outfit that I brought from Barresh, but that might be bland enough to pass for local tough wear.

The children were all blurry eyed, having been woken up so early.

Ayshada seemed to be quite keen to go. He had his little

backpack packed and sat next to the stack of luggage in the hall. He had always been fascinated by these stacks of bags from the moment he could crawl. "Packing up" and "getting all the bombs ready" were games he would play in Barresh where he'd drag all his possessions into the hall and collect the table coasters Eirani would use to protect the table underneath hot dishes, because they were round and flat like Sheydu's bombs.

He also loved bossing the younger kids around and now reminded the two Pengali kids that they had to pack their soap and bubble machine or they would have to leave it here—exactly in the way Eirani spoke to him.

The thought of the kids bringing the bubble-making contraption into the cabin on the flight horrified me. I reminded myself to double-check that the little backpack that the Pengali kids brought—a yellow thing—would be stowed in the passenger compartment where they couldn't reach it.

Nalya was quiet. He helped Thayu carry all of our bags into the hall and then waited while leaning against the wall. Then he asked me in a quiet voice if Mariola was going to come. I told him that I thought she probably had other tourists to guide today, and that answer seemed to satisfy him. For what reason, I had no idea.

Larrana was still talking about his collection. He had the catalogue open on his reader and was talking about how he could sell some of his loot for a profit and buy other rare items, but no one listened to him. Ayshada was playing a giggling game with the Pengali kids. Nalya held Emi. Ileyu was eating an energy bar, spilling sticky crumbs all over the floor, and Emi was trying to take it off her. Did I dare to hope that some of the kids had had enough of the plastic figurines and the fake cheerfulness of the resort? Or maybe that was just my wishful thinking.

Well, after this trip we would be on our way, returning to Athens, possibly via Rotterdam, if I managed to get onto Dekker. To be honest, his hide-and-seek routine was starting to get ridiculous.

I made sure I checked our messages before we left, but the only thing that had come in were a couple of messages from the Exchange that could wait, including one from Amarru with my travel details back to Barresh.

I would deal with all those when we came back here.

Someone had gone downstairs to the breakfast bar and returned with a tray of food. We had a quick breakfast while standing up. For one, I was looking forward to Eirani's cooking, fresh fruit and freshly baked bread. I was not impressed with the artificially sweetened and starchy offerings here. Many of the visitors looked like they'd had too much of this food, and the service staff looked like they could do with some.

I guess it was this way in many parts of the world, but at my father's community in New Zealand, and even in Auckland, I hadn't seen this level of segregation between rich and poor.

Then we were all ready, and the reception called to say that people were waiting for us downstairs.

We trooped out of the building.

Some went down the stairs and some of us caught the lift with all the equipment.

I thought we'd meet our guides in the foyer, but the two young men who waited turned out to be nothing more than pick up drivers.

The receptionist called a cheerful have a good day while we were leaving the foyer.

Have a good day indeed. Have a good day while the countries fought, while many lived in poverty and everyone was pretending there wasn't a war going on. They'd have a good day all the way to the end of the world.

Outside stood two people carriers.

Once we had deposited the bags in between the seats, there was barely enough space for all of us.

The drivers did not appear to understand us at all. They were there just to take us to the airport.

We were all in, and the convoy set in motion.

The vehicles took us through the busy boulevard that went past the park entrance, but we did not turn into it to join the small line of people already waiting there.

Instead, we went straight ahead and the sides of the street became a lot less glamorous, since the need to make everything appear pretty for the tourists evaporated.

There was a gate across the road, which was opened at our approach. These people knew that we were coming.

Outside the gate we returned to the dust bowl of a landscape that we had also seen on our way here and that darkness had hidden from us last night.

And it was dry and desolate. The sand was pale brown; the grass was all dry and dead. A mountain range rose from the plain in a blue-grey haze. The sky was pale blue.

A dry wind blew up eddies of sand. There was not a tree in sight.

Mariola had said that the trees were still dying back, and that you could tell how well off a community was by whether they had removed dead trees or made efforts to replace them. Keeping trees alive was a community effort. It meant giving up precious water and taking the time to look after them.

A short drive along the road with worn and cracked paving brought us to the airport.

Several aircraft waited on the other side. We were told to wait in a shelter. Dust had blown in through the open sides, covering the seats, even though I could see a woman using a broom to sweep it away in one of the adjacent similar shelters.

There seemed to be a separate shelter for each flight, so that the travelling parties didn't have to mix with the other plebs, or something along those lines.

The aircraft that stood closest to us was a gyrocopter.

Evi squinted at it.

"Is that African?" I asked him.

Ever since he had discovered the use of Indrahui technology during our illustrious trip to Ethiopia that had ended in the infamous "nuke from orbit" incident, he'd developed an interest in gyrocopters and related technology.

The brothers never spoke much of the time that they tried to escape Indrahui war lord Romi Tanaqan, but I understood that solar gliders featured in the story. Those gliders were also common in Ethiopia.

He nodded, slowly. "Sudanese make." His voice was dark.

A generation's worth of illegal imports encapsulated in two words. If ever there was an issue that illustrated the need for Earth to join *gamra*, this was it. African warmongering funded through the sale of technology illegally imported from off -world.

As soon as we had carried all our bags into the shelter, and the kids were blowing dust off the seats, a woman came from the vehicle. She was in uniform and introduced herself as Rosa.

"I'll be taking you for the first part of your trip today."

"I thought we were going to catch two vehicles," I said.

Also, with a craft of this size it would be impossible to get in an out of places quickly, besides the fact that this craft needed a lot of space to land.

And these gyrocopters were hardly silent.

"Oh no, we will transfer you to the smaller craft later. We need to cover quite a distance and we cannot fly those small craft all the way here. This is a big country."

Fair enough.

We followed her across the dusty tarmac. As we were walking to the craft in a long line, a gust of wind blew dust around us. I had to close my eyes to make sure the sand didn't get in.

"Windy day today," I said.

"Oh, this isn't too bad. You should have been here a few days ago. That's when all this dust blew across here."

I looked at the edges of the field where the cracked paving

blended into the dirt. Pale pink drift sand merged with the asphalt. A few dead blades of grass still stuck up out of the sand, but it was clear that this place had last seen rain a very long time ago.

We arrived at the vehicle and climbed up the stairs. I made sure that none of the kids carried anything that would disturb the pilots.

Again, we had to carry Larrana's wheelchair up, because the steps were too steep for the wheels to negotiate.

The inside of the cabin was well appointed, with a central aisle and seats on both sides.

We occupied every seat, especially when counting all the bags that Sheydu and her team insisted on taking into the cabin.

When we had all sat down and had strapped in, Rosa came in after us. She pulled up the stairs, closed the door, and then walked through the aisle to the cockpit. I assumed she was going to notify the pilot that the passengers were all ready, but when the door opened next, she came out in the company of a heavily armed man. He wore a traditional khaki military style outfit, a wide belt with many pockets for weapons and explosives, and carried an impressive gun.

Several people in my group stiffened. Hands went to upper arms.

Rosa also came out again.

"Because we are going to cross the border, America Free State requires us to carry a border patrol guard for your safety. This here is Chaz. He'll be with us until the first stop."

He nodded at us, his grey eyes roving over our assembly without emotion, not even when they lingered at the Pengali.

No one said anything. The children gave this heavily armed man puzzled looks. No doubt some of them were wondering whether this was another strange fake outfit.

He sat down at the front bench in the cabin.

Rosa went back into the cockpit, and moments later the blades of the machine started up.

I spotted Reida taking some measurements. He had also taken pictures of the craft. He was listening with keen interest.

I had never flown inside one of these machines and had to push aside the discomfort that came with associating gyrocopters with certain corrupt governments. The engine *sounded* like a PanAf gyrocopter, because this was exactly the same type of vehicle, and just the sound of it triggered my flight response. I'd spent most of my trip into Ethiopia running away from these things.

Outside the window, I could see the rotor blades go up and down, while the engines roared.

Then we were off the ground. The airport receded to be replaced with the streets and buildings of the community that surrounded the New World park.

You could see the park precinct as a green oasis, a community of interlinked covered spaces and domes in the middle of a desert.

Mariola's home suburb had to be that area on the other side, with its colourful houses that stood crowded along the streets. But the riot of colour still didn't dispel the dust bowl feeling.

I hadn't realised just how stark the difference between the park precinct and the outside world was.

In some other places, the drifting sand had invaded suburbs that were no longer in use. Houses poked half out of the dunes, their roofs fallen in.

A couple of people on motorbikes traversed a road with cracked paving, potholes and partially covered in drift sand.

Behind us, I could see the vague outlines of the city centre where we had been two days ago, an ugly concrete jungle.

I enjoyed the beach a lot more, but even it exuded an atmosphere of faded glory and many people who lived there were very poor.

The gyrocopter was not going in that direction. We gathered height. The noise from the engines became a drone in the background. The sun rose over the dusty landscape. Ahead, mountains peeked out of the haze. We soon crossed them and then flew over a dusty and desolate landscape.

The kids were playing games, but Nalya was looking out of the window.

Thayu had only re-established contact with her son recently, and that had only happened through a chance meeting when he and I had been welcomed into the Domiri clan together. My impression was that the poor kid was clamouring for guidance and an adult he could trust. After the debacle where his uncle had tried to grab Ezhya's position and had been killed, his family had fallen from grace.

It was customary that if a non-residential parent asked for their right to spend time with the child, the parent who normally looked after the child objected strenuously, and this led to long negotiations where favours and future favours could be extracted from either party. But Nalya's family had done none of this. They'd seemed happy to pass him off to someone else.

No one wanted to fight over him.

In the twisted ways of Coldi society, that was a sad thing for a child old enough to start mentoring.

It was not that he was a troublesome child.

Nalya was a thinker. He was quiet and studious. Someone I could draw into my circle of confidence, if only I could get him to trust me.

I sat next to Veyada, who briefed me on everything they had been doing to make sure that we went to the right places.

Since the previous trip to the office in San Diego had been so disappointing, I had hoped that we might meet people who still remembered the Southern California Aerospace Corps, because fifty years was not that long ago, was it?

Because everywhere we asked during our useless trip to San Diego, we had met with a deafening silence.

In space? People would say. We know nothing about space.

Some people would even laugh in our faces, assuring us that the capability of building vehicles to travel in space was long gone.

Sometimes, we had to tell them their own history, which they would then dismiss as propaganda. Because apparently anything I thought or said was untrue and said only to sell Nations of Earth or—heaven forbid—*gamra* ideas or power to gullible people.

"We stopped being gullible many years ago," those people then said.

So after that disaster, we concentrated on this complex in America Free State. My team had done a good amount of preparation, comparing old maps with satellite imagery, and filling in details provided by old photos we had found.

They had reconstructed a model of the complex and filled in the likely purpose for each building. They had labelled buildings as offices, as assembly plant, as electronics lab, even a chip-printing plant. According to old photos, there had been a good number of industrial 3d printers, and Reida had reconstructed a series of images showing what the full complex in operation might have looked like, complete with cars from fifty years back in the employee car park.

I was impressed, but Veyada added a warning.

"Mind you, the picture that forms the basis of this model is extremely old, and I don't know how much use the simulation is going to be, or what state the buildings will be in."

He informed me that my team had been unable to get more recent satellite imagery, because, apparently, there was an agreement that Nations of Earth would not spy on North America for as long as no one from the North American countries bothered Nations of Earth.

I'd had so little to do with this part of the world that even my study of its turbulent history hadn't brought up any information about that agreement. But as a lawyer, Veyada had uncovered it.

"It was Mereeni who told me," he confessed.

I had to stifle a chuckle. This stuff would make for interesting bedroom talk between the two of them.

He disliked being away from Mereeni and Ileyu as much as I disliked being away from Thayu and Emi.

I studied Reida's model despite the warning, familiarising myself with the layout of the complex. We'd have to visit the equipment assembly hall and the electronics plant.

After a while, I noticed that the craft was going down.

Outside the window, I could make out a small town with the streets laid out in a perfect grid pattern. Each house lay in its own little dusty plot of land. There was not a tree in sight.

This was where we were going to transfer to our two separate craft.

In fact, I could already see the airport with the two craft waiting for us.

CHAPTER EIGHT

OUR GYROCOPTER CAME DOWN NEXT to the two small craft and their crew.

On the far edge of the field stood a couple of dusty buildings with signs that were too flaked-off to read. The field looked clean and well used, and the control tower that overlooked it was well-maintained. People who had said that America Free State was all in ruins had given me the impression that we were about to fly into a war zone. It didn't feel like that at all. It felt like we had landed in a dystopian landscape.

The people who met us when we landed were a younger man with blond hair and a short beard in a neat shirt and trousers, and a middle-aged man old enough to be his father.

They both greeted our surly border patrol guard, who made straight for the building that held the control tower.

The young man turned out to be an airport employee, and the grizzled guy was our guide.

He dressed in camouflage gear, wore a shirt with the sleeves hacked off and fraying, wore his grey hair in a ponytail and had some kind of knitted ear warmer band on his head. His skin had the weathered appearance of someone who spent a lot of time in the sun. His dark eyes were set in a permanent squint.

He wore a broad belt on which he carried a large knife in a leather sheath and a serious gun.

He introduced himself as Junco.

I looked it up, re-typing the spelling a few times.

It was another bird.

He seemed to be a bit wary, glancing at the more unusual members of our team, in particular the Pengali and Evi and Telaris, when he started speaking.

"We have two smaller choppers for you. The very large ones are not as agile as the smaller ones and won't be able to get into the canyon as far as we can get down with the smaller ones. I understand that one half of the party will continue on after we've seen the canyon. You're with me. The young fellow here will take the other party. We'll be stopping at a couple of places and will serve refreshments at those places."

He continued with the safety briefing, which I had to translate for my team, because his accent was so strong that the translation module made a mess of it.

We boarded both craft.

Ileyu had been asleep on the other flight and was most displeased to wake up suddenly, to find herself in a sunny field about to be separated from her father Veyada. She made that displeasure known as Mereeni carried her up the stairs into the other craft.

I waved to Thayu and Emi as they went in. Emi looked around, bright-eyed. I was wondering if she'd remember this trip when she was older. I hoped she'd remember my father when we visited him.

The craft were both the same size, but the back seats of our craft were full of bags and crates stacked up and strapped into the seats with a transport harness.

"Camping gear," Nicha said.

I noticed Sheydu inconspicuously checking some of her equipment. She met Anyu's eyes and made the security hand sign for negative.

I assumed they wanted to know if there was any reception.

We were further away from any civilisation or rescue than I had ever been on Earth.

Junco took the pilot's seat.

While the engine started up, he gave us a description of the route, but it was very hard to understand him over the noise of the engine.

Then we were off.

The craft rose quickly, and not long after, we flew over the first rock formations.

They were round and jagged shapes, carved from dark red rock, enveloped in the misty haze that hung over the landscape. The ground was barren, covered in rocks with a few remaining skeletons of dead trees.

A road snaked in between the rock formations, but its cracked surface, subsided patches and encroaching sand dunes showed that it had seen little use, not to mention any maintenance, for many years.

A row of poles next to the road probably belonged to a power or communication line, but many no longer stood straight, and some had even fallen over altogether.

Way back when I was young and went to high school in Arcadia at New Taurus, we had a teacher who was very much into the rise and fall of empires and made us suffer through—so I thought at the time because I was no gifted pupil—countless lessons and essays about the downfall of Rome and that of the United States. Besides a lot of common political factors, they were different in one major aspect: a changing hostile climate. Extensive regions in the south of the former United States had grown so dry that they could no longer support a significant population. People fled to the cities on the coast and were treated like dirt. The wealthier ones made it across the border to Mexico and found employment in the massive solar farms, under terrible conditions with low pay, but they were the lucky ones.

Entire regions went empty of people. Towns were abandoned, industries died. Fertile agricultural land turned to dust.

We were seeing evidence pass underneath us.

The rock formations were pretty, but I could only see them through the lens of sadness. I remembered the pictures my teacher had shown of a landscape covered in grey-green vegetation with gnarled pine trees on rocky outcrops. It had never been lush, but wasn't desolate either. It was now.

In New Zealand, we had never suffered this badly.

The landscape grew more and more rugged, and after a while the canyon came into view: a deep cleft in the surface surrounded by rocky shelves and peaks eroded over many billions of years. The walls consisted of dark pink rock, hazy in the dusty air. The canyon narrowed down the bottom and to my surprise water flowed at the canyon's deepest point, fringed by ribbons of green.

The gyrocopter dived into the canyon until it flew at the height of the furthest cliff tops.

Everyone was looking out the windows now.

The other gyrocopter was just ahead of us.

Reida, next to me, took in the landscape with his dark eyes.

"What do you think?" I asked.

"It's a bit like the landscape in the Outer Circle," he said.

That had been my thought as well. We had spent some time in the canyon between the Outer Circle boundary and the military base. Although that canyon was broader, not so deep, and the riverbed was now used for agriculture. People were moving into the area instead of abandoning it.

"It's pretty," Reida added. "Are there any animals?"

"I'm sure there are." Wherever there was water, there would be animals.

Both craft followed the windy path of the river. Sometimes

the cliffs were close, at other times, they were further away. Impressive formations of red rock zoomed past. Flocks of birds took flight. We flew over stony rapids and deep, mirror-like pools, where the air disturbed by the craft in front made little waves on the water.

The two craft landed on a beach in a bend in the river next to a drop-off where a thin veil of water trickled over a rock shelf to join the main river.

We got out and walked along the beach for a bit.

After the sound of the engines had died down, it was deathly quiet. Every crunching footstep in the pebbles echoed between the rock walls.

The amount of water coming down the rock shelf was not enough to create a noise.

We climbed to the top and found a pool of vivid green water where a putrid smell of rot hung inthe air. A couple of dead fish floated in the water amongst foamy rafts of algae. Ynggi watched with wide eyes.

"This place is dying," he said. The sound of his voice echoed between the cliffs.

"It's like Asto, but the other way around. Athyl is becoming wetter. Creeks are flowing that haven't contained water for thousands of years. This landscape is drying up, going in the other direction."

"It's so sad. Are there any live animals left?" Deyu asked.

"There should be." I hoped.

Back at the craft, the pilots had set up refreshments for us, trays with fruit and sandwiches.

Unfortunately, Ayshada had discovered the echoes. He and the Pengali kids ran along the beach yelling at the tops of their voices.

I asked our guides about animals on Deyu's behalf.

"Squirrels," said the young pilot. "You will probably see some of them later."

"The damn goats are everywhere," Junco said.

"Why is there water in the river?" I asked. "Where does it come from?"

"It's because of the dam upriver," Junco said. "They get big winter rains up in the mountains, and the water collects in the dam. They let it out slowly."

"If they didn't do that, there would be no water in the canyon?"

"Probably not, except a few times a year, and then there would be enough to wash all the sand and vegetation away."

"There is less water every year," the young pilot said.

Junco nodded, his expression distant.

We re-boarded the craft and continued on.

We saw no other people at all. No other craft in the sky that I could see, and no settlements on the ground, except for a few... shacks that might not even be inhabited. Everything looked abandoned from up here.

For quite a while, we flew over this canyon that grew more and more intricate as the cliffs grew taller and the rocks at the various levels changed colour. The river down there looked so small, that I couldn't imagine that it had created this incredible landscape over millions and millions of years.

Then we arrived at the main visiting point: a lookout on the top of the southern end of the canyon.

The two craft landed in a patch of abandoned concrete that was being reclaimed by nature. Clumps of grass grew in the cracks between the paving, and sand had blown across, providing a footing for moss and small plants.

Along the edges of the paving were signs of human activity, past and present, with paths and roads and the remains of fencing. A small shop looked like it might open during busy times. A couple of tradesmen were working in a building that looked like a hotel. Closed right now, obviously, but maybe one day they'd offer tourists accommodation here, and this would become a little tourist enclave like the New World park.

We all got out of the craft.

A chilly wind blew across the deserted field.

Junco led us across the field to the lookout.

"Not very busy here," I commented to him while we walked.

He snorted. "It used to be very different. You see all the space here?" He gestured around where we stood. "This used to be a carpark, and every summer there used to be thousands, hundreds of thousands of people coming here. It was so busy that they had to pre-sell tickets because the lookout got too crowded."

"I presume that you're talking about a period before the Second Civil War?"

"Before that, before the great depression, before the other wars, before the border closure, people from all over the world used to come here."

"Are you sad they stopped coming?"

He shrugged. "Whether or not I'm sad about it, there is nothing I can do."

This was true.

Another craft had landed a bit further down, with five or six people standing around their guide. The latter was handing out drinks. His charges all wore blue shirts.

"Are there a lot of other people bringing tourists?"

"There are a few."

"Why are they all wearing those shirts?"

"Those guys take random tourists who can book in pairs or go alone, if they want. The guides are thinking about their safety. It doesn't look very good for us when accidents happen."

"Accidents?"

I felt uncomfortable. We were out of our depth. We were vulnerable. People could *make* us disappear if they wanted to.

"This canyon here." He pointed, while we were going down a

flight of crumbling stairs to a viewing platform. "It's responsible for many thousands of deaths. People who fell down, planes that crashed, people who drowned, people who thought they could climb the fence for a picture and slipped. People who got bitten by snakes."

"I can't imagine there being too many snakes here anymore."

"They are around, if you're unlucky."

We arrived at the viewing platform. Larrana was the last person to come down. The steps were low enough for his wheels, but he needed to make sure he didn't roll down the crumbling path by holding onto the railing. I asked if he needed help, but he said he was all right.

We stood at the edge of the platform. On the rocky shelf in front of us stood a dead tree. There was a bit of straggly vegetation on the ground, but most of the landscape was utterly arid. The wind was gritty and cool, and Nalya was clamping his arms around himself. He would not be used to the cold.

"That wind comes straight off the mountains," Junco said.

"Do you get snow?"

"A bit, sometimes, not enough to go skiing. It's rain, mostly."

I looked over the landscape, alien and beautiful as it was, I couldn't imagine anything more like a desert in the world. The idea that not so long ago thousands of people had come here to see this site, and now the visitor numbers were reduced to a handful per month, was difficult to comprehend.

"It's such a desolate place," I said.

"You could be mistaken. People still live here."

"Really? In that dilapidated town we just saw?"

"No, you won't see them from the air. People have built underground shelters, and others live in the town back where you changed planes."

And that was such a dusty hole that I couldn't imagine a full community living there. Not even the mushroom gatherers who lived in the aquifers of Athyl inhabited such poor surroundings. Or the *zeyshi* who lived in the old structures under the ground.

Most of those people at least had a nice place to live in, like the humid aquifers with their fields of crops and deep pools in between rock walls covered with plants, or the extensive and very comfortable caves where they lived.

Maybe it was because I was looking at this landscape from such a great height, and I couldn't see the nice places like the creek beds where there was water and vegetation. Although we'd landed on that beach and the stench of the green algae and dead fish in the stagnant pool still lingered in the back of my nose.

Up here, I only saw the remnants of a place that many people once visited: cracked paving, sagging fencing propped up with makeshift posts. Buildings that were no longer in use and had fallen to pieces. An old toilet block with discoloured walls where water seeped out of a crack in a wall and a squirrel came to drink from the puddle of dubious water.

I didn't know what to say.

Junco had probably never left this region and would have no idea that such places existed as my father's farm in New Zealand where it was so green that your eyes hurt, and where the little community that he and Erith were part of lived independently off the land with all the animals in their fields and their own energy generation plant.

Or even the Nations of Earth complex, where an army of gardeners did everything to keep the grass and the trees alive, or the little enclaves surrounding Rotterdam where, although much of the surrounding countryside was under water, farmers still grew flowers and vegetables.

This place looked so miserable, so poor, and so much like I'd accidentally taken a flight to Ethiopia or any of the Central African belt where large tracts of land were no longer habitable, but where people did things like generate huge quantities of electricity and turned electricity into hydrogen which they exported or used in local factories.

This land was just... empty, and war-torn, abandoned.

Junco was expecting me to say something about the view.

I didn't want to give the impression that I pitied him, because he was probably not to be pitied.

He was proud, adapted to the landscape, resilient and self-sufficient, the best he could do in this lousy situation.

"It's very nice," I said.

"Best view in the world."

"Yeah." And I left it at that. The view was nice, if you ignored the sagging building to the right and the collapsed walkway that had once led to it, if you ignored the skeletons of dead pine trees or you didn't think about the time they had been *live* trees.

I still didn't know what to think, or even what I had expected to find here.

I might have hoped to find a vibrant community that proved that not belonging to Nations of Earth was no disaster and that it was wholly possible to remain independent as a country.

Instead, it was just as bad as I had feared and I was overwhelmed with the desire to walk through that other desert valley, outside Athyl, where we discovered little plantlets in places where there had not been life for a long time, and where the creek flowed across the rocks from rains upstream that had started again after thousands of dry years.

And somehow I felt it should be possible for humans to fix this place, but it was impossible in conflict and when the locals saw nothing that needed to be fixed.

"Hey, are you all right?" Thayu came to stand next to me. She carried Emi on her arm, looking around with her big eyes.

"Yeah. Just thinking."

Thayu couldn't hear what I was thinking because we had no feeder connection.

"You look sad."

"I am sad. This part of the world has been forgotten and neglected. It's dying. Nature is dying. People are leaving. They can't live here anymore."

"Isn't that their own fault for not wanting to be involved with Nations of Earth?"

"It is, but there is more to it. All my life, I've heard stories of people coming here. I've seen it in movies and articles. This place is part of the natural heritage of this world. It shouldn't just be up to one country to look after it. We should all look after it."

"Clearly, they don't want anyone else here."

"I'm not so sure about that."

On a level below us, Ynggi and Jaki kept a close watch on the older children to make sure that no one came close to crumbling edges and rickety steps. The younger kids were getting bored, but Nalya walked along the fence taking pictures. Larrana followed him as much as he was able, but I thought he was getting bored, too.

"What do you mean, you're not sure?" Thayu asked.

"They took our money quickly enough. Someone in their government says their borders should remain closed, but clearly not everyone agrees with that. They need visitors to come and they've set up businesses for those visitors. They know what's happening to the land and even name their kids after plants and animals that have died out. Their governments might not be aware of it, but some people look ready to talk."

CHAPTER NINE

JUNCO and his young assistant pilot served a late lunch consisting of sandwiches with very appropriate toppings for each of us. There was no meat except fish for the Pengali and plenty of spicy offerings with clear handwritten labels that said what each box contained. I wondered which servant in Mariola's household had been responsible for these. There was also hot water for tea and juice for the children.

We ate at a picnic table overlooking the top of the canyon and the walkways of the lookout.

The weather was cool, thanks to a blustery wind laced with dust.

Junco said it was likely that a dust storm would whip up later in the day or tomorrow.

Our group was going to split up after this, and I spent most of lunchtime talking to Thayu and Emi. They would go back to the city to spend a few extra days on the beach while trying to contact Dekker.

Larrana had already asked me about the beach. He said he was cold up here and hated how the sand blew in his eyes.

To be honest, the kids looked tired and bored. They were

ready to go home, even if they had also behaved very well. There had been no mishaps with fences or—heaven forbid—bubble machines inside the aircraft.

I told Thayu we'd be back tomorrow. I told Emi to behave, although I doubted she understood me.

Nicha was saying goodbye to Ayshada, who was not happy about having to leave his father.

I gave a few last-minute instructions to Deyu, who was going to keep trying to get onto Dekker or anyone else at Nations of Earth. By now, I was also getting uncomfortable that I had heard little from Amarru. It was disturbing how much we relied on communication.

We were about to go deep into unknown territory and I feared that Dekker was going to want to contact me while I was out of range, and I wasn't sure I wanted to tell him what we were doing here. He would berate me that I hadn't applied for a million permits before travelling to this area, all layers of bureaucracy designed to stop people coming here.

The truth was that I would have told someone at Nations of Earth what we were planning and why, if only someone with a sympathetic ear had wanted to listen. Yes, Nations of Earth had their own issues to deal with, and a rogue decaying space ship ruin that was at least fifty years old buried in a remote rainforest on a faraway planet was probably not high on the list of priorities. But it was on mine. This was why I was here. It was none of Dekker's business.

Junco and his assistant packed up the lunch things.

Then I noticed that all the kids were standing around one of the gyrocopters, looking into the cabin. Two Pengali tails wriggled excitedly in the air, like black-and-white banded snakes. That was not a good sign.

"What's going on, kids?"

"Look," Larrana said. He pointed into the cabin.

I looked.

A grey squirrel sat on its haunches on the pilot's seat, tail held high above its head. It had acquired a piece of bread, which it held in both forepaws. Another squirrel had discovered the box of empty wrappers and was rummaging through it, scattering paper over the floor.

Junco came towards the craft. "Oh, for crying out loud, who left the door open? Shoo! Shoo!"

He jumped into the cabin. At least four squirrels skittered out, much to the delight of the kids.

The animals ran across the paving to the toilet block, scampered up the dead tree next to it and then onto the roof.

The Pengali kids ran after them, their tails straight up into the air.

Huh, that was weird.

As young as they were, the kids were trying to communicate with the squirrels in tail language, without even realising they were doing it.

"Those things are like ringgit," Veyada said, picking up wrappers the squirrels had scattered, and which were threatening to blow over the railing, adding to hundreds of years of plastic rubbish already scattered there. "They get into everything you're not watching."

The squirrels watched from the roof while Junco and his assistant finished packing up lunch and most of my team climbed into the larger of the two craft.

Jaki had to call the Pengali kids several times before they could tear themselves from their fellow tailed creatures.

Pykka wanted Nalya to take a picture of him and Amay with the squirrels. Nalya did this, very much like they had seen the tourists do. Pykka was disappointed that you could barely see the animals on the roof. Because clearly, to his mind, they were much bigger.

They all finally got into the craft.

The door shut.

I waved to Thayu with Emi on her lap behind the window.

Off to the beach. They'd loved that area, with its street markets and little shops and street performers. Larrana loved the roller skaters along the boulevard.

I almost wished we could go with them. It was a fun area, with lots of tacky Mexican hat references, colourful street theatre in Spanish, loud music and street painting.

But we would have some time off. I'd planned a brief holiday to see my father for just myself, Thayu, Emi, with a few others for security, because my father was keen to see his granddaughter.

We waited until the craft had departed, with Nicha waving to Ayshada who had wanted him to come. This would be easier on Nicha if he had a partner, but even if I'd said several times that I thought he should have someone, Nicha seemed happy to look after Ayshada by himself.

We then climbed into the other craft. I sat next to Junco and watched him start up the engine.

The last I saw of the lookout was the dusty roof on the toilet block. Two squirrels watched us, seated on their hind legs.

For a while, we followed the canyon rim.

I looked out the window into the dusty air and the tiny stream far below in the deepest part of the canyon.

Then the craft veered right, taking a shortcut over red-tinged desert. There was not much to see anymore, so I studied the craft's controls, figuring that Evi on the bench behind me was doing the same. It would probably help Evi if I asked where Junco had obtained the craft, but I wasn't sure how to frame that question in a manner that would not sound too political. There would be enough political stuff once we got to our destination.

After a long silence, Junco asked me, "So, tell me, that beautiful wheelchair the boy had, he did get that from over there, you know, off Earth?"

Out of all the questions I'd expected him to ask, this wasn't one.

"Yes, he did. I'm not sure exactly where, because you don't see a lot of disabled people over there."

Junco nodded and was silent while he adjusted some settings on his instruments.

I was still wondering why disabled people were so rarely seen in Coldi society and suspected that expectant women considered those children too costly and not meeting their contracted partner's expectations, so they aborted the pregnancy. This left me with all kinds of uncomfortable questions, like how badly affected a foetus needed to be for parents to take this action and whether there were laws regulating what you could and couldn't do. Could they test for mental conditions which didn't show up on a scan?

Taking away the kids born with disabilities left the kids who had accidents, like Larrana, but you never saw too many of them either. In theory, that meant either Asto was a very safe place and people didn't have accidents, or the medicos were much more reluctant to save people who could never return to their previous life. I could not argue in favour of the "safe place" option because I knew Asto was no safer than other places, but the alternative made me sick. Or were they really good at fixing damage to human bodies? I didn't think so, because on Asto, the Aghyrians ran a lot of advanced medical stuff, and if they had an altruistic bone in their body, I hadn't discovered it yet.

It was a subject I didn't want to discuss.

"Do you know how much those chairs cost?" Junco asked.

I glanced at him. It seemed a deeply personal question.

"A fair bit. I imagine the boy's father had this chair designed for him. He is a top government official." That was probably the best neutral description for the boy's father. "I imagine that a chair like this would be hard to get. Why? Would you be interested?"

"Yeah. You see, my boy needs a wheelchair. My wife was pregnant during the war at the time the Dixie Republic fighters dropped chemical bombs on us. He was born with his legs all deformed. She has since died of the cancer that it caused."

"I'm sorry."

He shrugged.

"How old is the boy?"

"Nine."

"Well, I could make some inquiries. If you give me your contact details, I can let you know what I find out."

"It might be best to contact me through Mariola. She'll know how to talk to me without..."

He shrugged again and blew out a breath. Without what? Arousing suspicion from a government keen to control its people? It seemed *he* was keen to discuss politics.

"Mariola regularly gets you customers?"

"Yes. It's a well-paying job. I'm talking to her all the time. She brings me a lot of business because she talks to tourists. Most of them don't even know that you can still visit the canyon."

"Yes, I can make some inquiries and let her know."

I had no idea how one would go about getting the wheelchair and getting it fitted, because I was sure that it would require an elaborate fitting process, but we would deal with that later. He might be a useful contact in America Free State. I needed to nurture that opportunity. It had been hard enough to find someone who would talk to us, even about the most mundane of subjects.

"Can I ask a bit more information about your son so I can make more detailed enquiries? What exactly would he need?"

"He is like the other lad. His legs are all crooked, and he can't walk. His arms are okay, but he has trouble with his shoulders so he can't use crutches. He just sits in a chair all day being miserable. He used to have a chair with wheels, but they had rubber tyres with inner tubes that needed pressure and the pump broke and I couldn't get hold of a new one. I tried using other materials, but it's just too bumpy, because the roads are rough. Then other bits started breaking. I could fix it, if only the supplier in Atlantia would send me the materials. I get so angry at those suppliers. My son tells me it doesn't matter because he doesn't like it when I'm angry. But he's lonely. He's got some friends, but most of the kids think he's weird and don't want to play or want to be seen to be his friend. Every week I carry him into church, and I cannot stand the look of pity on those people's faces. I come to church because I want to be a good man, but they're making it hard for me not to yell at their sanctimonious faces. The folk act like we're both contagious with a horrible disease. Do you go to church, Mr Wilson?"

"There are no churches where I live. I believe I can be a good person without having to visit a church."

He nodded. "Fair enough."

This was a question I always dreaded when I interacted with people on Earth. I had spent years preparing a variety of answers. If someone wanted, they could poke all sorts of holes in my inconsistent position on the subject of religion, mainly to justify that I wasn't the type of person they wanted to interact with. But the fact remained that I was not from a religious family. My parents had been nominally religious, but *gamra* had serious questions about religion and how it could coexist with science, one of the primary points they found baffling and incredible about Earth society.

I was reluctant to talk about it in public, especially since the subject of Earth's religions was such a hot topic in *gamra* and one that was used to ridicule Earth.

But one thing about that statement was absolutely true: I didn't think anyone needed to visit a church or be religious in order to be a good person.

Junco wasn't done with the subject. "Then what do you do on Sundays, over there?" he asked.

"There are no Sundays."

"Ha ha. I guess that answers that question."

"Where we live, there are five days in the week, and some other cultures don't have any week days at all but go by the days of the month."

"So you just got rid of weekends?"

"That's one way of looking at it."

"That sounds like a hard-working place to me."

"I guess so."

The concept of regulated days off was not something that we had in Barresh. I wasn't sure if that made the culture hard-working, especially not if it involved the Barresh counsellors. You could argue that if there was no weekend, then every day was a weekend. That was definitely how they lived their lives.

But if it made him happy, that was great.

"So, where are you from, then?"

"We are from a city called Barresh, which is the headquarters of *gamra*, which I'm sure you've heard of."

"Is that the thing that's called the alien union?"

"Yes." I cringed. I had not heard the word union for a long time, and definitely not preceded by the word alien.

"I was wondering where you were from before, because you're speaking funny."

"I grew up speaking Isla, and the version my parents spoke was more Asian than the version you know here. When I went to school, we spoke Cosla, the space settlement variety. They're not interchangeable, but close enough."

"Huh. We do none of that stuff here. We speak the good old language."

"Isla has international recognition. With many countries in the world contributing to economic activity and culture, the language is part of the international landscape, too."

He eyed me suspiciously. Then he dropped the subject. America Free State did not believe in an international economy.

"But where did you come from, or your parents?"

"I was born and lived until I was eight years old in New Zealand."

"Oh."

That answer seemed to satisfy him. I wasn't sure why, maybe because New Zealand was a country he approved of, as he didn't seem to approve of Isla, or influences by other cultures. It was a very quaint mindset, and one I hadn't encountered for a while. And he still wanted to talk to me.

"Why did you leave New Zealand?"

"Remember that I was only eight. I had no choice. My father got a job in Midway Space Station."

Now his face lit up. "That was a significant step up."

Obviously, Midway was also on the approved list. It was an *Earth* station and had nothing to do with *gamra*. In fact, the station management made a point of having nothing to do with *gamra*. I remembered how badly they had treated Erith there. I remembered the strange group of people who had tried to take over the station and assassinate a visiting delegation from *gamra*, which included the Chief Delegate Akhtari.

Back then, there had been a semi-militant movement of purist people on Earth to set up a space program that was separate from *gamra* and didn't use the Exchange.

What if... crap.

A cold feeling washed over me.

Had those people, many of whom were deeply religious, come from America Free State? Were they in any way related to the Southern California Aerospace Corps?

To think of it, that seemed likely.

Of course, Junco had grown up with those people painted to him as heroes. Those were the people who would further the cause of his country in space. Some were willing to sacrifice lives for that aim.

Damn, I hardly remembered any of them. There had been a man called Sullivan, and another man called Rocky, who wasn't part of the group. I didn't remember their full names. What did they even want and why were they there?

Those people had scared and tried to bully me, but I'd warned then-president of Nations of Earth Pedro Gonzales about them. I'd even spoken to him.

Knowing all the things I knew now, my youth experience looked like what I feared: these people were not friends of Nations of Earth and they weren't friends of *gamra* either. I didn't remember ever hearing from them again. After the attempt to steal a ship at Midway, they'd sort of... disappeared. Like these people we were looking for now.

Well, that was an interesting revelation. I'd have to investigate what had become of that group. I couldn't even remember what they called themselves. I'd been ten.

"So how long did you stay at Midway?" Junco asked.

"Just a couple of years, two or three, I don't remember. I was a young kid and went to primary school there. After that, my father got a job at New Taurus, and we moved to Arcadia."

"Huh, that would have been fun."

Did he mean that sarcastically?

"What do you mean?"

"With all the trouble after the crash at Taurus, and then all the bickering that led to the settlement being abandoned."

"That was after my time, but I don't remember it as being a very happy time for my father."

I'd been a teenager and obsessed with girls and bikes, and oblivious to the politics.

But damn it, there *had* been a rogue group of people who would rather die than work with *gamra* and it was entirely plausible that they had infiltrated and taken over aspects of the international space settlement effort, especially over fifty years ago, which would have been a very turbulent time that predated Nations of Earth.

As far as I knew, the human space program was still going,

with vibrant settlements on the Moon and Mars. As far as I knew, Taurus and New Taurus had been mostly abandoned. The people who were doing the work were also the same, the international group allied with Nations of Earth. They were scientists and international politicians, people who were sensible and diplomatic, if also boring and bureaucratic. The gung ho militants and military types had... vanished.

Well, damn.

But maybe I'd been looking in the wrong direction, maybe in that time of despair had those people made it to Barresh. The people who were trying to take over Midway Space Station had insinuated that they had a secret place where they were going to take the human space settlement effort, because they viewed Nations of Earth as pandering to the "aliens" too much.

Junco continued his questions. "So what about you? When did you decide to leave your own people?"

"I don't see it that way. We are all people. One of the little girls in the other group is my daughter. One of the guards here is her mother."

"You're kidding?"

"No, I'm not."

"I thought that was impossible."

"It's difficult, but it is possible. Have you heard of the Human Tree project?"

He hadn't, so I told him of the hundred-year-old project in Barresh to piece together the genetic relationships between all different kinds of humans, how the Aghyrians were at the base, how Earth humans had a place in it, and even the Pengali.

I said, "We're all people, and we're all related."

He looked me up and down, as if seeing me through a new lens.

"Well, that's interesting. Thank you for telling me that."

His appreciation seemed genuine.

He pulled out a map and started explaining about where we

were going. There was a town close to the site of the old factory, and there was another viewing platform where you could see over the canyon. He would take us there tomorrow morning.

I told him that I'd noticed there was accommodation for hire in the town. "Is the lookout that popular?"

"Not really, but people come for boat rides on the lake," he said.

The landscape underneath us had flattened out and looked old and dusty and incredibly ancient.

I could still see the canyon of the river out a left-hand window. Reida was following the contours of the land on his map.

He turned to me. "What is this here?" He pointed at a dark area.

"It's a lake," I said.

He frowned. "In the open? It's very hot and dry here."

"Yes, the water comes from somewhere else. There are mountains a bit further to the east. It's like the creek at Athyl. The water comes from somewhere else."

"But why the lake?"

"It's a dam," I said. "See how there is a wall here across the canyon?"

"Oh, yes. Why do people do that? The water goes all green and smelly if it doesn't flow. That's why the reservoirs at Athyl are underground. They'd just disappear in no time and the lake would become a smelly puddle, like the one we saw this morning."

Junco had been looking at us while we spoke.

I explained to him. "He comes from an area with a lot of desert, not unlike this area. He wondered why the lake was there."

"Well, there wouldn't be a lake if it wasn't for the dam."

"That's what I said to him."

"They don't have dams where he comes from?"

"They do, except they don't have a lot of water to fill dams. He wonders why the lake is in the open when the water is going to evaporate and algae is going to turn it green."

"Oh. I get that. The lake has been much higher in past years. We have to keep letting out some water to keep the river flowing, but there's folk who are afraid that it's going to empty sooner rather than later. But what can we do? Build a roof over the top?"

"Where he lives, the water reservoirs are all underground."

"Huh. That right, huh? I guess they have lots of money to build stuff, too."

"They have lots of people to build stuff."

Junco shrugged. "Well, the big guy up there hasn't been very kind to us. We've kinda earned it, I guess. We don't have lots of people. We don't have lots of money. We have all the oil in the ground no one wants to buy anymore and all the people who knew how to do it are gone. We have a government that prefers to keep us distracted with silly fights. It's all the design of the guy up there, isn't it? We screwed up, and he's punishing us."

I had to think about that for a while and then realised that he meant divine influence.

That was one way to think about it, even if not a viewpoint I subscribed to.

Meanwhile, in the valley of Asto, a huge irrigation program had sprung up and people were again growing plants in fields, and attempting to further soften the climate and bring greenery back to the landscape.

Once that was completed, the planet could support a lot more people.

But I wasn't here to discuss the problems of the world, and his government's failure to look after its people.

We were going down. I could already see the outline of the old buildings.

CHAPTER TEN

WE FLEW OVER THE TOWN.

It was getting later in the afternoon. The sun was turning yellow, spreading a golden glow over the dilapidated houses, the ruins, the cracked and dust-covered roads and the desolate landscape. Not a tree grew along the streets or in the yards, and the surrounding landscape was similarly barren.

I thought that it was a ghost town but then I spotted someone on a motorbike. A few people stood in the front yard of a house. Some shops in the centre of town also seemed to be operating. A man on a quad bike turned into a driveway.

What were these people doing in this barren place?

The lake lay to the left of us. The water was bright green, and well below the level etched into the rock over decades of use. A winding road ran along the far shore and ended at a couple of buildings where a walkway led to the water. There was a jetty with a few boats.

The lake and then the town slid from view. We continued following another road.

Once we came over a hill, the landscape became a bit more varied.

I could also make out a clump of buildings scattered against the hillside, overlooking a barren and dusty plain. The structures still stood upright, but only just. Part of the roof of a shed had fallen in. A pile of burnt rubble lay in the dirt outside another building.

"Is that it?" I asked.

"Sure is," Junco said.

At least we'd have something to look at. I'd feared that a combination of looting and the passage of time would have dismantled the entire site. We'd had trouble securing recent images.

Some worry fell off my shoulders. I hadn't come all this way for nothing. We'd do the work, write up the report, and I'd present it to Ezhya. We might even talk to some locals.

I'd had some ideas about the Southern California Aerospace Corps that I wanted to explore. I was now less certain than I'd been before that they'd been aligned with the Aghyrians. The people I'd known at Midway Space Station would never associate with "aliens". They'd vanished because they had re-absorbed back into the regular space programs. The militant groups amongst them had not stood the test of time, as such extreme groups were wont to do.

Yes, we'd do our jobs here, finish up and then concentrate on all the many important things waiting for me—after seeing my father and Erith with Emi.

The craft landed in a dusty field between the buildings. Several trees stood around the perimeter of the complex. About half of them were dead.

Patches of shrubbery dotted the landscape, but it was hard to tell if the shrubs were still alive. Their leaves were grey and dusty, but a few of them had green shoots, so those were obviously not dead.

The ground was dusty, with little sign that anyone had been here recently.

The site bordered a field that sloped down to a shallow gully.

Mountains in the far distance were purple against the late afternoon sun.

The buildings closest to us were still intact, but at some point in the past, squatters had been in here, and built a campfire and collected pieces of wood into a stack.

The roof of one shack had fallen in, and the wall of another was sagging. I didn't think those buildings were important.

We stood in an area that might once have been a carpark. Years' worth of dust had blown across the paving and various shrubs had taken a chance at colonising it, and had failed, judging by their dead skeletons.

"Well, here we are, for what it's worth," Junco said. "A friend of mine will be along shortly with dinner and the extra camping gear. We'll set up a camp and you can do... whatever it is you want to do."

My team took their gear and set about doing just that. First Deyu and Veyada set up the communication hub so that the solar panels would catch the last of the day's light to charge. Then they went inside the closest building. They each had their work plans. It was my task to ask questions.

"What do you know about this place?" I asked. "I understand from Swallow that you grew up in this area."

He nodded. "I lived in town. We used to do things here that weren't allowed when we were young boys. Jumping on the motorcycle, smoking, drinking. My folks are all pretty strict, you know. No smoking, no drinking, no girls until you're married. Not that it ever did me any good." He chuckled.

"Have you ever seen anyone else here?" I asked.

"Apart from us kids, no. This place was abandoned before I was born."

"Did anyone else in your family know anything about what used to happen here?"

"Not much. They made parts for ships. They put the ships together, and then they took the ships away."

"Space ships."

"Yes, but they built boats, too. People would come here for the lake. The family who owned this place used to also own the marina."

"Used to?"

"Yeah, hardly anyone comes out there anymore. We get stinking green algae in the lake in summer. Some people still come, but they're the foolhardy ones. It's pretty disgusting, to tell you the truth."

"I noticed that. Do you know what happened to the people who worked here?"

"Word is they all left to another factory. A friend's grandfather used to work out here when the factory was still in operation. My friend always said he grew bored with his grandad talking about it, about how wonderful it was and like nothing would ever be better."

"Have you ever seen pictures?"

"Oh, I have, but I always call bullshit on them. The pictures are all doctored to make it look bigger and more important than it really was, we know that."

"If I show you some pictures, would you be able to tell me what you know?"

"I can try, depends on what you want to know. Just so that you know, I was a kid when I lived here. I left before I finished school. My mate who'll be along later should be able to tell you more."

I showed him the pictures, and he was able to tell me where the buildings were and what used to happen inside. His observations coincided with many of ours. Occasionally he would tell me there used to be other structures that had not survived the test of time. I wrote his comments on my reader, and Deyu's hub made it so that my team would see them immediately.

Junco and I also wandered into the closest building through a large roller door that had become stuck halfway in its frame.

It led to a tunnel that looked like a loading dock, with a concrete floor and sides and a crane on rails still hanging overhead.

"I'm surprised all of this is still here," Junco said. "I haven't been here for ages."

"There is a canyon outside Athyl on Asto where the remains of a civilisation have lain in caves and under collapsed rocks for more than fifty thousand years. As long as there is no water, there is very little deterioration."

This area was like Asto in reverse. This place was becoming a desert, a living museum of times past. Humanity was witness to it. They were the cause of it.

According to the pictures, the main hall had been the factory floor, not as empty as I would have expected it to be. The towers that had surrounded the central space craft assembly pad that I'd seen on the pictures were mostly gone—sold for scrap metal, I assumed. The set of rails that led to the other end of the hall, that could be opened to allow the ship or ship compartment to be taken out of the hall, were still in place. Most of the calibrating and testing equipment was damaged, but the empty housings still lined the rails.

The members of my team had fanned out across the hall.

Deyu and Veyada had opened a panel and were studying the content. Reida, Nicha and Sheydu walked around the remnants of a piece of equipment. Ynggi had climbed onto a metal construction while Anyu threw him a handful of leads. That was an interesting pairing.

The concrete floor had collected years' worth of dust, blown in through the open roller door. Over time, the ceiling cladding and insulation had cracked and peeled. Bits of foam from the panelling lay in heaps in the corners.

A group of little birds sat on a ceiling support beam. By the look of things, they had made nests in the ceiling foam.

One picture I'd been able to find of this facility in the past had been taken at the door where I stood. Today, holding the picture up against the real thing, I could still recognise the shape of the building, and the positions of the machines in the assembly room. In the picture, a gleaming spacecraft sat on the assembly pad, ready for launch. This had been at the height of the space-craft production.

I meandered through the factory hall, comparing my pictures with the remnants of equipment.

Sheydu and Reida had found something that interested them. They stood inside the deep and round pit with metal walls that would have been underneath the assembly pad.

A narrow staircase wound along the outer metal wall and allowed me to go down to join them.

Reida was looking at some sort of schematic on his screen.

"Did you find something?" I asked.

"You know how we found that craft in Barresh?" he said. "There was a lot of rubbish that was too rusted to recognise, but other compartments had remained sealed and we found some intact parts. Look at this."

He showed me two pictures side by side. They were both of identical electronic parts.

"Can you guess which one is from Barresh?" he asked.

One of the parts—a tiny cream-coloured blob of plastic with metal "feet"—bore water stains. I pointed at that one.

"No. The other one. I found the stained one inside a panel just now. The two parts are identical."

"But how do you know they were both made here?"

"We just scanned it. Look at this."

He reached over the screen and showed me a bar graph that involved bright lines of light that represented chemical components. There were two bars, and the horizontal lines ran across them at the same spots for both.

It was a scanning device that he had brought from the industrial powerhouse of the Eighth Circle in Asto, where people used these gadgets to test the purity of manufactured parts. Apparently, if you calibrated the device in a certain way, one could identify the individual factory where the parts were made.

After the discovery of the craft in the rainforest, Reida had employed a team of local Barresh youngsters to go through all the scans he had made, and had done a fabulous job of reconstructing a model of the craft. He had even been able to get one of the Asto military engineers to look at it and make comments about how the craft worked.

Reida was a very capable young man these days.

"So this means that craft was made here?"

"Not necessarily. They use the same type of parts, which says more about who made them than where they were made."

Reida said he was going to look for other similar parts. He said Veyada and Deyu had found a bank of old computers which they were going to scan. I left my team to do their jobs and walked with Junco through the hall to look for a place where we could put up camp.

I thought he meant outside, but it seemed he preferred to stay in the shelter of a building, because of coyotes.

A set of stairs led up to the second floor of the office building.

It came out in a large room with the remains of work hubs on the floor, as if this had once been a data centre.

A biting wind blew through broken windows, but Junco said that he had some sheeting that we could use to create a sheltered spot.

Several broken plastic chairs and couches stood in the corner. Someone had made a fire in the middle of the floor. Part of the floor covering had melted.

From the top floor of the building, out the broken window,

you could see out over the surrounding plain. It was a pink desert landscape that reminded me of being on Mars. A few straggly bushes grew in sheltered depressions, but it was too dark and I was too far away to see if they were dead or alive. Other than that, the landscape was dead.

But, looking out over the valley, I was overcome by a strange sensation that I had seen this landscape before.

I remembered a picture in an article I read.

I flicked through the library on my reader to check, and found the article, but then wasn't sure whether this was the same place. Junco looked over my shoulder.

"I wonder if this is the same place," I said.

"It is," he said. "I recognise this here." He pointed at the hazy mountains in the distance.

Underneath the picture, it said, "view across the testing range from the head office."

There was a small rise to the right of the building, but beyond that the plain was very flat. So this was where they used to test the vehicles?

The article was about how they built planetary exploration vehicles, not necessarily space craft. Although it implied that those were being built too.

The article never said what they intended to do with the ground vehicles, and where they intended to take them.

Most of the pointers were that the organisation had enjoyed a very brief period of success before vanishing. Surely there would be someone who remembered something? Who had seen these factories in operation?

"Ah, there he is," Junco said.

I looked out the window.

A vehicle had turned into the dusty driveway.

I presumed it belonged to the mate he'd been talking about. We made our way to the stairs.

CHAPTER ELEVEN

BY THE TIME we got down, the vehicle had pulled into the space between the buildings.

It was a rough terrain buggy with an open tray at its back, containing many packs, a battered metal drum and a couple of boxes of the type I'd seen Junco use for food storage.

The driver was an old grizzled guy, wearing a battered hat. His grey hair hung in a ponytail over the collar of his jacket.

He stopped the vehicle and slid from the driver's seat. A brown dog jumped off the back, catching something that the driver took out of his pocket and threw in the air.

The man came towards us. He wore tall boots made from well-worn dark leather and carried a hunting rifle on a strap over his shoulder.

He greeted Junco.

"This is my friend, Sage," Junco said. "He's going to cook dinner."

"Nice to meet you all." His voice sounded old and gravelly.

Contrary to what I'd expected, he was easier to understand than Junco.

He continued, "You all had a good day? My friend here tells me you went to the canyon."

"We did," I said.

"What did you think? Quite something, huh?"

"It was nice."

No sense in mentioning the overwhelming feeling of passed glory I'd felt since coming here.

"Junco says there's seven of you."

"Yes, that's right. I'll do the introductions when they've finished working."

"And you're coming here to look at these old buildings, huh? All the way from..."

"Barresh."

"Yes." He didn't sound convinced. "Don't you have your own ruins?"

"We do, actually. Ruins tell stories of past civilisations."

"They sure do."

I wasn't sure what he meant by that.

Evi and Nicha had heard us talking and had come out of the building to have a look. Sage gave them suspicious glances.

Evi was taller than most people, and the afternoon sun made his black skin glisten. It was so dark that a couple of patches of dust showed up on his arm. His moss-green eyes took in Sage and his vehicle. Nicha didn't look as imposing or alien. Having lived in London for most of his younger years, Nicha blended in better.

The dog trotted over to them and sniffed at their legs. Nicha scratched the animal's head, but Evi stood as frozen. He was not a fan of dogs.

"Don't worry about the dog," Sage said. "He's as dumb as he's harmless."

Junco asked him about camping gear and Sage wanted to know where we were going to sleep. At least that was what I could decipher from the conversation in heavy dialect.

"On the top floor of the building? Pretty creepy place for a camp, if you ask me," Sage said.

"I don't want to have any trouble with coyotes," Junco said.

Sage snorted. "I'll be cooking outside, anyway. I'm not going to make a fire in that building. If you want to sleep there, that's your problem."

"I'll take the blame," Junco said. "I don't want to have any trouble."

Sage snorted again.

Why did I have a suspicion this was not about coyotes at all? Junco had also mentioned unruly locals. Did they sneak around at night trying to rob tourists?

The dog had decided that Evi wasn't interesting and trotted off into the building.

Sage opened the tailgate of the buggy. "Well, better do some cooking before it gets too late. Those rabbits won't cook themselves."

"I don't know if anyone told you, but many in our party are vegetarians," I said.

"Don't worry, the message got through. Did you see the pumpkins I brought? Grown by my own dear wife. But some of you might fancy a roast rabbit?"

I was about to say that I would not object to that, when the dog started snarling and barking inside the building. Someone yelled, and the bark turned into a growl.

Crap, what was that?

"What's gotten into that stupid dog?" Sage said.

We all ran to the entrance, where Reida and Anyu stood watching Ynggi and the dog. Anyu had taken her gun out of its bracket and held it with both hands, ready for action.

Ynggi had wrestled the dog onto the ground, leaning on its back, so it couldn't get up. The animal made soft growling noises. The whites showed all around its eyes.

"It tried to hunt me," Ynggi said, his voice indignant.

"Let it go," I said to Ynggi. "It was probably just trying to play."

Reida shook his head. "That didn't look like playing to me. Its hair was standing up, and it went straight for him."

Anyu glanced from Ynggi, to me, to Sage. She was still holding the gun.

Sage whistled.

The dog lifted its head and continued grumbling.

Slowly, Ynggi backed away.

The dog remained motionless for a moment, then scrambled up and ran to its owner.

Sage gave me a wide-eyed look. "How did he do that? That dog's vicious when he's angry."

And before he'd said the dog was harmless.

"You don't mess with a Pengali. Meet Ynggi, of the Thousand Islands tribe."

Ynggi climbed to his feet. When the dog had come for him, he'd been looking at a piece of equipment in a cabinet mounted on the floor and his scanner and leads lay scattered across the dirt.

The dog cowered and retreated behind its owner's legs, uttering a warning growl.

Sage grabbed its leather collar. "And what's gotten into you? Can't you greet our customers politely?" He looked at me and Ynggi. "Sorry about that. Seems the dog's met his match. His own stupid fault." He scratched the dog between the ears.

He looked at me and nodded at Ynggi. "Does he understand?"

"No, but I can translate."

I told him what Sage just said.

Ynggi looked confused. "The animal *belongs* to him?"

"Yes."

Ynggi gave Sage a suspicious glance. Pengali didn't own much, let alone other creatures.

"Was it wrong to hold it down?" he asked me.

"In your situation, probably not. Dog bites are not pleasant. He's just surprised that you could do it."

"The animal is strong," he said.

The emotions warred on his face. On one hand, you were supposed to compliment a person's belongings, but on the other hand, owning animals was a distasteful thing to Pengali.

He said, "Tell him that I didn't intend to hurt the animal."

I told Sage, and Sage nodded. He was looking at the fearsome knife that Ynggi wore on his belt, likely appreciating that he hadn't taken it out.

"I'm sorry that the dog thought he was fair game," Sage said.

Ynggi gave a small bow, mirrored with his tail.

Sage took in every detail of Ynggi's appearance, his plaited hair, his simple clothing, his muscled arms, his belt with the knife.

"He looks like a good hunter," he said, after a while.

"The tribe does a lot of fishing. They live in a forest and feed themselves through hunting and fishing and picking fruit." And trading diamond, but that was a different matter.

Sage looked at Junco. "You ever met any of these people before?"

Junco shook his head. "First time. We don't get many of them Union people. You should see their tailed little kids. They're patterned all over."

It was ages since I'd heard anyone use the patronising term Union. Its use had been common when I started at Nations of Earth.

Sage again glanced at Ynggi.

It was interesting. Sage and Junco hadn't said any of the things I was used to hearing at Nations of Earth. There was no comparison between Pengali and monkeys or any other animal. He'd correctly identified Ynggi as male and respected him for having outfoxed his farm dog.

"Anyway, I better start the fire."

He went to his truck and backed the vehicle up to the entrance of the abandoned loading dock.

Out of a box in the back, he produced the aforementioned pumpkins and two skinned and de-headed rabbits, strung by the feet.

He set up a metal drum with chunks of wood and opened a small box which turned out to contain burning coals.

With this, he had a fire going in no time. He strung up the rabbits to cook and placed cut-up pumpkin in a metal dish.

Meanwhile, we gathered up the last information for the day and found a place in the upstairs office for Junco to roll out the sleeping mats.

Whenever we passed the fire, the dog sat at Sage's feet, beating its tail into the dust and growling softly whenever Ynggi came near.

Sage told it to shut up and get over itself.

Ynggi was fascinated by the rabbits. He asked me what they were and where they lived. Could they swim?

I said, "I guess they can, but they live on the land. They eat grass."

"How do you catch them?" Ynggi wanted to know.

"I guess he shoots them, or maybe he traps them."

"With a line, like a fish?"

"I don't know. We can ask."

We were done for the day anyway, and went to join Sage at the fire.

The dog growled. There had to be something about Ynggi's scent it didn't like. Ynggi flicked his tail at him with a snap.

The dog stopped mid-growl and sat down. Its eyes followed the movement of Ynggi's tail.

I asked Sage how and where one caught rabbits.

"They're all around here," he said, waving his hand at the field that was golden in the setting sun.

"What do they eat?" Ynggi asked, without waiting for my translation.

I translated that for Sage.

Ynggi then remarked that he didn't see much grass, but Sage said that there was more towards the creek and that the rabbits didn't need that much.

"They're tough things and eat pretty much anything. Bark, wood, sticks, hay. Many birds and bigger animals have gone, but the rabbits just keep on breeding."

He turned the rabbits around over the fire. Fat was dripping onto the flames. The dog was looking at them, slapping its tail in the dust.

"I think the animal is hungry," Ynggi said.

I translated for Sage, who laughed.

He inserted his hand in the pocket of his jacket and pulled out something brown. Dried meat, I thought. He gestured for Ynggi to come over. The dog retreated with a soft whine.

He held the meat out. The dog came a bit closer. He gestured for Ynggi to come closer again.

You could see the warring emotions in the dog's eyes. The dog wanted food, but it was scared of Ynggi.

It came closer, stalking carefully, glancing at Ynggi.

Ynggi's tail gave a little flick, and it froze, the whites showing in its eyes.

Ynggi waved his tail at knee height, and the dog came closer again. The tail went up, and the dog stopped.

"Look at it," I said to Nicha, who stood next to me. "Tail language is universal."

The dog snatched the morsel out of Sage's hand and retreated.

Ynggi sat next to the fire, watching as the dog chewed the dried meat. It was gone in minutes, and then they just stared at each other.

Junco had finished preparing the camp and came to the fire. He brought a bottle with a dark fluid.

"Drink?"

I accepted some, and Veyada, being Veyada, had to try everything. Anyu was unsure and needed to consult with Veyada after he'd tried some, but Sheydu refused. Anyu took that as a cue to refuse as well. Ynggi very much disapproved of drinking, even in Barresh. But Evi accepted, and so did Reida and Nicha.

It was whiskey, I thought.

Ynggi sat next to me. Sage was turning the roasting rabbits on the spit.

"He hunts these animals?" Ynggi asked.

"Yes."

"And he grows these... fruit?" He flicked his tail at the pumpkins that were cut into pieces and cooking in a metal tray on the fire.

"Yes."

"People are all the same, right?"

"Yes. They live in a similar way to the Pengali." At least I hoped that this was what he meant. Ynggi could be infuriatingly opaque.

"What is the other animal, the *dog*, for?"

"It guards places. Dogs don't like intruders."

"We are intruders."

"To the dog, yes."

"How does it know the difference between people?"

"Dogs have very good noses. They can tell the difference between people by smell."

"Everyone can do that."

Well, the Pengali maybe, and my sense of smell had also increased since my transformation, along with the decline of my night vision, but nowhere near to a level to compete with a dog.

"The *dog* knows *which* people are the good people?"

"Yes."

"What does it do when bad strangers come?"

"It growls and makes a lot of noise, so that if this happens when everyone is asleep, the people wake up and can chase away the intruder."

"Hmmm."

He looked at the dog, and the dog looked back. It stopped flopping its tail into the dust and growled softly.

"It doesn't like me."

"Probably because it thinks you smell strange."

"Why does it listen to this person?"

"Because that's what dogs do, and this man feeds the dog."

"It's an animal. Can't it find its own food?"

"Probably, but I don't think people would like it. The streets would be unsafe, because the dogs would hunt."

"Hmmm. Animals are free. People shouldn't feed them."

"But dogs are useful. They can guard homes and they can be a friend."

Ynggi looked sideways at the dog, and the dog was still looking at him.

"Hmmm," he said again. "Some people in the tribe would probably like to try such a *dog*. Abri would probably say that animals should live free."

"I guess Abri will be glad to know that she would never get a dog through quarantine."

"Yes."

Ynggi turned around and left, presumably to find a jacket, because the air was quite cool.

"What was all that about?" Sage asked.

"He is fascinated by the dog and what it can do."

Sage laughed. "Even a silly bastard like this?" But he scratched the dog between his ears and threw it another morsel from his pocket.

"He says the tribe could use a dog."

"Somehow I doubt it's an option, huh?"

"Not in the slightest. Some of them also object to keeping animals as pets. He says animals should be free."

"That's not an option here, either. There is nothing to eat for them."

"I suspected as much."

Junco declared the rabbit done and took the basket with the pumpkin off the fire.

He carved up his efforts with a large knife that he cleaned in between the pumpkin and the rabbit.

The dog scored a few bones and crunchy bits.

We ate while the very proper and traditional members of my team—Sheydu and Anyu—ate from their own supplies, a sad selection of prepacked military rations, which they prepared with water to which they added red coded supplements. Veyada was happy to share the rabbit, Nicha got stuck into the pumpkin.

The meal was quite tasty, even if I wasn't used to eating much meat any more.

We discussed our project.

Reida showed the maps and 3D representations he was making of the factory, as it might once have been. Both men were impressed with his presentation. Sage said he'd never been inside when the factory was still in operation, but that he remembered the time that something was still happening inside the buildings.

He said he remembered talking to people in town about it.

"I was only little, mind, and I had some friends whose fathers worked here. Then one day, they were gone. The factory was closed."

"Did you ever hear why?" I asked.

"Suppose they ran out of money. There were a lot of rumours around town. They said some rich guy in Dixie bought the factory. Never found out if that was true."

"What happened to the people who worked there? This is such a small town. It wouldn't have been easy to find work elsewhere."

"No, it wasn't. A lot of people left, pretty much overnight, and that started a lot of rumours. They said that the engineers went in hiding, because they didn't want to give anyone in Dixie the stuff they'd been working on. Then we heard there was a big fuss about this ship that went down after launch."

I confirmed that he spoke about the very public failure of the launch of the first manned spacecraft by the organisation.

He was.

He told us the story as he had heard it. He'd been a little kid back then.

His story was pretty much like I'd already understood it to be, only uglier.

Sage said the SCAC started as an amateur society with a few rich members who bought up spacefaring technology when the technology was being retired. Their base was in San Diego, in the building we had already visited, but when Mexico took possession of that area, they moved inland. Mexico pledged to continue contributing to the space program, but I guessed that in reality, it was Nations of Earth that these people wanted to keep away from their technology.

President Gonzales—a Mexican—had argued that all parts of the world had to cooperate in space technology because nobody wanted rival factions in space. So the Europeans and the Indonesians and the Egyptians had all joined forces.

I knew about that part, but had been taught it was a good thing.

But the people of the American space programs—affiliated with the SCAC—had considered the president's requests for cooperation between space programs unreasonable. They had doggedly persisted on their own, culminating in a shuttle launch that may or may not have been planned to fail, and subsequent disappearance of the shuttle when it came down over Texas.

I asked if Junco and Sage had any idea where the shuttle had gone. We already knew it wasn't the same vehicle we had found in Barresh, because that was a much more advanced vehicle. But if these people could hijack a space shuttle, they could hide extra technology. I thought of the people at Midway Space Station talking about an escape route to a secret place. They could have pretended that the shuttle had crashed, but had landed it on the other side of the border instead. And then they had taken it to their secret hideout.

I had already asked Reida to check if the Exchange held any records about this launch as soon as we were back in range.

Hmmm. Maybe things weren't as simple as I thought.

Then I wondered. "Where is Ynggi?"

He'd left, and hadn't come back to the fire, and that had now been quite a while ago. He hadn't come down for dinner.

"Crap," Sage said. "Where is the stupid dog?"

CHAPTER TWELVE

I RAN into the building and up the stairs. It was pitch dark in the room where Junco had put the sleeping bags, but that would not be a problem for Ynggi.

I turned on the light of my reader and looked around. The sleeping bags lay in neat rows, each on its own mat, and with a pillow. Our luggage stood in the corner, all still untouched. The sky outside the broken and dirt-caked windows was dark.

"Ynggi?" I called.

There was no response.

I called again, "Ynggi, where are you? Dinner is ready."

Again, there was no response. I walked to the window, but it was too dark down there for me to even see the ground.

When I turned around, I noticed that Ynggi's bag was open and some of his clothes lay on the ground. I couldn't see the knife anywhere. What was the bet that he had taken the fishing gear and was trying his hand at catching something? I'd be highly surprised if the creek bed held any water.

Veyada had come up the stairs behind me.

"He's not here," I said.

Veyada said, "I don't get it. We would have seen him if he came down, wouldn't we?"

"I don't know. There may be another exit. To me, it looks like he's gone fishing." I pointed at the pack.

"But why?" Veyada asked.

"He was upset about the incident with the dog. He probably wants to bring Sage a fish."

"There are no fish here."

"There is a lake."

"You're kidding. That's too far away. He can do strange things, but he's not stupid." But his face displayed a concerned expression.

We looked around the room again, because it would be very handy right now if Ynggi turned out to be hiding somewhere. There were a few places along the walls where there had been cupboards, although the doors had long since been taken off and probably used to light someone's fire.

There was nowhere to hide.

Outside, Sage's whistles for his dog echoed in the dark.

"I don't like it that that animal has disappeared at the same time as Ynggi," Veyada said. "You should have seen it when it tried to attack him."

"I am more worried about the dog than I am about Ynggi," I said. "Dogs are not nocturnal. He seems capable of defending himself."

In fact, I was decidedly worried on the dog's behalf.

We checked and double-checked every nook and cranny. On this floor, there was nowhere except in the large office where Ynggi could hide. And the doors had been ripped off the cupboards, exposing broken shelving and collections of rubbish like bottles and food wrappers.

We went back down the stairs, and into the main hall, where we walked around, calling out for Ynggi. Reida and Anyu joined us, checking all the places where they had worked earlier. We couldn't see a sign of him.

A cold breeze came in through an open door on the far side of the hall.

"Strange. This door wasn't open earlier this afternoon," Anyu said.

I stared into the darkness.

The light from my reader only lit a section of stone-covered ground. Beyond that, the plain disappeared out of sight. The stars twinkled in the sky.

Then came the sound of footsteps and Sage and Junco approached from outside.

"You see him?" Sage asked.

"No," I said. "Any luck with the dog?"

"None at all."

His voice sounded as concerned as I felt.

"I think he left the building through this door," I said.

Sage stared into the darkness. "Does he often do this?"

"At home, he fishes at night," I said. "Pengali people are nocturnal."

"Not many fish here," Sage said.

"I'd be worried about coyotes," Junco said. "They hunt in packs. We can't even use the dog to trace him."

"The dog's with him for sure," Sage said. "He'll be following at a distance, because he's a curious bastard."

The rest of the party joined up with us, Evi first, because he had the best ears and excellent night vision. They confirmed what we already knew: they hadn't seen a sign of Ynggi either.

"All right," I said, as everyone gathered around. "We need to find him. What do we know about this area?"

Reida pulled up his map, which showed the creek intersecting the plain not too far from where we stood.

Sage confirmed there was no water in it. "Hasn't been for years that I remember."

Junco went to get Sage's buggy. It couldn't carry all of us, so I walked ahead with Veyada, Nicha and Evi, holding our lights in front of us.

Evi informed me that he could see a fair bit more than I could, because of the pale light of the almost full moon.

I remembered moonlight. I remembered sitting on the beach in front of the house where my father now lived, but that had belonged to my grandparents back then. The moonlight would reflect off the water and sometimes it was so bright, you could almost see without using a torch.

No more.

For me, everything was pitch dark. I knew that most in my team would feel the same. Dang Coldi night vision.

We fanned out from the building. The vehicle's headlights showed a landscape of stones with meagre clumps of dead grass and dried knee-high bushes with drooping leaves.

Sage told us to stay within shouting distance of the buggy, because of coyotes, which were vicious wild dogs, he told Reida.

"I really think they go overboard on the dogs," Veyada said to me in a low voice as we picked our way across the rocky ground together.

He was a big and comforting presence next to me, even if I knew he could see just as little in the dark as I could.

"I guess you don't like dogs?" I said.

"Not really."

"Not even Fred?" My father's poor old dog. I hoped he was still alive, even if I hadn't heard anything to the contrary.

"He's all right, but most are annoying."

"Worse than elephants?"

"Now you're just poking fun at me, right?"

Veyada did *not* like to talk about elephants.

"Personally, I'm not a fan of monkeys," I said.

"No." That sounded like a solid agreement.

"What about squirrels?" I asked.

"Squirrels are all right. But they can still be annoying, like they all got into the aircraft and made a mess of the lunch things. I don't get why all these creatures have to poke their noses into our affairs."

"Food."

"I guess. I just object to it being *my* food or even *being* the food."

I was still trying to convince him that the elephant that chased him over the fence hadn't been wanting to eat him, but I suspected that was a losing battle.

We continued slowly across the plain, our way lit by the headlights from the buggy.

Sage was right. The creek bed was quite close, down a mild slope. It consisted of more rocks and boulders, and as far as I could see, no water. I didn't see much of the promised grass either.

There was no sign of Ynggi. I didn't see any animals. No rabbits, no coyote. The night was deathly quiet and dark.

The only thing I could hear were the soft voices of Reida and Anyu who sat in the back of the buggy and were logging our progress.

Then there was a shout in the dark.

It sounded like Junco.

Reida shouted at us, "He's coming your way. On the other side of the creek."

I directed my light at the far side of the gully, where little clumps of grass clung to the stony ground.

First an animal ran out across the beam of light at incredible speed. It was the size of a cat, had big powerful legs and enormous ears.

The rabbit.

Then Ynggi followed, also at incredible speed. He had devised a weapon by tying a piece of string to a rock.

Pengali kids in Barresh used these improvised slings to catch meili out of the air. The rock would flip around the animal, pinning its wings together with the string and bringing it down. Meili were poor eating, so elders frowned on this behaviour as being cruel and undesirable. But kids did it, anyway.

Ynggi threw the rock. The string went neatly around the rabbit's neck, ensnaring the animal. It tried to get away but could not, jumping and kicking around. Ynggi reeled in the string and jumped on top of it.

Then he rose again, holding the animal by the foot.

On his back, on another piece of string, dangled a second rabbit.

The dog trotted after him.

Ynggi moved the tip of his tail down, and the dog sat down. They both looked like kids caught doing something naughty.

"Well well," Junco said. "That was quite something. I have to admit I've never seen anyone do that before."

Ynggi gathered up his two rabbits, dusted himself off and came across the creek bed. He was in traditional Pengali gear, which meant little clothing and no shoes. He had cut open his shin and one of his toenails was bleeding. This was very different country from where he was used to running around barefoot.

He went to Sage. He bowed and presented him with the two rabbits.

"Are these for me?" Sage asked, sounding a little puzzled, looking at me.

"I think so. The Pengali have a powerful tradition that involves offering food in reparation for misunderstandings and mistakes. They always bring fish when they come to visit me at my apartment. They don't feel happy if they can't bring food to an important meeting."

"Reparation?"

"About attacking your dog."

"I don't mind about the dog," Sage said. "They seem to have made up, anyway."

"I told him that, and I told him that the animal probably has a reaction to him because of his smell, but that doesn't matter. He needs to do what his tribe would consider the right thing. Even though the tribe is not here, he believes that they can see him if he acts dishonourably. He will have thought that by accidentally attacking your dog, he did something improper."

"Hah. Don't worry about it. The animal is stupid anyway, and it was a good lesson for him. I've long thought that sooner or later the stupid thing is going to have his nose bitten by a coyote."

"I have told him that, but that doesn't matter. Because if he is convince the tribe will think that he did something wrong, which he did, because he disrespected something that was someone else's property, then he will have to make repairs. The rabbits are yours. He would be honoured if you took them and if you told him you were going to eat them."

"I will certainly do that. Those look like good specimens. I'm amazed how he caught them."

Sage took the rabbits and said to Ynggi that he appreciated it.

The dog followed him, holding its tail low as Ynggi did.

Nicha was right. There were some tail dynamics going on between Ynggi and the dog. Just like the Pengali kids and the squirrel.

Sage chuckled. "Well, I guess we've all learned something. I'll put these in the cool box and will skin them tomorrow. I'm of a mind to make me some mittens."

"Does he like them?" Ynggi asked.

"Yes. He's happy."

I was going to say something else, but a thunder-like rumble in the distance made us all fall quiet. The sound echoed over the desert plain.

We all looked at each other by the glow of the buggy's headlights.

"What the hell was that?" Sage said.

"I think that's thunder," Reida said.

"It sounds different," I said.

"Thunder only sounds that way in Barresh because of the nearby rock wall of the escarpment."

I had to grant him that. Thunder sounded very different in Barresh. Quite scary actually. "But there are no clouds."

Both Sage and Junco studied the sky.

"It did sound like thunder, except it hasn't thundered here for as long as I can remember," Sage said. "It doesn't rain much here, especially at this time of the year."

"Then what was it?" I asked.

"I don't know." Junco sounded puzzled. "Something to do with a military exercise, I'm thinking. It's probably not as close as we think."

Ah yes, I remembered how my team had picked up talk about military activity. Atlantia was doing exercises. But that was an awfully long way from here. Maybe America Free State responded with its own exercises. Countries really were as childish as that.

Whatever the sound was, it killed the conversation. Both our guides didn't like it, even if they also acted like they didn't worry about it. We decided it was time to go to sleep.

CHAPTER THIRTEEN

THE FACT that Junco and Sage worried about the unknown sound disturbed me more than I liked to admit. They knew this area and its dangers well. They clearly didn't like what they heard.

Most likely, it was nothing that affected us, but it might affect Sage and Junco. Military exercises could be the precursor to armed conflict. This area was relatively stable, but that was only because few people lived here. The area housed military bases and training grounds that aided conflict elsewhere.

If nothing else, it reminded me of how vulnerable we were out here in this strange country.

When we returned to the buildings, and before we went to sleep, I told Reida to check if he could find out anything about it.

Reida spent some time fiddling with his equipment in the corner of the room. Anyu joined in for a bit, before he came over to my sleeping mat and told me that there was a military base not too far off and that it was his guess that there had been an exercise, but also that he couldn't verify that because there was no connectivity. He said he'd leave the receivers on overnight to see if they could gather something from passing satellites—most notably the Exchange's, one of which was due to fly over a bit after midnight.

Other than the sleeping mats, Junco had also collected a tank of water which sat downstairs in a room for us to wash, but most of us were used to desert living and I was the only one who used it, and then only not to give Junco the impression that he'd put in the effort for nothing.

It was dark and kind of creepy in the empty building when I went downstairs. Soft sounds came out of the dark hall. It was probably peeled-off cladding flapping in the breeze, but in my mind, I saw rats and other vermin crawling all over the place.

When I came back upstairs, many of my team were already asleep.

I thought I'd have trouble sleeping. The mats were quite thin, the floor was hard, and the icy breeze kept prying into places where I didn't want it.

But my body was finally catching up with me, and thinking I'd probably lie awake all night was the last thing I remembered.

I woke up when the window facing me was a pale purple rectangle, but everything else in the room was still dark. The members of my team I could see were still asleep.

I went to the window, trying to be as quiet as possible, and breathed the cool, earthy air.

The plain below stretched away from the building all the way across the valley to the gully and continued on the other side. I couldn't figure out where we had found Ynggi last night. I thought I could see buggy tracks in the soft sand directly underneath the window, but little else.

Not all of the mats were still occupied, so I went downstairs.

Junco and Sage must be up as well, because the sound of their voices and the smell of cooking drifted into the factory hall.

I found Reida and Anyu in a corner of the hall, using the metal structure that supported the roof as an antenna for the receiver.

They seemed busy, so I crossed the hall without disturbing them.

I stopped at the door. Junco and Sage had made a fire and sat drinking tea while warming themselves. The air was hazy with pale mist. What a peaceful, rustic scene in sharp contrast with the dystopian quality of the abandoned factory.

Someone else from my team came down the stairs, a dark shape too far away for me to see who it was. Sheydu, probably.

Veyada had also joined Reida and Anyu, and indeed Sheydu had appeared. They sat on the floor surrounding the transmitter. Its light was blinking. Sheydu was wearing the earpiece, pressing it to her ear. What were they listening to?

I went back to join them.

"Try that one," Anyu said.

Sheydu fiddled some more. She shook her head. "It's gone out of range."

"Is anything the matter?" I asked.

They turned around.

"We're not sure," Sheydu said. I didn't like the concerned tone in her voice. "We can't reach the Exchange right now. The satellites are out of range or the signal is too weak. We can get some local news. The translations suggest something may have happened, but it's hard to establish a source of reference in the local news sources. We need to understand their protocols and reporting framework."

Eh, yes, Sheydu. Thank you for that level of crystal clarity. "Maybe I can help. Do you want me to translate anything you've picked up?"

She handed me an earpiece, and after I put it on, Anyu cycled through several frequencies. One of them played music, another seemed to be some sort of talk show. Someone was discussing "affected areas", referring to a map I couldn't see, because we didn't have the accompanying visual channel.

Then a clear voice blasted into my ear from a broadcast

station that was featuring a news bulletin.

A male voice said, "... and there has been no news from the affected area. Rescue forces have been sent in to determine the extent of the damage. We would recommend that all residents remain indoors and keep listening for official announcements."

Affected area? Rescue forces? Damage?

I looked at them. "Something has happened."

"Yes, we agree. We got that far, but we have no idea what."

A crash, an explosion. Whatever we'd heard last night? It wasn't a military exercise? What was the "affected area"? Crap. My thoughts wandered to Thayu and Emi. But surely they were too far away and would be about to prepare for a day on the beach. They might worry about us, though.

Someone called outside for breakfast.

The breakfast offering involved eggs and meat, so most of my team resorted to their supplies, even if Ynggi appreciated the eggs.

He'd had eggs before and knew these were bird eggs, but he attempted to explain to Sage that in Barresh the Pengali ate lizard eggs. They were a bit smaller and soft-shelled. You ate them whole. Keihu would pickle them, often with the baby lizard recognisably inside. I was no fan of those.

Since having made up with his dog, Ynggi followed Sage around everywhere, watching precisely what he did.

I asked Sage if he had heard any local news, and he said he had not. He said he didn't care much about what other people called "news", unimportant gossip and other busybody stuff.

"Townsfolk are crazy people," he said. "They make a big thing out of stuff that's not important, and then they wonder why there is no food on the shelves or no water in the tanks and things like that. Dumb and ignorant. That's what they are."

"You weren't worried about the sound we heard last night?" I asked.

He shrugged. "Not much point worrying about something

unless I know what it is, right?"

"True."

"If we worried every time something unusual happened, I can tell you, we'd have no life."

I hoped he was right, but clearly, he *was* worried and he was being cavalier about it.

After breakfast we packed up, and handed Junco all our bags, before completing the scan of the buildings on the site.

Sage had already left without saying goodbye. I told Junco to tell Sage that we had appreciated his assistance when the two next met.

We finished the remaining work by mid-morning, by which time the sun was bright and the field outside had once again turned pale and dusty.

Junco announced that we were going to see one more tourist attraction before flying back.

"This is our best local spot," he said. "It would be a pity for you to miss it."

We all got into the craft and took off for a short flight over the desert landscape.

Again, we came over the town. The utter desolation of it made me wonder why anyone would want to live there. Maybe it looked better on the ground. Maybe it was because people were social creatures and stuck together, even if there was nothing to stick together for.

Sage didn't live in town, Junco said. He lived on the other side of the lake in the reserve, because he had enough native blood to do so.

Whether that area was any prettier, though, Junco couldn't say. I suspected he didn't see much wrong with the town. He said people lived there because it had a lake, there was always enough water, and now that the factories had closed, governments left the townsfolk alone. Being left alone was a big thing in America Free State, I understood that much.

We landed on a flat piece of land that again might once have been a parking area.

We followed a paved path that led up a slight incline and then down to a viewing platform.

It looked out over an incredible u-shaped canyon with water flowing at its very bottom. A dry wind whipped hair in our faces.

"That is pretty," Veyada said next to me.

"Finally, something Asto doesn't have?"

He grinned.

Deep in the canyon, the water flowed lazily around the bend past rock formations and little sandy beaches edged with a ribbon of green. There was not another person, not a bird, nor a squirrel in sight.

I turned around to ask Reida what he thought, but the other members of my team were not paying attention to the scenery. Anyu and Sheydu were again listening to something they had picked up, trying to communicate with the Exchange, or listening in on the various local broadcasts. Their actions worried me. Thayu said that an important aspect of being a spy was to develop a good gut feeling. Coldi used the word *berzhyu*, which translated as "what we don't know" and that translation didn't do the word justice. It was used very specifically by security when they spoke of things they couldn't prove but strongly suspected to be the case. Agents would not speak of facts they considered *berzhyu* until they had proof. I suspected that such a scenario was playing out right now. They *knew* something was happening. They might even have an idea what it was. They wouldn't tell me until they were sure. It was very frustrating.

I was ready to rejoin the rest of the team.

The trip had been reasonably successful. I hadn't found out amazing things, but little things I could work with. Enough for a report to Ezhya. Enough to figure out where the craft in Barresh had originated.

We returned to the patch of dirt next to the road where Junco's gyrocopter stood.

Someone shouted.

Sheydu, who walked in front of me, yanked her gun from under her jacket.

She called, "Watch out!"

Reida jumped next to me, also pulling his weapon from his belt.

Between him and Sheydu, I noticed a couple of figures running out of a gully, coming towards us. I counted five.

Young men, locals, judging by their clothing. They wore the same sand-coloured trousers that Sage had worn. They hid their noses and mouths under colourful scarves and the tops of their heads under wide-brimmed hats.

Junco swore.

"Who are they? What's going on?" I asked him.

The youths had stopped and faced us. One of them yelled a few words. All of them carried weapons.

Junco cursed. "They're idiots. Wait. I'll deal with them."

He pushed himself between Reida and Sheydu, but as he crossed the space in between us and the group of five, a quad bike came out of the gully with two more men.

It stopped on the path that led back to the gyrocopter.

So—they wanted to steal it? They wanted our luggage?

With the canyon at our back and a group of armed men at the front, we had nowhere to go.

"I can get rid of them," Sheydu said, putting her free hand in her jacket's pocket. I bet she could, too.

A small truck was coming up the road. It drove across the patch where the gyrocopter stood and parked next to it. Another five men came out of the cabin, and a further six out of the back compartment.

It looked like we were outnumbered.

Well, shit, what was this about?

Junco had reached the first group of men and was talking to them. They were too far away for me to follow the conversation. It didn't sound friendly.

We waited.

Assess, plan, carry out, that was Sheydu's motto.

My team watched and waited for an opportunity.

Meanwhile, a second and third quad bike arrived, and parked next to the other one. Each bike carried two additional young men, who went over to where Junco was still arguing with the youths.

A stiff breeze came up, blowing dust over the desert plain. The young man closest to me grabbed his hat that was about to blow off. He squinted at me over the top of the cloth tied over his nose and mouth. He eyed my clothing—still the jacket I'd brought from Barresh—my hair, my belt—if he was looking for weapons, that was the wrong place. I judged him to be no older than twenty. Maybe I could distract him.

I said, "Do you want to know where we're from? I can show you pictures."

He didn't react. It was not that he couldn't understand me. Isla had a large English component. He would understand at least some of my words.

He just stared at me, holding his gun with dusty hands that were the mark of someone who did manual work.

I tried again, "We were just at the old spaceship factory. Do you know anyone who used to work there?"

Again, no reply. He now avoided looking me in the eye.

The group with Junco had split up. One man shouted in our direction. Crap, where was Junco? I couldn't see him anywhere.

"Where is our guide?" I asked.

An older man jerked with his weapon. "Walk," he said, his voice like a bark.

The truck backed up the path. The back cargo doors were open.

They wanted us to go in there? Then take us where?

Sheydu made a hand signal to Reida and Anyu. *Be ready.* What for, I didn't know.

Ynggi's large eyes roved the countryside. He did wear clothes and shoes today, so he would be able to run, if needed.

Except where would we run? Who were these men and what did they want?

I didn't want to run.

All our equipment was in the gyrocopter except for the items we carried with us.

I saw Junco, just about to get into the gyrocopter. He was walking alone, although a man with a gun stood on a hill watching him.

Then a thought: Junco hadn't led them to us, right? Deliberately visited this "one more tourist spot" and told them to ambush us here?

I felt cold.

He didn't seem the type.

He probably had his business to consider, and having his customers kidnapped would look bad for his image.

I hoped.

It wasn't looking good. He reached the door to the gyrocopter's cabin, opened it and got in.

He was about to take off with our stuff. This didn't look good, not one bit.

Sheydu and Anyu glanced at each other. Veyada made a hand signal. Reida looked aside.

I mentally prepared myself to grab my weapon strapped under my shirt.

The truck came closer, turned a half circle and parked so that the back doors faced us.

We bunched closer together.

A man came out of the truck's cabin, and went to open the back doors, but one of them kept blowing shut with the blustery wind, so a second person had to show him where to secure the door.

But a bigger gust of wind yanked the door loose again. It hit the truck with a thud, narrowly missing the shoulder of one of the men. They scrambled to secure the door, and one of the others yelled something about not being stupid.

Sheydu took this moment of distraction as our opportunity. She dug something out of her pocket and lobbed it into the back of the truck. A man yelled, another slammed the back door shut. They both ran away.

Too late. The vehicle exploded in a ball of fire.

Veyada grabbed me by the arm, and we ran, dodging falling debris.

We ran off into a gully, and found the three electric quad bikes there.

Evi jumped on one of them, Anyu climbed behind him, and then Sheydu jumped on another bike, pulling me with her onto the back seat. Veyada secured the third bike with Ynggi and Reida.

"What about the gear in the gyrocopter?" I asked Sheydu.

"We'll worry about that later."

Hopefully, Junco could salvage it.

Fortunately, I had my reader with all the information we had collected in the pocket of my jacket. I'd learned my lesson well and truly on previous occasions.

We set off through a canyon. Since we had taken control of all their vehicles save the truck, which was out of action, the men had to follow on foot.

"Amateurs," Sheydu called. Her voice sounded smug.

I said, "Well, let's wait until we get to safety. There might be elephants."

And the big question was how we were going to get out of here.

CHAPTER FOURTEEN

THE THREE BIKES made good speed over the rocky ground.

We followed a bumpy path which ran along the top of the canyon.

We churned through deep sand and zig-zagged between sharp rocks. Several times we had to backtrack to find a better route.

I asked Sheydu where we were going, but she said only that we needed a safe base so we could meet up with the aircraft. I hoped that Junco would still be coming. How would he know where we were?

I judged it best not to disturb her with my silly questions.

They would have a plan. There was always a plan.

We arrived on the outskirts of the town, and along a deserted and dusty street, found a business that serviced trucks. A vehicle was sitting outside the office.

Reida, on the first bike, screeched to a halt in the yard. Sheydu also stopped the bike, jumped off and tried one of the truck's doors. It was locked, but Reida solved that problem.

He climbed in.

All those hours he spent running simulations of different types of technology were paying off in big spades.

Meanwhile, people had moved inside the business' office. Someone had figured out that we were *not* the vehicle's owners.

Too late.

We all piled in, with Veyada next to me, Nicha and Anyu in the back and Evi in the cargo compartment.

As we left the yard, a woman ran out of the office. She stopped in the middle of the road and pointed a weapon at us.

I yelled at Reida, "Watch out! Swerve!"

Too late.

A loud bang echoed in the street. A bullet ricocheted off the back of the truck's frame with a *ping*.

Sheydu cursed.

The truck moved as Evi was doing something in the back. There was a thud of a metallic and heavy object hitting the ground. The rear vision mirror showed me coils of fencing wire rolling and coming loose on the road.

We had pursuers—a man on a motorbike who dodged the wire with ease.

Reida got the vehicle up to maximum speed. He was not an experienced driver. At an intersection, he turned left, took the corner short, veered onto the wrong side of the road, almost hitting someone on a bike. That person was then almost hit again by the motorbike pursuing us.

We had come into the town's main street, with shops on both sides and people milling about talking to each other. There were pedestrians, older citizens, mothers with children, dogs. People stopped whatever they were doing to watch us.

We made it through without hitting anything—phew—turned left again onto the wrong side of a divided road that went down-hill. A vehicle coming up the hill honked at us and then turned around as we passed.

We raced down the hill, onto a bridge that spanned the canyon. On the left side was the deep abyss of the canyon, on the right the lake. As Sage had said, the water was a vile green colour, with salt-encrusted lines evidence that water levels had once been higher.

Up the other side.

Along the road stood a sign that read:

Warning. You are entering Native Land. No Access to main roads from here.

Oh crap.

A bit further, we hit a checkpoint with a closed gate across the road. A man sat in a white cubicle, to collect a toll or check a pass or something.

Reida veered to the side—again the wrong side—of the road and turned the truck in a big circle. I was going to have to talk to him about road sides and that this was not New Zealand, the only place where he had driving experience.

"Where are we going?" I asked.

Reida took us back down the hill. With solid rock walls on both sides, there was nowhere else to go. The motorbike and car had both stopped in the middle of the road, but Reida did not slow down. He made directly for the motorbike and when the rider ran off, steered the truck in between the bike and the road edge. The truck side-swiped an old traffic sign. In the screeching noise, I thought I could hear the discharge of Evi's gun, but I wasn't sure, and I lost sight of the road when Reida made a sharp left-hand turn into a narrow turnoff.

This road had eroded badly, with crumbling surface and big potholes, and sand mounds encroaching on the verges. The lake was to the right, visible as glimpses in between the rock formations.

Anyu in the back was yelling coordinates at someone in Coldi. Likely someone from the register.

The team had abandoned all efforts to remain covert and had pulled out the emergency plugs.

The road ended in another abandoned car park, with behind that, a low building with wide verandas. A white-painted walkway led from the veranda across the rocks. It didn't quite reach the water, but another such walkway did, and provided mooring spots for a handful of boats.

Damn, it was a marina, even if most of the jetties now lay dry.

Reida stopped the truck.

"What are we doing here?" I asked.

"Waiting for a pickup," Veyada said. He opened the door. "Get into the building. Take everything out of the vehicle."

"What? Did you just contact someone from the Coldi register and can they come all the way here?"

Sheydu replied, "They *could*, if they wanted to, but we don't want to create that much trouble yet. We'll see if this works."

I followed the team to the building. I had no idea what the "this" was that Sheydu referred to.

The door into the building was locked, but one kick from Reida solved that problem.

We entered what looked like a function room or dining room, with tables and chairs stacked up in the corner. There was a bar directly opposite the entrance. The entire right wall was taken up with windows overlooking the lake—vile green with white-encrusted edges.

Sheydu, Anyu and Reida set up a virtual security perimeter by placing monitoring devices pointed at strategic directions: the road, the lake, and the area behind the building, where a narrower, much rougher road continued alongside the lakeshore.

Evi and Reida took up strategic positions on the corners of the veranda with Evi's heavy-duty gun, which he clipped to the railing.

We made an inventory of all our other weapons. Sheydu was

unhappy with the result. We should have taken all the gear out of the gyrocopter, she said. I agreed.

It was as close as I had ever heard Sheydu come to admitting she had made a mistake. Had we been wrong to trust Junco? Was he a victim as well?

Then we pulled out a table and some chairs and waited.

The sun was beating down and a hot wind had come up.

Anyu and Reida went to the veranda facing the lake with their receivers. Sheydu went out, holding her gun, and spoke with them. Their voices drifted in through the window.

After a while, Sheydu came back in and sat next to me at the table. I had to admit I was starting to feel hungry and was of a mind to check if there was a kitchen in this place and if so, if there was anything edible in it.

"Did anyone from town follow us?" I asked.

"Yes. They've set up camp between the rocks over there."

She waved her hand at the opposite end of the abandoned car park, where the truck that had brought us here stood all alone.

"They're probably waiting for reinforcements, and if I have to make a guess, those will come from the military base nearby. So we don't have much time before we face trouble from that direction."

"Then what are we waiting for?"

"Junco has the aircraft."

"Do you expect him to turn up?"

"It looks bad for his business if we don't return from our excursion. He and the other fellow Sage will try to give us a hand."

"I wish I could share your confidence. There were a lot of those young guys. They could easily intimidate Junco. He doesn't live here anymore and is not part of their community."

"No, but he has his son and needs money from his business. He lives alone with his son. He needs to be there. He needs the money tourists pay him. The boy can't do much for himself."

She showed me an image of Junco's son. There was a lot more wrong with him than his inability to walk. He sat on the veranda of a house, strapped into a chair, his mouth open, looking cross-eyed at the ceiling.

I felt vaguely ill. I didn't really want to know as much as this, especially not from Sheydu, who came from a society where disabled children were second-class citizens.

"Where did you get this?" I asked.

"He gave it to me. He wanted wheels for the boy like Larrana's."

Damn yes, that was true. "But do you think he'll be able to control the chair like Larrana?"

She shrugged. "Junco says the boy can do more than people expect. My point is he wants this chair. He's not going to abandon us."

"But even if he can get Sage to help him, he's by himself."

"You didn't think *we* were here by ourselves, did you?"

Well, no, but I'd assumed that the surveillance she'd hinted at previously was safely tucked away in orbit, watching us from a distance.

"You don't have any military people following us, do you?" A vague horrified feeling crept into my stomach.

"Just some trustworthy locals."

"From this town?"

"No, from the city."

Of course. They were already in contact with the register and someone had followed us since we had arrived here, probably under direction of the military satellites. Some Coldi person with loyalty to Amarru whose loyalty was to Ezhya and through Ezhya, to me. I still had to get used to the fact that I warranted this sort of action these days.

"Was that who Anyu was talking to then?"

"Oh, that is not related to our immediate situation. But an

Exchange satellite was passing over and there was a brief window of connectivity. It's an observation satellite, not designed for communication, so the window was very short. She intended to do the usual thing—pass our details, log our trip—but found rather more chaos than she expected."

"Chaos?"

That cold feeling again. Something had happened. In my mind, I heard that distant rumble again. A bit like thunder, but not quite the same.

"This is about the sound we heard last night?"

"Maybe. This is what we've been able to gather so far. It's not complete, and we wouldn't speak of this outside security except in an unusual circumstance." And this, clearly, was such a circumstance. "Something has happened in the way of an attack. Several towns have seen unrest and destruction overnight and there is great instability in the region."

"Towns? Region?" I loved it when Sheydu was vague, but I also knew why she did it: during their training, it was hammered into Coldi security personnel to not speak aloud of suspicions until they were proven correct. It was indeed unusual that she spoke of it. She must be really worried or discomforted through the lack of communication.

And I became worried, too. "We need to get back to the rest of our association."

"Yes." A truer word was rarely spoken.

We had finished our brief excursion, which, all things considered, felt rather trivial now. If some political situation was about to blow up, I wanted to be nowhere near it, and the quicker we could get onto a flight out of Los Angeles, the better.

Sheydu continued, "Some people are going to provide help very soon. That is to get us out of this spot and back to the others. I don't know what we will do when we join up. Hopefully, they will have a better idea of what's going on."

Another reason she had left the others in the hands of a group of highly capable people, which included Telaris, who spoke Isla. Damn, I really wanted to know what this was about.

"Do we know who is causing all this trouble? Is this an extension of existing conflicts?"

"Nothing is known at the moment. I have not wasted any resources trying to find out. I want to be out of here first."

Fair enough. But help was taking a while to turn up. Meanwhile, the hostile town youth appeared to have come closer, and they had been joined by others, older men.

Several figures in dark clothing stood on the road next to a vehicle. None of them wore uniforms, but all of them were heavily armed.

I'd read about bands of heavily armed civilians patrolling the streets or marching in convoy to show their solidarity, but found it very hard to comprehend. In Barresh and on the *gamra* island, you could only carry weapons if you held specific permits and jobs. I'd thought those regulations were lax, because authorities in Barresh never checked permits unless a weapon had been fired.

The gear worn by these men was something on another level altogether. It was heavy-grade, military-style stuff. Where did they even get it?

We sat on the dusty floor to stay as much out of their view as possible. Sheydu said she wasn't afraid of them, but I knew that her training involved avoiding the use of weapons as much as possible.

Damn, I'd been stupid. It was one thing to go to the rainforest outside Barresh, where our enemies were the lack of communication, foul weather and forest creatures. That had been dangerous, but fellow humans were the most dangerous enemies of them all.

People had warned me not to come here. I'd snuck in under the noses of Amarru and Nations of Earth, defiantly stubborn, as always.

Now something had blown up.

The region was volatile, and I knew far too little about the political situation to navigate it safely. Not that long ago, when I was still in Barresh, we'd heard about an attack on Atlantia governor Celia Braddock. She was all the way on the other side of the continent in New York, but this sort of guerilla warfare was common in this part of the world. I had always known that. It was also common that the other countries took the bait and retaliated. So: Celia Braddock had survived the attack. She had ordered retaliation, which had involved trade sanctions. I'd known about this, too. America Free State's Governor Paterson had ordered a counter-attack on warehouses that held valuable goods that Atlantia had managed to import. He had a reputation for doing this, according to the news articles I'd read. He disliked luxury and anything that was produced outside his country. I'd known that, too. I'd been stupid enough to assume that we could just come here, ignore these problems and assume not to be affected by them.

The sound of a truck engine drifted in from outside.

Sheydu and Reida got up and went to the veranda. Both had taken their weapons from their brackets.

I sat on my knees so I could look out over the top of the veranda railing. Anyu handed me her binoculars.

A vehicle approached the group of townsfolk from behind.

This was also an unmarked vehicle, but when the back door opened, a couple of military personnel came out. If possible, they were even more heavily armed than the townsfolk.

Anyu and Veyada crouched next to me.

We watched between the slats of the veranda railing. This help that Sheydu had mentioned had better turn up quickly, or this would turn into a battle scene. And I still had no idea why.

Evi leaned the gun on the railing. Anyu was studying the surrounding landscape on her reader. A small dot was moving across it.

"They're coming," she said.

Sure enough, someone had gotten into a boat on the opposite side of the lake.

Of course. Make an escape in a dinghy. With a bunch of people who hated water. Across a lake that was disgustingly green and poisonous. What more could I have hoped for?

CHAPTER FIFTEEN

THAT WAS OUR HELP?

A single guy in a small boat by himself against a bunch of heavily armed townsfolk who seemed to have gotten reinforcements from the military?

My heart sank.

I don't know what I had expected, but in this situation, there was no way we could get into this boat and cross the lake safely, and then meet whatever was on the other side without being shot at.

As soon as we abandoned this house, the townsfolk would move in.

I still didn't understand what they were after, and why we had raised their ire so much, and even why they had requested assistance from the military.

But Sheydu and Anyu appeared to be getting ready to go down.

Reida was also packing all his gear, and Sheydu was reminding me to keep my weapon within reach. For all the good that would do.

We all gathered at the side of the veranda that faced the lake.

Sheydu's pockets were always a source of interesting items. She now pulled out a small, tightly wrapped package. She untied the band that held it together, unfurling some sort of grey camouflage netting.

Ynggi threw it over himself. His hands came out from underneath the netting to attach a clip onto a little box that Veyada wore on his belt.

And he disappeared. What the...? One moment he was standing next to me, the next moment... well, I could sort of still see him, or at least a vague, shimmery outline of him, especially when he moved, but the netting projected the scenery behind him, in this case the timber wall of the building, the window and stacks of chairs and tables on the other side of the glass.

Then I understood. A current ran along the outside of the netting that deflected the light, so we would be less visible. The Asto-made aircraft had a feature like this. Unfortunately, this effect grew more prominent during bright sunlight, and the sun was getting quite low.

We had little time to get away.

Sheydu told me and Nicha to get under the netting as well.

It was kind of awkward, and surprisingly warm underneath the fine mesh.

"When we're outside, we have a period in which we can be relatively unseen for as long as the charge lasts," Veyada said. He stood at the front of our hidden little group. I figured he could see more than the rest of us, and he'd be our "eyes".

Through the netting, I could see Reida and Anyu behind us, although their outlines shimmered. Anyu was busy with a communications program on her reader.

The townsfolk had noticed the dingy coming across the lake.

One of them was running towards the boat, yelling something, and pointing his gun.

The boat showed no sign of stopping.

Then a man strode up from behind. He reached around the

hothead's shoulder and pushed down the first man's arms, which were holding the weapon.

An argument broke out between the two.

A second man ran forward, also shouting at the man who tried to calm them. I was wondering: this man might be Junco or Sage, since both of them would be respected people in this small community. If anyone could calm the young hotheads, they could.

Sheydu shouted at us, "Move forward."

Crowded under the netting, we shuffled across the veranda. It was hard not to tread on the back of Veyada's shoes or trip over uneven patches I couldn't see from behind his back.

Sheydu stopped at the top of the stairs that led to the dilapidated and sagging boardwalk.

Veyada stood in front of me, but I could still hear the argument going on amongst the townsfolk. I wished I could see what was happening. All I could make out were the silhouettes of additional people running towards the group. The level of yelling increased. Or was that because the wind blew in our direction?

We started down the rickety boardwalk. The planks were uneven and had fallen victim to dry rot in some places. I had to concentrate on not tripping.

The breeze carried the acrid stench of the vividly green water.

It was very strange to walk in this tight group in the open, while I knew that we were almost invisible to casual onlookers. Ynggi had grabbed the back of my shirt. His tail held the netting over our heads. Nicha held the net behind me, so that it didn't slide off us.

Over my shoulder, I could see Sheydu and Evi standing at the corners of the veranda, while Anyu and Reida crouched behind the railing at the top of the stairs.

Anyu had taken bits of equipment out of her pocket and handed some of it to Reida. She was a highly competent, top-ranking security officer of the elite Palayi clan. He was a street urchin from the Outer Circle who had worked himself up to the point where he earned her respect. I was so proud of him.

Veyada at the front decided it was safer to abandon the boardwalk and continue on over the rocks. We negotiated the knee-high drop-off to the rock shelf while keeping the netting over our heads. The level of charge displayed on the screen on the box on Veyada's belt was going down alarmingly fast.

How far away was that boat? Would there still be any charge left by the time we got in?

The single man in the dinghy had gone to the far end of a rocky outcrop which appeared to be out of range of the townsfolk's weapons.

Veyada shuffled in that direction. We were slowly coming closer. The helpful man who might or might not be Junco or Sage had held up the townsfolk. I judged there was a real chance that we were going to reach the dinghy in one piece, even if Sheydu, Reida, Evi and Anyu were still on the veranda.

But then we reached a spot where a trickle of water seeped out of the rocks and trickled over the surface in the direction of the lake. The rocks were slippery as hell. Veyada noticed too late.

He lost his footing, fell on his backside and slid a short distance down the rock slope, taking the netting with him.

One of the townsfolk shouted.

And all hell broke loose. I lay flat on my belly, while weapons discharged and bullets bounced over the rocks.

"Stay down!" Veyada called.

Evi fired his gun several times in quick succession.

First, he hit the barricade on the road, making bits of truck explode into the air and their occupants run for their lives.

Then the next shot hit the truck that we had driven, turning it into a flaming ball of fire.

Next he hit a boat shack that stood between the main

building and the water line, and then the abandoned jetties, and next, the remains of the boats that lay there.

Holy crap, when Evi got going, he didn't take half-measures.

We belly-crawled over the rocks, trying to remain behind the broken boardwalk, while the breeze wafted acrid smoke over our heads.

The stone surface was rough, and we were now so close to the lake that we had to crawl through salt encrustations.

We kept close together. Several times, Ynggi's tail brushed my face. It felt like the pelt of a rough-haired dog.

Sheydu had abandoned her position and had come up behind us, and Evi was covering us from the corner of the veranda.

Anyu and Reida had run down the veranda and had tracked around the far side of the building back to the lake in a big arc. They were now much closer to the left of us.

The young men returned fire. Most of them were still out of range of their weapons—if not of Evi's—but they were coming closer. We were soon going to be outnumbered.

The dinghy drifted towards us.

The driver had taken cover behind the side, but he was also wearing an armoured jacket.

"Quick, get in!" he called out in Isla.

He appeared to be a local, quite dark-skinned with dark hair, which he wore in a ponytail.

Veyada got up. He crawl-walked to the shoreline, but the dinghy couldn't come close enough to allow him to get in without wading into the disgusting water. He tried to pull the boat up, but the underwater rock shelf was too slippery. He tumbled over the side into the dinghy.

Anyu went next, followed by Ynggi and Nicha.

I was the last one, getting my shoes thoroughly wet.

I whispered a "Thank you" to our unknown rescuer. He merely nodded.

We crouched in the bottom of the boat, between the seats. Veyada was folding up his net.

Sheydu joined us next, followed by Reida.

At this time, the townsfolk were held off only by Evi and his gun.

He descended the veranda, keeping the weapon aimed at the group of townsfolk. The man who had attempted to calm them down still stood with the group. He really looked a lot like Sage.

Next to him stood a couple of men in quasi-military gear. The real military waited a bit further back. I didn't think they had been involved in any of the action yet. They also hadn't tried to stop any of it.

Evi came closer and closer.

He arrived at the slippery patch, but fortunately, noticed the skid marks made by Veyada and circumvented the spot.

The fact that he was backing away from the townsfolk meant that he had to keep looking over his shoulder.

Reida rose from behind the side of the boat with an impressive weapon.

He yelled, "Mine!" to let others know that he was taking over cover.

Evi disarmed his gun and flung it on the strap across his back.

He ran.

I put one leg over the side of the dinghy to push off.

Bullets hit rocks around us.

Evi jumped into the boat, and the very force of his not inconsiderate body weight propelled us off the shore.

The boat rocked violently.

I lost my balance and went, head-first, into the green water.

Splash. Down into the darkness and the tepid, smelly, suffocating green soup.

My first thought was *poison!*

The second thought was *my gun*, but it was still in its bracket, and by now thoroughly soaked.

I spluttered to the surface. The water was oily and disgusting, and disturbing it made the smell even stronger.

The boat driver turned in a tight circle. Passing behind me, Veyada grabbed the back of my jacket and pulled me up over the side.

The boat swung around and sped across the lake at full throttle, the bow slapping on the water.

I lay on the metal bottom, panting, wet and smelly, with strings of slimy algae all over my clothes.

Well, that was not a terribly smart move.

I sat up. Water dripped from my hair into the collar of my jacket. With this wind, I would get cold very quickly.

The shouts of the townsfolk faded in the distance, replaced by the sound of rushing water.

The driver held the rudder, peering at the far shore.

"Thank you," I said to him, again.

He nodded, his brown eyes meeting mine.

"Where are we going?" I asked.

"Your transport is on the other side."

"Are you someone off the register?"

"What register?"

I guessed that answered that question.

He continued, "Junco is a friend of mine. He beamed in urgently, asking me to collect you. The townsfolk have gone nuts. They want revenge, but it's stupid. No way you had anything to do with it. I trust Junco. He brings in a lot of money. He's paying me to save his own job. I don't like the townsfolk much, anyway."

Revenge?

Had anything to do with it?

With what?

"Sorry, I seem to be missing part of the argument. What would the townsfolk want revenge for?"

"The attacks."

"Attacks?" I felt cold.

"Yeah, last night."

"What actually happened last night? Was that the sound we heard?"

"Yeah. I heard it, too. A lot of folk did. They say a number of places were attacked at the same time."

"Which places?"

"LA, New York, places like that. They said aliens did it. Well, maybe they did, but I don't know. People can figure that out for themselves. Not you, anyways."

"Aliens?" Even the word felt wrong to me.

"That's what they said. Aliens from space. So it kind of makes sense that they come to take revenge on the visiting aliens, because that's what the townsfolk are like. They like acting and don't like talking."

"But that's ludicrous."

"Don't blame me. I'm only repeating what I heard. I'm helping Junco getting you out safely. But if I were you, I'd leave quickly and don't come back in a hurry."

"No, I'm not blaming you. Thank you for helping." I meant it. I would have to make sure that Junco and Sage were properly compensated, too.

He nodded and said nothing further.

We arrived on the opposite shore of the lake. He took us to a rock shelf where we could step out of the boat into shallow water. The rocky bottom was slippery and the footing treacherous. The water was so murky green that it was impossible to see the bottom, even at that depth.

I was stiff from sitting on the hard bottom, and cold from being wet.

We gathered up all our gear, and our rescuer told us that someone would wait at the top, before pushing off and steering the boat back into the middle of the lake, away from the town. Apparently helping us only went so far.

I'd seen on the map that the lake was huge, with many nooks

and crannies. No doubt he would have another place to take his boat, out of reach of the townsfolk. Those men were still on the other shore, arguing with each other. A military vehicle had stopped next to the ruin of our truck, which was still smouldering. Actually, I better make sure we found the rightful owners and compensated them, too.

We ran up the incline, and over the crest of the hillock found the most welcome sight I had hoped to see: an Asto-built craft waited for us, the outline shimmering, visible only because the door was open.

There were two people with the craft, a man and a woman. Both were Coldi, middle-aged, didn't wear uniform, and looked nervous.

"Get in, get in," the woman sad. She spoke in a curious accent.

We all scrambled in. The craft was an older model, well used, but dated.

The woman shut the door and slipped into the seat next to the pilot. We strapped into the passenger seats, and then the vehicle took off. Into the safety of the air.

I said to the woman, "Thank you for coming to get us."

"It was a risky thing, to come here," she said, turning around to face me. "This is hostile country."

"I'm sorry." And I truly was.

Considering the current mysterious events, I wasn't sure how useful the visit had been, besides collecting some really old data about groups that were now irrelevant. Ezhya wanted the information, but was it worth the fuss and danger?

I added, "Have you heard anything about the rest of my team?"

"Don't worry, they're safe. We've been taking care of them. Amarru asked us to do it."

Phew. They were in contact with Amarru. We were safe. I sank into my seat and let them do the flying.

CHAPTER SIXTEEN

BECAUSE I WAS ALL WET, our hosts offered me a set of dry clothes and showed me the wash room cabin to put them on. The dark and sturdy wear looked suspiciously like Asto military gear.

The disgusting water had made my skin itchy. My wet clothes still smelled of the algae. I put them in the waterproof bag which the hosts had also helpfully provided.

The algae crap had already dried in a film of silk-like filaments over the panel of my weapon. I took it into the main cabin of the craft, hoping that someone would have a maintenance kit.

Of course, Sheydu did. She even offered to service the weapon for me, but I said it was my stupid fault that it had gotten wet, and also that I should practice my maintenance skills now and then.

Sheydu didn't believe in faults or karma, but the second part of my argument made enough sense for her to just nod at me and tell me to call her if I needed any help.

I found a seat in the back of the craft, letting its familiar feel come over me.

I folded out the seat's table, opened the maintenance kit, took out all the tools and little bottles with solvent, cleaning fluid and oil, unfolded the outside of the kit so it became a work mat.

Then I levered the barrel off the main body, took off the handgrip, the charge chamber and the control panel. There was water in all of them.

I spent the next while drying, cleaning, polishing and testing.

Our rescuers offered me some water and a few snacks. I didn't realise just how hungry and thirsty I'd been, not having eaten since breakfast.

The woman's name was Marisol, I learned from Nicha, who came to watch me perform my delicate task for a bit. Her male companion was her brother, and his name was Clay. I asked what their Coldi names were, but Nicha doubted there were any. Both had lived in Los Angeles all their lives, and they owned the house we were going to use as refuge. Apparently the rest of my team were already there.

They were third-generation immigrants. I didn't even want to ask for their clan. They would have truly lost touch with Asto clan politics.

But they *were* still on the register, which had to mean that they remained sympathetic to our cause, right?

I finished cleaning the weapon and put it back together and closed the maintenance kit back up. I was reasonably convinced no permanent harm was done, but I'd only know for sure tomorrow, when the control panel would have dried out enough that it was safe to be turned on.

Sheydu didn't even get angry or anxious about it, she said when I presented my work for her final approval. Stuff like this happened, she said. That's why she always made sure someone in the team had a spare. Adequate and timely maintenance solved most of the world's technical problems.

I looked out the window. The sun had sunk close to the horizon, spreading an orange glow over the landscape as the light hit the dusty atmosphere side-on.

The members of my team were all busy. I let them do their things, reconnect to their networks, hear all the news. I was sure I would hear more about it when they could establish connections and talk to a few people.

I tried to reach any media accessible to me, but I couldn't get onto the Exchange news. It had been available on and off for the last few days. Since the referendum had come out in favour of Earth joining *gamra*, the Exchange had set up a formal news channel which *should* be available worldwide, but evidently, was not. I was surprised that I couldn't even get it in this Asto-made craft.

Nicha said that it was because all communication was shut down in the region until they could establish where the attacks came from and how they had been coordinated.

All air travel was also suspended.

Well, crap.

"Certainly, you can still fly out of the country?" I asked.

Nicha didn't know.

Marisol didn't know either.

I went on a hunt for extra information. But it seemed like most of the news services had stopped publishing about the attacks, even respected services like World Newspoint. Its front page mainly stated how people could get assistance if they needed any. How localised was their service, anyway?

I scrolled through different services, some I knew about and others I didn't.

None of the services mentioned anything of note about the attacks. All had published information about where people could get help, and where *the young and brave* could sign up for the armed forces. Precious little was said about what had happened where and who was responsible.

Was this the normal way the news in this part of the world dealt with upheaval? Or were they just that jaded about conflict?

I remembered reading an article that discussed the role of the media in the Second Civil War, when news outlets had been accused of whipping up public anger by publishing articles that took liberties with the truth for the sake of getting attention.

One particular article had led to widespread rioting and many deaths over something that was, essentially, a lie.

From that moment on, authorities had used gag orders to stifle news in volatile situations.

Of course, those could also be misused, and they frequently were. Apparently the Dixie Republic once detained a bunch of farm workers from America Free State. The workers started a riot which spilled over to other farms and districts until America Free State used its military to force Dixie Republic to return their citizens.

The only way citizens of either country could find out about it was to follow the rogue news services in Mexico which attempted to broadcast news the old-fashioned way across the border.

Meanwhile, authorities could do as they pleased.

In the case of skirmishes between the countries—which happened quite often—the news services would simply stop reporting so as not to give the enemy the opportunity to gauge the effectiveness of their actions.

It was a quaintly old-fashioned world.

Meanwhile, travel was suspended. Offices were closed. Shops were closed.

Damn it. I could really use some anti-allergic cream, because my skin was breaking out in an itchy rash.

I looked out the window and thought I could see the border: a heavy fence that ran like a scar across the landscape, with dusty fields on one side and equally dusty wilderness on the other. A road led to the border but stopped there, and the part on the side of America Free State was half covered in sand dunes, and the paving got lost under decades of dust and feeble attempts at revegetation.

Damn, I was so itchy.

Sheydu was sitting with the others, discussing something over the screen. It didn't sound terribly good from what I picked up. No Exchange coverage at all. No one knew what was going on. The local news could not be trusted.

I told Sheydu how our rescuer had spoken about "aliens".

Marisol told us how she and a friend had driven across Los Angeles to pick up the other half of our team, and that they had seen lots of evidence of damage and explosions. Many large buildings were on fire.

But they had seen no evidence of fighting. They'd seen no attackers, alien or otherwise.

Clay told us that America Free State produced their own missiles, but why they would fire them into Mexico was anyone's guess.

"Do the Mexican authorities have anything to say about it?" I asked.

I could imagine that if conflict spilled over the border into Mexican territory, the government would have plenty to say about it. And Mexico was a prominent Nations of Earth member, so there would be statements from Rotterdam about incursions into sovereign air space and stuff like that.

But clearly, Sheydu's channels didn't receive that sort of news. Clay and Marisol couldn't raise any useful information either. Sheydu said she'd keep trying.

It was all a big, confusing mess.

Either communication was extremely poor here—always a possibility—or communication had changed so much recently that it went through channels not accessible to me and my team. I didn't know which option disturbed me most.

I looked out the window, and for now, the landscape below seemed quite normal. Brown, parched fields, stony hillocks, larger mountains. The occasional road, the occasional settlement, all often shrouded in dust. It was getting dark.

The number of settlements passing underneath was slowly increasing, and many of the settlements displayed street lights. Warm light radiated from the windows of houses. I spotted the occasional vehicle. We had to be getting close to the city.

Sheydu slipped into the seat next to me while I was looking down. I turned around. The way she fixed me with her gold-flecked eyes, I knew she had nothing good to say.

"We still can't get onto the Exchange," she said. "I've been able to raise a few local responses, but most of them are also wondering what's going on."

"What do you mean by local? How local?"

She showed me a map. Three of the four locations marked on the map were also in Los Angeles. One was further south in Mexico.

"The capital is also not responding."

"Mexico City? Has there been an interruption to communication infrastructure? Are we being jammed?"

I felt cold. My team's communication should bypass any blocks. She would use Exchange satellites. Those should be unaffected by anything that was going on locally.

Sheydu breathed in deeply. "Everything is possible. We know that there were several events of aggression in the city at the same time. Material I've seen suggests that they were attacks from the air. It's likely that communication equipment was taken out, potentially also power stations. We don't have any major relays in this part of the world so we're reliant on Exchange satellite communication and that is sporadic, since the satellites we use are not set up for this function, nor can they cope with the volume of messages currently directed at them. I suspect the latter is an issue. Simply too many people trying to use the satellites at the same time."

Sheydu hated not knowing. The stiffness in her language betrayed that she was deeply uncomfortable.

She didn't know what was going on.

She didn't speak the language and didn't trust translators—and with very good reason.

Her usual channels of communication didn't work.

She had the responsibility not just over me, but also over the entire team, which included the child of an influential rival.

And I insisted on doing things that pulled her deeper into the uncomfortable zone.

"What about our hosts? The owners of this craft? Have they said anything?" I had spotted Sheydu speaking to Marisol earlier.

"They live locally and have lived here for a long time. They suggest that communication outages are not uncommon. They say that usually, if they're unable to reach the Exchange, it's because the local network is out. But they're also saying that they haven't seen aggressive attacks this intense before. They say there is often unrest across the border, but it usually manifests at the street level with people gathering in large groups, looting shops or stopping the normal flow of life in the population centres. They say it never amounts to more than a few hundred people making demands, although it can also get violent and people can get killed and buildings get destroyed."

"Is there another way that we can reach the Exchange? What about Nations of Earth?"

She shrugged. "We don't have good contacts there as we used to. They continue to not answer our communication, but they were doing that already."

"Keep trying," I said.

"We will. We may need to wait until we're at our destination."

Yes. But being on the ground would cut us off from whatever tenuous connections we had with the Exchange while up here in this craft.

She returned to the others.

I resumed staring out the window into the murk of semidarkness outside.

Whatever had happened, at least I'd soon meet Thayu and Emi again. And then I should...

Wait.

I had an idea.

If all else failed, I could simply try to use the local communication channels to speak with my father. Not being in this area, he might have a less politically charged idea of what was going on. That was if news from this part of the world reached New Zealand. I had no idea if it did. I would think so, I hoped.

"Wow," Reida said from elsewhere in the craft.

His tone was genuinely impressed.

He was looking out the front window of the craft, over the pilot Clay's shoulders, pushing himself up in his seat so he could see more.

I got up from my seat.

The sky ahead faced west and should have been orange after sunset. Instead, it had gone dark with thick black smoke, which rose from numerous columns across the city. It hung in a murky blanket over the plain.

Clay lowered the flight altitude to avoid flying through the worst of it.

I moved to the seat behind him so I could look over his shoulder.

"What has happened here?"

"It looks like they came back while we were gone," Clay said. His voice was soft and horrified.

Much of the city was shrouded in black smoke, with the occasional spots of burning buildings.

We passed over several places where deep craters had been formed in the ground.

"Was it not like this when you left to pick us up?" I asked.

"Not as bad this. It looks like they've wiped out whole suburbs."

"Any idea at all who has done this?"

"Well, we assumed they were the army of the America Free State."

Could it really be that we had visited in the middle of the outbreak of another North American war? Hmmm, yes, "aliens" could just as easily mean people from other countries or continents.

"Has this happened before?" I couldn't imagine living like this. Also, I didn't think Amarru would have been happy to let me come here if this was a common occurrence. And Amarru was someone who always knew where I was going and why. She might be the only person on Earth who knew.

Clay said, "There are always tensions. Attacks used to happen quite a lot, but there haven't been any for a while. We thought that with the four countries now talking to each other, it might be over. I have to admit that I don't really keep up with the local politics."

But I bet he still knew a lot more than I did, and I wouldn't be surprised if someone like Ezhya was paying him for that knowledge.

"But everyone seems to say that last night's attack was different."

"It was. There seemed to be sophisticated equipment involved, operating from a very high altitude. That's as much as we heard before the news gag came into effect."

"I don't know why everyone seems to think that we were at peace," Marisol said. "In the last year or so, certain elements in America Free State have been spoiling for a fight, and Paterson is egging them on. First, there were the attacks on Braddock, because she 'gives in to the enemy', whatever that is supposed to mean. She did no more than have a preliminary meeting with Dekker, and nothing much came out of it anyway, and then

Paterson encouraged the emigrant America Free State populations to riot. The man is an idiot."

So, Dekker would have meetings with Braddock, but he ignored *gamra*.

Not that the sentiment surprised me, but the blatant expression of his disinterest in us was getting ridiculous.

Clay explained that it was impossible to land the craft anywhere near his house, so we'd have to go to a farm across the mountain range where a bus would wait for us.

We were going down.

It became hard to see through the shimmering outside the window where Clay had turned on the screening that reduced the visibility of the craft.

The craft was now flying over a mountain ridge. Pockets of suburbs occupied scattered areas of the bottom part of the slopes, but most of the top was a barren desert. We then descended the other side of the ridge, out of view of the city.

Not much later, we landed in a dusty field, next to a rickety farm shed.

A Coldi man waited outside the shed to guide the vehicle in.

Clay and Marisol spoke to him briefly in the local dialect that was hard to understand.

"He says there isn't much news," Clay said as we walked from the shed to the house along a driveway through a dusty field. "Sorry that it's not as you wanted. People are waiting for Paterson or Schuster to make an announcement."

That was Governor Schuster of Dixie Republic.

"Do you think either of them is responsible?"

"I expect so."

"What about blaming aliens?"

He snorted. "That's the first thing they all say. Aliens did it. If not, Nations of Earth. Then they'll have an investigation and find out that the problems are closer to home."

Well, in that case, we'd be happy to escape from this area. Los

Angeles should get help from the Mexican military, and Nations of Earth was likely to offer assistance. This wouldn't affect us once the passenger services started flying again. But it was probably a good idea to fly to Mexico City and return from there, rather than try to fly over these belligerent countries with short-fused leaders.

CHAPTER SEVENTEEN

AT THE END of the road, we came to the farmhouse.

Judging from the outside, the house was habitable and in use at least some of the time. The windows were intact, a section of the roof looked new, and an open carport to the side contained a vehicle.

We didn't go inside.

A bus sat on the packed dirt outside the front door.

We boarded the bus, a set of dusty and tired looking people, with dusty packs and not much to say.

Clay went into the house and returned a bit later wearing a local hat and jacket.

Marisol also clambered into the bus and sat on the seat behind her brother, turning around to watch us.

Neither she nor her brother looked particularly Coldi. Had they ever been to Asto? I guessed not.

We drove over a rough dirt road that zig-zagged up the mountainside. The landscape was rough, washed out, dusty, with straggly scrubs and occasional cactuses poking up from between the rocks. It was almost dark now.

By the headlights of the bus, we spotted a few small flocks of brown goats soaking up the lingering warmth from the rocks. Some animals had impressive curled horns.

By the time we crested the saddle of the mountain range and the city spread out before us, the sky was deep black.

Palls of smoke drifted low over the ground, lit from below by city lights in an eerie glow. Wafts of a burnt smell came in through the open window.

One stricken area at the bottom of the slope was close enough that we could hear the wailing of emergency sirens.

"There was a ground component involved in this attack?" I asked Clay.

"I don't think so, but few people are sharing information. Although I just heard that Celia Braddock is going to make an official announcement later tonight. We should be home in time to watch it."

Celia Braddock, of course, was the governor of Atlantia, and the leader most willing to speak to Nations of Earth.

"What do you expect her to say?"

"She'll claim responsibility. I didn't expect Atlantia to attack us, but there you go. I'm sure she'll call it a retaliation for the attempt on her life earlier this year."

"Really? Would she order an attack across the borders?"

"All the time, because the people who organised the attack on her were sympathisers with America Free State, and most of them lived in Los Angeles. This has been brewing for a while. They did this before, a few years ago."

Marisol said, "More than just a few years ago. It was at least ten, and it was nowhere near as extensive as this. I don't understand it. Braddock has been very keen on joining all the states together once more. She says we are making a stronger country. Why would she order this?"

Clay shrugged. "Retaliation."

The truck was rumbling down the hill, shrouded in its own cloud of dust.

"Is it far, where we're going?" I asked. I was getting really hungry now and worried about Thayu and Emi. I wasn't interested in these petty tit-for-tat wars. I wanted some sort of normality back in my life.

"Not that far, but we have to watch it. I suggest that you prepare to take defensive action, in case they question us at the perimeter fence."

My team didn't need to be told that twice.

Weapons came out, I was installed on the floor of the bus, with anyone else who was not in the first line of defence, like Nicha and Ynggi.

Sheydu checked my weapon and judged it was safe for emergency use.

I sat on the hard floor.

While he steered the bus, Clay explained that he and his sister lived in a kind of safe enclave, and that people in surrounding streets had put tall fences and wire around the pieces of land they owned.

"We want to make sure we can all stay safe," he said. "Some of them are funny about aliens."

It was hard holding on, because the bus was going at a crazy speed, and the road was rough. I hoped that there would be showers where we were going, because I needed to rinse the itchy lake residue off my skin.

We turned sharp corners, pushing us all into each other, and occasionally, I heard other vehicles.

But we reached our destination without trouble, and slowed down at the end of a winding road, at a solid wall with a gate that opened at our approach.

Once we were through, we could get off the floor and look out the windows.

We were in the long curved driveway of a house that stood on top of a rise on the mountainside, overlooking the city.

The yard must once have been an oasis, with a lawn and a pool and tennis court and a gazebo at the best vantage point. A railing ran along the cliff top from the house to the gazebo.

The garden had seen better days.

Several of the trees were dead, but some still clung on to life. The lawn resembled a crop of standing hay, and the pool was half empty, with a sad puddle of murky water at the bottom. A heap of sand had blown into one corner, forming a little beach. On this tiny sandy patch I spotted a welcome sight: two Pengali kids, fishing, tails in the air with excitement.

Sure enough, Ayshada stood at the edge of the pool, at the top of a rusty ladder, contemplating whether he would climb down, break the ladder and fall down, making an idiot of himself, or stay where he was and then let the Pengali kids make an idiot of him on his behalf.

He noticed us, abandoned his spot, and ran to the driveway.

I could hear his voice through the open windows of the bus.

"Daddy, Daddy, Daddy!"

The bus stopped in front of the house. Nicha was the first one off, scooping up Ayshada in his arms.

By the time we had collected our bags and stumbled off the bus, my entire team had come to the front door of the house.

I ran up the steps to Thayu and Emi, enclosing both of them in my arms.

"Thank goodness you're safe," I said.

"I could say the same." Thayu smelled clean and bathed, while I probably still smelled of algae. "You really chose your time to go on an excursion."

It was an attempt to be lighthearted, but Thayu didn't do lighthearted very well. I could hear the worry in her voice.

"We were all right. We didn't see any of the attacks and only had a slight run-in with some townsfolk." A little more than that, but no need to elaborate.

"You smell."

"I fell out of a boat in some dirty water."

"A boat? In the desert?"

"You know I always manage to find boats and water wherever I go?" It had been a standing joke in my team that in order to work with us, one had to have a working knowledge of boats.

"What's that gear you're wearing? It looks interesting."

"Is that interesting in the Thayu way? I suspect it's Asto military gear."

"Yeah. But years old. It's probably excess material from the military stores."

That made me wonder about Marisol's and Clay's affiliations.

"We were worried about you, too. How did you end up here?"

"This is a safe house. After unrest broke out, we got directions from the Exchange to seek out a safe place. We made our own way to a pickup point, and then they came to collect us. It was... interesting."

Yeah, I bet. I was sure I'd hear more about it later.

For now, I was so happy to see them.

"Any word from Amarru?"

"None directly, but the owners of this house have told us that the Exchange is arranging flights to take us out."

"Great. Have you heard from anyone else?"

"There have been some messages from Nations of Earth. You might want to look at them, but I don't think they're terribly important."

"Have you heard from my father?"

"No."

"I was going to contact him if we still couldn't get onto the Exchange, but I'll probably contact him, anyway. We should still visit him."

"That would be nice."

Veyada had also met his family, while Clay and Marisol had taken all the bags off the bus and had shut the vehicle's doors.

The Pengali kids had come out of the garden.

Pykka carried a kitchen bowl in which they had caught a small lizard. Amay carried the plastic bladder with the bubble device. She glanced at me, meeting my eyes for a moment before moving the contraption behind her back.

I struggled not to laugh. No, I hadn't seen that. Not at all.

Smells from inside the house suggested that food was forthcoming.

We followed the Pengali kids into the hall.

The house stood on top of the hill, and most of the windows and the veranda overlooked the plain where the suburbs of Los Angeles sprawled endlessly into the hazy horizon. Strings of white lights represented major roads, leading to clusters of multi-hued lights that were population centres, shopping precincts and groups of office buildings.

In the darkness, the smoke was not so obvious and at least eight hours had gone by since the last attacks. Fires had been put out.

This house, with its large block of land, surrounding wall, pool, tennis court and guest quarters had once belonged to a famous actor, Marisol explained when she'd joined us admiring the view.

"The name wouldn't mean anything to you, but he lived here with his mistress while his wife lived in the guest quarters. He was well known for holding loud parties every night. When the Civil War came, a lot of the movie production business went to other places like Glasgow and Jakarta. He died in disgrace while owing a lot of people a lot of money. No one lived here for a long time while the ownership passed from law firm to law firm. We acquired the house a few years ago."

She said they had also bought up surrounding properties,

many of them with ruined houses that had a similar history. One section of land, in a gully, they rented out to a community group who used it for growing vegetables and producing goat's milk. But apparently that was Marisol's sister's line of business.

We met the sister a bit later—her name was Vanessa—when she came to bring a tray of food.

With her came a bunch of other people, all Coldi, many dressed in dark featureless clothing, some even wearing earrings with blue stones. Palayi clan.

Asto military.

Definitely not local residents.

The smells of food also attracted a bunch of Coldi children, who mingled with ours. Other than Larrana, Nalya and Ayshada, I knew none of them. The unfamiliar kids wore local clothing. They spoke Coldi but used a lot of local words.

Vanessa told them, sternly, that they needed to wash their hands and wait patiently until the adult guests had eaten. She peppered her comments with local words, mostly Spanish, I thought.

I asked Marisol if they were Vanessa's children, but only one of them was. The others were children of people who lived in other houses that the family owned. This hill, the surrounding houses and the farms were a Coldi sanctuary.

Thayu had disappeared somewhere else in the house, and came back carrying Emi, now in a nightshirt, looking round-eyed at all those people around her.

We all sat on the couches overlooking the magnificent view of the city while Vanessa put trays filled to the brim with wonderful food on the table.

There was flatbread and cheese with olives and smoked vegetables, nuts, little quiches and many types of salads. It was all very proper, vegetarian and calibrated for the nutrient requirements for Coldi needs.

Ynggi muttered about the lack of fish, but that was the only complaint we got. I suspected he didn't even mean it, because the food was truly wonderful.

"They're Lingui clan, I'm guessing," Thayu whispered, while she sat next to me, making sure Emi ate the bread she was ripping into many pieces. "Business people. The Exchange pays them handsomely for providing a safe haven, and using their craft to assist Coldi in need in this region. The Exchange also pays them for gathering information, and they sell home-made food to well-off locals."

Sheydu and Isharu sat on Thayu's other side.

They'd attended some sort of general security meeting earlier on, but I thought Sheydu looked tired.

I told her that I was fine with them retiring early, but Sheydu said that she wanted to see the address by Celia Braddock that was scheduled to start soon.

I'd finished eating and took Emi so that Thayu could get her dinner.

The Coldi children had been set loose on the food, because the important adults—meaning the military—had finished, or because Vanessa had abandoned her surveillance of their actions in favour of setting up a screen in the living area so we could all watch the speech.

I went to put Emi to bed.

Thayu and I had been allocated two camp beds in the corner of what looked like an entertainment room. A fold-up cot for Emi stood between the two beds. I put her down and covered her with the blanket. Her eyelids were already drooping.

Several team members had congregated in the opposite corner of the room. I'd seen Reida, Deyu, Anyu, Evi, Telaris and Veyada in the main living area earlier in the evening, but had assumed that they'd gone to clean up or had gone to sleep.

But instead they were here holding their own security briefing. I joined the group, seated on two camp beds and the floor.

Deyu sat on her knees in the middle of the group and had

been showing my team something on her reader. She acknowledged me with a nod when I joined them.

"Any news?" I asked. "Do make sure you don't miss the governor's announcement."

"We're preparing for that," she said.

Apparently, they had been watching clips of other speeches Celia Braddock had given.

She showed me how they had created three sub-channels to record comments and observations over the top of the recorded speech, about whether her mannerisms were any different from usual. They had divided the screen in four areas for one person per area to observe. They had attached two translation devices and would cross-check each, and again check with Nicha and Telaris, both of whom should be able to follow the speech without the necessity to translate it.

There was even a special channel for making notes about the things that were in the background or immediately before and after the speech.

I was impressed.

I knew that Deyu had been taking classes at Asto's spy academy but hadn't seen any of it in action. Thayu assured me that the first year was so crammed full of theory about human behaviour that it could, in her words, *put the universe's biggest insomniac to sleep.* She'd warned me about Deyu and Reida going through this stage. They might seem impatient and restless, she said. Reida, sure, but as usual, Deyu drank it all in, turned it over in her mind, and then used every scrap of information she got, no matter how mundane or boring.

Spying was not about action and chases or gun fights.

It was about watching, comparing endless bits of data and waiting for someone to make a mistake. Not a big mistake, but a very small, dumb but crucial mistake.

They'd be watching Celia Braddock and judging her against all the other speeches she'd given in the last few years.

Judging her sincerity. Did she mean what she said? Was she honest? Did she seem nervous, distracted? Did she refer to other agendas?

Thank goodness for my team and Deyu.

One of the faceless, dark-clad military people came to the door. He said, "She's on."

CHAPTER EIGHTEEN

WE FOLLOWED him back to the living room.

In a corner, Clay and Marisol had set up a large screen on a stand. It was paper thin and had been rolled out from a cabinet in the wall.

Everyone at the house gathered at the couches that faced it, and others sat on the floor, stood behind the couches, or collected extra chairs from elsewhere in the house. The sheer number of people surprised me.

Besides my not inconsiderable team and Clay, Marisol and Vanessa, there were seven military people—a complete association—and the family I'd seen before, as well as an elderly couple, two young men who seemed to be friends, a woman with a teenage daughter and a family of five, all adults.

I hadn't been aware that there were quite this many people in the house.

It got very busy in the room.

Deyu and Reida had positioned themselves as close to the screen as possible, on the floor in front of it, with all their recording and monitoring devices spread out on the carpet in front of them.

The screen showed a presenter seated in front of a logo of a news service I hadn't considered for a long time: Flash News-point, the obnoxious gutter press that Melissa Heyworth used to work for. Of course. Their head office was in Los Angeles.

They were deeply political, anti-Nations of Earth, and forever tried to buy themselves credibility by appointing decent journalists like Melissa. And those decent journalists often had no option but to work for them because jobs in journalism were scarce.

The feed cut to a gathering of many people in front of a white-columned building, where an empty dais waited for a speaker to appear.

Somewhere off-screen, music started playing a kind of oohm-pah march with lots of blaring trumpets.

Then people in the audience started singing. They were not just singing along, but singing in rousing voices, with open mouths and balled fists.

Was this some kind of national anthem? It felt weird.

While the song finished up, a woman came out of the doorway behind the dais, flanked by two security guards.

She was of squat and stout build, in her middle age, pepper and salt hair cut into a bob. Her face was round, her cheeks full, and she squinted out of her eyes over the heads of the gathered crowd.

I recognised governor of Atlantia Celia Braddock from the pictures. A couple of people followed her out of the building and lined up behind her, including a man in a heavily decorated mili-tary uniform.

Celia Braddock waited until they had taken their places on a couple of seats to the side of the dais. During this, she nodded at a few people in the audience, but very little emotion displayed on her face.

Since I'd decided we were going to come this way, I had read a lot about her. She seemed like a shrewd operator, from a "proper" family, well-educated, well-spoken, a de facto spokesperson for this fractured, infuriatingly opaque and contradictory continent. There were a lot of people who hated her, and I had seen plenty of evidence for that, but most people here accepted her willingness to speak to Nations of Earth, because the other nations that used to be part of the United States, Prairie, Dixie Republic and America Free State, refused to speak with Nations of Earth, and Nations of Earth equally refused to speak with them. It all stemmed from a disagreement over international cooperation in the previous century. Since the United Nations used to have their headquarters in what was today Atlantia, they felt they should have been asked to play a part in the new organisation Nations of Earth, even if it seemed they only wanted this so that they could continue to argue with European members. Since that continual arguing had led to the downfall and eventual disbanding of the—by then utterly ineffective—United Nations, Nations of Earth had been reluctant to let any of the four nations join and had set conditions for joining that they knew the north American countries would not meet: proper separation of religion and state, rules on political funding and the legislated duty of care of the state towards individual citizens. These were precisely the issues that drove the United States to fall apart.

The world was damaged, peace was fragile, they needed cooperating voices to present a somewhat united front to *gamra*. Rightly or wrongly, they didn't want any members who refused to stick to the rules and refused to make a commitment to better the lives of their own poorest citizens.

Celia Braddock had been a player—albeit a minor one—on the international stage since securing a spot in the legislative assembly of Atlantia. She was a career politician.

I found it hard to understand her motivation for her involvement in international politics, which would be seen as a thankless job amongst her domestic peers. Ambition? Being seen as a serious player internationally? Behind closed doors, most people at Nations of Earth made jokes about this part of the world.

I'd wondered—and tried to research—the relationship between the four nations and the Pretoria Cartel, but the Cartel widely invested in off-Earth relationships, and the American countries were just... not interested in those. They just wanted the nasty "aliens" to go away.

The music had stopped and all the patriotic singing voices had fallen quiet. Celia Braddock took her place behind the lectern and faced the audience.

"I have a short and very important announcement to make," she began. "I won't be long, because, as you will understand after this press conference, I have better things to do than spend a lot of time talking. I will make a detailed announcement about all our findings later."

She was speaking quite a heavy local dialect. Several members of my team scrambled for their translators to make sense of it.

She put both her hands flat on the dais.

"At 9:41pm the night before last, we experienced two unprovoked, coordinated attacks on our capital. The airport and train stations were the main focus. The attacks came from the air and lasted only minutes. A second attack followed forty-three minutes later. Major infrastructure was destroyed. At present, the victim tally stands at two thousand and forty-five, mainly from the airport. The Atlantian Police and Rescue Service has mounted a significant rescue and recovery operation, which is still underway. If you live in any of the affected areas, you will have been contacted by local authorities, and if you have any problems, please make sure you contact them for help."

Someone in the audience yelled a question. I thought it was about terrorists.

She glared across the heads of the audience and ignored the question.

"I have to stress that this action was entirely unprovoked. Thankfully, the death toll will be somewhat depressed because the attacks came at night, and many people were at home. Things could have been worse, especially at the stations."

The same journalist repeated his question. He said, "This mode of operation is not typical for America Free State terrorist operatives. Who is responsible?"

Governor Braddock turned to him and pointed at him. "I'm getting to that in a moment." She sounded very much like a school teacher.

"As some of you have rightly concluded, this type of action is atypical for any of the entities that have recently perpetrated violence against us, or against me directly. The attempt to kill me last year came from terrorist operatives in America Free State and could be traced down to known enemy operators. This is different. Because there were two attacks following each other, our military were on high alert after the first incident. They scanned the skies. They picked up anything that shouldn't be there, and they managed to take out one of the attack vehicles, a drone carrying explosives, without triggering an explosion and destruction of the rocket. We know who they are now. We have their number. They will not be able to get away with this a third time."

People in the audience started yelling again. I picked up the questions I also wanted to ask: what about simultaneous attacks in other places?

She waved the audience into silence and continued, "I am aware that other cities have suffered similar provocations. Air attacks have been reported in America Free State, Mexico and Canada. Compared with what has happened in New York, those actions were fairly minor. More about this later. We're dealing with an enemy we haven't had to deal with before, an enemy of humanity that has, so far, left us in relative peace."

My heart jumped.

Damn, I had a feeling this was going to be about Aghyrians or the Pretoria Cartel.

She stepped back, allowing two uniformed men to come to the front. They were carrying a platform between them with on it, a cloth-covered object that looked disturbingly like a dead body, both in size and shape. They set this down on a couple of stone blocks that I'd assumed to be part of the landscaping, but appeared to have been placed there for the occasion. One of them whipped off the cloth cover. The platform held a curved fragment of metal about the length of a person, torn and blackened on one side.

The inside of the curved surface displayed a selection of electronic boards with singe marks. Coloured wires with little connectors hung loose or had been ripped from the rest of the device.

It could be part of a rocket or something like that.

Celia Braddock was still speaking. "I've spoken to General Bainbridge, Intelligence Chief Officer Dos Santos, and Science Bureau Chief Yau before making this public. All three of them agreed with each other over the origins of this device. It does not come from this earth. This is alien technology."

She let that sink in for effect.

I found the theatrics quite off-putting. Instead of turning this into a show, she might just tell the audience in plain language exactly where they thought this rocket came from. Last time I looked, the universe, even just our local galaxy, was a very big place, occupied by many different entities.

"This alien technology was used in the attacks that killed many people two nights ago. Why, we don't know. They have made no claims, but we can make some guesses. The aliens don't like us and never have. In my communications with Nations of Earth's President Dekker, I've expressed strong reservations about accommodating their wishes. Only the Atlantian military captured one of these drones, while the drones also attacked other countries. Isn't that strange that with all the might of their technology, countries like Mexico couldn't bring down a second drone? Is that because those attacks had the function to make it look like we weren't the only ones affected? Is that because Mexico and Canada accepted minor attacks for the sake of appearing to be on our side? In Los Angeles, the drones attacked a university building, an office tower, and the headquarters of a security firm, all of which were unoccupied because it was night. They lost four lives. In contrast, the drones attacked our airport and inflicted major damage and loss of life. Let's make no mistake, this was an attack on us specifically, to bring us into line or teach us a lesson."

What? Was she suggesting that *gamra* had sent these drones because they didn't like the fact that the small percentage of the North American population that had voted in the referendum had mostly voted against joining *gamra*? Really?

The broadcast's focus had returned to the governor, but the members of my team, including Sheydu, Isharu and Reida, had already captured the footage of the drone and had enlarged and enhanced it. Looking over Reida's shoulder, I judged the image quality to be quite poor. I hoped it would be good enough for them to derive at least some data. Isharu was running a simulation that inserted the fragment in a possibility of different vehicles based on its shape. Rockets, bombs, drone craft. None of the models that Isharu was flicking through looked familiar. There was also some activity going on in the group of Asto military, who had ensconced themselves in the other corner of the room, and had spread out their equipment over the dining table.

I presumed the two groups would join their efforts later.

Celia Braddock continued, "Make no mistake. This was a direct assault on the sovereignty of Atlantia. The aliens have always come here with one aim, and that is to destroy our planet's independence. They don't like us, they are afraid of us, and they think that the only way to deal with us is to beat us down and they can only do that by infiltrating our society. I have written to various world leaders to let them know that this is unacceptable. I am also about to consult with General Bainbridge about further action we will undertake, because there *will* be further action. I want there to be no doubt about that. While I will not be taking questions today—some of you have already asked your questions —I will be back here tomorrow and will return every day until this is solved and all your questions answered."

She nodded and turned around, flanked by the two security officers. The music blasted out of the loudspeakers and people started singing again.

The news service flicked back to a news presenter, and Clay turned off the screen.

Nicha met my eyes across the heads of those of my team who were seated on the floor.

While the others were still working on the translation, Nicha would have been able to follow the speech without devices.

He said, "What the fuck was that about? Did she just accuse *gamra* of military action against her country?"

His comment encapsulated my feelings perfectly.

CHAPTER NINETEEN

WHEN THE SOUND from the broadcast stopped, it became very quiet in the room.

Everyone who had come in to watch was looking at me, as if I had the answers.

Well, I knew what we should do, I thought, I hoped. But whether it would provide any answers remained to be seen.

Children had a perfect sensor for when something important was up. We had put them all to bed, but the older ones were all standing at the door. Nalya, Larrana and Vanessa's son and some other kids. Of course, the Pengali were also there. Jaki, because he looked after all these kids, and Ynggi and the kids themselves, watching with wide eyes.

No one moved to send them back to their room.

In Coldi society, kids were absolutely expected to be part of important decision-making processes.

I got up from the table.

"I presume that all of you have understood that in her speech, the governor of Atlantia accuses *gamra* of having taken military action against her country. I don't know if she realises how ridiculous this accusation is. For one, *gamra* does not command any military forces. She has no idea what she's talking about, other than that the fragment of the rocket they have brought down looks unfamiliar to them, and therefore, it is her misguided conclusion that it originated from *gamra*. I think you can all agree that our highest priority needs to be to establish the identity of this piece of equipment, where it came from and who made it, and communicate that clearly to all concerned. Can anyone report on what you've found out so far?"

I expected Sheydu or Isharu to get up, but it was Reida who gave the report.

He showed us the images they had captured and comparisons with similar devices, rockets or small-scale explosive delivery drones used by various militaries.

The seven Asto military officers in the corner watched and occasionally nodded.

Reida's main conclusion was that the design of the device was unfamiliar, but many of the components were not. He had circled a few items on the projection to prove his point. A control device matched a similar device that was produced on Asto and commonly used in aircraft. Another type of chip was commonly used in solar gliders at Indrahui. Part of the housing resembled metalwork done in Damarq. He also pointed out that the device contained many parts that the database didn't recognise at all, but also that this might be the result of poor image quality.

"In conclusion, the people who put this device together had access to markets for electronics at *gamra*, but may not have been from any of those entities, judging by the way they cobbled together the different components based purely on their function. Both Coldi and Damarcian designers would find the aesthetic arrangement of this device fundamentally displeasing. Neither of those groups would have designed a device like this. According to our modelling, the explosives delivery vehicles were small and are likely to have used simple hydrogen rockets. While powerful, they also require large storage tanks for fuel if operated over a distance. We haven't seen evidence of this, because these rockets would have shown up on multiple systems where we could track them. Besides, the only entity that still uses engines propelled by hydrogen is Miran, and this device looks nothing like anything built by Miran. This is a flimsy thing. No one in their right mind would design a rocket for atmosphere entry where the electronics are attached to the outer shell of the vehicle, but that looks precisely like what they have done here. Our conclusion is that these rockets came from a local source and never left the atmosphere."

Oh crap.

This was starting to look like some trick by the Pretoria Cartel. Yet I had looked for, but not found, evidence of any level of interaction between them and the North American countries.

Reida made a hand gesture to the military people in the corner.

One of them got up, a woman, carrying a reader.

She put the device face up in the middle of the floor where Reida had been sitting. Another black-clad, heavily armed man pulled shut the blinds to the largest window.

"We received this material just now during the governor's talk, and I apologise for not speaking of it earlier, but once you've seen it, you will appreciate why we made that choice."

Reida nodded at the officer. She touched a corner of the reader's screen. The familiar Exchange logo sprang up in the air. It was replaced with the image of the solar system and that damned approaching ship that we knew was coming, was still a way off, and I'd honestly pushed to the back of my mind because—damn it—Dekker refused to talk to me.

He continued, "I'm going to change the subject. Bear with me, because it will make sense when you've heard everything I want to say. Months ago, both the Exchange and the Asto military detected a single object coming towards this world. They were following it, expecting to engage with it at some point if it contained live technology and was not a piece of space junk. There were a lot of speculations about the origins of the object, but then again we know there are isolated communities in space, and they sometimes choose not to show themselves."

He looked sideways at Thayu. The Asto army, led by her father, very much chose to not show themselves most of the time.

"Anyway, during the night before yesterday, this single object emitted a burst of energy that jumped through space and split into multiple strands. You can see here how it has happened."

He showed us a moving image of the scan. It was blurry, but you could see the object we had been following for months, and that Amarru had been wanting to speak to Dekker about, that the Asto armed forces had classified as being of interest, had tried to communicate with, but ultimately, that all parties had ended up ignoring. Because it was only one small object and all signs were that it was a piece of dead space junk.

Mereeni said, "We've been trying to communicate with that thing for some time, but it wasn't answering."

In this, "we" was the Athens Exchange, and I knew that they had first spotted this object more than a year ago.

"That's because it looked like it was a piece of junk," Reida said. "But consider this. I'm going to overlay this rough scan with a map of this planet with the same scale and projection type and time schedule, and you may see the issue that worries us."

The projection of the filaments jumped over the top of a 3D projection of Earth, rotating slowly. I hadn't realised that the image of the filaments was also in 3D. The moving projection covered a few milliseconds, Reida said, and he slowed the image sequence down so we could see the flash of light bursting out of the unknown object and splitting and splitting into smaller and smaller filaments until they reached the Earth's atmosphere. There, they stopped as suddenly as they had appeared.

"What does that mean?" Telaris said. He had been on guard

duty for most of the time that my team had prepared for the speech and had, presumably, discussed these issues.

"We're not entirely sure," Reida said. "But consider the coincidences. This strong filament thread hit the atmosphere near New York." He pointed.

He also pointed out other filaments that went to other cities, including Mexico City and Los Angeles, and other parts of the world. Cities in Europe, Asia had also been affected.

"Is this as bad as it looks? Very clearly, the attacks were not limited to this continent, even if Governor Braddock acts like they were. Were other cities in the world attacked?"

Veyada said, "From what we've been able to gauge, yes, but we can't confirm that with certainty. It's probably a function of the fact that we're in a part of the world that doesn't communicate well with other entities."

Well, that was an understatement.

"Is anyone going to destroy this ship?" Like the Asto military.

"This is the difficult part. Because for *gamra* law, this world became a member when they signed the intent to join. Any entity of *gamra* can only send military intervention to any other entity when the receiving entity requests it, *and* the *gamra* assembly approves it."

"Has Asha ever been stopped by this kind of bureaucracy?"

"You'd be surprised. Yes, the Asto military sticks very rigidly to this rule. The only reason Asha could intervene in the earlier situation with Romi Tanaqan was because this world was not a member."

"So being a member is actually less useful?"

"Right now, it is. Until the president asks for help, and *gamra* can delegate Asto to provide that help."

"Has anyone else made a statement? Nations of Earth? Other countries? Has Dekker said anything? Has he asked for help?"

"Not that we know."

"What about the Exchange?"

"We've had little useful communication out of the Exchange for days."

Crap. Oh, crap.

A lot was starting to make sense.

I even understood why we had been attacked by the towns-folk. Because every local knew that we were at the old factory, we were seen to be part of the enemy, and we were "aliens".

I hoped Junco and Sage had extricated themselves safely. They seemed decent men and had been blindsided by the events as much as I had.

In the very back of my mind, I was trying to push away thoughts about a very similar situation.

A large Aghyrian ship disrupting the Exchange, almost causing a conflict to tear through Asto society. Aghyrians would never fight. They recruited others to fight on their behalf.

Meanwhile, the discussion between the members of my team had shifted to feasible ways for us to get out of here and back to Athens. Contact with the Exchange had been sporadic since the start of the trip, and as things were looking now, all commercial air travel had been suspended.

They discussed whether we should call in some additional favours from Clay, Marisol and Vanessa, and ask them to fly unauthorised across the continent back to Athens.

But Sheydu said that we were likely to encounter hostile military action because the military was on high alert and could not be trusted to act on messages informing them that an unknown craft of Asto make was going to fly across the country in the same way the Exchange notified other authorities if this was the case. We'd have to fly across America Free State and either Dixie Republic or Prairie and Atlantia and none of those countries were friendly to us, or had agreements with the Exchange.

None of the senior members of my team were keen to take the risk. Not Sheydu, or Isharu or Anyu.

Nicha asked if we could ask for assistance from the Asto military, but also agreed with Sheydu that it that would not be a good look.

According to Isharu, the Exchange could attempt to sneak in a craft over the Pacific Ocean if we could reach a place on the coast.

From where we sat in the living room in the house on the hill, I had a feeling that one might be able to see the ocean on a clear day. It wouldn't be far to travel. I was sure we could do that.

In that case, it might be possible to drop in on my father and Erith to see if they were all right. I'd just have to install the rest of the team in a hotel nearby. I could do that, too.

One thing we couldn't do was to stay here to ride out the crisis. No one knew how long this was going to take.

There was nothing we could do from here.

I wanted to get back to safe territory for the sake of the safety of the children with us. I could already hear complaints from Larrana and Nalya's families when they heard of the risks I'd subjected their sons to. Never mind that Larrana's family had most heavily pushed for the trip. When things went wrong, it would be my fault.

But a rebellious part in my mind wanted to do more.

I'd been through this rubbish before. When I started in Barresh, President Sirkonen had been murdered in similar circumstances: through means that didn't look familiar, and therefore were decreed "alien" and by extension, *gamra* should be blamed. Nations of Earth *would* have successfully blamed *gamra* had I not objected to that conclusion, even if I had less evidence back then than I did now.

I did not accept Celia Braddock's conclusions. Moreover, I wanted to prove that she was wrong. *Gamra* was not responsible. We needed to find out who were. And sneaking out of the country back to the Exchange did nothing to further that aim.

CHAPTER TWENTY

MY TEAM HAD CONCLUDED their deliberations and were now looking at me, waiting to decide on the choices they had outlined. Were we going to wait for assistance from the Exchange, ask the Asto military to rescue us, or try to make an escape via the coast?

But I had a different proposal to put to them.

Normally, we would have a team meeting in the hub in our apartment in Barresh, or if we were somewhere else, in the accommodation's bathroom, because if the accommodation was bugged, bathrooms were echoey and that messed with the quality of the recording.

I wasn't sure if we should include the locals in our planning. The fewer people knew about our plans, the better. But they might feel offended if we left them out, and I had no reason to distrust any of them. So my team gathered around me on the couches and the floor under the curious gazes of the others.

I began, "You were just looking at the images of the piece Celia Braddock said they found and claimed to have been responsible for the attacks. What conclusions do you draw from it?"

There were some frowns.

"We just discussed that," Deyu said. She sounded puzzled.

"No, we discussed what we know for certain. I want you to speculate about what the concerned parties are going to do about it."

"There is going to be trouble," Telaris said.

"That goes without saying. When Celia Braddock accuses *gamra*, what is Nations of Earth going to do?"

Deyu's eyes widened.

She pulled out her reader, opened an empty page and drew a circle in the middle. I was too far away from her to see what she wrote in the middle, but other members of my team now understood what this was about.

A doodle. Organising our thoughts until our best avenue forward became obvious.

"This is us," she said, pointing at the circle.

"Do you mean us, our association and people in the house, or do you mean us as *gamra* people? Or us as people who have been affected by the attacks?"

She formed an O with her lips.

She drew two more circles close to the first one, one being *gamra* and one Nations of Earth.

I asked, "Does Celia Braddock need a circle?"

Deyu drew another circle, close to the edge of the page.

"Why do you draw it all the way over there?" I asked.

"They're not related to us and are not sympathetic to us."

"True, but whichever organisation is behind these attacks is even less sympathetic."

She rubbed out the circle and drew it closer to ours.

"Who do you think is behind the attacks?" I continued.

"Aghyrians?" she said.

"The Pretoria Cartel," Evi said, his voice dark. "They didn't like losing the election and now they're trying to turn opinion against *gamra* to stop the joining process at the last moment."

"I don't know. They could have had many opportunities to do this before now, and much easier methods of doing it. We've been following this unknown approaching object in the solar system for over a year. I've spoken to Minke Kluysters about it. He says the Pretoria Cartel or Tamer Collective knows nothing about it. I am inclined to believe him."

Not everyone in my team believed him, and, in my case, the operative word in that sentence was "inclined". I was happy to change my mind at any time.

"Then Aghyrians?" Deyu said again.

"Probably. Or some group related to Aghyrians or related to the Cartel but not officially affiliated with them or sanctioned by them."

Reida frowned at me with a *did you just muddy your own argument?* look on his face.

Deyu was busily drawing on the reader with dotted lines and questions. She also drew in other circles. I wasn't sure what they represented.

Sheydu snorted. "Who these people are is not our immediate concern. The local authorities will sort this out. It's our concern to get out safely, especially with the youngsters in our care."

"But it is our concern. Nations of Earth signed to join *gamra* and we have to continue to act like that will happen, regardless of current developments with Simon Dekker. Under that contract, the agreement *gamra* signed with Nations of Earth, we are obliged to help them, if the source of a conflict originates off-world. And Governor Braddock clearly suggested that it was. Not only that, getting out of here is related to being able to determine the origin of the attacks. If people in this part of the world think we, *gamra*, are responsible, we'll have trouble getting out."

Anyu said, "Not if our sources have anything to do with it."

"I object to involving the Asto military unless we have no other option. Right now, we do have another option. We even have an option to find out about the governor's claim, because we're here, and because we know she has this fragment of the projectile that they managed to bring down."

"They should pass the images to Nations of Earth and Amarru," Sheydu said.

"Yes, but do you think anyone around here is going to give Amarru access to the information collected about this thing? Where it was brought down, how it was brought down, what they learned from it other than that their conclusion is that *gamra* was involved?"

"But we're not involved. Amarru will be able to confirm that."

"Amarru won't get the chance. Because these people have already decided it was done by *gamra*, never mind that there are many entities within *gamra* and if, for example, this is an Aghyrian thing, it's in the interest of all of us to know, especially for Nations of Earth, because we have the means to find out who within the Aghyrians or Tamer Collective is responsible. To broadly blame *gamra* is as ignorant as it is stupid. *Gamra* doesn't own equipment, doesn't have armies. Therefore, this cannot be *gamra* technology."

"We can't be entirely certain because the image quality is not very good," Isharu said.

"Yes," Sheydu said. I wasn't sure which part she intended to agree with. Then she added, "That's what the Exchange is for: communicate with the locals."

I continued, "They're not communicating very well at the moment. The *president* is ignoring me and Amarru. Amarru is too polite to tell me so, but I know it to be true."

Most of the members of my team and the others in the room gave me puzzled looks, but Thayu stared at me. She had seen this part of me before, and she knew what was coming.

"No," I said, and the members of my team, and the local Coldi, fell into silence. The security team stopped discussing security things, and everyone looked up to listen to me. I still found this a little embarrassing, because they had vastly more knowledge about many of these operational things than I did.

I continued, "As far as I can see, there is only one thing we can do."

After a further silence, I said, "The problem is that they think *gamra* means off-world. But *gamra* doesn't have distinctive technology. Its members do. And the non-members as well. This thing could be Aghyrian, it could be Tamerian, it could be something else altogether. But it's not Asto technology and has nothing to do with *gamra*. I think the best way of proving the truth, now that we are here on this continent, is to investigate this fragment. They should let us defend the accusations. Or at least let us look at this fragment, so we can analyse where we think it comes from. I don't hear any other reports of people having captured any of this technology elsewhere in the world."

"That's because this supposedly captured technology is staged," Nicha said. "I suspect they cobbled this together so they can blame us. They have a history of doing that sort of thing."

Sadly, this was also true.

"That could be true, but we won't know until we see this fragment," I said. "That's what we should do: demand to see it while we're here. No doubt they would prefer to kick us out of the country so that their theories can go unchallenged. Haven't you noticed how well the theory that *gamra* or some sort of *aliens* are responsible suits the local government's politics?"

It actually hurt me to say that word, aliens. I'd almost forgotten those derogatory terms that had marked my youth. Chans, ethies, aliens. They belonged to a different era.

"So what would you do?" Nicha asked. "We can't just walk up to them and demand to see this thing they shot down."

Clay said, "Yes. This piece of evidence will be held under tight security. You can't just barge in and look at it. These people are paranoid about their safety. Many years of conflict have scarred them deeply."

"I'm not sure if I'd want to bother with asking them," I said. "They'll never show us if we make a request. They'll shadow us and tell us to jump bureaucratic hurdles designed to keep us away."

Sheydu snorted. "Well, yeah. We're deep in hostile territory. Their armed forces are plentiful and make up for their technological deficiencies with their numbers and enthusiasm and brute force. We have children with us, whose parents will be seriously displeased if something happens to them. We're no longer nimble and invisible. I'm not in favour of splitting the team up again."

I chuckled. "Is this really Sheydu, telling me to give up?"

"I'm just warning you that the usual parameters for our team don't apply."

"Then I'm asking you to change our parameters to accommodate the plan. This is our story: we got marooned in the middle of an attack. Commercial travel has stopped and we're trying to get home. We'd be excused for attempting to travel overland to the Atlantic coast because this brings us closer to where we want to go. All of us will travel together. When we reach our goal, we might split up briefly, where a part of the team conducts the covert operation. We need to know how to make this travel happen, and we need to know where the governor keeps this piece of metal."

"That's likely to be on a military base," said Clay, his eyes wide.

"How can we find out where it is?" I asked, looking at him.

His mouth opened further.

"It's easy," Thayu said, "We ask my father. The governor gave her talk outside. The fragment was outside. They'll have satellite imagery of how it was brought to where we saw it, and then all we need to do is track the vehicles back to their origin."

She looked motherly, with Emi on her lap, but I had never seen a more dangerous version of Thayu.

"All right, I'll authorise that particular use of the Asto military. Find out. Then we'll find some way to get in and out of wherever this fragment is held. A small team will go, while the others stay in a safe location. We make sure that we have a means of escape lined up, either through Amarru or the register or a private transport company. We would prefer air travel, but would settle for travel across the ocean, maybe for a short distance just to get across the border. Do you think you could do that?" I looked at Sheydu.

"Hmmm," Sheydu said. "We could do that."

"Just make sure we don't have to travel on water," Anyu said.

"Yes," Isharu said, from the depth of her heart.

It was settled.

The locals were giving me *Is this guy for real?* stares. One of the military people in the corner gave me a small nod.

Sheydu rose and walked to the door, presumably to start preparations. On the way out, she turned to Clay, pointed at him and said, "And none of *you* heard this conversation."

CHAPTER TWENTY-ONE

THERE WERE a lot of preparations to be made.

Clay and Marisol offered to book ahead as many parts of the journey as possible. They had contacts in several places. They took me to the bottom floor of the house where room after room contained supplies: clothing, cooking gear, camping gear, stoves. I objected to taking too many things. We might not be able to return them.

"This material is here precisely for this reason," Clay said. "It's not ours, but it's here to distribute to people who need to travel inland and may have to avoid cities and towns."

He told me to make sure that Anyu and Reida came down to collect electronic gear that was better adapted to local systems.

Why did I have the feeling that the Exchange paid for this stash of stuff? Why did it make me feel uncomfortable to think that this was a safe haven for spies and that the presence of an association of Asto military officers was no coincidence?

We put the children to bed.

Nalya asked what was going on and what we were doing tomorrow.

Like this, with the light coming from the side, he looked a lot like Thayu. I'd found a lot of her quiet and resilient attitude in him.

Admittedly, I'd worried about having him along. The human part of me had trouble accepting that a family would send a child with someone who had murdered the child's uncle, even if it had been self-defense. But apparently not. Nalya's uncle, Taysha Palayi, had been killed in the pursuit of power, and that was acceptable, honourable even.

Nalya had been quiet, polite and easy to get on with from the time I'd collected him and Larrana from the apartment of Delegate Ayanu with whom they'd travelled from Asto.

Larrana had been racing around the hall, but Nalya sat on a bench, studying. I asked him what he was doing, and he'd shown me his text. Damarcian agriculture. Did he choose to study that, I'd asked him, and he said no. It was because teachers were told by the Inner Circle to raise a generation of people who knew about growing things and restoring landscapes, so that's what he did.

The maturity in this kid was quite something.

When he asked a serious question, I could not fob him off with a simple story. I sat on the edge of his bed, a narrow fold-out thing crammed in a small room at the back of the house. Larrana had the full-sized bed that stood in the room, and Ayshada slept on a mattress on the floor. Both of them were still in the bathroom with the Pengali kids. I could hear Ayshada's voice through the closed door. He was arguing in Pengali.

"We are being accused of being behind the attacks," I said to Nalya.

"I heard that, but I don't understand why. We were just in our accommodation. We were about to go to the beach because Larrana wanted to watch some kind of show. We saw the explosions in the sky. We weren't anywhere near them."

"They're not accusing us, our association, but they're

accusing Asto and *gamra* and because we're from *gamra*, they don't trust us."

"My father says that people always accuse Asto of these things," he said.

Yes, and his father wasn't the easiest person to talk to on the subject of Asto's relationship with *gamra*. That part of the Inner Circle wanted to send out the army when there was a perceived affront to Asto, and I was glad that the army wasn't on board with that.

"Unfortunately, when you're a big entity, that happens. People become vengeful or envious. You have to be forgiving when people accuse you of causing problems, because if you return the same level of viciousness, it's easy for things to get out of hand."

His face creased in a frown.

"So we should just let these people say we did it while we had nothing to do with it?"

"No. We shouldn't engage in their bickering. We should go by what is the truth. We should find out what that truth is."

His frown deepened. He was a thinker, and I hoped that maybe when he grew older, he might question some practices he saw happening at home.

"Where are we going?"

"We hope to get back home. All the commercial flights have stopped because of the attacks, so we will take alternative forms of transport."

At this point, there was a lot of commotion in the hall, so I said a quick good night, and went to see what the fuss was about.

The noise was coming from the room that served as the hub, which was small enough to have originally been intended as a broom cupboard. There was not enough room for all of us, with all security personnel wanting to cram in at once.

"What happened?" I asked their black-clad backs.

"We suddenly got Exchange coverage," Anyu said. "Apparently it's not very common that this happens, but they catch small patches of it when the right configuration of satellites exists."

Here was another strange thing.

If I, with my diplomatic, non-military background, were to plan an attack on Earth in the fashion that had just happened, I would make damn sure I'd disabled those satellites, in case they accidentally transmitted something that I didn't want to become public knowledge.

The Exchange was monitoring the satellites. Nations of Earth was monitoring the satellites.

If I were a general in the Nations of Earth forces, the first thing I'd do was to disable those satellites, in case they transmitted further commands that would cause more damage.

But nobody had disabled them.

It didn't make any sense for all the communication channels to still be open.

It was fortunate, if baffling.

Once they established the connection, Anyu hustled me into the room. Zyana vacated the seat at the hub. It was hot in there, with a powerful smell of hot stone that was the scent of Coldi sweat.

I sat in front of the unit. A very simple affair.

"I haven't seen one of these models in a while," I said. The hub in my apartment in Barresh used to have a unit like this, but even when I moved in, it was already outdated.

"These are simple but very powerful units," Anyu said. "They require little fine tuning or maintenance. Ideal for places where those things are in short supply. Do you know how to use it?"

"I do."

First stop was Amarru. But it was very early in Athens, and the junior Exchange operator told me she wasn't in. To his credit, he did try to contact her, but got no reply.

He told me they'd been through some gruelling days at work

and she might have turned off her communication. That didn't sound like Amarru at all. I assumed she'd gone for a walk, as I'd known her to do.

She had, however, directed her staff to send me a message. He asked if I'd received it.

I hadn't, so he re-sent it and told me about the gist of it. It was short and direct. Amarru was going to send a rescue team to pick us up from an as yet undisclosed locality on the coast, similar to the way she'd arranged to pick us up from Cape Town.

"You mean she's sending a craft to Los Angeles just for us?"

"There will be others who can use it, but she definitely wants you safe back here."

Oh no, I wasn't having that. I needed to have a look at the fragment that Celia Braddock had been parading as proof that *gamra* was responsible.

"Tell her to save our seats for desperate people with children and nowhere else to go."

"You're important to us."

"We are fine, honestly. Tell Amarru not to worry about where we are. We will make our own way back. I wanted to visit my father, anyway."

"She is clear about it: she wants you safe and on that flight. We'll let you know the flight as well. You can travel to the pickup point together. We'll let you know where it is."

I couldn't bring myself to tell him a lie, to promise that we would come, and that we would wait and register. I didn't want to talk about our plans, because it was very likely that people were listening in, in case Amarru thought it was a stupid idea, and in that case she was right: it *was* a stupid idea. Especially with such a large team that included children.

So I just signed off, telling him that people in my team wanted to use the link. I didn't like it.

Normally, if Amarru was informed about our plans, she would be fine with taking back part of our team, like the children and others we didn't need, to a safe haven, but she didn't know and I couldn't tell her.

We would have to give Amarru the slip. She worked hard and had not deserved me making a lot of trouble for her. But unfortunately, I saw no way to tell her why we wouldn't be at the rendezvous. Maybe in time, when she stopped being angry about it, she would even agree with me.

I was about to hand control of the hub back to Anyu when a message scrolled over the screen proclaiming that I had an incoming call.

Someone local, someone with a long identification number. I knew that number.

"Dad, why are you using the Exchange?"

My mind played horrible images in my vision. The safe haven where he and Erith lived destroyed in the attacks, houses burnt, people dead.

"Good evening, son."

"Well, yes, that, too. Are you all right? Where are you?"

"Erith and I are safe at home, but the lines are down, so I used the little doovey you gave me, a long time ago. Quite surprised that it worked, to tell you the truth. You might have heard that there was an attack on Auckland—"

"No, I hadn't. They're only talking about local attacks here. Which places are affected? How many?"

"Many big cities. Tokyo, Jakarta—"

"Athens?"

"Yes, there, too."

"How bad?" Why hadn't the Exchange operator said anything about that?

"Oh, I don't know. There is too much going on in this part of the world. I checked with the family. I know you haven't seen your cousins for years, but they all survived, although Jasmin and Morgan had to evacuate their home."

That was an unexpected right-angle turn into memory lane.

Jasmin was the daughter of my mother's older sister. I hadn't seen her—or any of my other cousins—since that fateful family gathering where that self-absorbed brat Dennis had thumbed his nose at my studies and desire to work at the Exchange. I'd decided that I had better uses for my hard-earned money than the suborbital to New Zealand to visit such rude gits, even for weddings.

"Has anyone said anything about where the attacks came from?"

"No. It's keeping a lot of people occupied. It's all so random. All we know is that the drones appeared as if out of nowhere. They didn't communicate, delivered their explosives and vanished without a trace."

"Celia Braddock says that the Atlantian military forces brought one down." Damn, why hadn't she mentioned the world-wide attacks?

"That's the first I hear of it. The security council of Nations of Earth has been in meetings since the event. Dekker has sacked the security chief and the head of the Special Operations unit. He made a very brief appearance that was stunning in its lack of information. Most governments have put their own defensive procedures in place. We've been supplied with emergency rations of medicines and have been given access to shelters, although we're probably too far away to get there in time if there is another attack."

"Dad, this is serious. You have to get to safety."

"Oh, I think we're quite safe here in our forgotten corner of the world."

"Dad, there is an unknown ship coming in this direction that we know nothing about. It's not answering any of our communication. It's the origin of these attack drones, even if we have no idea how they covered the distance between where the ship is and Earth. We know nothing else about this ship. When I say 'we' I mean *gamra* and the Asto military combined. We don't know what they want and we don't know who they are."

He said again that he'd be safe in rural New Zealand. And honestly, he was probably right.

I told him to take care, and that I was still planning to visit to show him his granddaughter if we could at all make it. He said he was looking forward to that, but I heard in his voice that he had doubts whether it was ever going to happen.

Reality sank in. Earth was under attack. We were on the brink of a war with an unknown enemy.

There wasn't much time to talk. Members of my team were lining up to speak with their contacts. I'd best get out of the way to let them do that.

I ceded the room to my team, and they went on to talk security things with security people. The connection would last perhaps half an hour before it phased out, and we were on our own again.

I found Thayu in the room where she had stayed overnight, packing away Emi's baby things. I told her about what my father had said. "One thing I don't understand is why the Exchange carried on as if nothing had happened. Why we heard nothing."

"That doesn't surprise me at all," she said. "You'll have heard Sheydu complain about the lack of connectivity here. This country is backwards."

"Yes, but what about the Exchange? I know connectivity is bad, but there has been contact. Earlier today, even. Why didn't they say anything?"

But I already knew the answer to that. Exchange communication was not secure.

Thayu confirmed my thought. "When the Exchange goes quiet like that, something is up."

In hindsight, I agreed. "Do you think they're badly affected?"

"Not badly enough to have stopped operations, but they're obviously keeping their heads down."

I then I told her about Amarru's directive to stay where we were so her people could pick us up.

"But I thought you wanted to see that drone?"

"Yup."

"Did you tell them?"

"We can't. The fewer people know about this, the better."

"I agree. What are we going to do?"

"I don't like it, but we have no option but to ignore Amarru. Hopefully, we'll be able to communicate with Amarru's people about where we are going, and they can come after us."

"She won't be impressed."

"Nope."

CHAPTER TWENTY-TWO

I RAN into Clay in the hallway when I was going to our room to pack. He held me back in the passage that led to the front door but was deserted right now.

"I'm worried. I heard that Amarru is sending people to pick you up. What am I going to say to them when they turn up?"

"Tell them we're held up getting to the coast."

"That's not going to keep them happy for long."

"Tell them we left, and to the best of your knowledge, we're on our way to meet them."

"They won't be impressed."

"Being impressed is not what they're paid for. When they come here to pick us up, they can wait for us to turn up, they can leave again with the other people they're rescuing, or they might like to chase us. That's up to them. We can't communicate our plans across any networks because there is a risk our information will fall into the wrong hands. If they turn up here in person, you can tell them the truth."

He still seemed very uncomfortable. What was his motivation and loyalty? It was hard to determine. He wore no clan earrings. He seemed close to Amarru. Very close.

I'd also never seen Coldi civilians who hosted units of the Asto military.

It made me think: was he a military spy? Thayu seemed to think Clay and Marisol were from the Lingui clan. I knew little about that clan or their relationships with the military.

By the time I went to bed, there was still a lot of activity in the communications hub. When I walked past, Deyu and Sheydu sat at the tiny table, going over some maps and satellite images while Zyana made notes. The trip would indeed involve trains, Deyu informed me when I checked on them.

Sheydu's team, with the help of the military satellite, had made a detailed analysis of the vehicles that had visited the garden of the government residence where Celia Braddock had given her talk.

They were still working on the identity of the vehicles in the car park outside the residence, but they had narrowed down the path that the fragment of drone had travelled and Reida was following the truck back to where it had originated, just like Thayu had said.

We had a pretty good idea of where this fragment was held. My team would confirm and crosscheck this with the military.

Thayu sat in a chair checking a security briefing, next to Emi who was out cold in her travel cot.

"Do you think we're doing the right thing?" I asked Thayu, sitting down on the bed. "I hate the thought of endangering the kids."

"What is the danger to them? That someone gets angry? That some in our party get taken into custody?"

"That would be unpleasant, especially since we know little about the norms and culture."

"When you operate at the level that we do, everything is about publicity and perception, even if it may mean temporary discomfort. You want to see their evidence. You can either see it by stealth or by forcing them to let you in. We all prefer stealth, because none of us can claim to comprehend this regime. I'm pretty sure you know this already. You've done stuff like this all your life."

"Yes, but I didn't have the responsibility for all these children."

"They'll be fine. It's a learning experience. We want Emi to follow in our footsteps, right?"

We both looked at Emi, on her belly on the mattress, her face scrunched into the sheet.

Yes, I wanted her with me, asking questions like Raanu when she was that age.

I really didn't have an option. Ezhya would want me to investigate while I was here. Once I took the proffered flight back to Athens, I would never get back into the country.

But I spent a long time looking at the ceiling in the darkness, listening for distant sounds.

I didn't know what I was waiting for.

Another attack to come out of the blue? Signs of unrest? Amarru's people coming up to the house sooner than I had expected?

But eventually, I fell into a dreamless sleep. I was awoken in the morning, while it was still dark, by activity in the hallway. People were talking, not bothering to keep their voices down.

I got out of bed, seeing that Thayu had already gotten up. Emi was still in her cot, looking at me with big bright eyes.

I lifted her out and dressed her in her travel clothes.

We had a sling we used to carry her.

When she was a little baby, we would carry it around the front, but now she was big enough to sit piggyback. That meant she would have to go over the jacket, and I needed to put on my armour and strap on my weapon, which would also have to go underneath my clothing. We had an extra piece of armour that went over Emi's sling to protect her.

It made for an interesting puzzle and combination of items.

With that done, I picked up our bags and went into the hallway.

By the sound of voices drifting through the hallway, I judged that most of my team was in the kitchen having breakfast. Indeed, I found all of them standing around the central bench. With them was another familiar face: Junco.

He greeted me with a crooked smile.

"I was worried about you for a bit," I said.

"No need. I've faced tougher situations."

"Even tougher than showing around a bunch of aliens when the aliens are supposed to have attacked your cities?"

"Yes. We do mostly tours for high-profile people, a lot of them world political leaders. Not all of them are particularly popular with the locals. Especially not the ones that come from across the Atlantic. When the townsfolk get wind of it, strange things can happen. You know, there are a lot of people with a lot of time on their hands out there."

It was heartening in a way that tourism still existed in a world like this.

I ate breakfast standing up—because Emi's armour made it difficult to sit. Emi didn't like the breakfast offering and refused to eat the sweet bread or the flavoured porridge. She had her mind set on getting yoghurt, but Coldi didn't tolerate milk very well, and we had no time for upset stomachs.

I had to remove her from the kitchen to stop her being grumpy.

I found Thayu in the security broom cupboard with the rest of the security team in a briefing where Sheydu handed out gear and weapons. Telaris and Nicha would each carry local weapons in addition to their regular pieces.

We were ready. We were heavily armed. The trip would take the best part of three days. Overnight, the Asto military had confirmed where the drone fragment was stored. All we needed to do now was go and see it.

CHAPTER TWENTY-THREE

BY NOW, everyone had packed, and people had moved into the hall.

The bus stood outside the front door, a bigger vehicle than the one that had brought us here.

We all climbed in. Nalya helped Larrana negotiate the steep stairs, Ayshada helped Ileyu climb in by pushing her backside and then Mereeni, Deyu and Thayu handed Zyana at the storage compartment all the bags and equipment so that they could be stowed underneath. We had accepted some of Clay's camping gear: sleeping bags, emergency rations, and tarpaulins that could be fashioned into makeshift tents.

He'd wanted no payment for any of it. I wasn't sure what arrangement he had with Amarru, but I was fairly certain he and his sisters had a close relationship with her and he either was an agent for the Exchange or was closely associated with agents.

And not only were we leaving against Amarru's wishes, I'd told him to lie to her about it. I hoped this trip was going to be worth the deceit.

Clay, Marisol, Vanessa, the local Coldi farmers from the

valley and the group of military people watched us from the veranda.

As the bus pulled out of the driveway, I thought I spotted one of the black-clad military people move to the side of the house. What was the bet they were going to follow us? I had no doubt that they were Asha's people.

The bus took us over the bumpy road back up the mountain-side, over the pass where the last glimpse of Los Angeles shrouded in dusty air slid from view, and down the bumpy and cactus-lined road on the other side to the same farm where we had arrived yesterday.

In daylight, the dry desolation of the landscape was all-encompassing. It was dusty, grey, washed-out. The remnants of previous agricultural activity dotted the hillside.

A half-collapsed house stood amongst a graveyard of dead olive trees. The ground between the skeletons was dusty and covered in rocks, but a group of brown goats—some with big horns—still found something to eat between the boulders.

Junco, at the wheel of the bus, complained about them.

"Those things have exploded everywhere. They even come into the suburbs. They eat any skeleton of a plant or bush that's still standing. Many people who wanted to farm out here have given up because of these damn pests."

The Coldi farmhouse lay in a gully where it was marginally greener than the surrounding countryside.

The doors to the shed with the Asto-made craft were closed, but a gyrocopter sat in a field outside the house.

The bus stopped a little distance away from it, facing the open cabin door. A man appeared at the top of the steps, in the company of a dog.

It was Sage and his canine companion.

As soon as the door to the bus opened, the dog jumped from the gyrocopter and tore across the field. It scrambled up the steps into the bus before Junco could grab it by its collar and came to a screeching halt at Ynggi's seat, barking furiously.

Several members of my team sprang into alert, especially those who hadn't seen the animal before.

The dog's tail was wagging, and Ynggi's tail was wagging. Jaki had taken the two Pengali youngsters on his lap, but their tails were up in the air, trembling with curiosity and excitement.

Had Ynggi told them about this strange creature called a *dog*?

He slid down from his seat and let the dog sniff him, and then let the dog sniff Jaki and the kids.

Junco had been about to interfere, but he relaxed.

He snorted. "Hmm. I think that stupid dog likes him after all."

We all got out of the bus. We collected our bags and trudged in a line to the gyrocopter.

Sage was still standing in the doorway, dressed in full military gear: a camouflage shirt and trousers, a broad belt with pouches, a knife strapped around his right leg, a gun in a bracket on his left leg. The gyrocopter's headset hung around his neck.

"I'm glad to see you safe and well," I said. "I'm sorry about causing trouble in your town."

He snorted. "Those idiots in town wouldn't harm me. I'm the reason the town still exists. We've been through tougher stuff than this."

He tossed us some jackets.

"It would be a good idea if you put those on," he said. "It might be a bit cold up there where we're going. This craft is not as nice as the other one."

We did as he said and then climbed into the gyrocopter.

Not as nice was an understatement. The other gyrocopters had been properly fitted with comfortable seats.

This was a military style vehicle with hard benches along the sides and a platform with netting in the middle of the hold where we had to deposit our luggage so it could be strapped down with a net. Junco was in charge of this operation.

We all sat down and did up the harnesses that hung from the wall.

With his harness and wheels, Larrana couldn't easily sit in a way that allowed the harness to be done up. The straps wouldn't extend far enough. We tried a few different spots.

"Oh, no, I got something different for the boy," Junco said when he noticed our efforts. He gestured. "Come here."

He opened a cabinet behind the pilot's seat and pulled out a shelf made from wood, fitted with something that looked like an old car seat.

"I rigged this up for you because I know life is hard," he said.

Larrana probably didn't understand what he said, but he pushed himself onto the seat.

From his new position, he could see over the pilot's shoulders to the controls and out the front window. His face was beaming.

I realised that he hadn't spoken of his collection all day.

Junco did up his harness and then walked past me to shut the door. Sage slid into the pilot's seat.

When Junco came back, I stopped him.

"Did you make that seat just for him?"

He met my eyes, and I was disturbed to see the emotion in them. He nodded.

"The poor kid's probably never had the best seat in the house before."

"What about your son? Isn't he going to miss you?"

"He's looked after by my partner. If he had wheels like this, he could probably come on trips and help me, but it still doesn't change who he is. Just makes him a bit more... human, you know?"

He spoke briefly to Sage, then took the spot next to me.

Sage started the gyrocopter's rotating blades. It became too noisy to keep taking.

Ayshada sat, very well-behaved, next to his father strapped in on the bench. He put his little hands over his ears. Telaris sat on his other side, and pulled out a pair of earmuffs and put them over Ayshada's head.

He was growing into such a big boy. He'd start formal tuition when we came back to Barresh.

Emi sat on Thayu's lap, looking around with big eyes. Her hair was getting quite long and Thayu had put it in a ponytail, which highlighted the spots of downy hair above her ears that were soft and purple. Thayu had also draped Sage's military jacket over her.

This behaviour was so typical of Emi. She loved being in noisy and busy places, but never contributed to either the noise or activity herself. She watched. She was, as Thayu would say, a perfect spy in the making.

The power of the engine made the craft vibrate. With a jump, we took off. The adventure was underway.

For a while, no one said anything. It was just too noisy inside the cabin.

But then the craft stopped climbing and increased its forward motion. Sage spoke to someone on the radio.

Larrana was looking over his shoulders out the front window.

From where I sat, I could only see a small window in the craft's cargo door. The Pengali were at that end, and Pykka was standing on the dog's back in order to look out. Both he and the dog were wearing a harness, attached to the side of the craft by a retractable cable. Were these harnesses especially for dogs?

Past him, I could see the dusty air. The sky above was pale blue. We were flying in an easterly direction. Pale sunlight came into the front window.

It was peaceful.

I didn't know what I'd expected. To be shadowed by the military? To be forced down?

Junco was looking at me.

"Thanks for helping us," I said.

He shrugged. "We're being paid."

"You don't normally work for Clay, do you?"

"Until this morning, I'd never seen him before. But that doesn't matter. He wants a guide to take people across the country, and we provide the service. He pays."

"You don't have to do this. It could be dangerous."

"Life is dangerous out here. We're used to it."

"I hope we haven't created any problems for you by escaping across the lake."

"Nah. That's not the first time something like that has happened. The young guys in town get a bit hot-headed. They're proud young men and they have nothing to do. Everything the town used to have that gave them jobs—the factories, the agriculture, the mines—is gone. They hate having to allow me and my business into the country. They hate tourists, especially foreigners. I understand. Hey, many of these kids are like the members of my family. They hear from older folk how great everything used to be and they don't have a lot of hope that things will get better in their lifetimes."

He appeared nonchalant, but his words and attitude filled me with sadness. Imagine being so jaded that you no longer viewed an armed attack on visitors as unusual.

CHAPTER TWENTY-FOUR

IT WAS WELL past midday when we came down.

Junco informed us that the craft needed to refuel, and that we had best stay inside while they did that.

We landed, and Sage got up from the pilot's seat and opened the door. A waft of air carrying the smell of hot and dry bitumen came in.

Several of the children had been asleep, and they woke up, looking around bleary-eyed.

Larrana wanted to know when we were going to get to Athens. It was a strange question. He hadn't asked about going back before, but I assumed that now that the visit to the park was over and done with, he might miss his family.

It was strange because he had never shown much interest in them. He'd travelled to my house in Barresh with Nalya, and while Nalya had dutifully contacted his family—even if I wasn't sure the family deserved it—Larrana hadn't shown interest. But clearly something was up.

These two boys were on the cusp of Coldi puberty. I didn't think they were friends. I didn't even think they got on very well, although they hid their dislike of each other well.

I had to tell Larrana it would be a while before we got back to the Exchange, cringing all the way, because his father would be unhappy to hear about this little excursion we had taken, one that was going to be more dangerous than bargained for.

The refuelling took little time. Sage and Junco climbed back inside and we kept going in an easterly direction, with the sun now at our back.

The landscape passing under us was mountainous, with red rocks and patches of snow on the tallest mountains.

It became increasingly covered in vegetation, green vegetation even. The amount of dust in the air decreased. Not long after that, we passed over the first patch of forest: thick dark green stands of pine trees that grew more frequent. The occasional road intersected the landscape, but otherwise we didn't see many signs of recent human habitation. I did spot an abandoned settlement, ruined buildings overgrown with weeds and tree saplings.

Junco told me that Sage deliberately picked a route that didn't cross commercial flight paths and that kept away from population centres. I asked him if many people lived here, and he said these areas had never been densely populated, but that most people now lived in the towns.

I was familiar with the phenomenon.

The big industrial food production complexes had made broad acre farming unnecessary. In New Zealand, the people in the community where my father lived traded farm produce and sold it for premium prices to urban cooperatives. But cities where few people could afford farm produce had no need for real meat when protein came cheaply out of a processing plant and no need for field-grown vegetables when they were grown in multi-storey complexes under artificial light.

When the sunlight turned golden, we arrived at a medium-size town close to a lake, surrounded by forest-covered mountains.

The lake was clear and dark, and shimmered in the evening

sunlight, its surface barely disturbed by the breeze. The shoreline consisted of a mixture of rocky beaches, rocks and marshland, set against a backdrop of dense pine forest. It was tranquil, secluded and pretty.

The paved airfield on the other side of the town was a simple affair with a small administration building, a shelter with benches and a hangar for maintenance. Another gyrocopter and a couple of fixed-wing planes stood on the tarmac.

While the gyrocopter was a recent model, like the ones that had taken us into the canyon, I wasn't sure that the fixed-wing craft were still operational. Leaf litter and sand had gathered underneath the undercarriage of one of the craft, a model with two propellors that I strongly suspected to date from before the wars of the last century.

Wow, the last time I'd seen an aircraft that ran on oil-based aviation fuel was... I didn't even remember. It must have been when I visited an aviation show with my father, in Germany if I remembered it correctly.

"Holy crap, look at those aircraft," Nicha said.

Reida took pictures.

Sage turned off the gyrocopter's engine.

"Well, this is as far as I can go," he said. "That land on the other side of those mountains is Prairie, and they're none too friendly with us. Someone else will come tomorrow and take you across the border. From there on, you'll have to find your own way."

"Thank you for helping us this far."

"It's the least we could do," Sage said.

Did he really feel the need to apologise for the events? That wasn't necessary. It had nothing to do with him.

A bus came up to the gate. The driver was a leather-skinned woman in middle age by the name of Poppy. Sage introduced her as a distant cousin of his and said that she would take us to our accommodation.

She took us through the town and along a narrow road that meandered through forested hills and came out on the shore of a small lake where a couple of wooden cabins sat on a grassy slope.

Our cabin was the one closest to the water. It had a large living area and communal kitchen. Two boxes with pumpkins, a bag of rice, onions and various other food items stood on the table.

The cabin had four bedrooms, each of which with sleeping benches and bunk beds.

Thayu and I dumped our bags and then took Emi for a walk while Sage, Junco and Poppy messed about making a fire in the outdoor fire pit for roasting the pumpkins.

Emi's legs were only short, and she tripped easily, so we kept to the paved paths, strolling past the other cabins, which were all locked up. Some cabins had been well-maintained, but others showed signs of age, with moss growing on the steps and leaf litter on the verandas.

Emi babbled away, leaving us to guess what she was talking about. The soft springiness of the grass and moss fascinated her. She placed her little hands into the moss cushions and then giggled when the imprint lingered in the surface.

"This is a sad place," Thayu said.

"It's the wrong season. People come here in summer. It gets very hot in the cities."

"Only a few people. No one would stay in the neglected houses. It's a sad place because people don't enjoy its beauty."

"That's a strangely philosophical thing for you to say."

She blew out a breath. "I like going to your father's house. The village is nice and you can tell that the people who live there love it. This... is a sad place. People live in deserts because rich visitors pay for an illusion that no longer exists, and they've abandoned places that are beautiful."

"There is no work here for people. They want jobs."

But of course the concept of paying jobs was alien to Coldi. People in Athyl worked because they had been carefully selected for positions they were good at and enjoyed, and most basic items were distributed over the population through a barter system that was only marginally related to work performed.

Emi said, "Oh!"

She looked around, wide-eyed, listening.

Down near the lake shore, Sage's dog was barking like an idiot.

The Pengali kids had found a piece of wood big enough for them to use as a raft. They floated a short distance from the shore. The dog stood with Ayshada, who was throwing sticks at the raft. And the dog was barking because, being a dog, it wanted to chase sticks, except it also seemed to object to jumping into the water. I assumed it was cold.

The scent of cooking hung in the air.

"We better go back," I said.

By the time we'd arrived at our cabin, most people in our team had gathered on the veranda. Poppy was carrying a large dish of roast pumpkin to the table.

The Pengali kids came running to the table with the dog, all three wet and muddy.

Ynggi said something to them. I thought it was a joke about their failure to bring a fish.

We sat by the lake until well into the dark.

Ynggi and the Pengali kids played with the dog until they were all tired. It was the first time I saw the Pengali kids voluntarily go to bed at night.

Thayu went to put Emi to bed. I spotted her a bit later out the back of the cabin with Anyu, setting up a device.

Gradually, everyone left until only Junco and I were left in the dark. We sat on opposite sides of the table, both of us close to the fire, which still radiated heat. The night was getting cold.

"Well, I better go to bed as well," I said. "We'll have a big day tomorrow."

"Wait," he said. "There is something I want to say."

I had been about to get up, but sat back down.

He continued. "Sage and I will leave you tomorrow because you'll be crossing the border and they don't like us in Prairie. I have something I want to give to you now because I won't get the chance tomorrow morning."

I frowned, and he continued, "I know you've been trying to get me to talk about political things. Finding out where I stand or what people in this country think. If you really need to know, most people here voted against joining you lot, if they voted at all, and to be honest, most of them didn't." He let a silence lapse in which I might have asked him which way he voted, but didn't. Politics was deeply personal here, I got it.

"But there are certain things... if they start, they cannot be stopped. If you try, bad things happen. We've seen that before, if you get what I mean."

I didn't.

He groped in his pocket and gave me a datastick. It was an older model, like I'd use in high school.

"You were wondering about the people who worked in the space vehicle factory, whether I knew anyone who had worked there when they still operated, because ten thousand people used to work there. I don't, and to be honest, I was too young to care. An old man in town gave this to me a while ago, but I hadn't done anything with it until recently. It doesn't look very exciting. It's a list of all the people who used to be employed in the factory. Just names, birth dates, previous employment, that sort of stuff."

"Anything can be useful. Thank you. I hope you've kept a copy for your own use."

"Sage would have one. I don't. I don't want it. Too hot for me. I really don't want to be political."

"A list of personnel is political?"

"I was getting to that. It looks pretty boring until you investigate these people. People warned me that if I looked I'd find stuff I didn't want to know, and I was too chicken to look at it, but I finally did last night." He shrugged, clearly uncomfortable. "You'd think that out of something like ten thousand employees, some would have stayed in town when the factory closed, especially since they were mostly locals. A workshop manager could easily find work in town. There wouldn't be *much* work, exactly, but there would be *some*, right? Enough to employ one or two people at the very least."

I frowned at him.

"They're all gone, like they never existed. I couldn't find any of these people anywhere. You know, even if some would have gone into the woods, at least a few would have settled in a town nearby. At least the women. They're not usually too keen on camping out and stuff." He shrugged. "I can't find any of them. They've just... vanished."

I felt cold and remembered the words of the old warehouse owner in San Diego. The Southern California Aerospace Corps had their headquarters in the building for a few short years. They packed up and disappeared.

If these were the same people who had occupied many of the administrator roles at Midway Space Station, those had tried to take a ship and disappear to a secret place.

They were people who didn't want to be found. They had sent ships to Barresh that no one knew about until recently. According to the Thousand Islands Pengali, they still visited, although I'd been unable to verify that.

This news was highly consistent with what I already knew.

"One thing I don't understand," I said.

He looked up at me, his dark eyes with a sad expression. It was as if he knew roughly what I was going to say.

"Why haven't you said anything about this before?"

"You don't understand. You're from a free place, and a place where, if you have proof, people will believe it and not try to twist it to suit their political views. You know, this land is tired. I might live across the border, but I'm a Free American by heart. This is my country. It pains me to see what's happened to it. Over the years and year and years, our leaders have worn us out. They've made division about us, the common people. They've told us we're good and the other countries are bad and that's why we should keep living like we're in a war zone. It's all based on twisted facts and lies. After a while, you're so tired that you even start believing their garbage, because not to believe it is setting yourself up to be an outcast. But if you press almost any decent person in this country, they know that great wrongs were done in the name of our corrupt governments. It's not just Patterson and his vile bunch in Denver. The other governments are just as bad. I could tell stories about the shit that goes on in Miami. I have a distant cousin who drives leisure boats out of Havana and gets to deal with the government people who can afford to come on holidays. You should hear the stories he tells. It's the same all over. People only looking after themselves. The rest of us being too poor to challenge."

He blew out a breath.

"Long story short, people around the canyon area know that this group of space scientists went missing. That they left Mexico because they didn't want to fall under Nations of Earth, and that they came to America Free State, and that they hijacked that shuttle that came down in Texas and took it God knows where. And that all their twelve thousand odd employees just vanished off the official records. And if you say that some of their stuff turned up on other worlds, I think we have a problem. Because many of them left San Diego for all the wrong reasons. But no one wants to say anything because there is a lot of garbage associated with it all. Bribery, thievery, slavery and stuff like that. You know we used to be a slave country? Well, we never got over that. Myself, I have ancestors who used to be slaves. I have native blood. I have African blood. I have Spanish blood. I want to stand up and look you folk in the eye as a proud man and say that we've done good things or died trying. That's why I give this to you.

Because no one else will do the investigation you're doing. We're too tired and too afraid to do it. We can't. We have no money and equipment."

"Thank you for your trust in me," I said. "I hope that I'll be able to live up to some of your wishes."

"Oh, you will. Anything is better than what we have now. It's sad, but there it is."

It was late and getting cold by the dying fire.

I went inside where it was also cold, and the air was laced with the scent of musty bedding. I didn't sleep very well, and, by the sounds of people wandering around the cabin at night, neither did most of my team.

A few people went outside very early in the morning. I heard them rummage in the living room, whispering to each other in Coldi. Apparently another communication window was about to open up.

I only got up when I could see light outside the window. The mist hung low over the lake, and the surface reflected the misty trees like a perfect mirror. It was incredibly still and peaceful.

Sheydu and Anyu sat at the table where we had sat last night, with all their devices on the rough wooden planks.

I went to stand next to the fire pit, surprised that it still gave off some warmth.

"We have limited coverage," Sheydu said. "I'm trying to get the news and get a few messages out."

"Anything I need to know about?" I asked.

"There is a lot of activity in the air."

"Where does it come from?"

"Nothing to do with us."

Judging by the tone in her voice, this worried Sheydu.

"Is that a problem?"

"Well, yes. They're unknown ships. We can't trace what they are."

"There have been attacks from the air. You wouldn't expect

the local military to carry out surveillance? I would think that sort of activity would be normal. I very much doubt they'd carry any type of identification that we can read."

"We don't know what they're doing."

"You mean they're tracking us?"

She gave me a dark look.

I was venturing into questions she wasn't at liberty to answer.

So what was going on? Was it that the Asto military couldn't shadow us with these craft here? Or that she had expected Asto military craft to be nearby, but the presence of these unknown craft meant they couldn't be? Was she meant to have received some intelligence from them?

As we sat there, Junco came outside, bringing steaming mugs of tea. He set them on the table and stood back, watching what Sheydu and Anyu were doing from a distance.

The bus was coming up the road along the lake.

It stopped in front of the house and Poppy came out, shouting, "Breakfast!"

She brought a big box down the steps, which she took into the cabin, leaving a smell of fried eggs in her wake.

There were plenty of eggs and baked tomato, and bacon for those who wanted it, and fluffy white rolls and a box with sauces.

The Pengali kids were highly amused by the mustard bottle. If you squeezed it, the mustard came out.

As it turned out, Pengali *liked* mustard, and when we had finished eating, the two kids wouldn't let go of the bottle.

"It's almost empty. They can have it," Poppy said.

Pykka still clutched the bright red bottle like a treasure when he got onto the bus.

We had to say goodbye to Sage and Junco.

I told them I'd try to update them with how we were doing. They'd been good to us, and I suspected they were at least somewhat sympathetic to a political change that allowed the region to re-join the world, and Nations of Earth. Living in Mexico, Junco was already part of this world, but his heart was with his roots across the border. I hadn't yet looked at his information. I'd give it to the team when I had a chance. Likely, Deyu and Reida could do wonders with it. Once we located a device to read it.

Poppy drove the bus down a winding path through a forest. This was one of the few dense living forests I had seen. On the West Coast, most of the trees had been dead, and I was told there were never very many to begin with.

It was pretty here.

Once, the bus had to stop for a group of three large-eared deer crossing the road. Poppy made noises that she thought it was a pity she didn't have a gun, because they were good eating, but I didn't think she would have survived Deyu's anger had she shot them.

Then it was into endless plains. We kept going for most of the morning. I looked at maps, the kids played games, Veyada slept and the Pengali kids giggled about his snoring. Deyu was drawing deer. On the same page, she had drawn a squirrel and a beetle. And Sage's dog. Towards mid afternoon, we came to another medium-sized town.

Here, we had to get on a train and we said goodbye to Poppy.

CHAPTER TWENTY-FIVE

THE TRAIN STATION was a disorganised sea of travellers.

A line of vehicles waited to drop off passengers. Long queues of people waited at the ticket machines. I'd thought people booked places electronically, but apparently that was not so.

The station had four platforms, and all were crammed with passengers.

Entire families lugged bags bulging with their possessions. Children sat in strollers and other contraptions. People argued over sparse seating on the platforms, and over who could stand in front of the boards with the timetable.

Clay had pre-purchased a ticket, so the attendants who determined who could get onto the platform only needed to see proof of payment.

A helpful man said that our train was about to come in.

A few people in the sea of passengers noticed us coming down the stairs to the platform.

The information that a "group of aliens" were getting on the train spread like a ripple across the waiting crowd. People looked at us and then looked away.

Telaris and Deyu moved to the front of our group. They were both impressive and visibly armed.

People moved aside, not meeting our eyes.

I'd have expected some shouted protests, but no one said a word. It was strange and eerie.

These people were scared.

I thought of what Junco had said last night. They were afraid of us and their own authorities and would rather stay quiet to protect themselves and their families.

In all conflicts of the past, tyrants were helped by complicity of people who saw themselves as unable to affect change.

This was one of the favourite lines my professor at Mars University used to say.

It was one of the things you'd busily scribble down as a student but never understood until you'd seen it in action.

If a regime wore down their citizens enough, it took a land-slide to move the people into protesting. That was the stuff that civil wars were made of. This part of the world had already seen two of those. They were tired. People were going to think of themselves first, and this made the problem of entrenched power worse. It was a vicious circle.

Nicha and Telaris had hired two adjacent cabins for us, where we installed the children and dumped all our gear. My team took off their most obvious weapons, while keeping the concealed weapons.

The weapons went with the bags into the rack above the seats.

Most of the team stayed with the children while Evi, Nicha and I went in search of the food carriage.

We walked through the public cabin in single file.

Evi attracted a lot of attention. He'd put on sunglasses and with a bit of goodwill, his bronze-coloured hair looked like it might have been dyed. But most dark-skinned people in Mexico had not been as dark as he was, and really dark people were definitely not as common across the border. He looked like a hired bodyguard and that, in turn, focused attention on the rest of us.

Several people were watching news on devices, and while we walked past, I tried to catch a glimpse of what they were looking at. The headlines were revealing.

Heroic army effort underway to protect citizens.

Some of those soldiers were also on the train, mostly young men travelling in groups of three or four. They wore a basic uniform in army green without many decorations. They seemed nervous, and I was wondering what the minimum age was for kids to join the armed forces, because many looked young enough to still be in school.

When I was at university, one of my professors placed a great deal of importance on knowledge of world history and we'd read about the young men who were so keen to sign up for the First World War that they lied about their birth date, only for masses of them to be slaughtered on the battlefield.

What good could an army of teenagers be in response to attack by an Aghyrian entity? Or was everyone lying about the origins of the attack and did they know where it came from? Like South Africa?

I was starting to see ghosts everywhere.

I caught a glimpse of a vid showing Celia Braddock declaring in a rousing speech that she would send the full force of the army to crush the bastards.

"You heroes can do a lot more than they expect," she shouted. "They won't be surprised. We will take back our country and avenge this cowardly attack."

The audience in the vid was cheering and yelling, and a couple of train passengers joined the owner of the device in watching it.

Whatever I saw of Celia Braddock, I liked her less and less. She seemed to thrive on short accusatory statements. Her speeches held little substance. They were full of angry rhetoric and low on details. She pretended that hers was the only country affected.

"What army?" I asked Nicha, who was walking behind me. Because I was unsure that the four countries would work together, and they were probably accusing each other, as well as Mexico and Canada, of collaborating with the attackers.

"I doubt she cares, as long as the people love it," he said. "You can't argue with her. She just makes up stuff just so that she is right. She's always done that."

He grew up in London, home of a large population of north American refugees. I had asked him to talk about what he knew before our trip, and he said he'd been very young and occupied with other things. However, since coming here, he'd made some valuable observations that stemmed from his internalised experiences. That people were protective of all four countries despite their differences. That they all viewed Nations of Earth as a bully. That they didn't take kindly to outsiders analysing the North American conflicts. That they viewed Mexico and Canada as invaders who had illegally obtained some of their land. That they had pride in self-sufficiency, even if that stubbornness also led to food shortages and the necessity of rationing.

They outwardly presented as a proud people who argued that they didn't need the rest of the world. Behind the scenes, though, Junco had told me that everyone was tired.

When we got to the food carriage, they only sold doughy rolls, and no vegetarian options were available, so I only bought food for the non-vegetarians and the others would have to use their rapidly dwindling supply of Asto military rations.

When we came back to our carriage, the first thing I noticed were two bubbles floating near the ceiling in the corridor.

Oh no.

We had two cabins. I'd noticed that the security team was holding a meeting in the first and all the kids sat in the second. I yanked open the door. An avalanche of bubbles spilled out. The cloud was so thick that I could barely see anything. Bubbles stuck to my face and in my hair and my hands.

Opening the door released a cloud of them into the hallway, which meant the density in the cabin dropped, allowing me to see in.

Ayshada was laughing so much that his face was bright red.

Pykka sat with the mustard bottle on his lap. He had attached its nozzle to the bubble blowing contraption with a small piece of hose. He was just squeezing the bottle, causing the contraption to release a cloud of bubbles into the tiny cabin.

He saw me, gasped and hid the thing behind his back, but this only caused the thing to blow out another puff of bubbles as it got caught between his back and the seat.

His eyes widened, like a frightened doggie that has just peed on the carpet.

"You know what I'm going to say," I said.

"I want to make bubbles!" he said.

"Not inside. It's very annoying. Look, Emi has soap in her eyes."

She was wiping her eyes furiously. I picked her up. She started crying. I tried to wipe her face, but the bubble soap was very sticky.

Pykka pushed himself back in his seat, his arms crossed over his chest. "This place is boring. There aren't even any fish to catch." He glared at Larrana in the corner, but refrained from mentioning the collection and how sick he was of listening to Larrana carry on about it. "I want to play and hunt."

"You'll get to blow your bubbles, I promise."

But clearly he didn't believe me.

Considering how active and free the Pengali kids were at home in Barresh, going fishing and collecting things and climbing things, I thought it was a wonder they'd behaved this well for this long. But they were getting tired. We were going to have a difficult few days ahead with them.

Junco had warned us that we'd soon cross the border and there might be shenanigans from guards if they felt like kicking up trouble. He had advised us to stay vigilant.

The train slowly slid into the night. There wasn't a lot of room to lie down in the cabins, so we tried to sleep sitting up. This wasn't as unsuccessful as it sounded. All the days' worth of travel had made all of us exhausted.

We took turns in sleeping on the pile of bags.

The children slept anyway, the Pengali youngsters curled up together with their tails wrapped around them.

As far as I knew, the train crossed the border without problems. I must have been asleep, because I didn't even notice that we stopped, although Deyu said that we had, and that guards had come aboard the train but hadn't entered any of the cabins.

We got off the train when it was still dark. Junco had told us to take a bus to a regular airport where it was also busy with panicked people with entire families and lots of bags.

We got something miserable to eat from a harried and too-busy food outlet and sat in a quiet corner while the sun came up over the eastern horizon. It was a cloudy morning, and the sky briefly went bright orange before the sun disappeared behind the clouds with an ominous flash of bright orange that lasted a few minutes.

Our flight to New York departed after breakfast.

It was one of the suborbital type, with comfortable seats, where the children soon fell asleep.

We were now so far out of the influence of anyone who could rescue us, I felt we might as well be back on the snowy surface of Tamer and surrounded by violent meat-eating dinosaurs.

But during a brief meeting with myself, Sheydu and Veyada, we had decided that it was time to prepare our escape after we'd seen the drone.

Sheydu and Reida had confirmed its locality in a military depot about half an hour out of New York. We needed to plan how, once we saw the drone, we would leave the continent. The first step was to let Amarru know, and then to contact Nations of Earth about what we were doing. Presumably, they would want to see proof of what we discovered. I wrote those messages and put them in our send queue.

We tried to look as inconspicuous as we could. Nicha had grown up doing this, wearing local types of clothes, dying his hair, trying to look like a local, but the others had not.

It was hard to shut the children up. The Pengali kids were cranky, Ileyu was cranky, and Ayshada had eaten something that made him thirsty. When we weren't looking, he had scored a container of a sweet drink that made him hyper-active, and in need to visit the facilities several times. Larrana's wheelchair was getting a fair amount of attention.

I was sure that the other passengers knew that we were from off world, and that they would report it to someone, and we would meet with trouble sooner rather than later.

This flight took us straight to New York in about two hours.

We arrived when a storm was coming in, and the tall buildings of the city were silhouetted ominously against the cloudy sky.

From the air, the damage done during the drone attacks was clear. Several buildings had collapsed, leaving rubble and smoking holes in the ground. A pall of smoke still hung over parts of the city.

This was much worse than Los Angeles. And other than the *Aliens!* accusations, we'd seen no clear evidence of where the attack had come from.

Reida and Deyu were preparing for the next, most dangerous, stage in our journey.

Taking the bulk of our group to a safe hotel.

Contacting Amarru with details of where we were and arranging a pickup through someone in the register.

Finding out the fine details of how to get to the base where the downed drone was held.

Getting enough materials to allow us to sneak in.

I was guessing it also involved communicating with the Asto military who were shadowing us on where we were going and what to do if things went wrong.

The craft landed, and we were allowed off the flight with the other passengers not much later.

But as we entered the arrival hall, a uniformed officer stopped Evi and Zyana at the front of the group and directed us to a room to the side. Sheydu and Isharu went into a heightened level of alert. Sheydu inserted her hand under her jacket.

A group of armed personnel was waiting for us in the room.

The officers surrounded us, a menacing wall of grey uniforms with badges that said Metropolitan Police. We were outnumbered.

"We'd like to speak to you," one of them said, his eyes searching the group for someone to address. Eventually, his eyes met mine.

I made a *back off* gesture to my team. We could absolutely not afford an incident right here, in a busy airport where people streamed past us and everyone would carry a device that could record what happened.

The use of off-world weapons would not be a good idea.

There was nothing we could do except comply with their demands.

CHAPTER TWENTY-SIX

THE OFFICERS TOOK us aside in a large and empty room inside the airport building, where we sat on hard seats while waiting for them to decide what they'd do with us. We needed escorts to visit the bathroom, which was down a long hallway—I went there several times with various kids.

The kids didn't take long to declare that they were bored, and, unlike us adults, had no inhibition to show it. The officers had not taken the bag containing the bubble device off the Pengali kids, although they'd looked at it and deemed it not dangerous. They might regret that decision.

After taking our IDs, and examining them slowly, in a different office, one by one, the officers declared that they needed to speak to a supervisor, and would take us to their head office, which was elsewhere. We were then all bundled into a van and taken across the city. By that time, it was mid-afternoon.

I wasn't quite up with the plan devised by Sheydu and the others, but I was sure they'd booked accommodation for tonight. I'd make sure I did my utmost best to get us there.

The police van was small and cramped. We still had all our luggage, but I wondered how long this would last and when and how many of our supplies and electronics would be taken off us. Veyada and Mereeni were busily reading up on legal stuff. The police could only hold us without a charge for a day, but in the past, I'd also found that all those rules didn't apply to those not holding an Earth-based citizenship, which was all of our group except myself.

While we were being driven, Reida collected data on where we were. He seemed to have limited Exchange coverage, and I asked him to send the prepared messages to Nations of Earth now, rather than later. I had a feeling this situation could get ugly very quickly.

The van took us through busy streets.

We passed an area affected by the drone attack, but a barrier stood across the side street that had sustained damage, and we couldn't see anything except construction equipment and emergency vehicles entering the area past a checkpoint.

I thought we were getting close to the city centre but didn't want to distract Reida to ask.

Old buildings took up both sides of the street.

There weren't many people about. Emergency crews occupied almost every intersection.

The main police office was in one of these streets, a modern building with an underground car park down a ramp with a steel gate.

Different officers waited for us here, with guns drawn, fanning around the vehicle as it stopped. These guys didn't mess around.

One of the officers came into the cabin when we had stopped.

We were told to leave everything except our personal items in the van. They searched us. We had to take all weapons and communication devices off. They even found the feeder in Isharu's hair. I had to explain what it was, and she had to take it off, too.

I watched Sheydu during this procedure, but she underwent

the search with a steeled look on her face. So did Thayu. So did Isharu.

Reida was the most upset when they asked him to leave all his electronics behind.

But the others? No. They'd expected it. They had contingency plans. They had backups. What they were... I guess I'd find out soon.

I made a fuss because that was my job. In absence of a reason for our arrest, I demanded a formal statement that our possessions would be returned as soon as we left this building. I said that I wouldn't enter the building until I had that statement. The officers were very obviously annoyed. A supervisor was called. I blustered my way through potential diplomatic disasters if they treated us improperly. I got my statement.

They took us through double security doors into a lift foyer. By now, there were at least twenty armed officers, keeping us separated in small groups.

Sheydu was in a different group. I met her eyes in between the uniforms. She gave a single appreciative nod, as if saying, *You keep doing your thing, we'll do ours.*

On second thought, Reida's protest at having to give up his equipment was probably an act, too.

Thayu stood next to me holding Emi, but she couldn't have looked less motherly had she tried. Her expression was lethal, her eyes took in everything that happened, every notice on the walls, every tiny move that the officers made.

Veyada's face held that distant look that he used to wear so often when I had first met him, and he was part of Ezhya's guard association.

Nalya stood next to him, his expression emotionless and hard.

Ayshada held his father's hand, his chin in the air.

The Pengali were in the group furthest from me. All I could see of them were three tails—one large and two small. The large tail, which I thought belonged to Ynggi, waved at thigh height and snapped occasionally, which startled the officers the first time he did it.

They took us five floors up in the lift in three groups, because the lift wasn't big enough to hold all of us at the same time.

I tried to remember as much of the details of the surroundings as possible.

They allocated us a room at the end of the corridor. It was a corner room with windows on two sides that looked out over the street and the buildings opposite the police station. From one of the windows, you could see through a gap between two buildings to a river.

The room contained couches and a low table.

"Someone will be along to bring something to eat," one officer said.

He didn't ask what we could or couldn't eat, so I told him in clear terms. When he objected to say that they might not have vegetarian food available, I demanded that we could go out to buy our own. He caved in on my demands then, because obviously, us leaving the building was out of the question.

He also said that we would be interviewed individually. I said that most of us wouldn't understand the questions, but that didn't appear to bother him.

I asked him if they had translators, but he didn't answer the question.

He left us, locking the door behind him.

If rolling eyes had been a Coldi thing, Sheydu would have done it. But my team were professionals, and they went into stealth mode straight away. Not a word was spoken about the situation. They did all of it with hand signals, after they had established where cameras were likely to be, and faced away from them.

The room contained an entertainment screen. The kids grew tired of exploring the very boring room, so we had to turn it on and let them watch some stupid, loud and shouty show. It included singing and dancing across the stage. The music was fake-cheerful and repetitive.

Ayshada seemed baffled by it.

He asked Larrana what this was, but Larrana said he didn't know. His voice sounded flat.

All the kids sat on the floor, watching it like zombies. They were worn out, physically as well as mentally.

The officers started the interviews not much later, with Deyu.

I silently wished them good luck getting anything out of her.

While Deyu was gone, Nicha paced back and forth in front of the window. He never spoke much about it, but I was sure that being questioned, yelled at, by police in a room by himself with no one to help him, brought back memories for him of the time when I'd just started my job, was still working for Nations of Earth, and President Sirkonen had been murdered. They had suspected Nicha with no evidence. They'd held him captive for weeks without allowing him contact with the Exchange or legal representation.

I went to stand in his way and stopped him when he walked past me.

"It's different now," I said in a low voice. "You have us. There are quite a number of us who don't have local ID."

He met my eyes, his expression intense. "That won't stop them."

"Yes, it will."

"I don't want my father to become involved in this." We all knew how close Asha had been to ordering an operation by the Asto army under his command to free his son.

"He won't be."

Deyu was back quickly, and this calmed Nicha. Next they took Isharu, who came back really quickly. She genuinely didn't understand any Isla.

My team communicated with each other and Deyu in sign language about the interview. She indicated that it was all right, as long as you pretended not to understand any of their words.

Next Anyu went in, then Zyana, and then Thayu. She gave Emi to me and walked out with the officers holding her back straight. Things like this never seemed to faze her much, but that was looking at it from our side. Even when we were wearing feeders, she usually kept that part of her thoughts well-hidden. Thayu did *not* like to admit fear.

I waited, feeling nervous. I presumed Thayu would be fine, and she'd been in worse situations, but still didn't like it.

Then I worried about the kids.

Ynggi and Jaki had kept them quiet, and the Pengali youngsters were asleep, but when they woke up, they'd be full of beans and the dreadful show that was still blaring from the screen would not keep them entertained much longer. Even Larrana had grown bored with it. He half-lay on the floor in the strange position that only he could take up with his harness and was using his thumb to spin one of the wheels.

When Thayu came back, she made a sign to indicate that she thought the officers were idiots. Nicha went in after Thayu, giving me a nervous look as he left.

Thayu went to inspect the tray of sandwiches an officer had brought in and put on the table.

Despite what I'd told them, most of them contained some type of meat, which other members of my team had already taken out, so she likewise fished out the floppy pink slices and deposited them on the tray. She pulled a face when biting into the bread. It was gluey and sticky. And as usual, too sweet. Emi didn't have a problem with it. She reduced a sandwich to crumbs in no time. She wanted another one, but Thayu didn't trust that it would end well, so she produced an energy bar from her bag. These were from our dwindling reserves of Asto military supplies. They were highly concentrated, very spicy, and usually kept Emi busy for a while. But today she decided she didn't want it. The gluggy sand-wiches were much more interesting. So Thayu took another one, making sure she scraped off all traces of meat and butter.

By this time, Nicha returned and told Evi to go in.

I looked for traces of discomfort on Nicha's face, but found none.

He stopped at the entertainment screen, and picked up Ayshada, who had fallen asleep. His little chubby hand twitched when his father carried him across the room to deposit him on the couch next to Larrana, who had borrowed Deyu's reader. Earlier, she had explained a mind game to him, which he'd been playing since. A very proper Coldi game.

Nicha then came to me.

"You were quick," I said.

"Yes, I had no interest in speaking to them. These people are really convinced that we are responsible for this, and there is not much we can say that convinces them otherwise. You should hear all the things they say about Nations of Earth and *gamra*."

Yes, having been here for several days now, I could completely imagine.

After Evi came back, Telaris went in.

Evi also came to me and repeated the things Nicha had said. Everyone was careful with what they replied, because the room was sure to be bugged. We weren't about to give the police any ammunition to further attack us, or make up additional conclusions aided through poor translation.

Deyu was fiddling with her equipment. She had told me in bits and pieces that they had taken photos of her from the side and the front and standing up and sitting down, and they had asked her to remove her suit so that she could be photographed only in a singlet. In case of Deyu, that seemed disturbingly voyeuristic, because she had an impressive physique.

This did not improve my opinion of the officers undertaking the questioning.

I was the last one to go into the interview room.

Two officers marched me down.

The room was a window-less concrete box, a couple of steps long in each direction. There was a table in the room's corner and a couple of darker coloured panels at the top of the wall where I assumed recording cameras to be. A single chair stood in the middle of the room.

Two officers I had not yet seen before sat behind the desk.

Each corner of the room was also occupied by a guard, one of them having stepped forward to open the door for me.

I was told to sit in the single empty chair in the middle of the room, surrounded by six armed officers.

One, who looked like a senior officer with extra decorations on his shirt pocket, met my eyes. He was an olive-skinned man with salt-and-pepper hair and dark eyes. His name tag said Santos.

"For the purpose of the interview, state your full name occupation and place of residence."

I had known that this was coming, and I had debated what angle to take. I legally had two identities, two legal names that I could use.

I had earlier decided to go with my Coldi name, which was the one I used for most of my official functions, but seeing these intimidating officers, I changed my mind at the last minute, because they would probably react better to my Earth name.

"My name is Cory Wilson. I am officially registered as a citizen of New Zealand. I have not lived in New Zealand for the past twenty-five years, and I currently live in Barresh which is the headquarters of *gamra*."

"Huh," the man next to Santos said. "Can you provide proof of that?"

He was younger. The shape of his face suggested that he was of African descent, although his skin was lighter than his colleague's. His name tag said Flynn.

"I have the documentation to back it up."

"You don't look like no one from New Zealand I know," Flynn said.

I was tempted to ask him how many people from New Zealand he knew. Not many, I would guess. Nor would he appreciate the question.

Santos said, "Explain to me how you are on this travel document under a different name."

So they'd gotten a warning through the airline?

"I have two legal names, one I was born with in New Zealand and one since I was accepted into the Domiri clan with my partner."

"You have been using these two names interchangeably with each other?"

"I have been quite consistent in using my Coldi name, because it is the capacity in which I am here. I have no wish to to disguise myself as otherwise."

Santos snorted. "You can give it any spin you want, but when you look at the facts, you've been playing a game with authorities."

"Do look at the facts. I have two legal identities. Both are attached to me and not to any other person. Looking up one identity will bring up the other."

"How do we know that you're not a spy?"

"If I was a spy, would I be travelling across the country with such a large group that includes children?"

He looked me up and down. Clearly, he didn't believe a word I said.

"So then, what are you doing here?"

"You will have seen that we have with us a young boy who uses a wheelchair. He is the son of an important official on Asto. It has been his lifelong wish to visit the theme parks. This was why we came."

"Hah. An alien boy wants to visit Earth theme parks?"

"Yes. It's been a bit of an ordeal to be honest, but it is what he wanted, and I promised it, because I owed a favour to his family."

"Huh," Santos said again, and then he said nothing for a while. Then he continued, "You were not exactly at the theme park any more. We have recorded you visiting Los Angeles, but then you came across the border, and there was no reason for you to do that."

"We travelled mostly overland to New York because most regular travel options were closed because of the attacks. Someone from the Exchange will pick us up here."

"Don't be smart. I'm talking about your inland trip prior to leaving on this overland dash."

"There were some natural sites that I was interested in. When we returned from those, the attacks had happened and all air traffic was cancelled."

"You were spotted in an area that's not regularly visited by tourists."

I wondered who had told them that. The townsfolk or the military.

"No. I wanted to see the Grand Canyon. It's been a dream of mine since I learned about it at school in New Zealand. We also have some team members who are interested in hunting. They wanted to hunt rabbits, and our guide knew a location where we could do this. Our guide grew up in this area and this is why we went there."

Santos glared at me. I wasn't sure if I had convinced him. Probably not.

"Hunt, huh? Weren't you just telling us that your team members are vegetarians?"

"Not all of them. The Pengali are keen hunters."

"Pengali?"

"The ones with the tails."

"Ah, the monkeys."

That again. Of course, the officers hadn't asked Ynggi or Jaki to come for their interviews. It was not a language thing. Most members of my team didn't speak any Isla either. It was because they thought the Pengali were not human. For fuck's sake, when were people on Earth going to can this attitude?

Santos made a signal to Flynn next to him, who had said little during the interview, and they both left the room, leaving me in the company of the four guards.

I was wondering how long this was going to take. My stomach was making gurgling noises. Those sandwiches weren't very filling or satisfying.

But Santos came back not too much later in the company of a female officer.

She was short and broad in stature, with short-cropped grey hair. Her uniform carried a lot more glittering pins and stars than Santos', so I assumed her to be a senior.

She took the seat that Flynn had earlier vacated, while Santos sat in the second seat.

She nodded at me and then asked all the same questions that Santos had already asked me.

I gave them the same answers. This was part of the game they were playing with us, and because I was the only one who understood their language adequately, they concentrated on me.

Then I asked, "Can I ask why we're here? What have we done that warrants this special and costly treatment? We have accommodation booked for the night. Are we allowed to go there? We have a group of children with us and we've been travelling for days, trying to get home."

"In this country, we have a policy investigate all unauthorised visitors."

"We have permits. We have cooperated with you. You've found nothing. I request that all our possessions be returned and that we are allowed to continue on with our travel."

She said nothing, but merely thanked me for my cooperation, and then she and Santos left the room.

Two of the guards returned me to the others.

Both Thayu and Nicha turned to the door, worry making way for relief on their faces.

"What kept you so long?" Nicha asked.

"The fact that they could talk to me for a change?"

"Did they say what they wanted or what they're accusing us of?"

"No, because there is nothing." I glanced at the sandwich plate on the table, now completely empty. Something was going to have to happen soon.

It did.

Flynn came to the door and told us we'd be taken to our accommodation.

I asked him if this meant we were free to go, but he didn't answer that question.

But going to the accommodation was better than sitting here, so we bundled up the kids. Emi had been asleep and was cranky. Ileyu kept insisting that she was hungry. In the last few days, she had picked up a few words that she could pronounce well enough for us to understand, and boy, she made sure we heard them.

We followed Santos and a bunch of guards to the underground car park, where a bus was waiting. Our luggage sat on the ground in a pile next to it.

Sheydu and Reida quickly went through and seemed happy that everything was there.

The officers had no reason to detain us and had found no reason to keep us here. I had no idea how long that would last. Especially considering our plans. If we wanted to sneak into this military depot shed where the drone was held, we had to be quick because they were on our case. Our easy run was over.

CHAPTER TWENTY-SEVEN

THE BUS TOOK us to the accommodation we had booked. We made sure every one of our possessions came with us. We'd have to double-check the content of the bags to see if anything was missing.

While we checked in with the receptionist, who seemed rather baffled by the size and composition of our team, the driver waited outside.

Oh yes, we were being shadowed.

The hotel had allocated us three adjacent rooms on one of the top floors of the building. The rooms all had internal doors and two of those could be opened so that the three rooms formed an apartment.

Ayshada had woken up and was so cranky that he didn't understand that not all of those doors opened. Some went to other rooms that we hadn't rented.

He had a screaming fit when Nicha suggested that he stop banging on the locked doors because there might be other people on the other side.

Yes, we were all hungry and cranky.

Finding something to eat was a priority.

Nicha offered to go with Evi and Telaris to buy something. I suspected that he offered so he could take Ayshada for a walk because once he was in a shouty mood, there was no stopping this kid.

They left, including Ayshada, and the rest of us took turns to freshen up.

One of the rooms had a kitchenette, and the surrounding smooth floor made for a suitable surface for Pengali dice and marble games which occupied the kids.

Not being interested in games, Nalya had inspected the drawer to the desk and found a book inside. He had taken a liking to books. Several of our accommodation rooms had contained books with pictures of attractions in the area for tourists to visit, but he was disappointed that this book was very plain and contained closely printed text and no pictures. It was left to me, while Thayu bathed Emi and showered, to explain the concept of "religion" to him.

Nalya tried very hard.

I didn't think he got it. Coldi were very good at numbers. They were also good at extrapolations and predictions. They were poor at concepts that were hard to prove or fictional. Whole *gamra* speeches had been written about whether Earth's religions were fictional and whether *gamra* should allow entities that used something you couldn't prove as a basis for government. Fortunately, I'd always managed to keep out of those discussions.

When I grew up, I was told that a person's beliefs were private and I preferred to keep it that way.

Not that this made it any easier to explain to an inquisitive thirteen-year-old.

Fortunately, Nicha and the others came back. Ayshada was proudly carrying a box which contained several smaller boxes and parcels.

He put it on the table with the words, "See, Dad, I didn't drop it." Clear words they were, too. He was growing up fast.

Once he opened the parcels, a wonderful smell spread through the room.

There was fresh bread and crumbed and deep fried squid and fish, oven-baked vegetables with cheese, vegetable curry and salads.

We were all hungry, and the food was gone in no time.

We installed all the children in one room where they could play or watch noisy shows.

It was time to plan our next move.

Evi and Telaris reported that while going out for food, they'd scouted the area for surveillance activity. Some guards had been sitting in our floor's laundry room, they said. They wore service uniforms but didn't act like hotel staff. There was also someone in the building's foyer pretending to be a business guest, and others were hanging around in the street.

Thayu and Deyu found out that our rooms were not bugged to the level that rooms at *gamra* would be. This was just as well, because our normal procedure to counter surveillance bugging was to meet in the bathroom, and the bathrooms attached to the rooms were tiny, too small even for two people, let alone our entire team.

"As soon as we leave this building, we will have people on our tail," Sheydu said. "We need to find another way out."

Nicha said, "Good luck with that. We're on the twentieth floor."

"I don't have a good feeling about this operation," Mereeni said. "Would there be a legal avenue that we can use to demand to see the remains of this drone instead of trying to break in?"

"Good luck with that, too," Sheydu said. Sometimes she still liked to needle Mereeni.

Veyada came to the rescue. "There might be such an avenue, if we were in a country that was a member of Nations of Earth."

Which we were not.

"But even so, I wouldn't like the prospect of it actually happening," he added.

"Why not? Atlantia signed the agreement on the exchange of information in conflict," Mereeni continued. "It's called the Bangkok Accord because that was where it was signed by most countries on Earth. It governs the right to demand verifiable data as a basis for conflicts and sanctions."

Yes, I'd almost forgotten about that, and I'd learned about it in my degree. There was a time that countries sought to limit information coming into their countries so they could control the news accessible to their population.

There had been wars, uprisings and boycotts based on information that later proved to be false. The accord gave the aggrieved country and international bodies the right to demand to see the data that was the basis of the policy or military action.

"I doubt it applies to *gamra*," I said. "Even if it does, someone will object to our interpretation of the accord and while we could potentially prove that it applies to *gamra*, who knows how long that's going to take, and how much the Atlantian government is going to manipulate the evidence?"

Veyada nodded. "Any time you take a fight to a court, it takes years."

"We don't have years," Sheydu said.

Isharu nodded. Thayu nodded as well. They had always signed up for my stealth operation.

"That doesn't change the fact that we're being watched," Mereeni continued. "They're looking for a way to arrest us and turn this into a diplomatic incident. If we create an incident, then this will harm existing agreements. Everyone will be upset with us, including Nations of Earth and *gamra*."

She was right, of course, but what was the thing they said about hindsight? If I'd known that there was going to be an attack by unidentified drones on the world's cities, I wouldn't have come to Earth at all, let alone this part of it.

"We just have to be quick," Sheydu said.

Several people nodded. Isharu, Anyu and Thayu all cared little for diplomacy.

"We could bust our way out of this room," Reida said. "We have enough people to overwhelm a couple of second-rate security guards."

"It's not those guards we need to avoid," Sheydu said. "I've seen the size of their military. Their equipment is not that good, but they make up for it in numbers."

"And I'm *not* having the Asto military involved," I said.

Nods all around. They knew this. I'd said it before.

I continued, "I would also prefer to do this without dead bodies. The relationship between Atlantia and Nations of Earth is precarious enough without us causing a diplomatic incident. Mereeni is right about that. We have to deal with two more years of Dekker, and that's if he doesn't get re-elected. I *have* to build up some sort of working relationship with the man."

"We can sneak out of here," Ynggi said.

Both Thayu and Isharu said, "How?"

And Nicha repeated, "There is security in the corridor and we're on the twentieth floor."

Ynggi gestured with his tail to Reida, and Reida gave him his reader. Ynggi didn't normally use devices—and I reminded myself that I should give him one and insist that he use it—and he asked Reida to bring up something.

A schematic.

A representation of the building.

We were on the third floor from the top, he said. The building had two lift shafts, one for general use and one for services only. The services lift gave access to one extra floor below ground, where things like storage and the laundry were located. The emergency stairs also led there. We could get out that way, he said.

"But I'm missing how we're going to get to these stairs," Sheydu said.

"It's easy. See this room?" He pointed with his tail. "That's one of our rooms. The room next to it has its main entrance in a little alcove next to the emergency stairs."

"But the door between our room and that room is locked."

"I can probably open it," Reida said.

"I'm sure you could," Telaris said, "but you'd also damage the door and set off an alarm."

"We don't need to do anything like that," Ynggi said. "We can just climb in. Over the balcony. The door is open."

"We're on the twentieth floor," Nicha and Deyu said together.

"That's not a problem," Ynggi said.

He jumped up and went to the balcony door. An icy breeze came in when he opened it.

"Keep it shut," Anyu said.

I squeezed through the gap before pushing the door closed.

Up here, the sounds from the street had faded and mingled with the general hum of traffic, the electric buses, the driverless vans that trundled along their designated paths.

The street lights and the pale pools of light they created seemed a long distance away. The light was hazy through the remnants of smoke from the extinguished fires.

I shivered. The breeze was cold indeed.

The balcony to the next room was not very far away.

Linking it and the balcony to our room was a thin stone ledge along the wall, and a gap twenty floors deep.

Ynggi said, "We can climb onto the ledge and get into the other room. Then we can open the door and you can come through. We can leave through the door without being seen."

I stared into the depth. "But it's an awfully long way down there."

"That doesn't worry us."

CHAPTER TWENTY-EIGHT

THE DEPTH of the drop freaked me out.

Ynggi repeated that it was no big deal, because they'd be careful and Pengali were good at climbing. And it was only a short distance. And was it really any different from climbing to balconies in Barresh?

Even Reida could do it, they said.

"I don't usually mind heights," I said. "But this is excessive."

"You don't have to do any of the climbing," Ynggi said. "You don't need to worry about it."

Was I allowed to be worried on their behalf?

We didn't have another option.

Before we did anything, we had to make sure that everyone was comfortable, fed and well-dressed.

When Nicha, Evi and Telaris had gone shopping, they had bought several non-perishable food items. They now distributed those to other team members, who stuffed the snack bars and packets in their bags or jackets.

In their minds, the group was already divided. Some supplies for me, Sheydu, Deyu, Reida, Ynggi and Evi who would go to look at the drone. The rest of the supplies for the others.

We needed to re-pack the bags to contain everything each group needed, but also so we could easily carry all our things. This meant removing personal items from my bag and replacing them with various boxes and packets Sheydu gave me.

Nothing that was explosive, she told me when I asked.

I wasn't sure whether to believe her. All that stuff was damn heavy.

Since Nicha and Veyada were the most senior team members who would be in charge of the larger group, they needed to be given all the necessary information.

Nicha booked accommodation for them in a town close to the base. Once we were out of the clutches of the police surveillance, they could make their own way there. Failing that, they could distract the surveillance from what we were doing.

Sheydu and Isharu passed around several scripts for potential scenarios and what each group member would do and what events would trigger certain actions.

Deyu was to be our communications person, and Anyu would be theirs.

While all this was going on, we all took short breaks to sleep, although I had to admit I slept little when my turn came.

Finally, we got the children out of bed just before dawn.

They sat in a tidy circle on the carpet, eating their portions without complaining. They were silent, tired probably, but I'd started to notice this odd behaviour in Coldi children. I wondered if they had an instinct that fired when they were in a stressful situation. They faded into the background, did what adults told them without question, and listened. I'd never seen this type of behaviour before, and it had to be an instinct because I would never expect it from Ayshada. But there he was, obediently doing as he was told.

We hadn't told the kids anything about our plans, but they seemed to understand that this was serious.

We gathered in our room, all dressed in warm, dark-coloured clothes.

Sheydu once again shared the plan and reminded each person of their task.

There was a tram line outside the building. It went to a terminal where one could hire driverless cars. We planned to take those.

Typing the name of the military depot in a driverless vehicle's destination menu would raise eyebrows, but the main road led not too far past it, and it went to the town where Nicha had booked the accommodation under his long-disused Earth identity that was no longer valid. But we'd worry about that once it came to paying the bill. In my experience, people cared much less about who you were when you presented them with money.

While using this driverless vehicle, we would make it stop along the road, and our smaller team would get off and walk across the fields to the military depot.

The major risk was getting out of this accommodation and out of the city unnoticed for long enough that we could sneak into the compound. Deyu and Reida had already done a lot of research about this locality.

Ynggi and Jaki got ready. They took off most of their clothes, because apparently, one couldn't climb while fully dressed. I made sure that they bundled their clothes in a pack on their backs. Then they went out over the balcony. Ynggi climbed over the edge and shuffled the short distance along the ledge to the next balcony. I was glad when he was over the railing. It was a very long drop down there.

He then caught the rope that Jaki threw him, and Jaki climbed over as well.

Then Jaki threw the end of the rope back so Reida could tie it on our balcony.

Reida climbed onto the railing. He hesitated ever so slightly, but let himself over the edge and shimmied along the two ropes.

He made it to the balcony, and climbed over, and then opened the balcony door to the room next to ours.

They went inside. A bit later, the lock to the connecting door clicked, and the door opened.

As quietly as we could, we carried everything across into that room.

The weapons were out, carried in Sheydu's, Deyu's and Telaris' arm brackets.

Sheydu and Deyu moved to the door. Telaris and Evi were behind them. They opened the door and looked into the corridor.

"The exit to the stairs is right here," Deyu said.

Ynggi nodded, a satisfied look on his face.

"Is it open?" I asked.

She went outside and tested the door handle. "It is."

It would be silly for an emergency exit not to be open, but stranger things had happened.

Since we were now out of view of the "hotel employees" who still occupied the laundry room by the sound of their voices, we could move without being seen, as long as we were quiet.

Sheydu held open the door to the room and Deyu held open the door to the stairwell and we all walked through as quietly as we could. Deyu shut the door behind us without making a noise.

It was a long way down the stairs. We counted down the numbers painted on the wall next to the doors on each landing.

On the ground floor, Deyu opened the door a fraction to peek out and shut it again almost immediately.

"There are people out there," she said.

So we went down one extra floor and the end of the staircase.

The door there came out in a concrete-lined corridor with doors at regular intervals. It led to a foyer for the service lift and next to that, an underground car park.

The rows of vehicles that stood there all carried the hotel's logo on the doors. The only vehicle that didn't belong to the hotel, a panel van, was double-parked in front of the lift entrance. The back door stood open.

Racks with tools lined the sides of the back compartment. Cardboard boxes were stacked on the floor.

It had been our plan to walk to the driverless vehicle terminal, but it would be better to use this van.

Reida ran across the underground space to open the gate that closed the car park off from the street.

We all piled into the van. I offered to drive it, but was told that Telaris would do that, because he knew how, and Deyu climbed into the seat next to him with the map. The rest of us, including the children, had to go in the back. We installed the children on a row of boxes behind the driver's seat. Nicha sat on his knees looking over Telaris' shoulder. Both he and Telaris were lapsed drivers. I hoped that between the two of them they could sort it out.

I understood why Sheydu didn't want me at the front. I was too visible, too recognisable.

But it was very cramped in the back compartment.

I ended up sitting on a box with Pykka on my lap. He was hanging onto his bag of goodies for dear life. As far as I knew, the bag contained sweets and energy bars, his woolly hat and mouse ears, and that blasted container with soap. I better make sure that didn't burst, or we'd have no end of trouble.

The back door only just closed with all of us inside. I wondered where Reida was going to sit.

The van started moving.

From my position, I could only see out a little window at the back.

The van slowed down. The front passenger door opened and Reida jumped in next to Deyu. We took off even before he'd shut the door.

We turned into the street.

It was very early in the morning. The road was not busy, but not deserted either.

We went for a few blocks before we had to wait for a traffic light. Isharu sat next to the window with her reader. In between her and Anyu, I could see her screen. It showed a scan of of the vehicles behind us, light-coloured patches on an IR screen.

Three of the vehicles were marked with a red dot.

"Are those following us?" I asked.

Anyu said, "We need to get rid of them before we can make our way out of the city."

"Go around the block," Sheydu instructed Telaris.

He did.

The vehicles still came around the corner. One peeled off into a side street. Two stayed behind us. We went around again, over a different route that went past a road that was closed off because of "emergency operations", an area where buildings had been damaged by the attack.

Several bored officers hung around the barricades, turning their heads as we came past. Did they know who was in the vehicles following us?

"Go a different way next time," I said.

Deyu scrolled over the map. "There are patrols in many places."

"That will be because of the attacks. They're not looking for us," I said. I hoped that was the case.

Deyu found a route for us to avoid the roadblocks and guards. But the three vehicles were still following us. It was now also fast getting busier as people came out, couriers came to work and deliveries started.

The day promised to be grey and misty, the latter a result of the fires. The scent still hung in the air.

Telaris steered the truck over the route that Deyu gave him. We passed the driverless vehicle terminal where we had planned to go. We'd already be on our way if it wasn't for these vehicles following us.

Damn, we needed to get rid of them if we still wanted to go to the military depot today. It was still a distance away.

But how could we get rid of them?

Create a chaos that closed the street and gave us time to swap vehicles and get away.

How?

I looked around the racks that lined the sides of the cabin. Surely, there had to be something we could use to create a disturbance?

"What are you doing?" Thayu asked. She stood next to me, one hand holding the shelving, the other holding Emi's shoulder while Emi sat next to Ileyu on Mereeni's lap.

"We need to throw something out the back that disrupts the traffic."

I studied the boxes in the racks.

Nails were good, but I could find only nuts and bolts. Those were not sharp enough to puncture tyres and stop traffic.

There was a packet with rolls of tape. Lengths of pipe, a knee-high machine with a long hose attached.

The owner of this van must be a plumber.

Behind me was another rack full of bits and pieces, pipe elbows, fasteners, bottles of glue. There were also two tall gas bottles strapped into a rack against the wall.

One said O_2 on the surface facing us.

Pressurised oxygen, huh?

A hose with a nozzle was attached to the top of the bottle. I reached over and turned the valve next to it. Gas hissed out the end of the hose.

Hmm. I might just have an idea.

I picked up Pykka and put him on Mereeni's lap with Emi and Ileyu. Then I opened Pykka's bag. I took out the bag of bubble soap. It was still attached to the empty mustard bottle. I pulled it off, opened a roll of tape and ripped off a decent length.

I taped the end of the bubble-blowing mouthpiece to the hose that came out of the oxygen bottle.

I turned the valve a fraction.

A burst of bubbles filled the cabin.

Telaris shouted, "Hey, stop that kid. I can't see."

He batted away bubbles with one hand. They stuck to his hair and his clothes and the inside of the window. Deyu scrambled to remove them.

I removed the tank from its bracket and lugged it across the cabin to the back door. The thing was damned heavy and awkward to manoeuvre in the crowded cabin.

"Tell me where the following vehicles are," I said to Anyu when I got to where she was sitting near the back door.

She showed me her screen. Two were behind us, and one was waiting in a side street ahead. I looked out the little window, but couldn't see anything unusual. I presumed Anyu had figured out which cars they were, but I wasn't going to waste her time by asking.

"Tell me when all three are behind us."

We passed the side street, and according to the screen, the third vehicle came out. A grey van, I thought.

I held onto the contraption with the oxygen bottle. The traffic wasn't moving fast enough for my liking. Once I set this thing off, we needed to get away in a hurry.

A few blocks later, we ended up first in line at a traffic light.

"When it's our turn, I want you to go fast," I said to Telaris.

I waited, one hand on the knob that opened the back door of the cabin, the other on my contraption.

And waited.

The light turned.

The van shot forward.

I opened the back door and turned the valve at the top of the bottle. A burst of bubbles blew into the cabin.

Crap.

They stuck to my face and jacket and my hair, and got into my eyes. The soap stung.

Crap.

The truck swerved. I swayed. I would have fallen out had Anyu not held onto me.

My eyes were full of soap. A stream of bubbles flowed out of the tank, most of them leaving the cabin through the open door which clanged into the side of the truck.

Through watery eyes, I could see that the other vehicles were behind us.

A decent space opened up between us and the next vehicle.

It was now or never.

I opened the valve fully and flung the contraption out the door.

The tank bounced on the paving, spewing a massive cloud of bubbles. A car crashed into the bottle and a second car crashed into that car.

Several vehicles tried to go around, but a light had just turned in the other direction and traffic from the opposite lanes plunged into the bubble cloud.

Bubbles stuck to their windscreens. Drivers couldn't see where they were going.

The last I saw of the chaos before we turned the corner was someone on the road trying to direct the vehicles to stop.

I shut the back door to the cabin.

CHAPTER TWENTY-NINE

WE KEPT GOING.

Pykka cried big tears over the loss of his bubble machine.

"I'll get you a new one," I said, knowing I'd regret this, and that Eirani in Barresh would have my hide, but the poor kid deserved some credit for having given me this idea, even if I'd regret it, too, over a death by ten million bubbles.

Two blocks later, we arrived at the driverless vehicle terminal again. Telaris pulled the van off the road, straight onto the footpath.

We got out, closed the doors and walked away as if nothing had happened. Just some maintenance being done at the terminal, right?

A few people gave us strange looks, but that was all.

There was no driverless vehicle big enough to fit all of us, so we divided our group into three parts, one with me, Evi, Sheydu, Reida, Ynggi and Deyu, the party who were going to break into the depot, one with Nicha, Mereeni, Telaris, Jaki and Veyada and all the children, and one smaller group consisting of Isharu and Anyu and Thayu which would shadow us, and which would include all our heavy gear that we didn't need or couldn't carry. I suspected that those people would talk to our mysterious military followers. I also thought that including Thayu in that party was significant. I would have thought she would have preferred to stay with Emi, but as I already suspected, there were other forces at work. Asto didn't take kindly to being accused of things it hadn't done.

On this part of the trip, Ezhya was looking over my shoulder.

We watched Nicha and Mereeni and the children go off. Thayu waved to Emi, who sat on Mereeni's lap.

Then we split up over the other two vehicles.

Isharu told us to go first. Were they waiting for additional operatives whom I wasn't supposed to see? If so, they'd just given away that these people would join them soon.

I met Thayu's eyes.

I thought she knew that I knew. She would also know that I didn't agree with the presence of Asto military on Earth. But they were there. They'd been present since we'd walked off the suborbital in Los Angeles, maybe even before.

We climbed into our vehicle, a bubble-shaped contraption with benches along the sides. I sat next to Reida, who operated the screen like a pro, and selected the destination as the town near the depot.

Where did my team find the time to study how to use all these things?

The menu warned us that the destination lay outside the vehicle's operating capacity.

"Does that mean that the kids can't reach the accommodation?" I asked.

"No, look, it's telling me to go to a different terminal. Nicha will follow those instructions. We can't."

"But we'll go out of range."

"We should be able to get close enough that we can walk."

At any rate, we needed to get out of here, because the bubble mess was only going to distract the local authorities for a limited time and it was already mid-morning. It would take us at least until midday to reach the destination, then maybe we needed extra time to walk and study the depot's perimeter fence.

Sheydu on the other side of me was already doing that, looking at satellite images of the area. Evi had opened his pack and had taken out a heavy box that I'd not been sure he'd possessed before. It folded out like a concertina into a worktable with a tiny screen which told him which parts to take out of the storage compartment in which order.

Damn it. I'd thought that the only weapons we had taken were our personal guns, and we had no explosives or any of Sheydu's usual gear, but I'd been wrong. This was some very nifty equipment, and someone had probably passed it to us recently. Like last night, when they went to buy dinner?

I didn't want to know.

Ynggi watched with big eyes. He had become very handy with equipment and I was of a mind to send him to do some training that cultivated that part of him. In the hands of a Pengali, a simple tool could become a magical item. Pengali had extraordinary spatial awareness. It was not for nothing that a number of young urban Pengali had found outstanding success in the Pilots Guild, and that they usually flew the largest of ships.

Soon, we came to a quieter part of the city where there were parks and trees and people lived in nice houses that looked quite pleasant.

We left the city via a six-lane road that was not terribly busy. A special lane was reserved for driverless vehicles like ours, and another lane was dedicated to driverless trucks. While those lanes were well-maintained, because the vehicles needed beacons at regular intervals, the remaining part of the road was not. Traffic barriers had rusted and collapsed. The road surface was rough. The few vehicles that used this lane were owned by the police, military or other services.

We turned off this road to a smaller two-lane road that meandered between hills and farms and the occasional cluster of houses. It was so peaceful that you would never guess that this part of the world had been wracked by conflict for many years.

It was just after midday that the vehicle warned us that we were getting close to the boundary of its operating capability, but we were now almost at our destination.

Sheydu and Reida had been keeping an eye on potential followers for a while.

Evi had completed his construction: some kind of explosive device with a display screen and sensors. It sat on the floor at our feet.

I knew better than to ask dumb questions about whether accidentally kicking it would set it off, but by the same token, kept my feet as far away from the device as I could.

I was distinctly aware of the presence of my gun under my jacket. We might have to use all this stuff soon. Veyada said that the best weapons were those you never had to use, and I agreed with him. This expedition was coming to a pointy end. The whole thing was my stupid idea, although I suspected that Asto—and Asto's military—very much supported it.

I was even wondering whether Asto had a particular interest in this part of the world. I'd never seen or suspected the presence of so many military people. Was this normal? Did they know something we didn't? Was it because this part of the world was not a member of Nations of Earth but still had an involvement in space travel?

The bubble car announced a warning that the signal from its base was too weak and it was going to put itself in "preservation mode". It trundled off the road into a bush and stopped there, the display flashing a red warning.

We got out and pushed the vehicle further off the road, behind a copse of trees. The weather had turned foul, with wind driving sheets of drizzle across the fields.

We got back into the dry cabin to eat some of our supplies.

Reida showed us where we were on the map. The depot was across a low hill to our right. We would have to walk a short distance across the fields. He'd spotted no evidence of anyone following us.

We needed to wait until later in the afternoon when it was about to go dark.

Right now, the only enemy we had was the terrible weather, and if we waited, we'd not only have the cover of darkness, but the rain might clear up, right?

Wrong.

It got worse.

The rain lashed against the windows of the cabin.

Only very few vehicles came past, most of them supply trucks without a driver. You could tell when one was about to come over the hill, because the beacon on the side of the road would flash.

One advantage of the truly atrocious weather was that it got dark even earlier than we had planned. But, being from Asto and a warm climate, we were not used to cold, driving rain. In fact, I barely remembered it from my youth in New Zealand.

We got dressed up as warmly as we could. Evi looked like a big bear with his jacket and woolly beanie. Sheydu resembled a scarecrow, since she had covered all her equipment in loose garbage bags to protect it from the rain.

Both Deyu's and Reida's clothing was probably inadequate, and we'd find out about it soon enough when they got wet and cold. This was really the worst kind of weather for a Coldi person to operate.

We left the vehicle, crossed the road, and walked along a little agricultural road that led between the fields. The path grew muddy very quickly. Rivulets of water trickled down the rutted tracks where farm vehicles had passed.

When we came over the crest of the hill, our destination

came into view, a couple of blocky buildings surrounded by a high fence.

It looked kind of... unimpressive. This was where the drone fragment was held? It looked like a bunch of storage sheds.

The data Reida had received from the military had better be right about this.

The farm road met another path at a t-intersection. We needed to go straight ahead, so we climbed the fence and made our way down through the soppy grass. We huddled under a sheet held up by Evi.

Reida's scan showed that there was one gate in and out of the compound, and that a couple of communication towers probably held security cameras. We needed to avoid those.

It was time for the invisibility net to come out again.

CHAPTER THIRTY

SHEYDU PULLED the net out of her pack and gave it, and the belt with the battery box, to Evi. He plugged it in and threw the net over all of us.

Reida cut through the fence until the hole was big enough for all of us to crawl through. Then he tied the sections of the fence back together with a few wire loops so the breach would not be immediately obvious.

So far, so good.

We walked unchallenged to the first of the dark sheds. The wind and flapping bushes kept triggering a motion-sensored light ahead. When it came on, the pool of light showed a concreted yard with yellow lines and a row of military vehicles. Some were ordinary trucks, others were work vehicles with scoops and caterpillar wheels. One of them sat on blocks of concrete instead of wheels. This looked like a place where those trucks were maintained.

We stopped under the overhang of an awning.

The net might stop us from being easily seen, but it didn't stop the rain. Water ran along the strands and into my hair and from there into the collar of my jacket. I was getting wet and cold and could only imagine what the others felt like.

Reida turned on the screen to re-orient himself. The pale light from the device showed his face glistening with water.

He pointed to a big shed across from where we stood.

Over there?

Well, for one, I'd be very glad to get out of the rain.

Until now, we'd stuck to the shadows close to the buildings, but we now had to cross a fairly large open space.

We came into view of a well-lit guard station a bit further down near the entrance of the compound. People were walking around behind the windows, seemingly oblivious to our presence.

But the upper part of the compound lay deserted. Even so, I doubted we had much time before someone alerted the guards that there was a big hole in their perimeter fence.

We arrived at the shed, which had a large door with a smaller door to the side. The large door was probably operated electronically, but the smaller door had an entry panel.

Reida made short work of unlocking it. He was really getting very good at this. I didn't think there were many locks he couldn't open.

As soon as Reida stepped inside, bright lighting came on.

Ouch. That was painful to my eyes.

Evi pulled the door shut behind us.

We had entered a freight delivery dock. There was an office to the side, and ahead the dark maw of the main hall opened up.

There was no automatic light in this part. We had to use our own lights.

The hall was huge and full of banks of equipment. A broad aisle led through the middle.

Reida led the way, directing his light in between the dark blocky and sometimes spindly, shapes of machines. If I'd had to guess, I would have said they were machines for scans, possibly medical. Each piece sat in its own demarcated lot surrounded by yellow painted lines. Was this perhaps a storage room for these things? It looked like it. None of the equipment showed signs of recent use. There was no sound, no blinking lights.

Sheydu, next to me, had inserted her hand under her jacket, clutching her gun underneath. Her gaze roamed the hall, even if it was too dark for her to see anything.

Evi behind us, who had much better night vision, appeared more relaxed.

We came to an almost empty lot where an object lay on a green sheet on the floor.

My heart jumped. This was the same sheet I'd seen in the news clip, wasn't it?

"This is it, right?" I asked Reida.

"I'm pretty sure."

Celia Braddock's evidence consisted of a tangled mess of metal and bent panels, exposed electronics and wiring. I knew it was the same thing by how the electronics boards were attached to the inside of the hull, as my team had noticed. This made the rocket unsuitable for atmosphere re-entry operations because anything attached to the hull would melt. That meant it was either a short-range vehicle or it was considered disposable, and both options went against anything Asto or *gamra* operatives would do.

Sheydu, Reida and Deyu got to their knees and crawled around the heap of twisted metal and electronics, taking pictures.

They agreed that this had very little to do with *gamra* technology.

It didn't look Aghyrian either. And from what I'd seen of the Tamer Collective, this differed greatly from their technology.

I let my team do their work.

No one spoke. I kept a lookout as we had agreed.

Sheydu and the others used their scanners to capture images of the chips and other inner workings of the device. I took several pictures from different angles while I watched them work.

Damn. This looked Earth-produced, some sort of Pretoria Cartel thing. If so, Minke Kluysters had lied to us when he said that the Tamer Collective couldn't develop this kind of technology.

But why the attacks? Did the Cartel have a disagreement with New York? Why the attacks on other cities, on Los Angeles, which was in Mexico, on Athens or other countries?

There seemed no political reasoning behind it.

While I stood guard and watched the others work, I was getting progress reports from them. Apparently some parts originated from various *gamra* worlds.

What the hell?

Reida sent me an enlarged image showing a little transparent part with a piece of circuit board inside that I recognised. I didn't need to see the diagnostic text overlaid by the program Reida used to identify the part. We used those things in Barresh. They could be programmed with simple routines to perform automatic actions. These things were made in Damarq.

Well...

There was also another part that looked familiar, because it was a type of connector that could be found in almost every piece of electronics that came from Asto.

Who the hell would mix up Asto-made and Damarcian parts?

He sent me another image of a different part, a little tube-shaped thing with a connector on one end. The overlaid diagnostic text said: source unknown.

Deyu and Reida broke into a command module that still appeared to be intact, and downloaded a lot of code.

Evi had taken charge of swabbing the surface down for micro elements that could help us determine where the thing had originated.

Then Deyu said, "Have a look at this."

Her voice was soft, but it sounded loud in the intense silence.

She showed us her screen, which displayed two images side by side of identical electronic parts.

"What about it?" Sheydu asked.

"They're the same," Evi said.

"Yes, they're the same," Deyu said. "These are not the only parts that are the same." She brought up another pair, and then another and another. All identical parts.

"These on the left are parts from this rocket here. The corresponding ones on the right are parts I scanned during our visit to the old factory."

What the....

Like what the actual fuck?

"These are the same people," I said, my voice hollow. "The missing members of the Southern California Aerospace Corps, or whatever they call themselves now."

We looked at each other.

"Who even are these people?" asked Deyu.

"They're are humans, they're from Earth, and they are likely to be very well organised as a military corps. They all seem to have fooled us into thinking that they disappeared. The craft in the forest in Barresh is not historic. These people disappeared fifty years ago, because they wanted to disappear. Of course they didn't disappear because someone pulled their funding and they were disbanded and spread out over other scientific organisations. They disappeared because they formed their own militia. And if I'm very honest with myself, I could have known because I might have watched them do it. They were highly trained space scientists and machine operators. Of course they got jobs in space, working for Nations of Earth, which they despised. I watched them plan to kill Chief Delegate Akhtari and flee to a new world when I was a boy. I assumed that because we defeated them, nothing of the sort was ever successful for them. But they could have had other plans, other ships—which they built in the facility we visited. Those ships could have gone to worlds we didn't know about. If they turned up in Barresh, that's likely to mean that they tricked the Exchange and if they did it once, they will have done it other times and have hidden in other places. And Earth didn't know of these worlds because they had no access to the Exchange and all travel went through natural anpar lines. No one who cared would have been able to track where they went."

"Wait—that's crazy," Reida said. "How can we not have known about this? Where are they, if they are not anywhere we can trace them?"

Sheydu snorted. "The universe is an enormous place. You can only find things in space if you have an idea where to look, or if you have a lot of people and a lot of patience."

I said, "There have been some records of unknown visitors buying things through the Pengali."

"But we know they were rogue Traders from Asto," Reida said. "That's why the Thousand Islands tribe all speak better Coldi than keihu."

Ynggi was nodding.

"Those, too, but there have always been rumours of other visitors." Even, I realised with a shock, from within the Pretoria Cartel who had considered these mysterious visitors dangerous. Abri had told me that Robert Davidson had spoken of these people and warned his own people not to stray too far.

And I had assumed that he had been talking about Pengali from the Misty Forest tribe, but although they'd obviously received help to build their modern forest-based technology, they had never come across to me as competent military operators. Pengali fights played out in a gathering of tribes around a set of betanka drums.

After our trip to the Thousand Islands tribe and our discovery of the old SCAC ship, the Pengali tribes were now negotiating.

Well...

Well, that upended a few assumptions.

"But what are these people doing here, attacking their own country of origin?" Ynggi asked. "Unless I misunderstand."

"No, you got it right. Their country kind of got the rough end of the stick when Nations of Earth was formed. I'm thinking they want their country back, they maybe want their entire planet back."

A cold shiver went over my back as I said that, not helped by the wetness of the collar of my jacket.

And I thought of that ship that was coming from the outer reaches of the solar system, that Nations of Earth, the Athens Exchange and the Asto military had all tried—and failed—to communicate with.

What was the bet that this had something to do with that ship? A re-activation of satellites left in orbit to carry out pre-programmed attacks as a warning shot across the bow?

It was not as if we hadn't seen any of that type of behaviour before.

We were looking at each other by the glow of our readers.

I could see the temptation hovering in their eyes to just say that this was nothing to do with us and that we should let humanity stew in its own mess. Sheydu would want me to say that. She had always been lukewarm about the idea of Earth joining *gamra* and that feeling had become stronger after Dekker had been voted in as president.

But this did have something to do with us, absolutely, since we had pushed for Earth to become part of *gamra*, and they had voted in favour.

But from *gamra*'s perspective, we had just imported a massive problem, the likes of which *gamra* had never seen.

Namely: a *gamra* entity was under hostile attack from another entity. The *gamra* entity being Nations of Earth, unwilling as they were right now to communicate with us. The other entity... I wasn't sure. Was America Free State in contact with the SCAC about these actions? Were they secretly part of a SCAC pact?

And what did Celia Braddock know about this? If Atlantia had known, why accuse *gamra*? If SCAC was friendly with Atlantia, why would New York have been the most heavily affected population centre? Or was there a randomness to the attacks caused by the age of the technology and pre-programming done fifty years ago?

And if this was just a shot across the bow, then we needed to destroy that approaching ship immediately.

And we couldn't do this without severe and far-reaching consequences for Asto, because of *gamra* law.

This was the worst possible option. If the ship had belonged to either the Aghyrians or the Tamer Collective, we would have been able to get away with military action that presumed future approval by the assembly because those groups were known as aggressors. This was an unknown group attacking a member entity which had not asked for assistance because, frankly, the current leaders at Nations of Earth were idiots. They'd known about this ship for months. Amarru had freely shared the information collected by the Asto military. And Dekker had simply ignored it.

CHAPTER THIRTY-ONE

THIS WAS NOT what I'd expected.

I'd thought that we would find evidence of involvement by a fringe group, funded and aided by either the Aghyrians or the Tamer Collective. Most likely the Aghyrians, because the Tamer Collective was too business-minded to attack their own future customers.

We'd dealt with Aghyrian-inspired splinter groups before.

This was different and required a completely fresh approach. An urgent approach.

We needed to get out of here. I wanted to speak with both Veyada and Mereeni, and Amarru, if I could get onto her.

We packed up all our things and made our way back to the hole in the fence. I probably imagined it, but the rain seemed to have eased up a little.

We patched the hole in the fence as much as we could. The driverless vehicle could not take us to the town where we'd meet up with the others, so we had to walk by the side of the road, through the wet grass, mud and ages' worth of rubbish.

It didn't look far on the map, but still took us the best part of an hour. In that time, only one vehicle came past, a large delivery truck that did not slow down or stop.

Fortunately, the rain really stopped while we walked.

None of us spoke much. In my mind, I was mulling over what was the best step to take. I knew what I wanted to do, but I didn't know if my team would support me. Of course I could just tell them what to do, but I wanted Veyada and Mereeni's opinion on legal matters, and hopefully a suggestion of how we were going to get out of here from the Exchange or whatever support services had been shadowing us.

The town barely deserved that name. It consisted of a gathering of a handful of houses, widely spaced around a bare intersection between two roads.

Neither of the roads looked busy or well-maintained. A road sign had faded so much that it was no longer legible in the light of the single street lamp that stood at the intersection. Weeds sprang up through the paving. Both roads disappeared into nothingness on all sides.

The accommodation Nicha had booked lay across the intersection, across a field of grass and rubble.

It was a sprawling conglomerate of rooms, each with a door that opened onto the courtyard where there was room to park vehicles.

I'd seen these types of accommodation buildings in old movies and had no idea that they still existed. At one point they had existed in New Zealand, but they had disappeared by the time I was old enough to notice.

When we trudged across the intersection and up to the building, the door to one of the rooms opened. The bright light inside backlist a silhouette. That looked like...

"Thayu!"

She came out and ran across the car park.

Her arms were warm, her clothing dry and clean.

"You're so wet," she said.

I mumbled something about the weather. Until now, I hadn't realised how cold and miserable I'd been.

"I hope there is food. I hope Emi is still awake. We have a lot to discuss."

We went inside. I was happy to find the entire team in the room, spread out over the bed and the floor. The heater blasted hot air in the direction of the table where Nalya and Larrana sat.

Nicha said that the owner of the accommodation had been puzzled at the presence of this large group, but he and his wife had done their best to make everyone comfortable. They had provided us with plenty of food. No meat, no milk for the kids, but plenty of surprisingly fresh bread and fruit. Nicha reported that the Pengali kids had discovered tomatoes and were obsessed with them, especially the little ones which you could put into your mouth whole and bite them until the content squirted into the face of the person next to you.

Pykka seemed to have forgotten about the bubbles, but I made a mental note for myself not to forget.

Sheydu, Evi, Reida, Deyu, Ynggi and I got changed. I sneaked in a hot shower. My skin burned. That was how cold I was.

The rooms themselves were quite basic. This was the biggest room, and the only one with a table. There were only three chairs, so everyone sat on the beds and the floor. Telaris distributed hot tea.

We had some big plans to make.

I told the gathered team of everything we had discovered. Reida backed me up with images.

They were looking on, expressions of shock coming to their faces.

"Wait, so we are dealing with an unknown entity?" Nicha said after I'd finished.

"That's right, and there is every sign that it's the same one that we'd already been investigating, and they probably came to our attention because they've been stirring. The same entity that years ago misappropriated a space vehicle, had factories all around the country, sent a ship to Barresh, and made thousands of people disappear overnight. That disappearance may be a poorly kept secret in the depths of America Free State, but I don't think too many other people know about this."

Nicha said, "And the ship that's coming in this direction, do we know any more about that?"

"It wouldn't surprise me if it's also a drone." Hence the lack of response.

"Then they should destroy it," Sheydu said.

I presumed that by "they" she meant Nations of Earth, the entity she now believed no longer wanted to join *gamra* unless they made serious steps in that direction. She didn't say *we* should destroy it, because she would not make suggestions as stupid as I had made.

"Does Nations of Earth have the ability to destroy it?" I asked.

"Isharu may have something to say about that," Sheydu said.

Yes, and while we had been at the base, she, Anyu and Thayu had met up with our military shadowers.

I bet the Asto military was keen to intervene. They were a fan of short, sharp action that prevented later problems. But after speaking to Veyada, I also understood why it was not going to happen unless Dekker came around. And for the time being, no one at Nations of Earth was speaking to me.

Damn, why did this always happen at such inconvenient times?

"So, what are we going to do?" Thayu asked.

She knew me well enough to know that I *would* attempt to do something, even if most members of my team saw this as being outside my responsibility. They would probably suggest that we return to Barresh as soon as possible for our safety.

"This is what I really wanted to talk about," I said.

Yes. They understood. They all looked at me from their positions around the room. On the bed, on the floor, the children at the table. Deyu even opened a blank document on her reader to start a doodle.

I began.

"We can take several paths from here. I can argue that it was Ezhya's directive to investigate the ship we found in Barresh. We did that. But now, we found a problem and we can report it back to *gamra*. But we all know that *gamra* won't act because in the first place, we're talking about people from America Free State, a non-member entity that's related to Nations of Earth, a prospective member entity that has been dragging their feet on membership. One might see it as akin to trying to meddle in the perpetual conflicts at Indrahui. It's not our business."

Sheydu nodded. She very much wanted to get back to Barresh and continue securing *gamra* against spying from the Tamer Collective or the Aghyrians.

Evi briefly glanced at me and then at her. He and Telaris were victims of those eternal conflicts at Indrahui and would very much like *gamra* to take greater interest in solving the problems, even if some of it was outside their mandate.

I continued, "I tend to step back and look at the overall picture. When I started working for Nations of Earth, the entity we were watching was *gamra*. It ruled travel through the Exchange and it determined which were acceptable standards for joining. It controlled too much, people at Nations of Earth said. Then we got the Aghyrians lurking in deep space and threatening our relatively peaceful society. They're still out there, watching us. We don't know what they want, but we know they *could* do a lot of damage to our bubble of safe space. They haven't shown interest in doing so. But they could. Then we ran into the Tamer Collective. We definitely know that they are not terribly interested in talking to *gamra*. They're obsessed with trade. We're talking to them, and generally, the talks have been fruitful. But they could do a lot of damage to *gamra*'s authority and credibility if they chose, *especially* if they collaborated with the Aghyrians. I don't think they'd want to collaborate, but again, we don't know. So we already have two entities outside *gamra*, that could seriously damage the cooperation between entities that allows us to have the Exchange, and to have peace."

While I'd spoken, Deyu had drawn the circles for *gamra*, Nations of Earth, the Aghyrians and the Tamer Collective and the arrows between them.

"It now seems that we have *another* entity. This group, descendants of a disgruntled space army, has been lurking in the shadows. For those who say that we haven't discovered any people yet—and no, we haven't—I'd like to remind them of Ezhya's principle of the technology pyramid. In order to have produced this drone technology, there needs to be a large independent population of people somewhere."

"They borrowed some of our technology," Veyada said.

"Even so, they will need to have the people to put these drones together and launch an attack on an entire planet. I suspect that if we start looking, we will find small signs of their presence everywhere. Unlike the entities I mentioned earlier, but especially the Aghyrians and Tamer Collective, they seem to be prepared to use acts of war to make their point. We don't know who they are: where they are, or how many of them there are. We can guess what they want: recapture their planet. Back when I briefly dealt with them, when I was a young boy, they didn't have the technology to travel through space. They've developed it. They want to use it not to make money, like the Tamer Collective, but to attack."

"They attacked their homeland," Isharu said. "They could have sent the most destructive drones to the Exchange, but instead they attacked their homeland."

"I think they want to build distrust against *gamra*. They want others on Earth to think that *gamra* was responsible."

"That seems like a roundabout way to do it."

"It's one way to do it, and it may be a smart way. No one will question Celia Braddock's speech where she announced that the drone is *alien*. Technically, she is right. It won't change anything politically, because most people in this part of the world already believe that Earth shouldn't join *gamra*."

Isharu gave me a *see, I'm right* look.

"But the biggest player in this world is not Braddock. It's Dekker. And *he* has just received confirmation of his already strong opinion that it may not be such a great idea to rush into joining *gamra*. If there was ever a chance that Dekker would react rationally about the issue of *alien* attacks, this has well and truly blown it."

Sheydu snorted. "That's just another illustration of why we shouldn't get further involved. Pass the information we have to the *gamra* assembly, to the ineffective Nations of Earth assembly, if you want. This is not our fight."

"Isn't it? So you don't agree that these people have been trying to do exactly the same thing in Barresh recently? They tried to set up a Pengali war in Barresh that would have seriously destabilised Barresh. Fortunately for us, the Pengali are very big on making a lot of noise about small incidents, but they're far more likely to hold a betanka fight that will render the entire city deaf for the next ten years than they are to actually go to war. Sorry for saying this, Ynggi and Jaki, but Pengali might murder a few people in the shadows, and have a huge argument about it, but will then negotiate. They also love making beautiful things, including armour and weapons and aircraft, but they would rather sell them than use them. They suck at going to war. This is a good thing. The SCAC tried to destabilise Barresh. They couldn't get it to work."

Sheydu looked at me. She opened her mouth to say something and shut it again. She blew out a breath, looking at Deyu's doodle.

I continued, "We have, at the moment, several entities involved that are barely talking to each other. Atlantia, America Free State, Nations of Earth, which the first two hate, *gamra* which they all hate, the Pretoria Cartel, whom many consider to be criminals and refuse to talk to, and the Tamer Collective which is doing secretive stuff we barely know about. The Aghyrians who may support an action of war, or they may not. This previously unknown group turns up, seeking to destabilise the ruling order, which maintains peace. We can get involved now and fail, but if we don't get involved, I think there is a very high chance that for the rest of our lives, we will regret that we never tried."

A deep silence followed my words.

Sheydu blew out another breath. Her shoulders slumped.

Thayu said, in a low voice, "Doing something would involve —what?"

"Breaking down perceptions. Every single one. Resisting the cause-and-effect avalanche we find ourselves in. Finding the truth."

Sheydu snorted. "Translate into non-diplomatic speech, please."

"I'm going to see the governor."

"Which one?"

"All of them, as many as I can see. Starting with Celia Braddock."

CHAPTER THIRTY-TWO

SEEING THE GOVERNOR, of course, was not simple, especially without invitation. I'd been trying to get an invitation to see Dekker for almost a year, and he was supposed to be friendly to us. I had no illusion that I could just walk up to Celia Braddock's office and get in. Trickery was needed.

We discussed options and their inherent problems. I didn't want violence. This restricted the options somewhat, but my team agreed that violence would be unhelpful. I was trying to convince the leaders, not kidnap or threaten them. It would be helpful if Celia Braddock saw my evidence and understood who was responsible for the attacks. She was in a good position to communicate with these people, when they chose to come forward. Maybe they already had, who knew? She was going to be an important link in the future.

Fortunately, while my team would use violence—and explosives—if needed, they specialised in covert operations. They could get me in, Sheydu said, and Isharu agreed. If I authorised them to use military surveillance data. I was surprised that they asked, and I told them I didn't hear that suggestion.

I left them to plan the operation and walked with Thayu to

our room along the front of the building. The glow from the single streetlight at the intersection reflected in the puddles on the pavement. It had started raining again.

"I've never seen Sheydu so completely surprised," Thayu said.

"Yes. Do you know why that was?"

"I think because she had never thought to make the link between what's happened the last few days and what's happened in Barresh."

"That link is obvious," I said.

"Obvious to you maybe, but not to everyone."

"That's what's wrong with people, and with institutions. They don't look beyond their own boundaries and their own experiences. They look at what happened in Barresh and they'll say 'That's just Pengali', because... Pengali. Obviously Pengali are not proper people and whatever happens to Pengali could never happen anywhere else. They tried to stoke a *war* between the Pengali by giving tools and designs to the poorest, most disenfranchised tribe. And to draw the parallel, they chose a handful of the least listened-to, most ridiculed countries to start the destabilisation of Nations of Earth."

"I know, I know," Thayu said, putting her hand on my arm.

I blew out a breath. "I get really fired up about this, don't I?"

She chuckled.

"Is it annoying or do I get people like Sheydu to feel stupid about themselves?"

"That shouldn't worry you."

"But it does. I like Sheydu and she's very useful. She's not stupid at all, not in the slightest."

"She's also someone who belongs to an older generation. So old that she never went to the spy academy, and she feels sore about that, even though she taught there. There are things younger people get to learn and have to do that are new to her. She doesn't like being defeated."

"But I didn't go either."

"You're part of our generation. It's the generation where conflicts are not solely about *sheya* loyalty networks and Asto anymore. There is virtually nothing you learn at the academy that you can't also learn through experience. But she feels that, if only Ezhya had allowed her to go, she wouldn't have this gap in her knowledge. But it's just Sheydu being Sheydu. She wouldn't have seen those things even if she had gone. It's not the way she thinks. Large-scale political situations bore her. She's like, if you want that door open, I'll open the door. Just tell me how much damage you're happy for me to inflict."

We both chuckled.

"Sheydu knows a lot of good stuff that I don't," I said. "I can tell her that."

"Don't," Thayu said. "It will just make it worse."

We reached the room.

It was dark inside, because Emi was already asleep. Thayu had told me that Pykka and Amay and Nalya also slept in the room. We sneaked into the room and no one had stirred by the time we got into bed.

I was exhausted, but not enough to skip a certain activity.

Ynggi and Jaki came in when I was about to doze off in Thayu's arms. I didn't know where they'd been. Most likely Ynggi had wanted to show Jaki rabbits, but it was cold and wet out there, so I wasn't sure how successful that would have been.

The constant level of exhaustion caught up with me. It was as if, now that we'd decided what to do, my mind had been freed of the indecision.

I slept and didn't wake until it was light. The two Pengali kids stood giggling at the side of the bed.

Nalya said, "Don't be stupid."

Thayu lifted her head. "What is stupid?"

"They are," Nalya said. "They were saying dumb things about you."

Thayu pulled back the blanket and patted for him to come into bed. Like a little boy, he did.

When he lay on the pillow next to his mother, the similarities between them were obvious. Not only did he have the same nose and same thoughtful expression, but he expressed himself in the same reserved way.

Thayu spoke in a low voice. "I'm sure they don't mean what they're saying or don't understand what they're saying."

I had a pretty good feeling that the Pengali would have been talking about our night-time activity. Pengali were overly fascinated by how things worked for other types of people and other creatures. The adults were much better at hiding this fascination than the kids.

"I still think it is stupid," Nalya said.

"You're getting a bit tired of being with us?" Thayu asked.

"Why do you think that?" The horrified tone in his voice disturbed me. I knew that this kid couldn't possibly have a happy life back in Athyl. Not with a family like that.

I put a hand on Thayu's arm, hoping that she might get the message and ease off, but like a true Coldi person, she ploughed on.

"Because of Larrana's obsession with his collection?" she asked.

He shrugged. "I think Larrana understands that we don't like it. He's been better recently."

That was true. He had.

"Because you don't like babysitting small kids?"

"You have to get used to small kids. They can be annoying, but they get better when you know that they don't understand you because they can't."

He'd been very protective of the young kids. The first time I watched him with Emi on his lap had brought home to me just how isolated and lonely he was. At thirteen, he had no idea how to hold a toddler.

And Emi was all over Ayshada. She thought Larrana was cool, but she had no idea what to do with Nalya, her own half-brother.

It came not from his awkwardness, but because he desperately wanted it to work, despite having no experience and skills.

"We'll be very busy this morning. Do you want to give Emi her breakfast?" I asked.

His eyed widened briefly, and then he sprang out of bed.

"Emilu!" He never called her Emi.

"You chased him off," Thayu said.

"Watch him."

He went to the bag with our supplies and retrieved a pre-packed cube that contained sweet porridge from the Asto military supplies.

Emi was such a human vacuum cleaner that she'd go after anyone who took something from this bag, no matter who they were.

Nalya opened the packet. He sat on the ground. Emi dropped to her backside in front of him, her mouth open.

Thayu and I watched the two of them.

"I don't want to send him back to that horrible family," Thayu said in a low voice.

"I'm sure we can keep him at our house a bit longer."

We got up as well, grabbed some breakfast and packed up.

Everyone gathered in the large corner room where most of the team had slept.

The day was bleak and windy, and low-hanging clouds promised more rain.

Nicha had been up for several hours already, trying to figure out the best way to return to the city.

We only had two driverless cabs here. All of us could fit in, but it would be too cramped for a longer distance. Also, we could not split the team into a small spearhead group and a larger group with the children.

Nicha said that the next town had a train station. It also had a driverless cab hub, and hopefully if we abandoned the vehicles there, it wouldn't raise too much suspicion.

Reida had also monitored the area and had detected some activity from people who may have tracked us after we escaped our followers in the city. Of course, the police still had seen no reason to arrest us, so we weren't officially under investigation.

But we had to be careful, especially with this step of the plan. Things could go pear-shaped very quickly.

We split up when we came to the cab terminal. We entered the train station in four small groups and made sure that we travelled on different carriages.

I entered the second carriage of the train with Thayu and Veyada and Mereeni and the children.

The trip was uneventful, taking us through country with rolling fields that still lay barren after winter, even if a few flowers already grew in the road verges.

It was not very busy in the train. Several people spoke to us to inform us that they thought going to the city with young kids was a bad idea. Did we know there had been alien attacks on the city?

More than in Europe, the people here were of mixed ethnic origin. I'd read that during the Second Civil War, many non-whites had fled to Atlantia or across the border to Mexico, like Mariola and her family, but it was another thing to see it in front of you. I was by far the whitest person on the train, and my Coldi entourage, or even Evi and Telaris, whom I could see at the end of the carriage, didn't look out of place.

Thayu got a message from Deyu, who sat in another carriage, that she had established contact with the Exchange. I could only imagine the consternation in Amarru's office when she realised that we had disappeared. Whatever else happened, at least that manoeuvre had been worth it.

Thanks to the Atlantian air force and my stubbornness, we

knew where these drones came from. I was not sorry about leading Amarru up the garden path at all.

The train arrived at the station. We got off at a busy platform where many people with bulging bags were waiting to get on. Families were still trying to escape the city.

Several soldiers stood at the platform.

We kept to our small groups. Each of us made our separate ways out of the station and got into separate driverless cabs.

Government Hill was a pretty parkland area situated across the water from the city centre. I understood it had once been the home of the famous Statue of Liberty, but it had been damaged through rising water levels and in the Second Civil War, removed, restored and was now housed in a museum—I forgot which one—because the footings of the original monument were under water.

These days, the area held the governor's residence and offices, and some government buildings.

The park was pleasant and well-maintained. Rows of trees lined wide boulevards. They were still without leaves, but dandelions bloomed in the grass.

Modern buildings stood well back from the streets, behind stone walls and metal gates. The streets were closed to all private traffic, but the driverless cabs were allowed to enter at slow speed.

The day had turned sunny and families were out walking. Compared to the devastation downtown, the scene was surreal.

But I didn't feel peaceful. I'd be happy when we had completed this part of the plan successfully and we were on our way to Athens.

We got out of the vehicle at the very end of the boulevard where a heavy metal gate barred the way. From here, you couldn't see the governor's official residence, but I'd seen pictures of the glass and concrete modern building that looked out over the water.

The group that included Deyu had also gotten out of their

cab. We gathered on the grass like a bunch of friends meeting for a picnic. Nicha had done his job admirably and had even noticed a pancake stand—and had looked up the times it opened. We bought several boxes and sat eating them to add to the impression that we were just day trippers.

But while we were eating, and the children played on the grass, several of us were hard at work.

Anyu went for a walk around the series of ponds that lay on the other side of the residence and office. Reida monitored who went into the office and who came out and where they did this.

We only had a short time to find out how to get in, and the team needed to fine-tune the plan.

I'd once barged into Danziger's office in the presence of heavily armed guards, but that was to scare Danziger. I wanted to convince the governor, so I needed a more delicate approach. Still, without Reida and Anyu, I would never get in. I needed all the help I could get for one of the more brazen moments in my career.

CHAPTER THIRTY-THREE

WHILE WE HAD BEEN SITTING in the park, I had noticed groups of black clad people about. They had been too far away for me to see if they were Coldi, but I'd been reasonably sure that they were. I'd seen these types often enough to recognise them by the way they watched and observed, and always wore clothing that was slightly odd, usually in dark colours. Usually very sturdy, often too thick for the weather.

When discussing our plan last night, Sheydu had warned me we might need to ask for "assistance from others". That they were from the Asto military went unspoken. But I had not imagined there to be so many military people. The only ones I had seen were the seven at the safe house in Los Angeles. There were more than seven. A lot more.

They walked around, strolling along the tree-lined paths. They never had children or dogs as company. They didn't talk to each other, and now that I had started to notice them, there were really a lot of them.

Creating a security breach was a critical part of the operation, and while I said that Anyu and Reida could do it, Sheydu had

said that she didn't want any of our team on the front line, in case
something went wrong.

The plan was to release a bug that created a security issue.
They'd released it before we came here. Now they needed to
establish which of the building's systems were down and how
security was covering the problems. Presumably they also knew
this by now.

The final blow would be to release a further bug that attacked
a part of the system that was already weak.

I was very much not up to speed with the meaning of those
terms. I understood that the jargon could apply to both computer
systems that controlled the flow of information between members
of a security team, or physical items like cameras, locks or face
recognition scanners.

Those things would be reprogrammed to let us through, or to
convince the guards that I had a legitimate appointment with the
governor. It was a delicate operation and none of it was in my
hands. My task was to talk once we got in.

The military people walked past the gate.

The fact that they weren't casual tourists was painfully
obvious to me. Would it be as obvious to the guards at the gate,
who had barely seen Coldi people in the course of their duty, let
alone Asto military? How good were these guards?

Reida said that while our not-tourists strolled past the gate
and the tall walls that surrounded the compound, they released
scanning routines which would allow them to judge the weak
points of the site. Were there guards on the other side of the wall?
Was there just a camera that fed back to a security station?

I'd impressed upon Sheydu and her team that I wanted no
violence. In that light, her earlier comments about the large
numbers of local military put me somewhat at ease.

Sheydu had a healthy respect for all her opponents. Underes-
timating one's adversary was a sure way to disaster. I was sure she

wouldn't do that. She'd want to stay well clear of that local military.

Now the local police... that might be a different story. They'd roughed us up already. For what aim, I could only guess. They didn't seem to have a learned a lot, and although they would be following us around, monitoring what we did, they didn't seem to act with any kind of purpose. If they believed they had reason to detain us, they would have done so already. Either they didn't know that we'd broken into the military depot —which I found hard to believe—or they were waiting to see what we would do now. Something was about to come to a head.

Reida now rose and went to the group sitting on a park bench. They spoke briefly, and then he came back, while the group got up and joined the others closer to the compound.

"We have to wait here. There will be action soon," he said.

He would have spoken with hand signals for the others, but this was to the benefit of all of us.

I looked around the park where many people were still enjoying picnics. It was surreal.

Jaki and Ynggi sat with the kids on a park bench. The Pengali kids were playing a game with acorns, Larrana watched them, and Nalya watched us. He knew something was up.

I hoped someone would take these kids to a safe place once the plan was underway.

Thayu sat next to her son, but looking or acting motherly was not in her arsenal today.

Zyana crouched on the other side of her. He kept glancing at a device in his pocket. I was reminded that I intended to speak with him one on one to establish his history other than having worked for the Third Circle guards. You did not catch Sheydu's attention while working for the Third Circle guards.

Deyu sat on a stone wall with her backpack casually at her feet. It looked like a normal pack one might bring for a day trip, but it contained the transmitter that everyone was using to talk to each other.

We waited. We watched.

Then, some action started at the far end of the central tree-lined road that lead through the park. This road was off-limits to vehicles because of a row of bollards at the park's entrance.

Now, a great number of uniformed men arrived on heavy duty motorbikes. The bollards went down. People in the park stopped to watch.

The riders advanced in a phalanx to clear the road of pedestrians. As they went, individuals peeled off the group and stationed themselves along the roadsides. They were wearing communication headsets and helmets. They wore weapons slung across their backs.

Curious park visitors converged along the roadsides, held at a distance by these guards.

Well, crap. It looked like a VIP was arriving. That was not the sort of action we'd expected.

My team sprang into action.

Sheydu made a few hand signals. She indicated that I should stay seated and listen to Thayu.

Deyu heaved her backpack onto her shoulders. She and Anyu set off in the direction of the wall surrounding the governor's residence. A large group of people had gathered at the complex's gates, but three dark-clad people stood off to the side. They looked and acted like guards and didn't look out of place at all. But I noticed something else. A fourth person was with them.

Ynggi had earlier declared that he needed to visit the amenities. He hadn't returned to us, but I now noticed him sheltering behind the much larger members of this group.

As the crowd cheered, as everyone was watching the empty road while waiting for what they probably assumed to be the governor's car, Ynggi simply... vanished.

Crap. Invisibility nets.

One of the group's members extended his arm to lean against the wall. A shimmering patch hovered at his shoulder, then jumped up to a support strut that held a light, from there to a small recess in the concrete that probably held a security camera —and what was the bet that the camera was already disabled through a bug sent by Reida?—and from there to the top of the wall.

The patch vanished. Ynggi was in the compound of the governor's residence. Crap, what had I said about not wanting my team members involved in illegal activities? Knowing Ynggi, he'd probably offered.

While this was happening, most other members of my team packed up their picnic things and casually strolled in the direction of the road, as if they were going to join the crowd in groups of two and three.

Deyu and Anyu were already there.

Reida and Sheydu went closer to the gate into the compound. Another group of Coldi military people was already there.

Thayu, Nicha and Veyada stayed with me.

Jaki and Mereeni took the children. Mereeni carried Ileyu in a sling. Nalya carried Emi, his face very serious. The two Pengali kids hitched a ride on Larrana's shoulders. They walked in the direction of the three guards who had helped Ynggi over the wall.

Then Thayu got up. Nicha and Veyada got up. I followed them across the grass to the area where the crowd was the thickest: the entrance to the compound.

A dark coloured van followed the motorbikes, then a dark coloured car and another one, followed by more bikes.

The column of vehicles progressed slowly along the path. People gathered along the road cheered and waved. All vehicles had darkened glass windows that made it impossible to see the drivers or passengers.

The governor was in that car? Had my team known this?

The gate to the compound opened, letting the dark van into the compound.

But it stopped halfway inside the gates, so that the next car, presumably the governor's, was half out of the gate. Apparently, there was a hold-up in the middle of the compound. Some issue created by Ynggi?

We had now arrived at the back of the crowd that had gathered there. The people parted. A man yelled protest at being shoved to the side. That was Deyu's doing.

Nicha walked through, followed by Veyada. Then I followed and Thayu was behind me.

We walked straight up to the gate. While most of the motorcycle guards at the gate were occupied with the commotion ahead, one of them had gotten off his bike. He greeted me.

Reida opened the door to the car and let me get in.

Of course there was someone already in the car. Governor Celia Braddock.

Part one of the plan was completed.

CHAPTER THIRTY-FOUR

IN REAL LIFE, Celia Braddock was shorter than she looked in the media, and slightly dumpy. I imagined her to be in her fifties, with her hair cut short just below the ears, and peppered through with grey.

Far from being alarmed to see me appear in her car, she seemed bemused.

"I take it you're Mr Wilson?" she said.

Well, how was that? She knew and had been informed that this was going to happen. Likely, her inner circle of security knew. Thank the heavens for Sheydu's machinations.

"I am. Nice to meet you."

"It's an interesting way to meet up. I was always a fan of old spy movies."

She extended her hand, and I shook it, an old-fashioned gesture most people in the rest of the world had given up long ago. I'd read that some areas of the world had never shared that European-origin greeting, and it was uncommon enough already when the rapid spread of a disease had forced people to rethink how often they touched strangers. Very formal people at Nations of Earth sometimes did it, and it was common in this part of the world which, ironically, had never controlled the disease very well.

The convoy had started to move again. I glanced over my shoulder, hoping, presuming, that Thayu, Veyada and Nicha were in the car behind us.

The driveway crossed a green lawn—where I couldn't see a sign of Ynggi or of the commotion he may or may not have created.

The convoy swung around a sweeping driveway to a stop in front of the lakeside residence, a modern structure with a glass-fronted entrance hall where several people waited.

When the car stopped, one of them came down the few steps to open the door. His eyes widened when I came out first, but the governor nodded to him.

We went up the steps into the building. The other car had also stopped. I was happy to see Veyada, Nicha and Thayu come out and follow us up the steps in the company of some uniformed guards.

"Those people are my security," I said. "It's customary for them to come as far as the security station. One of them is also a lawyer, if we need one."

"Noted."

She didn't say what would happen to them. I presumed they could look after themselves, and also that a large Asto military team watched from the shadows. I absolutely hoped that they could stay right where they were.

We walked down a corridor with glass on one side and a view across the lake. There was a fountain in the middle, spewing a jet of water into the sunlight. Trees and bushes grew on the far shore. The map had shown me that there was a security wall over there, on the bank of the river, but I couldn't see it from here. Instead, the buildings of the inner city poked over the top of the trees. It was a peaceful setting, unless you knew that the lingering haze came from fires that were still smouldering.

We came to another security door at the end of the corridor, opened by a guard at our approach.

As soon as this door slid aside, a dog barked and ran across the airy foyer.

And a magnificent dog it was, too, a tall, slender creature with a pointed nose and drooping ears. The most amazing feature was its light brown hair that was long and flowing and almost dragged over the ground. It was glossy, having been trimmed, shampooed and combed to within an inch of its life. Another dog followed the first one, this one darker, and without barking.

Both animals trotted to the governor, sniffed her hands and then came to me.

"What gorgeous dogs," I said. "I've never seen these before. My father has a dog, but it's a farm animal."

"A kelpie. A sheep dog?"

"Yes."

Obviously she had spent some time studying me. Or she knew a lot about dogs. Or both.

I followed her out of the foyer into a large office.

The entire far wall consisted of thick glass—probably bullet-proof—and looked out over the lake.

Everything about the office reminded me of Sirkonen and his office at Nations of Earth on that fateful day that changed my life. The similarity of the opulent Victorian style of furniture was so uncanny that I felt a certain discomfort creeping up on me, as if some gunman or a ship in orbit was going to shift the world out from under me yet again.

A big wooden desk sat in the middle of the room, with a chair that looked like it came straight out of the Victorian period. The matching furniture was all polished and gleaming.

Old-fashioned paintings adorned the walls, some of them even so old that the people wore horse hair wigs.

As we came in, I spotted movement in the corner of the room. A third dog got off a bench that seemed to have been put there for the governor's furred companions, and padded across the room. This animal was almost white, and its appearance was regal. It had a dark nose and dark, mournful eyes, with which it observed me.

The governor crossed the room to her desk and sat down. A small couch faced the desk, and it was the most natural place for me to sit.

The dog came up to me and sat down. The other two dogs were still at the door.

Celia Braddock gave a sharp command, and all three animals padded to the bench.

They were such amazingly graceful creatures. Deyu would love to see them.

"There is a lot of history in this room," I said.

"You cannot adequately understand the present if you don't understand the past," she said. "These were the founders of our city and our nation, people of great resilience and drive."

I remembered that it was precisely this adoration for old revered figures that had caused so many troubles between the states. Which history to keep and which to let slide into the obscurity of time. I also noticed that she spoke of one nation. Last time I looked, there were four. I was reasonably certain that the belligerent Governor Patterson of America Free State might start a war over what she just said.

"I'm sure that you're aware of the reason I want to talk to you."

"Your people have mentioned it. But, to start off our conversation, let me be clear: we're independent. We're not shackled to the slavish doctrine of Nations of Earth. We're not seeking membership, nor are we out to stoke conflict with them."

No, I bet she wasn't. International sanctions had crippled several of her predecessors.

"I have no desire to comment on your relationship with Nations of Earth. There is only one reason I needed to speak with you: that is about the source of the invading drones and specifically the one your forces brought down. We have discovered some interesting facts about it."

"You are here because you broke into their facility illegally."

"I would never have gained access otherwise. There were things we needed to know."

"Members of my government might say that you would have been kept out for a very good reason."

"But you obviously didn't agree?"

"No, you misunderstand. I agreed with them, but I wanted to give you some rope to hang yourself. We've been collecting data of all of you folks sneaking around here, probing into our systems. It's time to face the music, Mr. Wilson. This room is a fortress. There are eyes everywhere. I'm not afraid of you. You represent a spineless organisation that's too afraid to call out what's been happening. What business do you think you're conducting?"

"I'm here for only one thing: the truth." And she was wrong: I didn't represent Nations of Earth.

She snorted. "The truth? The truth is that this gormless woman made a pact with the devil and now they're all so wrapped up in their referendum result that they can't even stand up against the bully."

"I'd prefer to conduct this talk without insults to presidents."

"This is my house and I dictate the terms. You've already taken way more liberties than I would have allowed for most other self-absorbed lobbyists."

"I'm not a—"

"A lobbyist. That's what you are. Make no mistake, Mr Wilson. You're here because I'm curious, not because I think your words will be important. You better get on with it, because my curiosity is fast running out."

I took a deep breath. "The reason I've come here is to show you what we have found about the origin of the drones. I'll give you a copy of all our materials so you can check it for yourself. I won't need much of your time. I'll present the facts to you and then I'll leave the country with every member of my team."

She said nothing, folding her arms over her ample chest.

I took it as a sign to continue.

One of the dogs let its front legs slide from underneath so it landed gracefully on its stomach. All three dogs were watching us.

In the intense silence, I started my story. I told her about the buried ship in the territory of the Misty Forest tribe, about the attempted destabilisation of Barresh, about the ship that was still approaching Earth and no one had been able to communicate with. I told her about the entities we thought might have been responsible, about the Aghyrians and the Tamer Collective.

Then I pulled out the images Reida had prepared for me, showing her the parts that were of Asto origin, the parts that were of Indrahui origin, the parts that we didn't recognise, and the parts that were exactly the same as the ones we had found in the craft in Barresh. When I finished, she gave me a hard look.

"So, what are you saying? That *we* attacked our own cities? Mr Wilson, are you out of your mind?"

"Do you want me to assume that the people behind these attacks are *yours*? Because I doubt it, and I never suggested that they were."

"Yet, you do. That's clear to me."

"Many years ago, they left a country that you have been in conflict with several times in the last fifty years."

"We disagree, but the group you're talking about came from all over the region. They were our best and finest minds. I don't like the insinuation that they formed an army in space and attacked their home. Frankly, that's ludicrous."

"I am merely telling you what the data suggests."

"Suggests. Let's start with that. You suggest that the highly trained people in our forces haven't studied this fragment and haven't done a lot of work to come to our own conclusions?"

"Would they have the knowledge about *gamra* technology that we have?"

"You would be surprised."

"If so, why do they come to the bizarre conclusion that *gamra* is responsible?"

"I don't question the opinions of my experts. That's why they are experts."

"The experts would have found the same parts. The experts would have scanned the parts and obtained the same data. On top of that, your experts would have had the benefit of the knowledge of what became of the great institution that was NASA once they lost government funding, and where the people and resources went. They would have been aware that a fundamentalist organisation splintered off and started building their own ships. They would have been aware that many of the people who worked in those factories disappeared."

"Don't tell me how to do my work."

"Were you not aware of those things, then?"

"I can't see how this has anything to do with this attack."

"Because these people or their descendants are behind the attack."

"I already told you that makes no sense whatsoever. Why would they attack their country of origin?"

"Why did they leave?"

Again that hard stare. "The Southern California Aerospace Force is a proud chapter in our heritage."

"Then tell me: why did they vanish? Why did about ten thousand people vanish fifty years ago? Have they been in contact with you?"

"They didn't vanish. They were re-absorbed in other programs. The organisation isn't active anymore."

"They are active. It's what the evidence suggests: that we're dealing with a third entity beyond Nations of Earth or *gamra* that we haven't encountered before and haven't been aware could pose a threat until recently. We know that they arose from the SCAC. That is all I'm here to tell you about the drones. *Gamra* didn't send them. Nations of Earth didn't send them. Suggesting that they did is...unhelpful."

"Unhelpful, huh? I think your suggestions are unhelpful. Preposterous. I think your theories are crazy. I trust my experts. Your presentation does not change my view in any way."

"That would be to your detriment. It would also hamper our ability to enact an adequate response. These drones will keep coming. We need to be prepared."

"And what's that? A threat? Some sugary motherhood statement about how we should all come together to fight against a greater evil? An evil that's the result of the softness of Nations of Earth? They try to sell us the lies that they want to join the aliens to protect us. That's nonsense. They don't want to protect us. The world doesn't care about us. The world hasn't cared about us for close to a hundred years. The world is not going to care now. We can solve this ourselves, and I will have no further dialogue with people like you. In fact, I'd urge you to leave. I will allow you safe passage out of the country, but don't get any illusions that you are ever going to be welcome here again. Good day, Mr Wilson. I've stuck to my promise and listened to you. Now you can go."

She waved her hand at the door, which slid open, letting in two uniformed officers.

I rose. Took a few steps to the door.

Then I turned around again. "I'd urge you to study the fragment closely, and you'll come to the same conclusion as I have."

"I would love to show you where you can stick your data, but I think I better give it to my security officers who will pick it apart to see the trickery you've performed on this so-called data. Expect to hear from me again. Expect to be presented with a bill for the damage you've inflicted, and the wages of security staff I've been forced to put on you."

I nodded. "Thank you for seeing me."

She snorted.

I followed the guards out the door, and walked down the corridor flanked by them, while trying to remember if I had ever been to a more unproductive and hostile meeting.

Yet, I'd come here because this was important. Also, because I had hoped that I could bring her closer to Nations of Earth.

I believed in those things, and I didn't appreciate her mocking of them.

But keeping lines of discussion open was hard to do when Nations of Earth itself was in a state of flux and not communicating with me. And *gamra* didn't care about these issues yet.

This was the worst possible thing to happen at the worst possible time. We couldn't afford disunity and distrust.

From my own perspective, I intensely disliked failure.

But it was what it was.

I'd thought Celia Braddock would see sense if presented with the data, but I'd forgotten that this was a government that considered facts optional.

I'd failed and Celia Braddock would continue to spew her crap on the world stage, and the world would continue to mock her for it, instead of getting organised to counter further attacks, devise a plan to take out that approaching ship.

I could talk to Nations of Earth, but Dekker didn't want to see me either.

Why did I even bother?

CHAPTER THIRTY-FIVE

THAYU, Veyada and Nicha waited in the airy foyer of the building, accompanied by a bevy of uniformed guards. We kept silent as I re-joined them and were escorted out of the building to a van that took us the very short distance back to the gate.

Another, larger, van waited there, behind a line of uniformed motorcyclists holding back a crowd of onlookers.

We left the smaller van on the side facing away from the crowd, and briefly came into their view when being escorted from one vehicle to the other.

People shouted. I couldn't hear their words, but they didn't sound friendly or curious. We were in hostile territory. I didn't know why I'd thought I could negotiate away more than a hundred years' worth of division by just talking to people. They didn't like us here. Many would be civil enough to deal with us, especially when there was money to be made, but behind our backs, they hated us. They wanted to believe that we were responsible for the attacks. They weren't interested in proof.

I didn't even know if Junco or Sage's apparent friendliness was real anymore.

Inside the other van, we encountered the rest of the team.

Mereeni and Jaki sat at the very back seat with the kids and behind the pile of luggage. Mereeni looked relieved to see Veyada.

Ynggi sat next to Evi, with Telaris and Zyana across the aisle.

Anyu was there with Reida, and Deyu with Isharu.

Sheydu sat in the front seat, next to an officer holding a weapon. Nothing about him was casual. A second armed guard stood on the steps. They were both eying Sheydu.

Thayu and I sat down on the bench behind her.

"What's going on?" I asked her.

The officer next to her looked over his shoulder and gave me the stink-eye.

"They really don't like us here," Sheydu said.

"Did they touch any of you?"

"No. Deyu made sure of that."

I shuddered inside. She was putting on a stoic face, but there clearly had been an altercation. And when Deyu was involved...

"Did anyone die?"

"No. Nothing was harmed except his pride," Deyu said from the seat behind us.

"His ability to reproduce might be temporarily impaired," Sheydu said.

Ouch.

The guard was looking from one to the other. I didn't think he understood a word of what we said.

I made the hand signal for *careful*.

My team understood. Oh, they understood. Things would have to have been pretty bad for a confrontation to have happened already. Talking to each other in front of these very nervous guards, while they couldn't understand a word we said, would not end well.

So we fell quiet.

The vehicle started moving down the tree-lined road. Most of the earlier crowd had already dispersed or had gone back to their picnics.

The bollards at the park's entrance sank into the paving at our approach.

The van inserted itself into the traffic.

We drove for quite a while, over a main road that followed the river bank. The tall buildings of the city centre rose from the opposite shore. From this distance, the effects of the drone attacks were no longer visible.

I worried about what Celia Braddock was going to do now that she continued to believe—and tell her lackeys and everyone who would listen—that *gamra* was responsible for the attacks. There *would* be people worldwide who would listen to her, because there were always conspiracy theorists who wanted to believe that the source of all ills in the world was "Aliens!"

We could absolutely not use that attitude now, or at least not from any of the world's leaders.

And I was being taken further and further from its source, while being powerless to do anything about it. Celia Braddock wasn't listening to me. Simon Dekker wasn't talking to me. Amarru was likely to be angry with me. Ezhya... well, he was smart and would not get involved.

What sort of conflict was this, even? A domestic one? What else could I do to help people see sense?

We were indeed being taken to the airport. I recognised the buildings when we turned off the main road. We went in not through the regular passenger entrance but through the Customs office.

Here, a different group of guards was waiting for us.

They took us out of the vehicle one by one. Sheydu was the first one to go. Her face spelled thunder.

But I motioned for her to keep calm. I knew that she would do this anyway, because she was a professional. But deep down, she still appreciated solidarity, even if she would never tell me so.

I was in the next batch off the bus, with Deyu and Isharu.

It was getting dark, and an icy wind blew over the open space of the airport. A small solar plane was coming in to land.

They took us into the building, into a waiting room with rows of seats.

Fortunately, Sheydu's planning and foresight had made sure that we carried at least some food, enough for the kids.

We waited. I was sure the room was bugged, so none of us said much. We looked out the window, which offered a view over a boring expanse of concrete where some trucks and other aviation-related vehicles were parked.

We were tired. This trip had turned into a disaster, and we needed to go to a safe place to regroup and re-think our strategy.

The kids were restless. Emi and Ileyu ran around and slid over the lino floor, which was disgusting and soon their knees and hands were black. There was a small toilet cubicle at the back of the waiting area, but the washbasin was so tiny that trying to clean unwilling toddlers resulted in a mess. I held Emi while Thayu tried to wipe the dirt off her hands. After a long day, Emi was so tired that she flew into a rage every time something didn't go her way. She was screaming and worming to get out of my grip, while Ileyu "helpfully" made a washcloth wet and dripped water all over the front of her shirt.

In the middle of all this, the sound of an unfamiliar male voice came from the waiting room behind us.

I turned around, still holding Emi, both of us wet.

Emi fell quiet. Thayu took her from me, and quickly wiped her little hands before she got the chance to object.

A strange man had entered the room and looked around for someone for him to address, someone who could understand him.

At least I thought it was a man, but with his shoulder length pink hair, and his long flowing jacket and plenty of jewellery, I could be made to think otherwise.

"You're Cory Wilson?" he asked.

Even the tone of his voice was ambiguous.

"Yes, that's me."

"I have been told to come and get you. There is a vehicle waiting outside the building. We have a very short departure window."

"Wait. Where are we going?" And who was he, anyway? An introduction would be nice.

"I'm taking you back across the Atlantic. I'm not sure where we will be able to land, but it will be somewhere from where you should be able to return to Athens."

"Well, that's welcome news, but can we know a bit more about who sent you and why you're here?" I'd have expected someone from Nations of Earth or the Exchange, not this character.

"I am here because I happened to be visiting New York for an art exhibition. My name is Jayde Colwin. I am an agent of Nations of Earth of sorts."

"Do we know each other? I've heard your name mentioned before."

"I work for Simon Dekker."

And now I remembered why I knew his name. Simon Dekker had an American partner. This man was sure to be him. That was interesting. So he wouldn't talk to me, but would send someone to stop me being an embarrassment to him?

"Ah, I see. I have a lot to say to President Dekker, but let's deal with the important things first. When are we leaving?"

"Right now. The plane is ready."

I told my team to gather up all their things, and within five minutes, we were out the door.

He took us through the corridors and courtyard out the back where a minibus waited.

There was only a driver with it, no security personnel.

"You don't have any guards?"

I was beginning to feel iffy about this again.

If he turned out to have nefarious intentions, we could easily overpower the driver. Maybe that was what he wanted us to do: bait us. Was he really from Nations of Earth?

"Mr Wilson, you have to understand that we're both on hostile territory. I'm not normally allowed to take any security guards when I come here. They're waiting in the plane."

"They really hate Nations of Earth, don't they?"

"They don't trust each other, that's right. They view me, as native born New Yorker, with even greater suspicion. I know you have your doubts about me, but regardless of our differences on other subjects, trust me on this one."

"I just want to get out of here."

"I bet you do."

Whatever that was supposed to mean. An air of superior morality dripped off him. OK, they didn't like what I'd tried—and failed—to do. They saw him as a good samaritan rescuing me from an embarrassing position.

A small private aircraft was waiting, large enough to fit my entire extended team.

When our luggage was stowed, we all strapped in, and finally left this cursed continent. I watched the coastline recede in the deepening dusk.

I still didn't like failure and kept thinking about alternate ways I could have presented my data to make Celia Braddock believe me and willing to cooperate. But I had to concede that this desire had probably been doomed from the moment I conceived the plan to reason with her. She had her own agenda, shaped through decades of mutual distrust. I wasn't going to change anything with just one visit. She wasn't interested in reason. Or the truth.

From *gamra*'s perspective, I had found important information. That would have to be my focus. Deliver this to the assembly and discuss it there, with Melissa and the other bureaucracy. But still, the stupidity...

The craft came with a single cabin crew member who provided us with decent food for the first time in days.

The children ate so much that he needed to scour the kitchenette for additional portions.

Then, when we were all satisfied, and I was starting to begin to feel very comfortable and sleepy, Jayde came out of the cockpit and sat down on the bench next to me, enveloping me in a smell of perfume.

He began, "There are several things you need to know. Once we're over international waters, we will restore access to your devices, and you will see that the world has changed."

I frowned at him.

"We've only been away from news for a few days." We'd already heard about the attacks on other cities, right? Did this mean there was more?

"The attacks that were perpetrated on the major cities on the American continent were repeated throughout the world."

"I know that. I spoke to someone about it."

A hand of fear clamped around my heart. My father was all right, wasn't he?

"Celia Braddock likes to make out that the New York attack was the worst. It was, but only in the Americas. Athens took a direct hit."

"You're kidding." That's what I'd feared. That would be why Amarru was so coy with information, and why her people weren't out here already. Why all assistance to us had been rendered by Asto military. Because Ezhya had sent them, because Amarru and the Exchange didn't have the bandwidth. Damn.

"Sadly, I'm not kidding."

"Has any country taken any type of action?"

"Against what? We know nothing about the assailants."

"I know who they are. We got to check out a drone that was shot down."

His eyes widened. "You captured one?"

"No, we didn't, but the day after the attacks, Celia Braddock boasted on the news that the Atlantian Air Force shot a drone down. She paraded the fragment in a press conference. We could see that it wasn't *gamra* technology, as she claimed. This was why we went across the continent to have a look at this thing, to see if we could determine its origin. They were not very helpful, as you might understand. They were even less helpful when we pinpointed where the drone came from."

"Let me guess, the Aghyrians?"

"No."

"Then the Pretoria cartel?"

"No. Not them either. "

"You can't suggest that Asto or any other *gamra* entity would do something like this?"

"Did you hear me say that? That's what she wants to believe."

"No, but I am out of ideas."

"I will tell you something. Please understand that this is highly in sensitive information and I have only told the members of my team, and Celia Braddock, who banned me from the country in response. She didn't like my conclusion."

"That's not unusual. She doesn't like a lot of things."

I sensed there was a lot of experience behind that remark. I was beginning to like this man. He had to have been forward-thinking to leave his home and the likes of Celia Braddock to come to live in Rotterdam. I might not like his partner, but this man at least was prepared to listen. I told him what we had found out, and as I spoke, his eyes widened.

He nodded when I spoke of the reports that people had just disappeared. He agreed that there had been a rebellious element within the spacefaring community after having their programs cut again and again. He agreed that they had been infiltrated with a paramilitary vibe. He said it was not unexpected, because many of them came from the military. And they would not have taken kindly to being told to stand down and disband.

He said, "Presuming you're right—and I think your arguments are good—one thing I don't understand is this: how did they manage to get a lot of this stuff off Earth? We're talking about large ships to get into orbit, interstellar ships and space stations that nobody knew about."

"I suspect they built a lot of their larger hardware in space. There are many questions we need to answer, but we need to speak with whichever governments will listen to us on how to prepare for their next action, because this is an emergency. We don't know what they'll do next. They sent drones, leaving us with no avenue to retaliate. There is that one ship approaching Earth that's not communicating. I can arrange for it to be shot down, but I'll absolutely need the agreement from the Nations of Earth assembly to do this. I would appreciate if you could raise this with the president."

"One ship?"

"It's only one ship, and it's not very big. It might contain weapons, or it might contain a delegation to negotiate with us, or put forward their demands. We don't know. We need to present a unified force to them. I would like to see the president as soon as possible."

His expression closed. "You will understand that the president is very busy at the moment. Many cities are in ruins, and there is a need to render assistance to people who have lost property or loved ones."

"The president needs to make sure that this doesn't happen again. The drones may have self-destructed, but it's clear what these people are capable of. They will have no hesitation to do it again. I don't know why I can't seem to get onto the president. It's like he's been avoiding me since he was elected."

It seemed too ridiculous that it might be over a petty grievance about something that happened years ago.

"As I said, he is very busy."

"I'm sure that's not all of it. Are you sure there isn't some sort of political pressure on him not to join *gamra*, even though the world has voted in favour?"

"I'm not in a position to comment on how he chooses to allocate his time."

"At least tell me why he avoids me."

"He's not avoiding you."

"Avoidance, being busy, whatever you want to call it, this has been a frustration ever since he was elected. With Margarethe, even with Danziger, I had a working relationship. When something happened, they would contact me. It wouldn't always be nice for me. I've had Danziger shouting at me on several occasions, but he would reply to my messages." Eventually, and quicker when he needed something from me.

"I'll see what I can do."

"Please, do."

"Mr Wilson, I hope you understand that you're a private citizen—granted, one with a bit of influence—but with no official function that justifies an urgent meeting with the president."

I stared at him.

What the...

What the actual fuck.

I was going to ask him whether he didn't think being Ezhya's *zhayma* warranted a meeting, but I realised that it didn't.

Any Coldi person would simply feel the loyalties, and official announcements or elaborate appointment diaries would be unnecessary, ridiculous even. But people at Nations of Earth had no understanding of the *sheya* instinct. For them, I *was* an arrogant upstart without official status. If I wanted to speak with the president, I could stand in the queue with all the lobbyists and minor politicians.

I let out a deep breath.

"I know he doesn't want to or like me, but I'm asking for a bit of sensibility. Bury the political differences. There are people's lives at risk. These people who attacked us will do this again. They only lost drones, and I'm sure they have a lot more where those drones came from. We can provide a lot of people and military power to snuff this attack out. It probably wouldn't even take all that long. But If we don't cooperate, Earth is going to be a sitting duck."

"I'm sure he understands that."

I got no further with him. It was all very frustrating.

He retired to the private cabin in the front of the craft, and we tried to sleep in our seats.

We arrived on the other side of the ocean without further incident.

It was dark, and from the air, I couldn't make out where we were.

During the flight my team had regained Exchange coverage. They had been very busy with whatever things that security were busy with.

I scrolled through the news channels and read a lot of words on nothing. Everyone was still guessing about the drones. Several articles mentioned *gamra*. That *gamra* must know something, or that they would have seen something. Either way, *gamra* was assumed guilty by association. I even spotted an article that said that Earth should withdraw from the process of joining *gamra*.

Apart from who was responsible for the attacks, I had nothing to give them. No names, no planet of origin, no reasons.

The attacks seemed pointless, because they had achieved nothing. They might be a warning about what they might do to Earth if we didn't give into their demands, or something. If they just told us what the demands were, that would be helpful. We would also have someone to communicate with. And know where their base was.

It turned out that we had landed somewhere close to Paris.

A bus waited at the airport building to take us to the train station, and we hired cabins on the fast train that took us across the continent.

The pale morning light showed us sporadic evidence where attacks had hit, as smoke plumes hanging over the horizon. I was hitting myself on the head for believing that the attacks had only affected New York badly. How easy it was to be deceived when you became isolated from independent information.

There were very few passengers on the train. Our team spread out over the seats and adjacent cabins.

Any of us not asleep tried to raise responses from Nations of Earth. The lines were out or extremely busy.

We arrived in Athens without having spoken to Dekker or anyone else at Nations of Earth. We went from the train station to a taxi-bus to take us to the Exchange.

It was mid-afternoon, and a line of vehicles waited to get to the entrance of the building. It stretched all the way along the date palm lined driveway, through the gate and onto the street outside. The other vehicles were also taxis or buses.

Damn, this reminded me of the time immediately after the attack on Sirkonen. People were being taken off-world. Large numbers of people.

My courage sank, then.

My life's work lay in pieces.

Had I really worked my butt off in the past few years for nothing? Had I wasted my time supporting the referendum and Margarethe? Would it have been better to just let Earth be Earth and ignore it?

CHAPTER THIRTY-SIX

IT TOOK us a fair amount of time to make it to the entrance, where a few harried attendants tried to organise the chaos of desperate travellers into groups. *Anyone who needs tickets, this way please, regular passengers, this way.*

But when the attendant spotted us, he ushered us straight through. Amarru was waiting, he informed me.

The team were going to get the craft ready, and I went straight from the entrance to Amarru's office.

I found Amarru standing in the corridor outside her office talking to someone.

As soon as she saw me, she ended the conversation and came towards me. It had only been a short time—about two weeks—since I'd last seen her, but she looked old.

"I'm so glad you're back," was the first thing she said. The worried look in her eyes disturbed me.

"Well, it was interesting."

I was trying to sound light-hearted, but a worn out feeling hit me like a freight train. This was the safest I had felt since leaving this same place two weeks ago, when we were yet unaware of what would happen.

"I thought we lost you, when you slipped our guards in Los Angeles."

"Well, I'm sorry about that."

"I have to admit, I wasn't impressed. I sent my people on a wild chase after you. You could have told me about your plans and I might have saved the resources that I could have used to retrieve other people in difficult positions."

"I said I'm sorry, and truly am, but we got important data, and I think the trip was worth it, even if it didn't achieve any of what I had hoped it would. Have you had any communication with Nations of Earth?"

Amarru snorted. "I wish I understood this man better. I've had a very short talk with him, over a video link, and that is it."

"Before or after the attacks?"

"Before. It was a diplomatic call. I was going to propose a long string of measures that should be taken cooperatively to get our joint systems going, but he just keeps stalling on all of it."

"What is the bet that he voted against joining? "

"Oh, there is no doubt about that."

"He seems to be a vindictive and petty little man. I had some trouble with him a number of years ago, when we got rid of Romi Tanaqan. That almost cost me my citizenship."

"Yeah I remember that. It was very effective but very risky."

"I can't believe that he is still sore over that. It solved the problem."

"Well, at the time, he was responsible for the joint Armed Forces at Nations of Earth, and they all missed the presence of Asto ships in orbit and had no idea that they were within striking distance."

Yes, I could imagine that that would be a sore point to his ego.

"But why let it derail his relationship with us for so long? Tanaqan was a rogue and was always going to create a problem. None of us wanted him. Not him, not Asto, not *gamra*, not the

Zhori mafia really either. He was building up a base of supporters."

"You tell me. You don't have to convince me."

I looked over her shoulder out the window.

"And your systems have also been affected by the attack?"

"They tried. Fortunately our alarm warning system is better than that. When these drones came within a certain distance, we had all alarms going off in this building, and some technology was dispatched."

"I am guessing I better not ask too much about that technology?"

"That would be a good idea."

"Does that also mean there could be pieces of debris that came down in the area surrounding Athens that are going to be found and analysed?"

"In theory, yes, although you will probably find them a lot more damaged than the sample you saw."

"I'm going to leave a copy of all that data with you. I've already sent it to Dekker, for all the good that will do."

"Save yourself and give it to Ezhya."

I detected a kind of finality behind her words, and that disturbed me.

"What do you mean?"

"We're closing up shop for the time being. We are evacuating."

I stayed at her. "What?"

"I want to show you something."

She got up from her desk and accompanied me the short distance down the corridor to the Exchange's central hub.

Even though it serviced an entire planet, the level of technology was only about the same as the one in Barresh. This would have to change massively once all the systems were integrated and people from Earth could formally travel.

The hub's operator seemed to have been waiting for her.

Of course, they had known that we were on our way.

She showed me the visual representation of the attack as it had been captured by the Exchange. Deyu and Reida had shown me something like this, but there was a bit more detail to these images. You could see the drones approaching Earth and vaporising in the atmosphere after delivering their payload. You could even see how the Atlantia Air Force had intercepted one of them, which went down before it could deliver its payload. She played the sequence over a few times and enlarged certain areas.

Amarru continued, "We can prove that the attack drones came from the approaching rogue ship. It is still some distance away, but these drones appeared in lower orbit. How did they get here so quickly?"

"The Asto military can't be the only one with a one-way Exchange sling."

"Yeah. And look at this."

She flicked to another frequency where the ship split off in five different strands. "This is from yesterday. These haven't reached us yet."

"Shit," I said.

"Yup. Now when you consider that distant ship, we tried to communicate with it, but I don't think it has that capability. In fact, you can see here the moment the drones split off. The lines that come from it are the same strength as the ship itself. Brightness equates size, so it basically duplicates itself several times here," she pointed back at the original picture.

"So what did the ship do at that point?"

" Well that's an excellent question, isn't it? We have no idea."

"Is the original ship still approaching?"

"Yes. So are several of its duplicates."

"Shit. This is really no time for Dekker's antics. Did you show him this?"

"We tried."

"And?"

"I have no idea. He didn't reply."

"We can't afford to have this type of behaviour."

"Nope. But he seems adamant that we have something to do with it."

"What else do you know?"

"Not much. We're dealing with an unknown technology that they have developed independently, even if they also used some of our parts. We don't know who this is, and we don't know what they can do. There could be an entire army of these things on its way to us. Each of these five vehicles might give rise to additional attacks. We don't know. We don't know what they want. We have not been able to communicate with them. Nations of Earth also isn't communicating with us. We remember what happened when we were all trapped here because we acted too late. We will not let that happen again. This is why I have given the evacuation order for everyone who wants to be evacuated. We are ready."

I very much wanted to say that this was a very radical measure, and surely things wouldn't be that bad, but I remembered that time very well. I remembered just being able to get out in time. I remember thinking about all those people who did not. I remember seeing that mother whose young child was left behind. I didn't want to see anything like that ever again.

"Are all *gamra* people taking up this offer?"

"Not all of them. Many of them have lived here long enough, they've got nowhere else to go, but quite a lot of them have. About half have given me their intention to leave. We will get them to come here in orderly fashion without overwhelming any of the local systems."

"You really have thought about this for a long time, haven't you?"

"Only about eleven years. Letting people become trapped here was a failure that I've never allowed myself to forget."

"So, where do we fit in?"

"I'd go home if I were you."

"I presume my craft is still here?"

My pilot Leisha had been attending some talks about future changes and things all pilots would need to know when the Athens exchange officially opened for all.

"I've told everyone with private craft to evacuate first. I wanted the hall to be as empty as possible, so that I had the space to put all the odd sundry of craft that are going to arrive."

"But how am I going to get back?"

"Don't worry. We have all that sorted. I've reserved spots on a shuttle that's leaving soon."

She was right.

We barely had time to get something to eat.

While we were eating in the large upstairs canteen where I used to sit with Nicha, I briefed the team on what I had heard from Amarru.

Like me, they were shell-shocked. Every time I spoke to someone else, the situation became more serious than we had assumed.

The children all listened quietly.

I know I still couldn't get over how well-behaved they all were, and how much I needed to prepare some really smooth talking to Nalya's father, because I was sure that I would be blamed for taking his son into a war zone, never mind that problems had only started breaking out when we were already here, and that they were not my fault, anyway.

I expected a writ to be on my desk when I came back. Make that two writs, once Larrana's family heard about our adventures.

Sigh.

We collected all our things. It was amazing how, with so many kids, stuff ended up in strange places. For example, why was there a game triangle under the table next to ours?

We walked through the corridors of the building, so familiar to me. I wondered when I would be back again.

If Asto couldn't help stave off an invasion because Nations of Earth was being stupid, what would it mean for all the people on Earth? Would SCAC be joining up with the anti-*gamra* cause and taking over Nations of Earth?

Those were all horrible questions that I didn't want to think about.

The shuttle was quite large and was full to overflowing with people who clearly normally lived on Earth. Many of them hadn't even bothered to change back into Coldi clothing. I wondered where they were going. I thought of the people I had left behind, Clay, Marisol and Vanessa and their community. I thought of the Zhori community in South Africa, and in Ethiopia, of the Coldi in London, who could get out because they belonged to the Palayi elite, and of the many, many Coldi in Athens, many of whom would probably not get out because they had no money and nowhere to go.

I thought of my father. I'd tried to send him a message that we weren't in a position to see him, but there had been no reply. Likely, he and Erith were feeding the llamas, sailing in the bay or chatting to the neighbours.

After a while, the crew announced that we were due to arrive at the "way station".

A vast dark shape loomed in the projection on the wall screen, against the glare of the planet and the back-lit crescent of the Moon. It was too big to fit onto the screen. I thought I spotted a few pinpricks of light in the darkness.

Well, crap, a giant Asto military ship was hidden away on the far side of the Moon at the LaGrange point.

The blue marble slid from view, and not much later, the shuttle docked. The crew informed us that they had a short window in which they had to return to the Exchange, so *Please leave the craft in timely fashion and ask for assistance if you have difficulty.*

When the doors opened and we were allowed out, we

emerged in a hall where the walls bore the attachment points for the fighters that would hang here in the ship's normal operation, but had clearly been moved elsewhere, probably outside the hull.

There was a clear path marked over the smooth curved floor and passengers streamed out towards an entrance that led to a light-filled room. There were a lot of people here, and the smell of food hung in the air. The room gave a view over Earth, a blue marble over the top of the dark shape of the Moon. My heart ached.

Someone came towards us.

A man's voice said, "Oh. There you are, finally."

Ayshada called out. "Grandpa!"

Thayu, who carried Emi on her arm, whirled around.

I witnessed a very rare emotional encounter between Asha, Thayu, Nicha and both the children. Then Asha faced me. He was in full uniform, the desert pink flight suit, rank designation and everything. I rarely saw him like this.

"You knew we would be back?" I said flippantly.

"You're indestructible, so yes, but I didn't like it. When first news came out of what had happened, we were ordered to go here immediately."

And that order could only have come from Ezhya because he was the only person who could order Asha.

"Where is Ezhya?"

I was beginning to have a very bad feeling about this.

Asha glanced over my shoulder. I turned.

Sure enough, the man himself was walking through the room.

Only two guards walked in front of him, a sign of how much things had changed since I had brought the Omi clan into line. Before that, surrounded by all these people from the rival clans, he would be in the company of a lot more guards.

But he was not alone.

Two other people followed him.

But that was...

"Dad, Erith."

I rushed to them and closed them in my arms.

"I'm so glad you're all right," my father said.

"What are you two doing here?"

"We received a strong suggestion from someone to take up the offer to come here."

"Why? Is New Zealand that unsafe?"

"It's likely to become less safe, but also, we wanted to see you, because after this visit, it may be a long time before you can come back, if the Exchange is closing."

"But certainly that is a temporary situation?" I glanced at Ezhya, who was talking to Sheydu.

"It's only a short visit, but I wanted to make sure we took advantage of it. Now, where is this young lady I've heard so much about?"

Thayu had joined the group with Sheydu and Ezhya. Rather than take her attention off what looked to be an important discussion, I took Emi from her. She was wide awake, looking around with big eyes.

My father had not seen his granddaughter before. She was happy being held by him and Erith. He told me he was happy that I'd named her after my mother. It was so good to see him again.

But my attention kept going to the group next to us, where Ezhya lingered an uncharacteristically long time talking with Sheydu, and even Deyu.

I picked up snatches of the conversation.

He was here with a sizeable contingent of the Asto military.

A full-scale operation. The Asto military had certainly learned from its previous mistakes.

"So that's it?" I said to Ezhya when he came to stand next to me. His presence was familiar and comforting. Coldi never truly spoke of friends, but if one had to translate, those people in a well-functioning association would be called friends.

"I've tried to approach them," Ezhya said. *Them* being Nations of Earth. "I offered help."

"And not getting anywhere?"

"Oh, they're talking, but no one is making any commitments, and the president seems to change the subject every time I talk about joint military operations."

"He actually wants to talk to you?"

"I suspect not. That's the problem."

"He was in charge of the Nations of Earth guard and peace-keeping forces when I asked Asha to do a little job for me. He didn't like it."

Ezhya told me that failing a request from Dekker for assistance, there was nothing he was willing to do.

We all knew that there had been a time of double standards within *gamra*: that Asto got away with a lot more than the other entities. No more. Chief Delegate Marin Federza made damn sure of that.

This ship was going to start taking passengers to Asto once the available room on board was filled up. That would take a while, because the ship could carry thousands, the shuttles only had room for a hundred or fewer passengers, in case of the smaller private craft.

Because Amarru had shut down the core of the Athens Exchange, we needed to use the military sling, but that required us to travel a bit because that very secretive military ship did not make a habit of coming close to planets.

Ezhya assured me that there would be a way for us to go back to our ship, which was stored on another military vessel. We decided to stay until my father and Erith would have to go back home. We spent as much time as possible with them. In my mind, I made plans to bring them to Barresh for an extended visit. Fred the dog was fifteen years old and wouldn't be with them much longer, but once he had passed on peacefully, my father and Erith would be free to spend some time with us.

While the loading of passengers was expected to continue at least overnight, we were allocated a military-style cabin to clean up and have a rest.

We shared a very basic meal in the—bare and military—canteen with my father and Erith. Afterwards, I found most of the children already asleep in the hammocks, and we joined them soon, all jammed together.

I was so tired that I didn't even mind that I had to share the hammock with Thayu. The passage outside was a noisy place, with people talking, meeting up and yelling at each other. Heavy things were being dragged through the corridors. The door didn't shut.

I woke up briefly when the gravity dropped and the ship stopped its rotating habitat to engage the engines.

I thought I'd have a brief rest. Some people could sleep in noisy environments. I wasn't one of those people.

But when I woke up, it was several hours later, and most of my team had already left the room.

Some gravity had returned, but the soft hum of the walls and floor indicated that the ship was moving. The ship had to be a personnel carrier, because most military ships wouldn't have a rotating habitat, or if they did, they wouldn't operate it in flight.

Smells of food drifted in from the hallway. I followed my nose to the canteen, where civilian passengers occupied every table and spare bench along the perimeter.

I found my team with my father and Erith at one of the tables. My father held Emi on his lap. She held a biscuit in both chubby hands and was chewing on a very soggy corner of it.

"Give her some porridge," I said.

"She already had some. She can really eat. That young lady reminds me of you when you were this little."

I went to the serving area and collected my ration, including a serving of highly red-coded mushrooms.

The pilot had turned on the large screen at the far end of the room. It showed Earth and the Moon as two bright dots in a dark sky.

When I was about to return to the others, Asha came into the canteen. The way he strode in my direction, I knew that something was up.

"We've got contact with Nations of Earth," he said.

I snorted. "And *now* they want to talk to me?"

But I dumped my breakfast on the table with a sigh, and followed him to the hub, a room shrouded in semidarkness with screens along the walls. More than half of them idled in sleep mode, since the ship had shut down its military operations.

Asha guided me to a seat and handed me an earpiece.

There was no visual, he said, and the signal was not very good.

He was right.

Through the crackling of static, a clear voice said, "I hate to have to talk to you, Mr Wilson. You've presumed far too high a status without justification."

"What's changed?" It was the least snarky response I could muster. Once I would have attempted to be polite to the office of president, but Dekker had shown me how much of a wasted effort that was. You made connections with *people*, not positions. If the people weren't up to your standard, then it shouldn't matter what position they held.

"I am talking on behalf of all the people on this planet, which I hope you would feel some kind of responsibility towards."

That was Dekker all over. Trying to guilt trip me.

"Just tell me what you want. It's late in this process. We're on our way out. If you'd started talking to us earlier, maybe we could have avoided this situation altogether."

"I don't ask this lightly. We need help. Any help you can get. From anyone at all."

And then the link dropped out.

I sensed someone was standing behind me. I looked over my shoulder and found Ezhya there.

"Any idea what this means?" I asked.

"Something happened. Maybe they discovered the five extra ships. They realised they can't fight this enemy without us. It's war."

Thanks for Reading

THANK you for reading Ambassador 11: *The Forgotten War*. As the author of this book, I would hugely appreciate it if you could return to where you purchased it to write a short review. Thanks so much!

The next book in the series is Ambassador 12: The Unfolding Army.

NEVER AGAIN MISS a new release and get four books free if you sign up for my newsletter.

ABOUT THE AUTHOR

Patty Jansen lives in Sydney, Australia, where she spends most of her time writing Science Fiction and Fantasy.

Her story *This Peaceful State of War* placed first in the second quarter of the Writers of the Future contest and was published in their 27th anthology. She has also sold fiction to genre magazines such as Analog Science Fiction and Fact, Redstone SF and Aurealis.

Patty has written over thirty novels in both Science Fiction and Fantasy, including the *Icefire Trilogy* and the *Ambassador* series.

pattyjansen.com

BOOKS BY PATTY JANSEN

MORE INFORMATION:

PATTYJANSEN.COM

Lightning Source UK Ltd.
Milton Keynes UK
UKHW011842240521
384311UK00009B/582/J